W9-BDA-582

By Timothy Zahn

The Blackcollar
A Coming of Age
Cobra
Spinneret
Cobra Strike
Cascade Point and Other Stories
The Backlash Mission
Triplet
Cobra Bargain
Time Bomb and Zahndry Others
Deadman Switch
Warhorse
Cobras Two
Distant Friends
Conquerors' Pride
Conquerors' Heritage
Conquerors' Legacy
The Icarus Hunt
Angelmass
Manta's Gift
Starsong and Other Stories
The Green and the Gray
Night Train to Rigel
DRAGONBACK BOOK 1: *Dragon and Thief*
DRAGONBACK BOOK 2: *Dragon and Soldier*
DRAGONBACK BOOK 3: *Dragon and Slave*

STAR WARS: *Heir to the Empire*
STAR WARS: *Dark Force Rising*
STAR WARS: *The Last Command*
STAR WARS: *The Hand of Thrawn*, Book 1: *Specter of the Past*
STAR WARS: *The Hand of Thrawn*, Book 2: *Vision of the Future*
STAR WARS: *Survivor's Quest*
STAR WARS: *Outbound Flight*

OUTBOUND FLIGHT

OUTBOUND FLIGHT

TIMOTHY ZAHN

BALLANTINE BOOKS
NEW YORK

Published in the United States by Del Rey Books, an imprint of The Random House Publishing Group, a division of Random House, Inc., New York.

DEL REY is a registered trademark and the Del Rey colophon is a trademark of Random House, Inc.

Illustrations by A. J. Kimball

ISBN 0-345-45683-1

Printed in the United States of America on acid-free paper

www.starwars.com
www.delreybooks.com
www.readstarwars.com

2 4 6 8 9 7 5 3 1

First Edition

To Michael A. Stackpole
For his contributions to the *Star Wars* universe:
Words of prose, words of advice, and, occasionally, words of somewhat less consequence.
And in regards to that last category,
one of these days I *will* beat you at
Star Wars Trivial Pursuit.

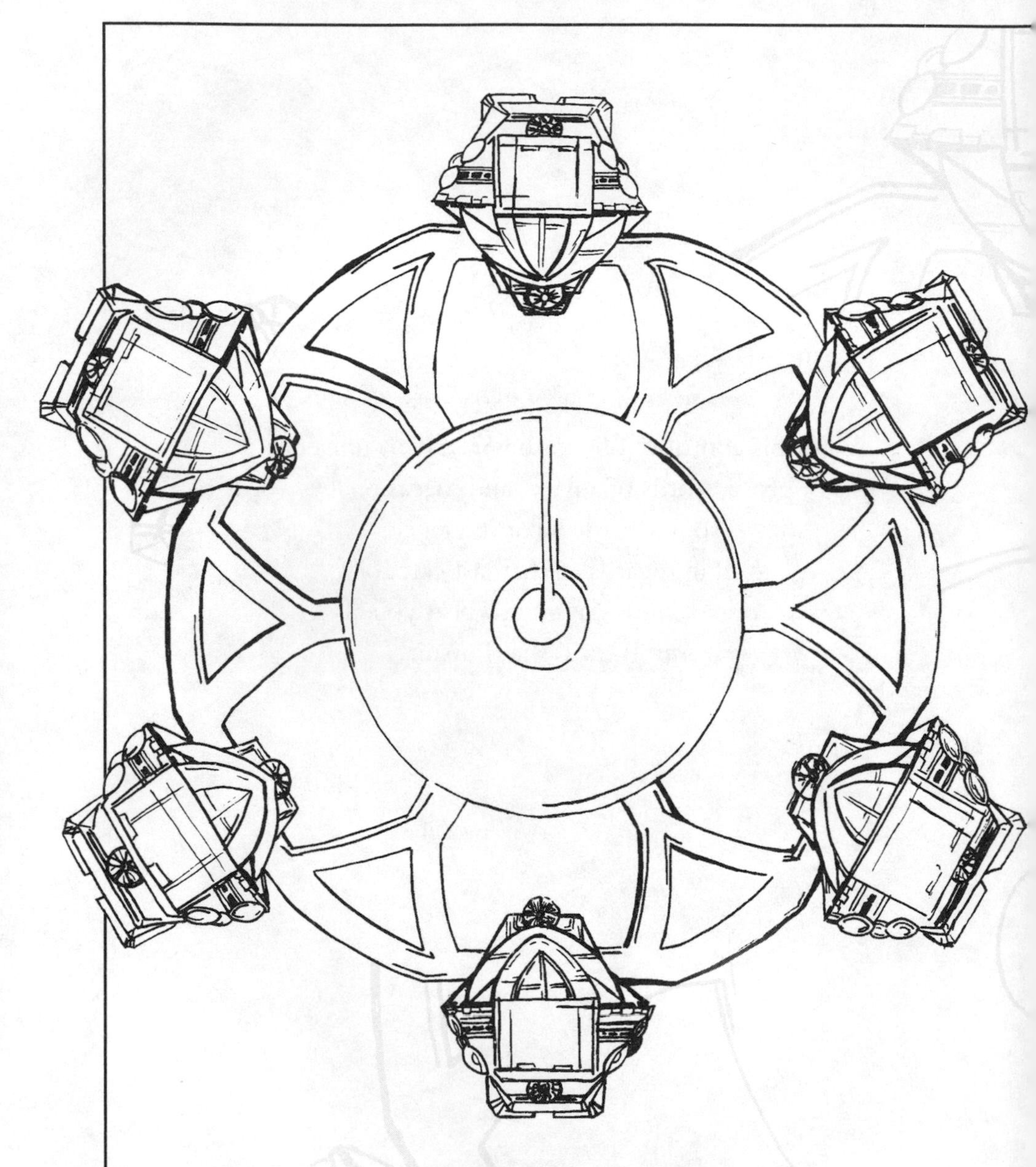

OUTBOUND FLIGHT:

Dreadnaughts and core,

front view

OUTBOUND FLIGHT:

Six Dreadnaughts arranged around a central core.

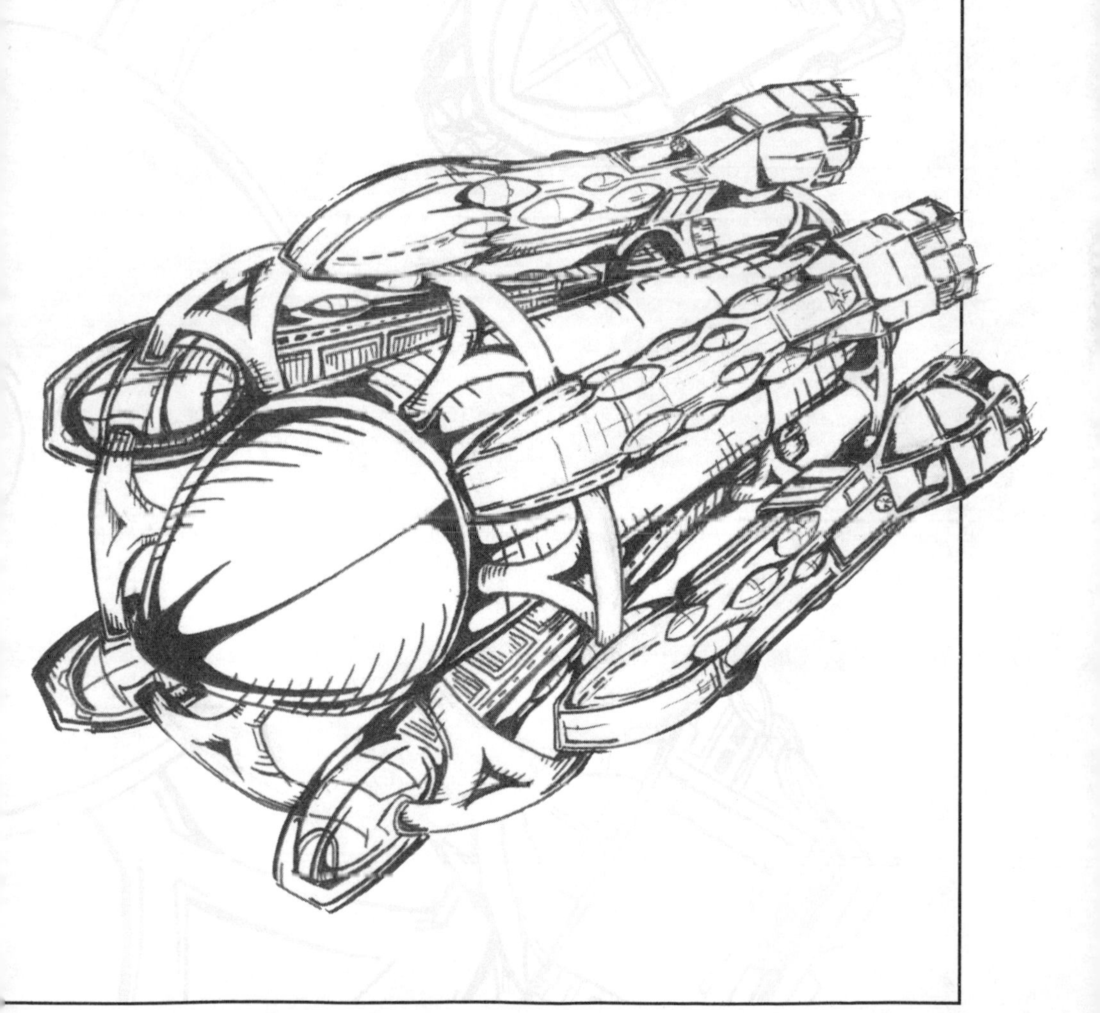

OUTBOUND FLIGHT

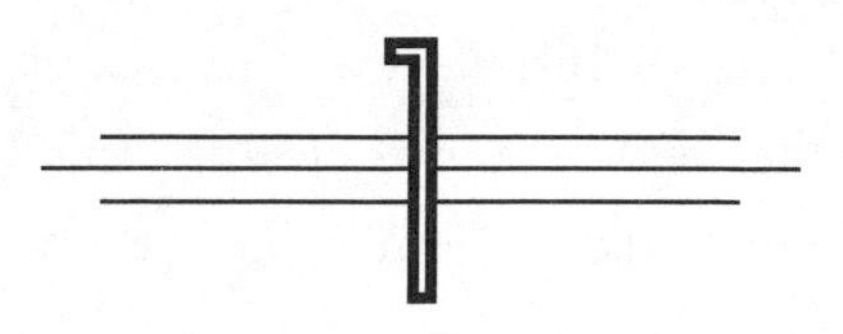

The light freighter *Bargain Hunter* moved through space, silver-gray against the blackness, the light of the distant stars reflecting from its hull. Its running lights were muted, its navigational beacons quiet, its viewports for the most part as dark as the space around it.

Its drive gunning for all it was worth.

"Hang on!" Dubrak Qennto barked over the straining roar of the engines. "Here he comes again!"

Clenching his teeth firmly together to keep them from chattering, Jorj Car'das got a grip on his seat's armrest with one hand as he finished punching coordinates into the nav computer with the other. Just in time; the *Bargain Hunter* jinked hard to the left as a pair of brilliant green blaster bolts burned past the bridge canopy. "Car'das?" Qennto called. "Snap it up, kid."

"I'm snapping, I'm snapping," Car'das called back, resisting the urge to point out that the outmoded nav equipment was

Qennto's property, not his. As was the lack of diplomacy and common sense that had gotten them into this mess in the first place. "Can't we just talk to them?"

"Terrific idea," Qennto bit out. "Be sure to compliment Progga on his fairness and sound business sense. That always works on Hutts."

The last word was punctuated by another cluster of blaster shots, this group closer than the last. "Rak, the engines can't hold this speed forever," Maris Ferasi warned from the copilot's seat, her dark hair flashing with green highlights every time a shot went past.

"Doesn't have to be forever," Qennto said with a grunt. "Just till we have some numbers. Car'das?"

On Car'das's board a light winked on. "Ready," he called, punching the numbers over to the pilot's station. "It's not a very long jump, though—"

He was cut off by a screech from somewhere aft, and the flashing blaster bolts were replaced by flashing starlines as the *Bargain Hunter* shot into hyperspace.

Car'das took a deep breath, let it out silently. "This is *not* what I signed up for," he muttered to himself. Barely six standard months after signing on with Qennto and Maris, this was already the second time they'd had to run for their lives from someone.

And this time it was a *Hutt* they'd frizzled. Qennto, he thought darkly, had a genuine talent for picking his fights.

"You okay, Jorj?"

Car'das looked up, blinking away a drop of sweat that had somehow found its way into his eye. Maris was swiveled around in her chair, looking back at him with concern. "I'm fine," he said, wincing at the quavering in his voice.

"Of course he is," Qennto assured Maris as he also turned

around to look at their junior crewer. "Those shots never even got close."

Car'das braced himself. "You know, Qennto, it may not be my place to say this—"

"It isn't; and don't," Qennto said gruffly, turning back to his board.

"Progga the Hutt is *not* the sort of person you want mad at you," Car'das said anyway. "I mean, first there was that Rodian—"

"A word about shipboard etiquette, kid," Qennto cut in, turning just far enough to send a single eye's worth of glower at Car'das. "You don't argue with your captain. Not ever. Not unless you want this to be your first *and* last tour with us."

"I'd settle for it not being the last tour of my life," Car'das muttered.

"What was that?"

Car'das grimaced. "Nothing."

"Don't let Progga worry you," Maris soothed. "He has a rotten temper, but he'll cool off."

"Before or after he racks the three of us and takes all the furs?" Car'das countered, eyeing the hyperdrive readings uneasily. That mauvine nullifier instability was definitely getting worse.

"Oh, Progga wouldn't have racked us," Qennto scoffed. "He'd have left *that* to Drixo when we had to tell her he'd snatched her cargo. You *do* have that next jump ready, right?"

"Working on it," Car'das said, checking the computer. "But the hyperdrive—"

"Heads up," Qennto interrupted. "We're coming out."

The starlines collapsed back into stars, and Car'das keyed for a full sensor scan.

And jerked as a salvo of blaster shots sizzled past the canopy.

Qennto barked a short expletive. "What the *frizz*?"

"He *followed* us," Maris said, sounding stunned.

"And he's got the range," Qennto snarled as he threw the *Bargain Hunter* into another series of stomach-twisting evasive maneuvers. "Car'das, get us out of here!"

"Trying," Car'das called back, fighting to read the computer displays as they bounced and wobbled in front of his eyes. There was no way it was going to calculate the next jump before even Qennto's luck ran out and the fuming Hutt back there finally connected.

But if Car'das couldn't find a place for them to go, maybe he could find all the places for them *not* to go . . .

The sky directly ahead was full of stars, but there was plenty of empty black between them. Picking the biggest of the gaps, he punched the vector into the computer. "Try this one," he called, keying it to Qennto.

"What do you mean *try*?" Maris asked.

The freighter rocked as a pair of shots caught it squarely on the aft deflector. "Never mind," Qennto said before Car'das could answer. He punched the board, and once again the star-lines lanced out and faded into the blotchy hyperspace sky.

Maris exhaled in a huff. "That was *too* close."

"Okay, so maybe he *is* mad at us," Qennto conceded. "Now. Like Maris said, kid, what do you mean, *try* this one?"

"I didn't have time to calculate a proper jump," Car'das explained. "So I just aimed us into an empty spot with no stars."

Qennto swiveled around. "You mean an empty spot with no *visible* stars?" he asked ominously. "An empty spot with no collapsed stars, or pre-star dark masses, or something hidden behind dust clouds? *That* kind of empty spot?" He waved a hand toward the canopy. "*And* out toward the Unknown Regions on top of it?"

"We don't have enough data in that direction for him to have done a proper calculation anyway," Maris said, coming unexpectedly to Car'das's defense.

"That's not the point," Qennto insisted.

"No, the point is that he got us away from Progga," Maris said. "I think that deserves at least a thank-you."

Qennto rolled his eyes. "*Thank* you," he said. "Such thanks to be rescinded if and when we run through a star you didn't see, of course."

"I think it's more likely the hyperdrive will blow up first," Car'das warned. "Remember that nullifier problem I told you about? I think it's getting—"

He was cut off by a wailing sound from beneath them, and with a lurch the *Bargain Hunter* leapt forward like a giffa on a scent.

"Running hot!" Qennto shouted, spinning back to his board. "Maris, shut 'er down!"

"Trying," Maris called back over the wailing as her fingers danced across her board. "Control lines are looping—can't get a signal through."

With a curse, Qennto popped his straps and heaved his bulk out of his seat. He sprinted down the narrow aisle, his elbow barely missing the back of Car'das's head as he passed. Poking uselessly at his own controls, Car'das popped his own strap release and started to follow.

"Car'das, get up here," Maris called, gesturing him forward.

"He might need me," Car'das said as he nevertheless reversed direction and headed forward.

"Sit," she ordered, nodding sideways at Qennto's vacated pilot's seat. "Help me watch the tracker—if we veer off this vector before Rak figures out how to pull the plug, I need to know about it."

"But Qennto—"

"Word of advice, friend," she interrupted, her eyes still on her displays. "This is Rak's ship. If there are any tricky repairs to be made, he's the one who'll make them."

"Even if I happen to know more about a particular system than he does?"

"*Especially* if you happen to know more about it than he does," she said drily. "But in this case, you don't. Trust me."

"Fine," Car'das said with a sigh. "Such trust to be rescinded if and when we blow up, of course."

"You're learning," she said approvingly. "Now run a systems check on the scanners and see if the instability's bled over into them. Then do the same for the nav computer. Once we get through this, I want to make sure we can find our way home again."

It took Qennto over four hours to find a way to shut down the runaway hyperdrive without slagging it. During that time Car'das offered his help three times, and Maris offered hers twice. All the offers were summarily refused.

Sometime during the first hour, as near as Car'das could figure from the readings tumbling across the displays, they left the relatively well-known territory of the Outer Rim, passing into a shallow section of the far less well-known territory known as Wild Space. Sometime early in the fourth hour, they left even that behind and crossed the hazy line into the Unknown Regions.

At which point, where they were or what exactly they were flying into was anyone's guess.

But at last the wailing faded away, and a few minutes later the hyperspace sky collapsed into starlines and then into stars. "Maris?" Qennto's voice called from the comm panel.

"We're out," she confirmed. "Running a location check now."

"I'll be right there," Qennto said.

"Wherever we are, we're a long way from home," Car'das murmured, gazing out at a small but brilliant globular star cluster in the distance. "I've never seen anything like *that* from any of the Outer Rim worlds I've been to."

"Me, neither," Maris agreed soberly. "Hopefully, the computer can sort it out."

The computer was still sifting data when Qennto reappeared on the bridge. Car'das had made sure to be back at his own station by then. "Nice cluster," the big man commented as he dropped into his seat. "Any systems nearby?"

"Closest one's about a quarter light-year directly ahead," Maris said, pointing.

Qennto grunted and punched at his board. "Let's see if we can make it," he said. "Backup hyperdrive should still have enough juice for a jump that short."

"Can't we work on the ship just as well out here?" Car'das asked.

"I don't like interstellar space," Qennto said distractedly as he set up the jump. "It's dark and cold and lonely. Besides, that system up there might have a nice planet or two."

"Which means a possible source of supplies, in case we end up staying longer than we expect," Maris explained.

"Or a possible place to settle down away from the noise and fluster of the Republic for a while," Qennto added.

Car'das felt his throat tighten. "You don't mean—?"

"No, he doesn't," Maris assured him. "Rak always talks about getting away from it all whenever he's in trouble with someone."

"He must talk that way a lot," Car'das muttered.

"What was that?" Qennto asked.

"Nothing."

"Didn't think so. Here we go." There was a screech, more genteel than the sound from the *Bargain Hunter*'s main hyperdrive, and the stars stretched out into starlines.

Silently, Car'das counted off the seconds to himself, fully expecting the backup hyperdrive to crash at any time. But it didn't, and after a few tense minutes the starlines collapsed again to reveal a small yellow sun directly ahead.

"There we go," Qennto said approvingly. "All the comforts of home. You figure out yet where we are, Maris?"

"Computer's still working on it," Maris said. "But it looks like we're about two hundred fifty light-years into Unknown Space." She lifted her eyebrows at him. "I'm thinking we're going to have a stack of late-delivery penalties when we finally get to Comra."

"Oh, you worry too much," Qennto chided. "It won't take more than a day or two to fix the hyperdrive. If we push it a little, we shouldn't be more than a week overdue."

Car'das suppressed a grimace. Pushing the hyperdrive, if he recalled correctly, was what had wrecked the thing to begin with.

There was a twitter from the comm. "We're being hailed," he reported, frowning as he keyed it on. He threw a look at the visual displays, searching for their unknown caller—

And felt his whole body go rigid. "Qennto!" he snapped. "It's—"

He was cut off by a deep rumbling chuckle from the comm. "So, Dubrak Qennto," an all-too-familiar voice rumbled in Huttese. "You think to escape me so easily?"

"You call that *easy*?" Qennto muttered as he keyed his transmitter. "Oh, hi, Progga," he said. "Look, like I told you before, I can't let you have these furs. I've already contracted with Drixo—"

"Ignore the furs," Progga cut in. "Show me your hidden treasure hoard."

Qennto frowned at Maris. "My *what*?"

"Do not play the fool," Progga warned, his voice going an octave deeper. "I know your sort. You do not simply run *from* something, but run rather *to* something else. This is the lone star system along this vector; and behold, you are here. What could you have run to but a secret base and treasure hoard?"

Qennto muted the transmitter. "Car'das, where is he?"

"A hundred kilometers off the starboard bow," Car'das told him, his hands shaking as he ran a full scan on the distant Hutt ship. "And he's coming up fast."

"Maris?"

"Whatever you did to shut down the hyperdrive, you did a great job," she said tightly. "It's completely locked. We've still got the backup, but if we try to run and he tracks us again—"

"And he will," Qennto growled. Taking a deep breath, he switched the transmitter back on. "It wasn't like that, Progga," he said soothingly. "We were just trying to—"

"Enough!" the Hutt bellowed. "Lead me to this base. Now."

"There isn't any base," Qennto insisted. "This is the Unknown Regions. Why would I set up a base out *here*?"

A light flashed on Car'das's proximity sensor. "Incoming!" he snapped, his eyes darting back and forth among the displays as he searched for the source of the attack.

"Where?" Qennto snapped back.

Car'das had it now, coming from directly beneath the *Bargain Hunter:* a long, dark missile arrowing straight toward them. "There," he said, pointing a finger straight down as he stared at the display.

It was only then that his brain caught up with the fact that this wasn't the vector a missile would take from the approaching Hutt ship. He was opening his mouth to point that out when the missile burst open, its nose ejecting a wad of some kind of material. The wad began to expand as it cleared the shards of its container, opening like a fast-blooming flower into a filmy wall stretching over a kilometer across.

"Power off!" Qennto snapped, lunging across his board to the row of master power switches. "Hurry!"

"What is it?" Car'das asked, grabbing for his board's own set of cutoffs.

"A Connor net, or something like it," Qennto gritted out.

"What, *that* size?" Car'das asked in disbelief.

"Just *do* it," Qennto snarled. Status lights were winking red and going out now as the three of them raced against the incoming net.

The net won. Car'das had made it through barely two-thirds of his switches when the rippling edges came into sight around the sides of the hull. They folded themselves inward, curling around toward the bridge—

"Close your eyes," Maris warned.

Car'das squeezed his eyes shut. Even through the lids he saw a hint of the brilliant flash as the net dumped its high-voltage current into and through the ship, sending a brief coronal tingling across his skin.

And when he carefully opened his eyes again, every light that had still been glowing across the bridge had gone dark.

The *Bargain Hunter* was dead.

Through the canopy came a flicker of light from the direction of the Hutt ship. "Looks like they got Progga, too," he said, his voice sounding unnaturally loud in the sudden silence.

"I doubt it," Qennto rumbled. "His ship's big enough to have cap drains and other stuff to protect him from tricks like this."

"Ten to one he'll fight, too," Maris murmured, her voice tight.

"Oh, he'll fight, all right," Qennto said heavily. "He's way too stupid to realize that anyone who can make a Connor net that big will have plenty of other tricks up his sleeve."

A multiple blaze of green blasterfire erupted from the direction of the Hutt ship. It was answered by brilliant blue flashes vectoring in from three different directions, fired from ships too small or too dark to see at the *Bargain Hunter*'s range. "You think whoever this is might get so busy with Progga that they'll forget about us?" Maris asked hopefully.

"I don't think so," Car'das said, gesturing out the canopy at the small gray spacecraft that had taken up position with its nose pointed at the freighter's portside flank. It was about the size of a shuttle or heavy fighter, built in a curved, flowing design of a sort he'd never seen before. "They've left us a guard."

"Figures," Qennto said, glancing once at the alien ship and then turning back to the green and blue flashes. "Fifty says Progga lasts at least fifteen minutes and takes one of his attackers with him."

Neither of the others took him up on the bet. Car'das watched the fight, wishing he had his sensors back. He'd read a little about space battle tactics in school, but the attackers' methodology didn't seem to fit with anything he could remember. He was still trying to figure it out when, with a final salvo of blue light, it was over.

"Six minutes," Qennto said, his voice grim. "Whoever these guys are, they're good."

"You don't recognize them, either?" Maris asked, looking out at their silent guard.

"I don't even recognize the design," he grunted, popping his restraints and standing up. "Let's go check on the damage, see if we can at least get her ready for company. Car'das, you stay here and mind the store."

"Me?" Car'das asked, feeling his stomach tighten. "But what if they—you know—signal us?"

"What do you think?" Qennto grunted as he and Maris headed aft. "You answer them."

The victors took their time poking or prodding or gloating over whatever was left of the Hutt ship. From the number of maneuvering drives Car'das could see winking on and off, he guessed there were just the three ships that had been involved in the battle itself, plus the one still standing watchful guard off their flank.

Connor nets, like ion cannons, were designed to disable and hold rather than destroy, and Qennto and Maris had most of the systems back online by the time their keeper finally made its move. "Qennto, he's shifting position," Car'das called into the comm, watching as the gray ship drifted leisurely past the canopy and settled into a new spot with his stern above and in front of the *Bargain Hunter*'s bow. "Looks like he's setting up for us to follow him."

"On our way," Qennto called back. "Run the drive up to quarter power."

The gray ship was starting to pull away when he and Maris

returned. "Here we go," Qennto muttered, dropping into his seat and easing them forward. "Any idea where we're going?"

"The rest of the group's still over by the Hutt ship," Car'das said, squeezing carefully past Maris as he headed back to his own station. "Maybe he's taking us there."

"Yeah, looks like it," Qennto agreed as he fed more power to the drive. "So far, they're not shooting. That's usually a good sign."

There were indeed three alien vessels hovering around the remains of Progga's ship when they arrived. Two were duplicates of their fighter-sized escort, while the third was considerably larger. "Not that much bigger than a Republic cruiser, though," Car'das pointed out. "Pretty small, considering what it just did."

"Looks like they're opening a docking bay for us," Maris said.

Car'das measured the opening port cover with his eyes. "Not much room in there."

"Our bow will fit," Qennto assured him. "We can use the forward service tube to get out."

"We're going to go into their ship?" Maris asked, her voice shaking slightly.

"Unless they want to use the tube to come in here instead," Qennto told her. "The guys with the guns get to make those decisions." He lifted a warning finger. "The key is for us to keep control of the situation while they're doing it."

He half turned toward Car'das. "That means *I* do all the talking. Unless they ask you something directly, in which case you give them exactly as much answer as they have question. No more. Got it?"

Car'das swallowed. "Got it."

Their escort led them to the larger ship's side, and two

minutes later Qennto had the *Bargain Hunter*'s bow snugged securely inside the docking collar. A boarding tunnel began extending itself toward the service hatch as Qennto shifted the systems to standby, and by the time the three of them had made it down the ladder the exit sensors indicated the tunnel was in place and pressurized. "Here we go," Qennto muttered, drawing himself up to his full height and keying the release. "Remember, let me do the talking."

Two of the crew were waiting outside the hatch as it slid open: blue-skinned humanoids with glowing red eyes and blue-black hair, dressed in identical black uniforms sporting green shoulder patches. Each of them had a small but nasty-looking handgun belted at his waist. "Hello," Qennto greeted them as he took a step into the tunnel. "I'm Dubrak Qennto, captain of the *Bargain Hunter*."

The aliens didn't answer, but merely moved to either side and gestured down the tunnel. "This way?" Qennto asked, pointing with one hand as he took Maris's arm with the other. "Sure."

He and Maris headed down the tunnel, the ribbed material of the floor bouncing like a swinging bridge with each step. Car'das followed close behind them, studying the aliens out of the corner of his eye as he passed between them. Aside from the unusual skin color and those glowing eyes, they were remarkably human looking. Some offshoot of humanity's ancient expansion into the galaxy? Or were they their own people, with the resemblance purely coincidental?

Two more aliens were waiting just inside the ship proper, dressed and armed the same way as the first pair except that their shoulder patches were yellow and blue instead of green. They turned in military precision as the three humans arrived and led the way down a smoothly curved corridor made of a pearl-like material with a soft, muted sheen. Car'das ran his fingertips gently along the wall as they walked, trying to decide whether it was metal, ceramic, or some kind of composite.

Five meters down the corridor their guides came to a halt outside an open doorway and planted themselves on either side. "In there, huh?" Qennto asked. "Sure." He squared his shoulders the way Car'das had often seen him do just before a negotiating session. Then, still holding Maris's arm, he headed inside. Taking one last look at the corridor walls, Car'das followed.

The room was small and simple, its furnishings consisting of a table and half a dozen chairs. A conference room, Car'das tentatively identified it, or possibly a duty crew meal room. Another of the blue-skinned aliens was seated on the far side of the table, his glowing eyes steady on his visitors. He wore the same black as their escorts, but with a larger burgundy patch on his shoulder and a pair of elaborately tooled silver bars on his collar. An officer? "Hello," Qennto said cheerfully, coming to a stop at the edge of the table. "I'm Dubrak Qennto, captain of the *Bargain Hunter.* I don't suppose you happen to speak Basic?"

The alien didn't reply, but Car'das thought he saw his eyebrow twitch slightly. "Maybe we should try one of the Outer Rim trade languages," he offered.

"Thanks for that brilliant suggestion," Qennto said with a touch of sarcasm. "Greetings to you, noble sir," he continued, switching to Sy Bisti. "We're travelers and traders from a far world, who mean no harm to you or your people."

Again, there was no response. "You could try Taarja," Maris said.

"I don't know Taarja very well," Qennto said, still in Sy Bisti. "How about you?" he added, turning to look at the two guards who had followed them into the room. "Do any of you understand Sy Bisti? How about Taarja? Meese Caulf?"

"Sy Bisti will do," the alien behind the table said calmly in that language.

Qennto turned back, blinking in surprise. "Did you just say—?"

"I said Sy Bisti will do," the alien repeated. "Please; be seated."

"Ah . . . thank you," Qennto said, pulling out chairs for himself and Maris and nodding to Car'das to do likewise. The chair backs were contoured a bit oddly for humans, Car'das noticed as he sat down, but not uncomfortably so.

"I'm Commander Mitth'raw'nuruodo of the Chiss Ascendancy," the alien continued. "This is the *Springhawk*, Picket Force Two command vessel of the Expansionary Defense Fleet."

Expansionary Fleet. Car'das felt a shiver run up his back. Did the name imply this Chiss Ascendancy was in the process of expanding outward?

He hoped not. The last thing the Republic needed right now was a threat from outside its borders. Supreme Chancellor Palpatine was doing his best, but there was a lot of resistance to change in the old business-as-usual attitudes and casual corruption of the Coruscant government. Even now, five years after its little misadventure on Naboo, the Trade Federation had yet to be punished for its blatant aggression, despite Palpatine's best efforts to bring it to judgment. Resentment and frustration simmered throughout the galaxy, with rumors of new reform or secession movements surfacing every other week.

Qennto loved it, of course. Government bureaucracies with their dozens of fees, service charges, and flat-out prohibitions were an ideal operating environment for small-scale smuggling operations like his. And Car'das had to admit that during his time aboard the *Bargain Hunter,* their activities had earned a very respectable profit.

What Qennto perhaps failed to understand was that while a little governmental instability could be useful, too much would be as bad for smugglers as it would be for anyone else.

A full-scale war, needless to say, would be as bad as it got. For everyone.

"And you are . . . ?" Mitth'raw'nuruodo asked, shifting his glowing red eyes to Car'das.

Car'das opened his mouth— "I'm Dubrak Qennto, Commander," Qennto put in before he could speak. "Captain of the—"

"And *you* are . . . ?" Mitth'raw'nuruodo repeated, his eyes still on Car'das, a slight but noticeable emphasis on the pronoun.

Car'das looked sideways at Qennto, got a microscopic nod. "I'm Jorj Car'das," he said. "Crewer on the freighter *Bargain Hunter.*"

"And these?" Mitth'raw'nuruodo asked, gesturing to the others.

Again, Car'das looked at Qennto. The other's expression had gone rather sour, but he nevertheless gave his junior crewer another small nod. "This is my captain, Dubrak Qennto," Car'das told the commander. "And his—" *Girlfriend? Copilot? Partner?* "—his second in command, Maris Ferasi."

Mitth'raw'nuruodo nodded to each in turn, then turned back to Car'das. "Why are you here?"

"We're Corellian traders, from one of the systems in the Galactic Republic," Car'das said.

"K'rell'n," Mitth'raw'nuruodo said, as if trying out the word. "Traders, you say? Not explorers or scouts?"

"No, not at all," Car'das assured him. "We hire out our ship to take cargo between star systems."

"And the other vessel?" Mitth'raw'nuruodo asked.

"Pirates of some sort," Qennto put in before Car'das could answer. "We were running from them when we had some trouble with our hyperdrive, which is how we ended up here."

"Did you know these pirates?" Mitth'raw'nuruodo asked.

"How could we possibly—?" Qennto began.

"Yes, we've had trouble with them before," Car'das interrupted. There'd been something in Mitth'raw'nuruodo's voice as he asked that question . . . "I think they were gunning specifically for us."

"You must be carrying a valuable cargo."

"It's nothing fancy," Qennto said, shooting a warning look at Car'das. "A shipment of furs and exotic luxury garments. We're most grateful to you for coming to our aid."

Car'das felt his throat tighten. The bulk of their cargo was indeed luxury clothing, but sewn into the filigree collar of one of the furs was an assortment of smuggled firegems. If Mitth'raw'nuruodo decided to search the shipment and found them, there was going to be a very unhappy Drixo the Hutt in the *Bargain Hunter*'s future.

"You're welcome," Mitth'raw'nuruodo said. "I'd be curious to see what your people consider luxury garments. Perhaps you'll show me your cargo before you leave."

"I'd be delighted," Qennto said. "Does that mean you're releasing us?"

"Soon," Mitth'raw'nuruodo assured him. "First I need to

examine your vessel and confirm that you're indeed the innocent travelers you claim."

"Of course, of course," Qennto said easily. "We'll give you a complete tour anytime you want."

"Thank you," Mitth'raw'nuruodo said. "But that can wait until we reach my base. Until then, resting quarters have been prepared for you. Perhaps later you'll permit me to show you Chiss hospitality."

"We would be both grateful and honored, Commander," Qennto said, inclining his head in a small bow. "I'd just like to mention, though, that we're on a very tight schedule, which our unexpected detour has made that much tighter. We'd appreciate it if you could send us on our way as quickly as possible."

"Of course," Mitth'raw'nuruodo said. "The base isn't far."

"Is it in this system?" Qennto asked. He lifted a hand before the Chiss could answer. "Sorry, sorry—none of my business."

"True," Mitth'raw'nuruodo agreed. "However, it will do no harm to tell you that it's in a different system entirely."

"Ah," Qennto said. "May I ask when we'll be leaving to go there?"

"We've already left," Mitth'raw'nuruodo said mildly. "We made the jump to hyperspace approximately four standard minutes ago."

Qennto frowned. "Really? I didn't hear or feel anything."

"Perhaps our hyperdrive systems are superior to yours," Mitth'raw'nuruodo said, standing up. "Now, if you'll follow me, I'll escort you to the resting area."

He led the way another five meters down the corridor to another door, where he touched a striped panel on the wall. "I'll send word when I want you again," he said as the door slid open.

"We'll look forward to further conversation," Qennto said, giving a truncated bow as he eased Maris behind him through the doorway. "Thank you, Commander."

The two of them disappeared inside. Inclining his head to the commander, Car'das followed.

The room was compactly furnished, containing a three-tier bunk bed against one wall and a fold-down table and bench seats on the other. Beside the bunk bed were three large drawers built into the wall, while to the right was a door leading into what seemed to be a compact refresher station.

"What do you think he's going to do with us?" Maris murmured, looking around.

"He'll let us go," Qennto assured her, glancing into the refresher station and then sitting down on the lowest cot, hunching forward to keep from bumping his head on the one above it. "The real question is whether we'll be taking the firegems with us."

Car'das cleared his throat. "Should we be talking about this?" he asked, looking significantly around the room.

"Relax," Qennto growled. "They don't speak a word of Basic." His eyes narrowed. "And as long as we're on the subject of speaking, why the frizz did you tell him we knew Progga?"

"There was something in his eyes and voice just then," Car'das said. "Something that said he already knew all about it, and that we'd better not get caught lying to him."

Qennto snorted. "That's ridiculous."

"Maybe there were survivors from Progga's crew," Maris suggested.

"Not a chance," Qennto said firmly. "You saw what the ship looked like. The thing'd been peeled open like a ration bar."

"I don't know how he knew," Car'das insisted. "All I know is that he *did* know."

"And you shouldn't lie to an honorable man anyway," Maris murmured.

"Who, him? Honorable?" Qennto scoffed. "Don't you believe it. Military men are all alike, and the smooth ones the worst of the lot."

"*I've* known quite a few honorable soldiers," Maris said stiffly. "Besides, I've always had a good feel for people. I think this Mitth'raw—I think the commander can be trusted." She raised her eyebrows. "I don't think trying to con him would be a good idea, either."

"It's only a bad idea if you get caught," Qennto said. "You get what you bargain for in this universe, Maris. Nothing more."

"You don't have enough faith in people."

"I got all the faith I need, kiddo," Qennto said calmly. "I just happen to know a little more about human nature than you do. Human *and* nonhuman nature."

"I still think we need to play completely straight with him," Maris said.

"Playing straight is the last thing you want to do. Ever. It gives the other guy all the advantages." Qennto nodded toward the closed door. "And this guy in particular sounds like the sort who'll ask questions until we die of old age if we let him."

"Still, it wouldn't hurt if he kept us around for at least a little while," Car'das suggested. "Progga's people are going to be pretty mad when he doesn't come back."

Qennto shook his head. "They'll never pin it on us."

"Yes, but—"

"Look, kid, let me do the thinking, okay?" Qennto cut in. Swiveling his legs up onto the bunk, he lay back with his arms folded behind his back. "Now everyone be quiet for a while. I've got to figure out how to play this."

Maris caught Car'das's eye, gave a little shrug, then turned and climbed up onto the bunk above Qennto. Stretching out, she folded her arms across her chest and gazed meditatively at the underside of the bunk above her.

Crossing to the other side of the room, Car'das folded down the table and one of the bench seats and sat down, wedging himself more or less comfortably between the table and wall. Putting his elbow on the table and propping his head up on his hand, he closed his eyes and tried to relax.

He didn't realize he'd dozed off until a sudden buzz startled him awake. He jumped up as the door opened to reveal a single black-clad Chiss. "Commander Mitth'raw'nuruodo's respects," the alien said, the Sy Bisti words coming out thickly accented. "He requests your presence in Forward Visual One."

"Wonderful," Qennto said, swinging his legs onto the floor and standing up. His tone and expression were the false cheerfulness Car'das had heard him use time and again in bargaining sessions.

"Not you," the Chiss said. He gestured to Car'das. "This one only."

Qennto came to an abrupt halt. "What?"

"A refreshment is being prepared," the Chiss said. "Until it is ready, this one only will come."

"Now, wait a second," Qennto growled. "We stick together or—"

"It's okay," Car'das interrupted hastily. The Chiss standing in the doorway hadn't moved, but Car'das had caught a subtle shift of light and shadow that indicated there were others wandering around out there. "I'll be fine."

"Car'das—"

"It's okay," Car'das repeated, stepping to the doorway. The Chiss moved back, and he walked out into the corridor.

There were indeed more Chiss waiting by the door, two of them on either side. "Follow," the messenger said as the door closed.

The group headed down the curved corridor, passing three cross-corridors and several other doorways along the way. Two of the doors were open, and Car'das couldn't resist a furtive glance inside each as he passed. All he could see, though, was unrecognizable equipment and more black-clad Chiss.

He had expected Forward Visual to be a crowded, high-tech room. To his surprise, the door opened into something that looked like a compact version of a starliner's observation gallery. A long, curved couch sat in front of a convex floor-to-ceiling viewport currently showing a spectacular view of the glowing hyperspace sky as it flowed past the ship. The room's own lights were dimmed, making the display that much more impressive.

"Welcome, Jorj Car'das."

Car'das looked around. Mitth'raw'nuruodo was seated alone at the far end of the couch, silhouetted against the hyperspace sky. "Commander," he greeted the other, glancing a question at his guide. The other nodded, stepping back and closing the door on himself and the rest of the escort. Feeling more than a little uneasy, Car'das stepped around the near end of the couch and made his way across the curve.

"Beautiful, isn't it?" Mitth'raw'nuruodo commented as Car'das arrived at his side. "Please; be seated."

"Thank you," Car'das said, easing himself onto the couch a cautious meter away from the other. "May I ask why you sent for me?"

"To share this view, of course," Mitth'raw'nuruodo said drily. "And to answer a few questions."

Car'das felt his stomach tighten. So it was to be an interrogation. Down deep he'd known it would be, but had hoped against hope that Maris's naïvely idealistic assessment of their captor might actually be right. "A very nice view it is, too," he commented, not knowing what else to say. "I'm a little surprised to find such a room aboard a warship."

"Oh, it's quite functional," Mitth'raw'nuruodo assured him. "Its full name is Forward Visual Triangulation Site Number One. We place spotters here during combat to track enemy vessels and other possible threats, and to coordinate some of our line-of-sight weaponry."

"Don't you have sensors to handle that?"

"Of course," Mitth'raw'nuruodo said. "And usually they're quite adequate. But I'm sure you know there are ways of misleading or blinding electronic eyes. Sometimes the eyes of a Chiss are more reliable."

"I suppose," Car'das said, gazing at his host's own glowing eyes. In the dim light, they were even more intimidating. "But isn't it hard to get the information to the gunners fast enough?"

"There are ways," Mitth'raw'nuruodo said. "What exactly is your business, Jorj Car'das?"

"Captain Qennto's already told you that," Car'das said, feeling sweat breaking out on his forehead. "We're merchants and traders."

Mitth'raw'nuruodo shook his head. "Unfortunately for your captain's assertions, I'm familiar with the economics of star travel. Your vessel is far too small for any standard cargo to cover even normal operating expenses, let alone emergency repair work. I therefore conclude that you have a sideline occupation.

You haven't the weaponry to be pirates or privateers, so you must be smugglers."

Car'das hesitated. What exactly was he supposed to say? "I don't suppose it would do any good to point out that our economics and yours might not scale the same?" he stalled.

"*Is* that what you claim?"

Car'das hesitated, but Mitth'raw'nuruodo had that knowing look again. "No," he conceded. "We *are* mostly just traders, as Captain Qennto said. But we sometimes do a little smuggling on the side."

"I see," Mitth'raw'nuruodo said. "I appreciate your honesty, Jorj Car'das."

"You can just call me Car'das," Car'das said. "In our culture, the first name is reserved for use by friends."

"You don't consider me a friend?"

"Do you consider *me* one?" Car'das countered.

He regretted the words the instant they were out of his mouth. Sarcasm was hardly the option of choice in a confrontation like this.

But Mitth'raw'nuruodo merely lifted an eyebrow. "No, not yet," he agreed calmly. "Perhaps someday. You intrigue me, Car'das. Here you sit, captured by unfamiliar beings a long way from home. Yet instead of wrapping yourself within a blanket of fear or anger, you instead stretch outside yourself with curiosity."

Car'das frowned. "Curiosity?"

"You studied my warriors as you were brought aboard," Mitth'raw'nuruodo said. "I could see it in your eyes and face as you observed and thought and evaluated. You did the same as you were taken to your quarters, and again as you were brought here just now."

"I was just looking around," Car'das assured him, his heart beating a little faster. Did spies rank above or below smugglers on Mitth'raw'nuruodo's list of undesirables? "I didn't mean anything by it."

"Calm yourself," Mitth'raw'nuruodo said, some amusement creeping into his voice. "I'm not accusing you of spying. I, too, have the gift of curiosity, and therefore prize it in others. Tell me, who is to receive the hidden gemstones?"

Car'das jerked. "You found—? I mean . . . in that case, why did you ask me about it?"

"As I said, I appreciate honesty," Mitth'raw'nuruodo said. "Who is the intended recipient?"

"A group of Hutts operating out of the Comra system," Car'das told him, giving up. "Rivals to the ones you—the ones who were attacking us." He hesitated. "You *did* know they weren't just random pirates, didn't you? That they were hunting us specifically?"

"We monitored your transmissions as we positioned ourselves to intervene," Mitth'raw'nuruodo said. "Though the conversation was of course unintelligible to us, I remembered hearing the phonemes *Dubrak Qennto* in the Hutt's speech when Captain Qennto later identified himself. The conclusion was obvious."

A shiver ran up Car'das's back. A conversation in an alien language, and yet Mitth'raw'nuruodo had been able to memorize enough of it to extract Qennto's name from the gibberish. What kind of creatures *were* these Chiss, anyway?

"Is the possession of these gems illegal, then?"

"No, but the customs fees are ridiculously high," Car'das said, forcing his mind back to the interrogation. "Smugglers are often used to avoid having to pay them." He hesitated. "Actually, considering the people we got this batch from, they may also have been stolen. But don't tell Maris that."

"Oh?"

Car'das winced. There he was again, talking without thinking. If Mitth'raw'nuruodo didn't kill him before this was over, Qennto probably would. "Maris is something of an idealist," he said reluctantly. "She thinks this whole smuggling thing is just a way of making a statement against the greedy and stupid Republic bureaucracy."

"Captain Qennto hasn't seen fit to enlighten her?"

"Captain Qennto likes her company," Car'das said. "I doubt she'd stay with him if she knew the whole truth."

"He claims to care about her, yet lies to her?"

"I don't know what he claims," Car'das said. "Though I suppose you could say that idealists like Maris do a lot of lying to themselves. The truth is there in front of her if she wanted to see it." He took another look at those glowing red eyes. "Though of course that doesn't excuse our part in it," he added.

"No, it doesn't," Mitth'raw'nuruodo said. "What would be the consequences if you didn't deliver the gemstones?"

Car'das felt his throat tighten. So much for the honorable Commander Mitth'raw'nuruodo. Firegems must be valuable out here, too. "They'd kill us," he said bluntly. "Probably in some hugely entertaining way, like watching us get eaten by some combination of large animals."

"And if the delivery is merely late?"

Car'das frowned, trying to read the other's expression in the flickering hyperspace glow. "What exactly do you want from me, Commander Mitthrawnuruodo?"

"Nothing too burdensome," Mitth'raw'nuruodo said. "I merely wish your company for a time."

"Why?"

"Partly to learn about your people," Mitth'raw'nuruodo said. "But primarily so that you may teach me your language."

Car'das blinked. "Our *language*? You mean Basic?"

"That *is* the chief language of your Republic, is it not?"

"Yes, but . . ." Car'das hesitated, wondering if there was a delicate way to ask a question like this.

Mitth'raw'nuruodo might have been reading his mind. Or, more likely, his eyes and face. "I'm not planning an invasion, if that's what concerns you," he said, smiling faintly. "Chiss don't invade the territories of others. We don't make war against even potential enemies unless we're attacked first."

"Well, you certainly don't have to worry about any attacks from *us*," Car'das said quickly. "We've got too many internal troubles of our own right now to go bother anyone else."

"Then we have nothing to fear from each other," Mitth'raw'nuruodo said. "It would be merely an indulgence of my curiosity."

"I see," Car'das said cautiously. Qennto, he knew, would be into full-bore bargaining mode at this point, pushing and prodding and squeezing to get everything he could out of the deal. Maybe that was why Mitth'raw'nuruodo was making this pitch to the clearly less experienced Car'das instead.

Still, he could try. "And what would *we* get out of it?" he asked.

"For you, there would be an equal satisfaction of your own curiosity." Mitth'raw'nuruodo lifted his eyebrows. "You *do* wish to know more about my people, don't you?"

"Very much," Car'das said. "But I can't see that appealing to Captain Qennto."

"Perhaps a few extra valuables added to his cargo, then," Mitth'raw'nuruodo suggested. "That might also help mollify your clients."

"Yes, they'll definitely need some mollifying," Car'das agreed grimly. "A little extra loot would go a long way toward that."

"Then it's agreed," Mitth'raw'nuruodo said, standing up.

"One more thing," Car'das said, scrambling to his feet. "I'll be happy to teach you Basic, but I'd also like some language lessons myself. Would you be willing in turn to teach me the Chiss language, or to have one of your people do so?"

"I can teach you to understand Cheunh," Mitth'raw'nuruodo said, his eyes narrowing thoughtfully. "But I doubt you'll ever be able to properly speak it. I've noticed you don't even pronounce my name very well."

Car'das felt his face warm. "I'm sorry."

"No apology needed," Mitth'raw'nuruodo assured him. "Your vocal mechanism is close to ours, but there are clearly some differences. However, I believe I *could* teach you to speak Minnisiat. It's a trade language widely used in the regions around our territory."

"That would be wonderful," Car'das said. "Thank you, Commander Mitth—uh . . . Commander."

"As I said, Cheunh pronunciation is difficult for you," Mitth'raw'nuruodo noted drily. "Perhaps it would be easier if you called me by my core name, Thrawn."

Car'das frowned. "Is that permissible?"

Mitth'raw'nuruodo—Thrawn—shrugged. "It's questionable," he conceded. "In general, full names are required for formal occasions, for strangers, and for those who are socially inferior."

"And I'm guessing we qualify on all three counts."

"Yes," Thrawn said. "But I believe such rules may be broken when there are good and valid reasons for doing so. In this case, there are."

"It will certainly make things easier," Car'das agreed, bowing his head. "Thank you, Commander Thrawn."

"You're welcome," Thrawn said. "And now, a light refreshment has been prepared for you and the others. After that, the language lessons can begin."

The receptionist set down her comlink and smiled up at the man and woman standing over her. "The Supreme Chancellor will see you now, Master C'baoth," she said.

"*Thank* you," Jedi Master Jorus C'baoth said, his voice cool and brooding.

Beside him, Lorana Jinzler winced to herself. Her Master was angry, and under the circumstances she couldn't really blame him. But C'baoth's quarrel was with Palpatine, not a lowly receptionist who had no power or authority over the orders that issued from the Supreme Chancellor's Office. There was no reason to vent his annoyance at her.

That wasn't the way C'baoth did things, however. Without another word, he strode away from the woman's desk and headed for the doors to Palpatine's inner office. Lingering half a step behind him, Lorana made sure to catch the receptionist's eye and give her an encouraging smile before following.

A pair of Brolfi came out the door as they approached, their yellow-and-green-patterned hornskin quivering with emotion beneath their leather tunics. C'baoth didn't break stride, but continued straight ahead toward the two aliens, forcing them to move hastily to either side to let him pass. Wincing again, Lorana took a couple of quick steps to catch up with her Master, reaching him just as he passed through the doors into the office.

Supreme Chancellor Palpatine was seated at his desk, an expansive view of Coruscant's skyline visible through the wide window behind him. A young man wearing a tooled tunican and vest was standing beside him, leaning over the desk with a datapad and speaking in a low voice.

Palpatine looked up as C'baoth and Lorana entered, his face breaking into one of his famous smiles. "Ah, Master C'baoth," he said, gesturing them forward. "And your young Padawan, of course—Lorana Jinzler, isn't it? Welcome to you both."

"Let's dispense with the pleasantries, Chancellor," C'baoth said stiffly, pulling a datapad from his belt pouch as he strode forward. "This isn't a social visit."

The young man beside Palpatine straightened up, his eyes flashing. "You will not speak to the Supreme Chancellor in that tone," he said firmly.

"Mind your tongue, underling," C'baoth growled. "Take your bureaucratic trivia and get out."

The young man didn't budge. "You will not speak to the Supreme Chancellor in that tone," he repeated.

"It's all right, Kinman," Palpatine said soothingly, holding out a restraining hand to the young man as he rose to his feet. "I'm sure Master C'baoth doesn't mean any disrespect."

For a moment C'baoth and Palpatine stared at each other across the wide expanse of the desk, an almost visible tension rippling the air between them. Then, to Lorana's relief, the Jedi Master's lip twitched. "No, of course not," he said in a marginally more courteous voice.

"As I said," Palpatine said, smiling fondly at the young man. "You haven't met my new assistant and adviser, have you, Master C'baoth? This is Kinman Doriana."

"Pleased and honored," C'baoth said, in a tone that made it clear that he was neither.

"As am I, Master C'baoth," Doriana replied. "It's always a privilege to meet one of those who've dedicated their lives to safeguarding the Republic."

"As it is for me, as well," Palpatine agreed. "What can I do for you, Master C'baoth?"

"You know very well what you can do for me," C'baoth growled. Without waiting for an invitation, he seated himself in one of the chairs and set his datapad on the desk. "In a word: Outbound Flight."

"Naturally," Palpatine said tiredly, gesturing Lorana to the chair beside C'baoth as he reseated himself in his own chair. "What is it now?"

"This." Waving a hand, C'baoth used the Force to send the datapad sliding across the desk to stop in front of the Supreme Chancellor. "The Senate Appropriations Committee has cut my funding again."

Palpatine sighed. "What do you want me to say, Master C'baoth? I can't dictate to the Senate what it should do. I certainly can't force a stiff-necked group like Appropriations to see things our way."

"*Our* way?" C'baoth echoed. "It's *our* way now, is it? I seem to remember a time not very long ago when you weren't at all enthusiastic about this whole project."

"Perhaps you should examine your memory more closely," Palpatine said, a slight edge creeping into his tone. "It's the Jedi Council, not me, that's been backing away from Outbound Flight for the past few months. In fact, I was under the impression Master Yoda had even changed his mind about allowing more than one or two Jedi to join the expedition."

"I will deal with Master Yoda when the time comes," C'baoth said firmly. "Meanwhile, *you're* the one holding the project's fate in your hands."

"And I've done everything in my power to assist you," Palpatine reminded him. "You have your ships—six brand-new Dreadnaughts, straight off the Rendili StarDrive assembly line. You have the central storage core you wanted, and the turbolift pylons ready to connect the whole thing together. You have the crews and passengers in training on Yaga Minor—"

"Ah!" C'baoth interrupted, jabbing a finger at the datapad still sitting untouched in front of the Supreme Chancellor. "In fact, I do *not* have my passengers, not at all. Some idiot bureaucrat has changed the population profile to consist of crews only, with no families or other potential colonists."

Reluctantly, Lorana thought, Palpatine picked up the datapad. "A cost-saving decision, most likely," he said, scrolling through the data. "Having all those extra people aboard would mean more supplies and equipment."

"What it would mean is a cancellation of the entire project," C'baoth countered. "What sense does it make to send an expedition to another galaxy if there's no chance of planting any colonies once we're there?"

"Perhaps that's the committee's point," Palpatine suggested quietly. "The political situation has changed considerably since you and the Council first proposed this project."

"Which is what makes Outbound Flight all the more important," C'baoth said. "We need to find out what dangers or threats might be lurking out in the Unknown Regions, or poised to invade us from another galaxy."

"Dangers?" Palpatine echoed, lifting his eyebrows. "I was under the impression that Outbound Flight's purpose was to search for new life and potential Force-users outside our borders. Certainly that was the rationale given in the original proposal."

"There's no reason it can't do both," C'baoth said stubbornly. "For that matter, I would think adding a security angle to the mission would make it *more* acceptable to the Senate, not less."

Palpatine shook his head, his gray-white hair glinting in the light from the window behind him. Lorana could remember when that hair had been mostly brown, with only touches of gray at the temples. Now, after five years of carrying the Republic's weight on his shoulders, the brown had all but vanished. "I'm sorry, Master C'baoth," the Chancellor said. "If you can persuade the Senate to override Appropriations' cuts, I'll be more than happy to support you. But at the moment, there's nothing more I can do."

"Unless," Doriana put in, "Master C'baoth is able to do something about the Barlok situation."

"There's nothing more I can do," Palpatine repeated, throwing a cautioning look at his assistant. "At any rate, the Council's hardly going to send him out to Marcol sector when there are so many pressing matters to be attended to here."

"Not so fast," C'baoth rumbled. "What exactly is this problem?"

"It's hardly even worth mentioning," Palpatine said reluctantly. "A small dispute between the Corporate Alliance and one of Barlok's regional governments over some mining rights. Those Brolfi who left as you came in were just presenting their case and asking for assistance in negotiating a settlement."

"And you didn't immediately think of me?" C'baoth said drily. "I think I've been insulted."

"Please, Master C'baoth," Palpatine said with a smile. "I have far too many enemies on Coruscant already. I don't wish to add you to their number."

"Then make a bargain with me," C'baoth offered. "If I can resolve this dispute for you, will you instruct Appropriations to restore Outbound Flight's full funding?"

Lorana stirred uncomfortably in her seat. This was, it seemed to her, perilously close to the sort of under-the-desk speeder swapping that was steadily corroding the whole concept of justice in the Republic's government. But she didn't dare suggest that to C'baoth, certainly not in the presence of Palpatine and his aide.

"I can't make any promises," Palpatine cautioned. "Certainly not where the Senate is concerned. But I believe in Outbound Flight, Master C'baoth, and I'll do everything in my power to make sure your dream is realized."

For a long moment C'baoth didn't reply, and again Lorana felt the tension between the two men. Then, abruptly, the Jedi Master gave a short nod. "Very well, Chancellor Palpatine," he said, rising to his feet. "We'll be on our way to Barlok before the end of the day."

He leveled a finger at Palpatine. "Just make certain that when I come back I have my funding. *And* my colonists."

"I'll do my best," Palpatine said, giving the other a small smile. "Good day, Master C'baoth; Padawan Jinzler."

Lorana waited until they had passed through the outer office and were striding down the wide corridor before speaking. "What did you mean we'd be off to Barlok tonight?" she asked. "Doesn't the Council have to approve any such trips?"

"Don't worry about the Council," C'baoth said brusquely. "Back there, on our way into Palpatine's office, you broke stride for those two Brolfi."

Lorana felt her throat tighten. "I didn't want to just run them down."

"You wouldn't have," he countered. "I'd already measured the gap between them. Neither would have needed to move aside for us."

"Yet they *did* move," Lorana pointed out.

"Because they wished to do so, out of respect," he said. "Understand this, my young Padawan. Someday you will be a Jedi, with all the power and responsibility that it entails. Never forget that *we* are the ones who hold this Republic together—not Palpatine, not the Senate, not the bureaucracy. Certainly not the small-minded people who can't make it through the day without running to Coruscant for help. They must learn to trust us—and before there can be trust, there must be respect. Do you understand?"

"I understand that we want them to respect us," Lorana said hesitantly. "But must they fear us as well?"

"Respect and fear are merely two sides of the same coin," C'baoth said. "Law-obeying citizens hold the coin one way; those who wallow in lawlessness hold it the other." He lifted a finger. "But with neither group can you appear weak or indecisive. Ever."

He lowered the raised finger, tapping it against the lightsaber tucked into her belt. "There are times when you'll wish your identity to remain unknown, and at those times you'll hide your lightsaber and all traces of who and what you are. But when you travel openly as a Jedi, you must *behave* as a Jedi. Always. Do you understand?"

"Yes, Master C'baoth," Lorana said, only half truthfully. Certainly she understood the words, but some of the attitude was still incomprehensible to her.

For a moment C'baoth continued to stare at her, as if sensing her partial duplicity. But to her relief, he turned away without demanding any more. "Very well, then," he said. "I'll go to the Temple and speak with the Council. You call the spaceport and arrange transport for us to the Barlok system. Once you've done that, go and pack."

"For how long?"

"For a simple mineral-rights dispute?" C'baoth scoffed. "Travel time both ways plus three standard days. I'll have this sorted out in no time."

"Yes, Master," Lorana murmured.

"And then," C'baoth continued, half to himself, "we'll see to Master Yoda and his shortsighted fears." Picking up his pace, he strode off down the corridor.

Lorana slowed to a halt, watching as the messengers and bureaucrats walking along on their own business moved hastily out of the way for the tall, white-haired Jedi Master. C'baoth, for his part, never even slowed, as if he simply expected others to make room for him.

When you travel as a Jedi, you must behave as a Jedi.

She sighed. It didn't seem right to her, this firm belief in the inherent superiority of Jedi over all others.

Still, C'baoth had studied long and hard through many years, delving deeply into the mysteries and subtleties of the Force as he grew in power. Lorana, in contrast, was a young

Padawan learner, barely started on her own path. She was hardly in a position to challenge him on any of these things.

In any event, her Master had given an order, and it was her task to obey him. Stepping to the side of the corridor, out of the way of the bustling pedestrians, she pulled out her comlink.

She was about to key for the Jedi Temple's transportation service when, across the corridor, an all-too-familiar face caught her attention.

She froze, her breath catching in her throat, her eyes and mind and Jedi senses stretching out through the crowd of people between them. She'd seen this man many times before in the past few years, generally in the public areas of the Senate chamber but occasionally other places as well. He was young, probably a year or two younger than her, of medium height and build with short-cropped dark hair and a strangely bitter set to his mouth. She'd never gotten close enough to see what color his eyes were, but she assumed they were dark as well.

And every time she'd seen him, she'd had the distinct sense that he was watching her.

He was doing so now, studying her out of the corner of his eye as he pretended to work with a wiring panel he'd opened. She'd often seen him at wiring panels or fiddling with droid modules, but whether he actually knew his way around circuit boxes or whether he just used them as a pretext to hang around, she'd never figured out.

At the beginning, she'd assumed it was all coincidence. Even now, she had no actual proof it was anything else. All she had was the fact that, as her Jedi skills had grown, she'd been able to stretch out even through crowded corridors like this one to sense his mind.

And as she did so now, she found the same simmering resentment that she'd always felt before. Resentment, and frustration, and anger.

Directed at her.

Someone she'd harmed or slighted in a past so distant she couldn't even recall the incident? But she'd been in the Jedi Temple since she was an infant. One of the non-Jedi employees at the Temple, then? But surely her instructors would have taken action if they'd sensed any threat from him.

The man looked in her direction. Then, deliberately, he turned his back on her and gave his full attention to his wiring panel. Lorana watched him work, fighting against her own flurry of discomfiting emotions. Should she go over and try to find out what he had against her? Or should she go first to the Senate records and see if she could track down his identity, holding off on any confrontations until she had more information?

Or should she let it go entirely, and assume that the meetings were a coincidence and that his anger was merely directed at Jedi in general?

She was still trying to make a decision when he closed the panel, collected his tool kit, and stalked away. He glanced back once as he reached the corner, then disappeared around it.

There is no emotion; there is peace. Lorana had been taught that dictum from her earliest days in the Temple, and she'd tried her best to incorporate it into her life. But as long as the question of that man remained unresolved, she knew somehow that she could never have complete peace.

She also knew that now was not the time. Taking a deep breath, lifting her comlink again, she keyed for the spaceport.

* * *

The door closed behind the two Jedi, and for a moment Kinman Doriana gazed at the spot where they'd exited, a sour taste in his mouth. As a general rule, nearly all Jedi struck him as pompous and arrogant and obscenely sure of themselves. But even with that head start Jorus C'baoth was in a class by himself.

"You really don't like him, do you?" Palpatine asked mildly.

Setting his expression carefully back to neutral, Doriana shifted his attention back to the Chancellor. "I'm sorry, sir," he said. And he meant it. Whatever his personal feelings, it was bad policy to let emotions of any sort rise to the surface. Especially where Jedi were concerned. "I just think that with all the other problems facing the Republic, a massive exploration and colonization project should be relegated to the bottom third of the priority list. And for Master C'baoth to insist that you personally do something about it—"

"Patience, Kinman," Palpatine interrupted soothingly. "You must learn to permit people their passions. Outbound Flight is Master C'baoth's."

He looked across the office toward the door. "Besides, even if they find nothing of real value out there, it may be that just the news of their expedition will spark the imaginations of people across the Republic."

"If they ever *do* actually announce it," Doriana said. "The last I heard, the Jedi Council still had the whole project wrapped in secrecy."

Palpatine shrugged. "I'm sure they have their reasons."

"Perhaps." Doriana hesitated. "But I'd like to apologize to you, sir, for speaking out of turn during the meeting."

"Don't concern yourself about it," Palpatine assured him.

"Actually, it was an inspired suggestion. Master C'baoth is quite good at the sort of mediation the Barlok situation so sorely needs. I should have thought of it myself."

He snorted under his breath. "And to be perfectly honest, I'll be just as happy to have him off Coruscant for a couple of weeks. It'll give me a chance to consider how I'm going to persuade the Appropriations Committee to restore Outbound Flight's funding."

"As well as find a way to persuade the Council to give Master C'baoth all the Jedi he wants?"

"That one I can do nothing about," Palpatine said. "If C'baoth wants more Jedi, he's the one who'll have to persuade Yoda and Windu."

"Yes, sir," Doriana murmured. "Well . . . maybe he'll succeed so well at Barlok that they'll have no choice but to give in."

"Or else they'll give in simply to get him off their backs," Palpatine said drily. "He's as persistent with them as he is with me. At any rate, that part is in C'baoth's hands now. Speaking of matters in hand, when are you leaving for your own trip?"

"Tonight," Doriana said. "I have a ship reserved, and all the necessary files and documents are prepared and packed. I just need to stop by my apartment after work to pack my personal items and I'll be ready to go."

"Excellent," Palpatine said. "Then you might as well go now. There's nothing more I need from you for the rest of the day."

"Thank you, sir," Doriana said. "I'll keep you informed on what happens at the various meetings."

"Yes, do that." Palpatine raised his eyebrows. "And be sure you deliver those data cards to Governor Caulfmar personally."

"Yes, I read the reports," Doriana said, nodding. "Actually, if the timing works out I may take an extra day to poke around and see if I can identify the traitor in his inner circle. With your permission, of course."

"Granted," Palpatine said. "But be careful. There are rumors of growing dissatisfaction in that sector."

"There are rumors of that sort everywhere," Doriana said. "I'll be all right."

"I trust so," Palpatine said. "But still be careful. And hurry back."

It was a twenty-minute air taxi ride to Doriana's home in the Third Ring Apartment Towers northeast of the Senate complex. He split the time between datapad and comlink, checking on his travel plans and smoothing out the inevitable last-minute details. The taxi let him out on the 248th-floor landing pad, and he rode the turbolift ten stories down to his apartment. Unlocking the door, he went in, locking and privacy-sealing it behind him.

He had told Palpatine that he still had to pack his bags. In actual fact, they were already packed and sitting in a neat row just inside the conversation room. Passing them by, he went to the desk in the corner and sat down. From behind the false back in the bottom right-hand drawer he took a holoprojector and plugged it into the computer. The access/security code was a simple matter of twelve letters and eighteen digits; punching them in, he picked up his datapad again and settled back to wait.

As usual, the wait wasn't very long. Barely three minutes after he sent the call, the hooded face of Darth Sidious shimmered into view above the holoprojector. "Report," the other ordered in a gravelly voice.

"Jedi Master C'baoth is on his way to Barlok, my lord," Doriana said. "Depending on what kind of transport he was able to get, he should be there in three to six days."

"Excellent," Sidious said. "You'll have no trouble arriving ahead of him?"

"None, my lord," Doriana assured him. "My courier is faster than anything the Jedi can provide. He'll also have to stop off at the Temple and persuade the Council to give him official permission, while I'm ready to go right now. And all the groundwork has been laid."

"Then he should arrive to a warm reception indeed," Sidious said, his lips curving in a satisfied smile. "What about Chancellor Palpatine? You're certain he won't notice this little side trip?"

"I've built the necessary slack into my schedule," Doriana assured him. "I can spend up to three days on Barlok without falling behind. If it ends up taking longer, there are a couple of items on my agenda I should be able to resolve via HoloNet conference. I can do that from Barlok or anywhere else along the way, without having to actually travel to those systems."

"Again, excellent," Sidious said. "I have many servants, Doriana, but few as clever and as subtle as you."

"Thank you, my lord," Doriana said, a warm glow flowing through him. Darth Sidious, Dark Lord of the Sith, was not a man who was generous with his compliments.

"It will be a distinct pleasure to get Jorus C'baoth out of our way," Sidious went on. "All indeed goes according to my plan."

"Yes, my lord," Doriana said. "I'll report as soon as we've achieved our victory."

"Just make certain we *have* that victory," Sidious said, the note of warning in his tone sending a chill through the lingering warmth of his earlier compliment. "Proceed with your work, my friend."

"Yes, my lord."

The image vanished. Shutting off the holoprojector, Doriana

disconnected it from the computer and returned it to its hiding place. Then, pocketing his datapad, he retraced his steps to where his packed bags waited. Yes, the punishment for failing the Sith Lord would undoubtedly be severe. Nearly as severe, he had no doubt, as that which would descend upon him if Chancellor Palpatine ever learned that he had a traitor in his inner office.

But if the price of failure was great, so were the rewards of success. Doriana's apartment, his position, and his quiet but far-ranging authority were proof of that. It was, in his estimation, a gamble well worth taking.

Besides which, he did so enjoy the game.

Pulling out his comlink, he keyed for a taxi to take him to the spaceport. Then, gathering his bags together, he headed for the turbolift.

The door to the Jedi Council Chamber slid open. "Come," Jedi Master Mace Windu called.

Squaring his shoulders, wondering what this was all about, Obi-Wan Kenobi stepped inside.

And stopped, feeling his forehead wrinkling in surprise. A person summoned to the Jedi Council Chamber naturally expected to find the entire Council waiting for him. But aside from Windu, standing over by the windows gazing out at the city, the room was deserted. "No, you haven't misunderstood where you were supposed to go," Windu said, half turning to give Obi-Wan a faint smile. "I need to talk to you."

"Certainly, Master Windu," Obi-Wan said, still frowning as he crossed to where Windu stood. "Is this about Anakin again?"

"No," Windu said, raising his eyebrows questioningly. "Why, what's young Skywalker done now?"

"Nothing," Obi-Wan assured him hastily. "At least, nothing

in particular. But you know what fourteen-year-old Padawan learners are like."

"Strong, cocky, and amazing naïve," Windu said, smiling again. "I wish you luck with him."

Obi-Wan shrugged. "If there *is* such a thing as luck."

"You know what I mean." Windu turned back to look out the window. "Tell me, have you ever heard of a project called Outbound Flight?"

Obi-Wan searched his memory. "I don't think so."

"It was proposed as a grand exploration and colonization mission," Windu said. "Six Dreadnaught warships were to be linked to each other around a central equipment and supply storage core, the whole thing to be sent out into the Unknown Regions and from there to another galaxy."

Obi-Wan blinked. To another *galaxy*? "No, I haven't heard anything at all about this. What's the proposed time frame?"

"Actually, it's mostly ready now," Windu said. "Just the final assembly and some disagreements about the passenger list."

"Who's in charge of it? The Senate?"

"Nominally, it was the Council's plan," Windu said. "In practice, it's been Master C'baoth who's been the chief driving force behind it."

"Jorus C'baoth, master of the designated interview?" Obi-Wan asked drily. "And yet the project hasn't made HoloNet newscasts? Incredible."

"You shouldn't talk about a Jedi Master that way," Windu reproved him mildly.

"Am I wrong?"

Windu shrugged, a slight lift of his shoulders. "The fact is, everyone connected with Outbound Flight has had their reasons for keeping the project out of the public eye," he said. "Chancellor Palpatine has been concerned that spending time and money this way in the face of the Republic's other problems might not go over very well. Ditto for the Senate, which provided the Dreadnaughts they'll be using."

He pursed his lips. "As for the Council, we had reasons of our own."

"Let me guess," Obi-Wan said. "C'baoth is hoping Outbound Flight can find out what happened to Vergere."

Windu looked at him in mild surprise. "You *are* growing in Jedi insight, aren't you?"

"I'd like to think so," Obi-Wan said. "But this doesn't really qualify. Anakin and I never did get the whole story on her disappearance; more to the point, we weren't able to find her on our last trip out that direction. Never mind what C'baoth wants; *I* want to know what happened to her."

"Careful, Obi-Wan," Windu warned. "You mustn't allow your emotions to intrude on this."

Obi-Wan bowed his head. "My apologies."

"Emotion is the enemy," Windu went on. "Emotion of all sorts. Yours *and* Master C'baoth's."

Obi-Wan frowned. "You think Master C'baoth is getting too close to this project?"

"To be honest, I don't know *what's* happening with him," Windu admitted reluctantly. "He insists that we need to send a strong force out into the Unknown Regions to find Vergere and bring her back, which is all well and good. But at the same time he talks about how the Republic is teetering on the brink and how it might be good to transfer some of the best Jedi out of the Republic entirely, settling them in new colonies in the Unknown Regions where Coruscant politics can't touch them."

"You're not really considering doing that, are you?" Obi-Wan asked. "We're spread thin enough as it is."

"Most of the Council would agree with you," Windu said. "Unfortunately, the majority also think that by now Vergere's trail is so cold it will probably be impossible to follow. Most of those who still hold out hope think a smaller probe would still be worthwhile, something larger than your attempt but far below the scale C'baoth wants." He grimaced. "The bottom line is that C'baoth is about the only one still pushing for the full Outbound Flight."

"Are you suggesting he might defy the Council if you try to cancel it?"

"Why not?" Windu countered.

Obi-Wan turned back to face the window, and for a moment the room was silent. "So what exactly does the Council want me to do?" Obi-Wan asked at last.

"At this moment, Master C'baoth and his Padawan, Lorana Jinzler, are on their way to the spaceport," Windu said. "Apparently, Chancellor Palpatine mentioned some bogged-down negotiations on Barlok, and C'baoth persuaded the Council to send him there to mediate."

"Is this something major?"

"Major enough," Windu said. "The Corporate Alliance versus the local government. And you know how anything involving any of the big corporate players makes headlines these days."

"Yes," Obi-Wan murmured. Center-stage negotiations, so of course C'baoth would be headed in that direction. "Again, what do you want me to do?"

A muscle in Windu's cheek tightened. "We want you to go to Barlok and keep an eye on him."

Obi-Wan felt his mouth drop open. *"Me?"*

"I know," Windu agreed soberly. "But you're here, and you're available. Besides, Skywalker seemed to get along well enough with him the one time they met. Maybe you can frame the whole thing as a desire to show your Padawan how Jedi negotiations are done."

Obi-Wan snorted. "You really think C'baoth will buy that?"

"Probably not," Windu conceded. "But if you don't go, it'll have to be either Yoda or me. You think he'll be less explosive if one of *us* shows up?"

"You have a point," Obi-Wan said with a sigh. "Fine. We're between assignments anyway. And you're right; Anakin *was* rather impressed by that take-charge single-mindedness of his. Maybe a little youthful hero worship will keep him calm."

"Maybe," Windu said. "At any rate, there'll be a ship waiting by the time you and Skywalker get to the spaceport."

"Any instructions other than to just watch him?"

"Not really," Windu said. He pursed his lips, and his gaze seemed to stretch out toward infinity. "There's something else going on, though. Something deep inside the man that I haven't been able to get a grip on. Some private thoughts, or agenda, or . . . I don't know. Something."

"Right," Obi-Wan said. "I'll be sure to watch for that."

Windu gave him the sort of wryly patient look Jedi Masters seemed to do so well. "And keep in touch," he said.

Thrawn had told Car'das that his base wasn't far from the spot where his task force had run into the *Bargain Hunter*. What he hadn't mentioned was that the trip would take nearly three standard days.

"About time," Qennto muttered under his breath as the three humans stood together at the back of the *Springhawk*'s bridge and watched as the handful of ships flew in formation across a small asteroid field. "I'm about to go stir crazy."

"You could always join Maris and me for the language lessons," Car'das offered. "Commander Thrawn really is decent company."

"No thanks," Qennto grunted. "You two want to aid and abet a potential enemy, be my guests. Not me."

"These people are *not* potential enemies," Maris said firmly. "As you'd realize if you'd made any effort to get to know them. They're very polite and extremely civilized."

"Yeah, well, the Hutts have a civilization, too, or so they

say," Qennto retorted. "Sorry, but it'll take more than good manners to convince *me* the Chiss are harmless."

Mentally, Car'das shook his head. Ever since that first night aboard when he'd been frozen out of the negotiations, Qennto had been nursing a grudge against the Chiss in general and Thrawn in particular. Car'das and Maris had both tried to talk some sense back into him, but Qennto was more interested in brooding than in reason, and after a few attempts Car'das had given up. Maybe Maris had, too.

Thrawn had been across the bridge, standing beside the crewer at what Car'das had tentatively identified as the navigation station. Now the commander stepped back and circled to where the humans waited. "There," he said, pointing ahead out the wide viewport. "The large asteroid with the slow rotation. That's our base."

Car'das frowned at it. The asteroid wasn't rotating so much as it was doing a slow wobble, nearly but not quite end over end. Not for pseudogravitational purposes, obviously; the *Springhawk* showed that the Chiss had artificial gravity. So why pick a rotating asteroid?

Maris was obviously wondering the same thing. "That wobble must make it hard to dock with," she commented.

"It *does* require a certain degree of skill," Thrawn agreed, lifting his eyebrows slightly like a teacher trying to draw an answer from a group of students.

Car'das looked back at the asteroid. Could Thrawn have set up a deliberately tricky docking procedure as a training exercise for new recruits? But he could do that more easily and safely with a separate practice station.

Unless this asteroid was merely a training facility and not his main base at all. There were certainly no lights or indications of construction showing anywhere that he could see. Was that the conclusion Thrawn expected them to come to?

And then, suddenly, he had it. "You've got a passive sensor array at one end," he said. "The wobble lets it sweep the whole sky instead of just one spot."

"But why spin the whole asteroid?" Maris asked, sounding puzzled. "Couldn't you just rotate the array?"

"Sure he could," Qennto growled. "But then there'd be something moving on the surface an enemy might spot. This way everything's all nice and quiet and peaceful, right up to the minute when he blows their ships out from under them."

"Essentially correct," Thrawn said. "Though we're not expecting enemies to actually come calling. Still, it's wise to take precautions."

"And they didn't blow *our* ship out from under us," Maris said, tapping a finger on Qennto's chest for emphasis.

Qennto turned a glower toward her. Car'das spoke up quickly: "So we're in Chiss space now?"

"Yes and no," Thrawn said. "Currently, there are only some survey and observation teams here, so it's hardly representative of a proper Chiss system. However, the second planet is quite habitable and within a few years will probably be opened up to full colonization. At that point, it will come officially under the protection and control of the Nine Ruling Families."

"I hope you're not expecting us to stay for opening ceremonies," Qennto muttered.

"Of course not," Thrawn assured him. "I tell you this simply because you might wish to return someday and see what we've made of the Crustai system."

"You've named it already?" Maris asked.

"The initial survey team always has that honor," Thrawn said. "In this case, the name Crustai is an acronym for—"

"*Crahsystor* Mitth'raw'nuruodo," a Chiss called from across the bridge. *"Ris ficar tli claristae su fariml'sroca."*

"Sa cras mi sout shisfla," Thrawn replied sharply, striding back to his command chair in the center of the bridge and sitting down. *"Hos mich falliare."*

"What did he say?" Qennto demanded, grabbing at a nearby chair back for balance as the *Springhawk* veered sharply portside and began to pick up speed. "What's going on?"

"I'm not sure," Car'das said, mentally replaying the Cheunh words and trying to sort out the various prefixes and suffixes. The Chiss grammar was logical and relatively easy to learn, but after only three days of lessons he didn't have much vocabulary to work with. "The only word roots I caught were the ones for 'stranger' and 'run.' "

"Stranger. Run." Qennto hissed between his teeth as the stars in the viewport stretched into starlines. "They're after someone."

"Someone not too far away, either," Maris murmured. "Isn't *stae* a word root for 'near'?"

"Yes, I think you're right," Car'das agreed. "I wonder if we ought to go back to our quarters."

"We stay right here," Qennto said firmly. "We already saw how they treated one ship that wandered in too close. I want to see what they do with another."

"They only took out Progga because he fired first," Maris pointed out.

"Yeah," Qennto said. "Maybe."

For the next few minutes the bridge crew worked busily at

their stations, the silence punctuated only by an occasional command or comment. Car'das found himself staring at the back of Thrawn's head as the commander sat motionlessly in his chair, wondering if he dared sidle up behind the other and ask for an explanation as to what was going on.

A few seconds later he was glad he hadn't. Less than a minute after entering hyperspace, they suddenly dropped back out again.

"Already?" Qennto muttered, sounding stunned.

"He did a *microjump,*" Car'das said, hardly believing it himself.

"Ridiculous," Qennto insisted. "You can't hit the side of the Senate Building with a—"

Abruptly, the deck jerked beneath them, nearly knocking them off their feet. Reflexively, Car'das grabbed Maris's upper arm with one hand and a nearby conduit with the other, keeping both of them on their feet.

Just as a pair of small ships roared past the viewport, spitting laserfire and missiles at the *Springhawk*.

"I'd say he did a little better than hit the side of the Senate Building," Car'das managed as the deck again shook beneath them. "Looks like he's right where he wants to be."

"Terrific," Qennto bit out. "I'm glad *he* wants to be here."

The shaking subsided as the attackers flew out of optimum firing range, and Car'das focused on the visual displays. There were just three ships indicated: the two fighters now coming around for another pass, plus one larger ship considerably farther away. Unlike the fighters, the larger vessel seemed to be trying to move away from the battle zone instead of into it.

"Here they come," Qennto said.

Car'das looked back at the viewport. The *Springhawk* had

swiveled to face its attackers, and in the distance he could see the glow as the fighters kicked their drives to full power. "Grab on to something," he warned, resettling his fingers around the conduit as Maris got a grip beside his. The fighters split formation as they approached, veering toward opposite sides of their target, their lasers opening up again. The *Springhawk*'s weapons returned fire.

And both attackers exploded.

"Whoa!" Qennto said. "What in the—?"

"They blew up," Maris breathed. "A single shot, and they just blew *up*."

"Don't start cheering just yet," Car'das warned. The *Springhawk* was swinging away from the expanding clouds of debris and picking up speed. "There's still the big one left."

The dizzying sweep of stars settled down as they finished their turn, and in the distance he could see the drive glow of the larger ship. "I don't suppose we could be lucky enough for it to be unarmed," Qennto said.

"Thrawn wouldn't attack an unarmed ship," Maris told him firmly.

"Why not?" Qennto growled back. "*I* would. Those fighters attacked first. That makes the whole bunch of them fair game."

"And probably dead meat," Car'das muttered.

Maris shivered but said nothing.

The other ship saw them coming, of course. Even as the *Springhawk* closed to firing range, it swung partway around, and a handful of missiles streaked out. The Chiss lasers flashed in reply, and the missiles vaporized in midflight. The enemy responded by rolling ninety degrees over and launching a second salvo. This group, too, was dealt with at a safe distance. A third missile group followed, then a fourth, all destroyed en route.

"Why don't they jump to lightspeed?" Maris murmured.

"I don't think they can," Car'das told her, pointing to one of the tactical displays. "Looks to me like someone took out their hyperdrive."

"When?" Qennto asked, frowning. "I don't remember hearing any firing before the fighters attacked."

"Someone had to be here to call in the news," Car'das reminded him. "Maybe he got in a lucky shot."

Whatever the reason, the other ship was definitely not getting away. The *Springhawk* continued to close the gap, and as they neared it, Car'das noticed for the first time that its hull was covered in what looked like ovoid bubbles, each roughly two meters across and three long. "What are those things?" he asked. "Qennto?"

"No idea," the other said, craning his neck. "They look kind of like tiny observation blisters. Part of the navigation system, maybe?"

"Or cabin viewports," Maris said, her voice suddenly tight. "Could it be a passenger liner?"

"What, with four clusters of missile launchers?" Qennto countered. "Not a chance."

The Chiss helmsman moved the *Springhawk* alongside the alien vessel, compensating almost casually for its sluggish attempts to veer away, and nestled up against the other's hull. There was a quick stutter of dull thuds as maglocks were engaged, and Thrawn tapped a key on his command board. *"Ch'tra,"* he called.

" 'Go,' " Car'das translated. "Looks like we're boarding."

The commander rose from his chair and turned around. "My apologies," he said, switching to Sy Bisti as he crossed to the three humans. "I hadn't intended to take you into danger this way. But the opportunity presented itself, and I needed to take it."

"That's all right, Commander," Car'das assured him. "And it didn't look like we were in *that* much danger."

"As it turned out," Thrawn said. Stepping to a bank of lockers along one wall, he opened one and pulled out an armored vac suit. "Your quarters are too close to the boarding area for safety, so I'll ask you to remain here until we return."

"You're going in personally?" Maris asked, frowning.

"I command these warriors," Thrawn said, climbing into the vac suit with sure, practiced movements. "Part of my duty is to share in their danger."

Maris glanced at Qennto. "Be careful," she said, sounding almost embarrassed.

Thrawn gave her a small smile. "Don't worry," he said. Slapping the final seal closed, he pulled a helmet and large handgun from the locker. "The vessel is most likely severely undercrewed, and Chiss warriors are the best there are. I'll return soon."

Car'das had wondered at first why none of the rest of the bridge crew had joined with Thrawn in the boarding party, the sounds of which they could occasionally hear wafting along the corridors and through the open door. It was soon clear, though, that they weren't just sitting around waiting, but were actively engaged in some project of their own.

It was only as the melee was winding down that he was able to piece together a few recognizable snatches of conversation and figure out what that project had been. Using the *Springhawk*'s sensors, they'd been assisting the boarders in tracking down enemy combatants, whether hiding or gathering together for an ambush. Even charging pirate-style onto an enemy vessel, Commander Thrawn made use of all available resources.

It took less than an hour for the Chiss to secure the enemy

vessel. Another two hours went by, though, before one of the warriors came to the bridge with instructions to bring the humans aboard.

Car'das hadn't traveled very much before hooking up with Qennto and Maris. But most of his recent travel had been to the seedier parts of the Republic, and as he stepped into the boarding tunnel he was confident he could handle anything they found at the other end.

He was wrong.

The vessel itself was bad enough. Dank and dirty, its entire interior showed signs of multiple repairs done in a hasty and careless manner, and the mixture of odors swirling through its corridors made his nose itch. Worse than that were the dozens of blast points and scorch marks on the walls and ceilings, mute reminders of the short but vicious battle that had just taken place.

Worst of all were the bodies.

Car'das had seen bodies before, but only the serene and neatly laid-out ones he'd encountered at funerals. Never before had he seen bodies haphazardly stretched out wherever the Chiss weapons had thrown them, twisted into whatever grotesque contortions their own death throes had sculpted for them. He winced as the Chiss warrior led them through various clumps of the dead, not wanting to look at them but forced to do so if he didn't want to step on them, hoping desperately that he didn't completely shame himself by getting sick.

"Relax, kid," Qennto's voice muttered at his side as they reached yet another scattering of corpses. "They're just bodies. They can't hurt you."

"I know that," Car'das growled, throwing a surreptitious look at Maris. Even she, with all her genteel upbringing and idealistic sensitivity, was doing better with this than he was.

Ahead, a door opened, and Thrawn stepped into the corridor. He was still wearing his vac suit, but the helmet now hung on a fastener on his left hip. "Come," he called, beckoning. "I want to show you something."

Nearly there. Taking a deep breath, focusing his attention on Thrawn's glowing eyes, Car'das managed to make it the rest of the way.

"What are your thoughts?" Thrawn asked as they reached him, gesturing to the corridor around them

"I think they were probably very poor," Maris said, her tone mostly calm but with an edge of disapproval. "You can see where they've had to patch and repatch just to keep everything operating. This isn't a military ship, certainly not one that could have been a threat to the Chiss."

"I agree," Thrawn agreed, turning his glowing eyes on her. "So; poor people, you think. Nomads?"

"Or refugees," she said, the disapproving edge growing a little sharper.

"And the missiles?"

"They didn't do the passengers much good, did they?"

"No, but it wasn't from lack of trying." Thrawn turned to Qennto. "And you, Captain? What's *your* reading of this?"

"I don't know," Qennto said calmly. "And I don't especially care. They fired first, right?"

Thrawn shrugged microscopically. "Not entirely true," he said. "One of the sentries I had stationed here happened to be close enough as they came through to disable their hyperdrive. Car'das? Your opinion?"

Car'das looked around at the faded and motley walls. He might not have had a lot of schooling before running off to space, but he'd had enough to know when a teacher was still looking for an answer he hadn't yet gotten from anyone else.

But what *was* the answer? Maris was right; the ship did indeed look like it was falling apart. But Thrawn was right about the missiles, too. Would refugees have weapons like that?

And then, suddenly, it struck him. He looked behind him, locating the nearest alien body and doing a quick estimate of its height and reach. Another look at the wall, and he turned back to Thrawn. "These aren't the ones who did the repairs, are they?"

"Very good," Thrawn said, smiling faintly. "No, they aren't."

"What do you mean?" Qennto asked, frowning.

"These aliens are too tall," Car'das explained, pointing to the wall. "See here, where the sealant pattern changes texture? That's where whoever was slopping it on had to go get a ladder or floatpad to finish the job."

"And whoever that worker was, he was considerably shorter than the masters of this vessel." Thrawn turned back to Maris. "As you deduced, the vessel has indeed been repaired many times. But not by its owners."

Maris's lips compressed into a hard, thin line, her eyes suddenly cold as she looked back at the dead bodies. "They were slavers."

"Indeed," Thrawn said. "Are you still angry at me for killing them?"

Maris's face turned pink. "I'm sorry."

"I understand." Thrawn's eyebrows lifted slightly. "You of the Republic don't condone slavery yourselves, do you?"

"No, of course not," Maris assured him hastily.

"We have droids to handle most menial chores," Car'das added.

"What are droids?"

"Mechanical workers that can think and act on their own," Car'das explained. "You must have something of the sort yourselves."

"Actually, we don't," Thrawn said, eyeing Car'das thoughtfully. "Nor do any of the alien cultures we've met. Can you show me one?"

Beside Maris, Qennto rumbled warningly in his throat. "We didn't bring any on this trip," Car'das said, ignoring his captain's thunderous expression. Qennto had warned him repeatedly not to discuss the Republic's technology level with the Chiss. But in Car'das's opinion this hardly qualified. Besides, Thrawn had surely already examined the *Bargain Hunter*'s records, which must show a dozen different types of droids in action.

"A pity," Thrawn said. "Still, if the Republic has no slavery, how is it you understand the concept?"

Car'das grimaced. "We do know a few cultures where it exists," he admitted reluctantly.

"And your people permit this?"

"The Republic hasn't got much pull with systems that aren't members," Qennto put in impatiently. "Look, are we done here yet?"

"Not quite," Thrawn said, gesturing toward the door he'd just come through. "Come and look."

More bodies? Steeling himself, determined not to go all woozy again even if the whole place was piled high with them, Car'das stepped past the commander and through the doorway.

And stopped short, his mouth dropping open in amazement. The room was unexpectedly large, with a high ceiling that must have stretched up at least two of the ship's decks.

But it wasn't piled high with bodies. It was piled high with treasure.

Treasure of all kinds, too. There were piles of metal ingots of various colors and sheens, neatly stacked inside acceleration webbing. There were rows of bins, some filled with coins or multicolored gems, others stocked with rectangular packages that might have been food or spices or electronics. Several heavy-looking cabinets against one wall probably held items that would have been too tempting to leave within easy reach of the slaves or perhaps even the crew itself.

There was also a good deal of artwork: flats, sculpts, tressles, and other forms and styles Car'das couldn't even categorize. Most of it was stacked together, but he could see a few pieces scattered around throughout the room, as if some of the loaders either hadn't recognized them as art or else hadn't much cared where they put them.

There was a sharp intake of air and a slightly strangled gasp as Qennto and Maris came in behind him. "What in the *worlds*?" Maris breathed.

"A treasure vessel, carrying the plunder of many worlds," Thrawn said, slipping into the room behind them. "They were not only slavers, but pirates and raiders as well."

With an effort, Car'das pulled his eyes away from the treasure trove and focused on Thrawn. "You sound like you already know these people."

"Only by reputation," Thrawn said, his almost gentle tone in sharp contrast to the tightness in his face as he gazed across the room. "At least, up until now."

"You've been hunting them?"

A slight frown creased Thrawn's forehead. "Of course not,"

he said. "The Vagaari have made no move against the Chiss Ascendancy. We therefore have no reason to hunt them."

"But you know their name," Qennto murmured.

"As I said, I know their reputation," Thrawn said. "They've been moving through this region of space for at least the past ten years, preying mostly on the weak and the technologically primitive."

"What about their slaves?" Maris asked. "Do you know anything about them?"

Thrawn shook his head. "We haven't found any aboard this vessel. From that, and from this room, I presume they were en route to their main base."

"And they off-loaded the slaves to keep them from finding out where that base is?" Car'das suggested.

"Exactly," Thrawn said. "The crew complement is smaller than one would expect for a vessel of this size, as well. That indicates they weren't expecting trouble, but instead intended to go straight home."

"Yes, you mentioned back on the bridge that they were undercrewed," Car'das said. "How did you know that?"

"I deduced it from the fact that their defense was sluggish and mostly ineffectual," Thrawn said. "They did little but launch missiles, all running the same countermeasures we'd already seen. A fully crewed vessel would have had laser gunners in place and would have shifted the defense patterns of their missiles. Clearly, they were expecting their escort to do any fighting that became necessary."

"And boy, were they wrong," Qennto muttered. "You had them outclassed from the start."

"Hardly outclassed," Thrawn told him. "I merely noticed that in both of their attacks a laser salvo preceded their missiles in a distinct and predictable pattern. When they launched their third attack, I was able to fire back just as the tubes' protective doors opened, detonating the missiles before they could be launched. Fighters that size never have sufficient armor to withstand that sort of internal blast."

"You see?" Car'das said drily. "Nothing to it."

Qennto's lip twisted. "Yeah," he said. "Right."

"So what happens now?" Maris asked.

"I'll have the vessel towed back to Crustai for further study," Thrawn said, giving the room one last look before turning back to the door.

"Question," Qennto put in. "You told Car'das you'd be giving us some extra stuff as payment for teaching you Basic, right?"

"That wasn't precisely the way I stated it," Thrawn said. "But that's essentially correct."

"And the longer we stay, the more extras we get?"

Thrawn smiled faintly. "That may be possible. I thought you were in a rush to return home."

"No, no, there's no hurry," Qennto assured him, giving the treasure room a leisurely sweep of his eyes. His earlier impatience, Car'das noted, seemed to have vanished without a trace. "No hurry at all."

Come, Padawan," C'baoth said tartly, half turning to throw a glare behind him. "Stop lagging."

"Yes, Master C'baoth," Lorana said, picking up her pace and hoping fervently that at her increased speed she'd be able to get through the early-morning marketplace crowds without running down any of the shoppers. Up to now the browsing Brolfi had been able to get out of C'baoth's way as he strode through their midst, but she suspected part of that was the fact that he was as hard to miss as an approaching thunderstorm. She, unfortunately, didn't have nearly the same commanding presence, and there had been some near misses already.

The frustrating part was that there was no need for them to walk this fast in the first place—they still had plenty of time before the day's negotiations began. No, C'baoth was simply angry: angry at the stubborn Brolf negotiators, angry at the equally stubborn Corporate Alliance representatives, angrier still at the careless drafters of the original mineral-rights contract who had left matters open to multiple interpretations in the first place.

And the angrier C'baoth got, the faster he walked.

Fortunately, the Force was with Lorana, and she made it to the end of their particular market segment without bowling anyone over and crossed onto one of the wide promenades that divided up the marketplace. One more segment to go and they would climb the steps to the wide western door of the city administration center where the negotiations would soon resume.

Unfortunately, C'baoth responded to the open area by picking up his pace all the more. Grimacing, Lorana sped up as much as she could without breaking into a trot, which she knew would bring an instant rebuke as being undignified and unbecoming of a Jedi.

And then, without warning, C'baoth braked to an abrupt halt.

"What is it?" Lorana asked, stretching out with the Force as she came to a stop beside him. She could detect no danger or threat nearby, only C'baoth's own suddenly heightened annoyance. "Master C'baoth?"

"Typical," he growled, his hair and beard rustling against his robe as he turned his head. "Nervous and distrusting, the whole lot of them. Come, Padawan."

He strode off toward the market square to their right. Lorana craned her neck to look as she followed, trying to figure out what he was talking about.

And then she saw two men coming toward them through the crowd: a Jedi and his Padawan, both of them familiar looking, striding confidently through the ordinary people like lights amid a swirl of dead leaves.

She frowned, the mental image suddenly catching her conscious attention. *A swirl of dead leaves . . .*

When in the worlds had she started to think of non-Jedi that way? Surely that wasn't how she'd been brought up to think of the people she had dedicated her life to serve. Could it be an attitude she'd picked up from some of the people she'd traveled among since becoming C'baoth's Padawan? Certainly many of them had seemed to consider themselves inferior to those who carried the lightsaber.

Or had she picked it up from C'baoth himself? Was that how *he* thought about people?

C'baoth stopped a few meters from the edge of the square and waited, and as the two figures threaded their way around the final group of shoppers and continued toward them Lorana finally matched their faces with their names. "Master C'baoth," Obi-Wan Kenobi said, nodding in greeting as he and his Padawan, Anakin Skywalker, walked up.

"Master Kenobi," C'baoth greeted them in turn, his voice and manner polite but with an edge of intimidation beneath the words. "This is a surprise. Have you come all the way from Coruscant just to shop for prisht fruits?"

"It *is* said that Barlok horticultural techniques produce the best specimens," Obi-Wan replied calmly. "And you?"

"You know perfectly well why we're here," C'baoth said. "Tell me, how *is* Master Windu?"

Kenobi's lip twitched slightly. "He's well."

"That's good to hear." C'baoth shifted his attention to the young teen standing at Kenobi's side, and a slight smile finally touched the corners of his lips. "Master Skywalker, isn't it?" he said in a friendlier tone.

"Yes, Master C'baoth," Anakin said, and Lorana couldn't help but smile herself at the earnest gravity in the boy's voice. "It's an honor to see you again."

"As it is likewise an honor for me to meet once more with such a promising Padawan," C'baoth replied. "Tell me, how goes your training?"

Anakin glanced at Kenobi. "There's always more to learn, of course," he said. "I can only hope my progress is satisfactory."

"His progress is more than satisfactory," Kenobi put in. "At this rate, he'll be a full Jedi before he's twenty."

Lorana winced. She herself was already twenty-two, and C'baoth had made no mention of recommending her for Jedi Knighthood anytime soon. Was Anakin that much stronger in the Force than she was?

"And yet he began his training so much later than usual," C'baoth pointed out, smiling almost fondly at the boy. "That makes his development even more impressive."

"Indeed," Kenobi said. "In hindsight, I think it's clear that the Council made the right decision in permitting me to train him."

There was just the slightest emphasis on the word *me,* and for half a second a dark cloud seemed to hover at the edge of C'baoth's face. Then the darkness faded and he smiled again. "This has been a pleasant meeting," he said. "But the negotiators are assembling, and I have work to do. I trust you'll excuse me if I go and deal with legitimate Council business."

"Certainly," Kenobi said, his cheek tightening slightly at the implication that he and his Padawan were not, in fact, on legitimate Council business themselves.

"But I forget my manners," C'baoth continued. "This is a full and rich city, and you and Master Skywalker will undoubtedly wish to sample its amusements while you're here." He gestured to Lorana. "My Padawan, Lorana Jinzler, would be honored to escort you on your explorations."

"Thank you, but that won't be necessary," Kenobi said, throwing Lorana a measuring look. "We'll be fine."

"I insist," C'baoth said, and there was no mistaking the command in his tone. "I wouldn't want you getting in the way of the talks, or accidentally running afoul of any of the negotiators." He looked at Anakin. "Besides, I imagine Master Skywalker would enjoy the company of another Padawan for a while."

Again, Anakin looked at his teacher. "Well . . ."

"And I'd take it as a personal favor, as well," C'baoth added, looking back at Kenobi. "There's really nothing for Lorana to do in the negotiations, and thus no real reason for me to keep her there. I'm sure she'd prefer to be out and about, and I'd feel better knowing she was touring the city with someone reliable."

Kenobi's lip twitched. He wasn't at all happy about this—Lorana could see that even without the Force. But he'd been outmaneuvered, and he knew it. "As you wish, Master C'baoth," he said. "We'd be honored to have your Padawan's company for the present."

"For as long as you wish," C'baoth said. "Now I must go. Farewell." Turning, he strode away.

Lorana watched him go, her throat tightening. She'd been perfectly content to sit behind C'baoth during the negotiations, and up to now he'd seemed equally content to have her there. Had she done something to displease him?

Still, whatever the reason, she had her orders, even if they'd been largely unspoken. Bracing herself, she turned back around.

To find Kenobi and Anakin gazing expectantly back at her. "Well," she said, wincing at the inanity of the word. A Padawan of Jorus C'baoth's should be more urbane and eloquent than that. "I've only been in the city for a day, but I did pick up a guide card for visitors at the spaceport."

"So did we," Kenobi said, lifting his eyebrows slightly.

Clearly, he wasn't going to make this easy on her. "Master Kenobi—"

"You know anyplace to get good tarsh maxers?" Anakin spoke up hopefully. "I'm hungry."

Kenobi smiled at his Padawan, and when he looked back at Lorana she could feel the tension between them fading away. "Actually, that sounds good to me, too," he agreed. "Let's hunt down a diner."

Seated on the balcony of his hotel room, Doriana watched as the three of them headed off toward one of the city's more mid-scale restaurant districts, scowling as he followed their leisurely progress through his macrobinoculars. So the Jedi Council had pulled a fast one on him, sending Obi-Wan Kenobi and his up-start Padawan to keep an eye on C'baoth. *That* hadn't been part of Sidious's plan.

But then, these two seemed to be making a career of that sort of thing. He remembered vividly Sidious's anger after the Naboo incident and the unexpected defeat of his Trade Federation allies. Their army should have been able to occupy the planet for months or years, creating a turmoil and paralysis in the Senate that Sidious and Doriana could have used to devastating effect.

But all that had been lost, thanks to Skywalker and his dumb luck in taking out the Trade Federation's Droid Control Ship. Darth Maul's death at the hands of Kenobi and Qui-Gon Jinn had been equally devastating, short-circuiting a quiet reign of terror that would have distracted the Jedi even as it pruned the edges of their close-knit group.

And now here they were on Barlok, threatening to interfere with Sidious's plan to eliminate Jorus C'baoth.

He set his lips firmly together. No—not this time. Not if Kinman Doriana had anything to say about it.

Inside his pocket, his special comlink beeped. Still watching Kenobi and his companions, he fished out the device and flicked it on. "Yes?"

"Defender?" a hoarse Brolf voice asked.

"Yes, it is I, Patriot," Doriana said. "I have returned as I promised to help you in your time of need."

"You are late," the other growled. "The negotiations have already begun."

"But nothing is yet decided," Doriana said. "There's still time to send a message that the Brolf people will not be cheated. Has everything been prepared according to my instructions?"

"Almost," Patriot said. "The final components should be on the way. The question is whether *you've* brought the contribution you promised."

"I have it right here," Doriana assured him.

"Then bring it," Patriot said. "Third North from Chessile and Scriv Streets. Two hours."

"I'll be there."

There was a *ping* as the connection was broken. Putting away his comlink, Doriana glanced at his chrono. Excellent. The address wasn't more than half an hour's walk away, which would give him time for a leisurely stroll and a careful survey of the neighborhood before he arrived.

But first, he would see what he could do to keep Kenobi on the sidelines where he belonged.

Fortunately, that shouldn't be a problem. Whatever his purpose here, chances were he wouldn't make any serious moves without first consulting the Jedi Council. A little tweaking of the city's HoloNet computer access system, and there would be nothing coming into or going out of Barlok for the next day or two. Plenty of time for him and his Brolf allies to finish the job.

Stepping over to the desk, he opened his computer and set to work.

The cantina they found didn't have the most promising décor Obi-Wan had ever seen. But like Dex's Diner on Coruscant, appearances could be deceiving, particularly where food was involved. The hearty aroma of roast tarsh was definitely in the air, maxers were the headliners on the menu, and Lorana's guide card gave the place a triple-porken rating. All in all, it looked like a pretty good bet.

A WA-2 droid scuttled up as they chose a booth overlooking the street and sat down. "Welcome to Panky's," it said, its electronic voice somehow managing to convey both courtesy and the fact that it was being severely and unfairly overworked. "What may I provide for you?"

"I want a tarsh maxer and bribb juice," Anakin said eagerly.

Obi-Wan suppressed a smile. Anakin had discovered bribb juice on his first trip as a Padawan, and ever since then he'd ordered it every chance he got, whether it really went with the rest of the meal or not. "Same maxer for me, but make my drink a Corellian noale," he told the droid.

"I'll take the bribb juice, but with a prisht-fruit salad," Lorana said. She gave Obi-Wan a hesitant smile. "After all, Barlok *does* produce the best specimens."

"So I've heard," Obi-Wan said, studying her. She was about medium height, with dark hair and striking gray eyes. She had an intelligent face, a nice smile, and that sense of global awareness that came from knowledge of the Force. To all appearances, she seemed well on her way to becoming a typical Jedi.

And yet, there was something about her that felt odd to him, something that didn't quite ring true. Her air of dignity and confidence felt strained, like an accessory she put on every morning instead of something that was truly a part of her innermost being. Her smile had a similarly tentative edge to it, as if she was afraid it would get her into trouble.

On the surface, she had everything down just right. Beneath it all, she was still a Padawan learner with a lot of work yet to do.

"I don't think I've ever met anyone before who was trained by Master C'baoth," he commented as the droid bustled away. "What's he like to study with?"

The corners of Lorana's mouth compressed, just noticeably. "It's been a valuable learning experience," she said diplomatically. "Master C'baoth has a depth and strength in the Force that I can only hope I'll someday be able to approach."

"Ah." Obi-Wan nodded, his mind flicking back to his last conversation with Master Windu. She might be right, or it might also be that C'baoth wasn't nearly as deep into the Force as she thought. Possibly even not as deep as C'baoth himself thought.

But discussing a Jedi with his Padawan was considered poor form, particularly in front of another, younger Padawan like Anakin. "I'm sure you'll make it," he told her. "In my experience, a Jedi can gain as much depth in the Force as he or she wants."

"Within his or her limitations, of course," Lorana said ruefully. "I don't know yet where that line lies for me."

"No one does until the line is reached and tested," Obi-Wan pointed out. "Personally, I don't believe there *are* any such limits."

Another droid bustled up with their drinks balanced precariously on a tray. Obi-Wan leaned back, ready to reach out with the

Force to rescue the glasses if it became necessary, but the droid set them down without spilling a drop and bustled away. Picking up his drink, Obi-Wan sent a slow look around the room.

Small, unassuming places like this, he knew, were usually passed over by casual visitors looking for flash and sparkle. Sure enough, most of the patrons were locals: hornskinned Brolfi in varying shades of yellow and green, plus a counterpoint sprinkling of the more delicate arboreal Karfs from the vast tisvollt forests that edged the city on two sides.

But there were also a few other species represented, including three more humans. Perhaps the guide card recommendation was actually having some influence on the visitor trade. His leisurely gaze drifted to the genuine duskwood bar at the far end, where a skinny, mostly yellow skinned Brolf was serving drinks.

He frowned. "Lorana, that human over there—black vest, gray shirt, talking to the bartender. Have you ever seen him before?"

She turned to look. "Yes, he was in the group waiting outside the negotiating chamber when the talks ended yesterday. I don't know his name."

"You know him, Master?" Anakin asked.

"Unless I'm mistaken, that's Jerv Riske," Obi-Wan said. "Former bounty hunter; currently top enforcer for the magistrate's office of the Corporate Alliance."

"What does an enforcer do?" Anakin asked.

"Pretty much anything Passel Argente tells him to," Obi-Wan said. "Bodyguard, investigator, and probably extra muscle if there are bad debts to be collected. I wonder which of those roles he's performing here."

"Probably the bodyguard one," Lorana said. "Magistrate Argente's leading the Alliance's negotiating team."

An unpleasant sensation crept up Obi-Wan's back. The head of a powerful, galaxy-spanning organization such as the Corporate Alliance hardly had the time to deal personally with a minor contract dispute like this.

Unless the Barlok dispute wasn't as minor as everyone seemed to think.

He looked back at Riske. The man was still talking with the bartender, both of them leaning slightly over their respective sides of the bar, their heads close together. "Anakin, you see that dish of quartered nuts on the bar near Enforcer Riske?" he asked, setting down his drink. "Go and grab a few of them."

"Sure," Anakin said. Sliding out of his seat, he started threading his way between the rows of tables.

"What are you doing?" Lorana asked.

"Giving myself an excuse to go over there," Obi-Wan said, watching Anakin's progress across the room and judging his timing. One more table . . . now. "Wait here," he added, standing up and heading off after his Padawan. Focusing his attention on the conversation at the bar, he ran through his Jedi sensory enhancement techniques.

He got within eavesdropping distance just as Anakin reached the bar, squeezed himself in between an Aqualish and a Rodian, and started helping himself to the nuts. "—centered in Patameene District," the bartender was saying in a low voice. "But that's just a rumor, mind."

"Thanks," Riske said. His hand brushed over the bartender's, and Obi-Wan caught a glint of metal as the bartender straightened up, his closed fist dropping casually behind the bar. The Brolf's eyes shifted to Obi-Wan, the hornskin puckering a little as he frowned. Riske caught the change in expression and turned, his right hand dropping casually to his belt, the fingertips dipping inside the edge of his vest.

"That's enough, Anakin," Obi-Wan said, keeping his voice light but firm as he came up behind Anakin and took casual hold of the boy's shoulder, carefully keeping his eyes away from Riske and the bartender.

"Just one more?" Anakin asked, turning and holding up a large tashru.

"All right, but for *after* your lunch," Obi-Wan said firmly. Out of the corner of his eye he saw Riske's hand drop the rest of the way to his side and sensed both his and the bartender's suspicions fading. "You don't want to spoil your appetite."

The boy sighed theatrically. "Okay," he said. Closing his fist around the nut, he started to turn around.

And as he did so, his shoulder bumped the Aqualish's back just as the burly alien was lifting his drink to his mouth, sending a small wave of bright red liquid sloshing over the rim and down the alien's massive hand.

Obi-Wan winced. It was a minor accident, as such things went, with equally minor damages. But such subtleties were lost on the typical Aqualish mind and temper.

And this one was very definitely typical. "You child human troublemaker—" he grunted in his native tongue, spinning around fast enough to slosh a little more of his drink over the edge. "What do you do to bother me?"

"It was an accident," Obi-Wan said quickly, pulling Anakin back to just in front of him. "I apologize for his carelessness."

"He is no babe in leafwrap that you must clean up his messes," the Aqualish retorted, glaring at Obi-Wan with his huge eyes. He looked back at Anakin, his hand dropping to the blaster belted at his waist. "He must learn manners and self-discipline."

Obi-Wan tightened his grip on Anakin's shoulder as he sensed the boy's flash of anger. Self-discipline was one of Anakin's biggest problem areas, something Obi-Wan had to call him on probably twice a week. The last thing the boy wanted to hear was the same lecture coming from a grumpy alien. "Easy, Anakin," Obi-Wan warned, aware that every eye in the cantina was on the confrontation. His little playacting had alleviated Riske's first suspicions about the would-be eavesdropper, but those suspicions would be back with a vengeance if Obi-Wan was forced to reveal himself as a Jedi. "Come, friend," he said soothingly to the Aqualish. "Surely you have more worthwhile ways to spend your energy. Let me get you another drink, and we'll be on our way."

For a long moment the Aqualish glared at him, his hand now openly gripping the butt of his blaster. Obi-Wan stood motionless, his mind slipping into combat mode, his hand ready to dart beneath his tunic and snatch his lightsaber if and when it became necessary.

And then something seemed to flicker in the Aqualish's anger. "A Likstro," he said, lifting his hand off his blaster and pointing at his half-filled glass. "A large one."

"Certainly," Obi-Wan said. The other's glass was nowhere near large size, but this wasn't the time or place to quibble over details. Senses still alert for a last-minute sneak attack, he turned and caught the bartender's eye. "A large Likstro," he said, gesturing to the Aqualish.

The bartender nodded and busied himself with his tap. A minute later the drink was in the alien's hand, the payment was in the bartender's, and Obi-Wan and Anakin were heading back toward their booth.

"That wasn't a large drink he had," Anakin muttered as they maneuvered between the tables.

Obi-Wan nodded. "I know."

"That means he stiffed you," Anakin said, an accusing edge creeping into his voice. "Probably what he had in mind all along."

"Possibly," Obi-Wan acknowledged. "What if he did?"

"But we're *Jedi,*" Anakin growled. "We shouldn't have to put up with that kind of shakedown."

"You have to learn to see the bigger view, my young Padawan," Obi-Wan reminded him, glancing around. "All we really wanted to accomplish here—"

He broke off. Riske was gone.

So was Lorana.

It was apparently her lot in life, Lorana thought as she wove her way through the crowds on the walkway, to be forever trying to keep up with someone. Earlier it had been C'baoth; now, she was struggling just as hard to keep Riske in sight.

She had to admit, though, that it was an interesting study in contrasts. C'baoth's technique was the straightforward one of intimidating others out of his way. Riske gained the same result by taking advantage of every opening or opportunity for advancement, seldom disturbing any of the other pedestrians, slipping through the crowd like a night animal through the trees of a forest.

Master Kenobi had said that the man used to be a bounty hunter. He'd probably been a very good one.

Unfortunately, she hadn't thought to get Obi-Wan's comlink frequency before they split up. C'baoth might have it, but she knew better than to interrupt him during the negotiations for anything short of an imminent catastrophe.

But the Jedi Temple on Coruscant surely had the listing. Dodging around a strolling Ithorian, she pulled out her comlink and keyed for the city communications center and a HoloNet relay.

"Vast apologies, citizen," a mechanical voice said from the comlink. "All connections offworld are unavailable. Please try again at a future time."

So much for that approach. Lorana shut off the comlink and returned it to her belt, sidestepping as a pair of large Brolfi suddenly loomed in her path. They passed her by and she started forward again, craning her neck to see over the crowd.

To find that Riske had vanished.

She hurried forward, scanning the street and stretching out to the Force. But there was no sign of him.

Calm yourself, Padawan, C'baoth's oft-repeated admonition whispered through her mind. Riske couldn't have gotten very far in the brief time he'd been out of her sight. He must have either gone into one of the dozens of little shops that lined the street or else ducked down one of the pair of narrow alleyways branching off to the left and right just ahead.

Briefly, she weighed the options. The shops would be constricting, drastically limiting his freedom of movement. A man like Riske, she decided, would more likely go for one of the alleys.

She reached them and looked both directions. No one was visible. When she'd last seen Riske, he'd been closer to the left alleyway, which made that one the more obvious choice. But he didn't strike her as an obvious sort of person. Weaving around another pair of pedestrians, she stepped into the alley to the right.

The passageway was fairly narrow, about one and a half landspeeders wide, with one side stacked with tall but neat piles of garbage containers awaiting pickup. Halfway along its length, another alley cut across it at right angles, dividing this particular block into quarters. If Riske had gone this way, he would have had two additional directions to choose from once he reached the center. Slipping her hand inside her tunic, she got a grip on her lightsaber and headed in.

She reached the central intersection without incident and looked in all directions. Riske, unfortunately, wasn't visible in any of them.

For a moment she stood there, looking back and forth down the cross-alley, the sour taste of defeat in her mouth. Nothing to do now but retrace her steps and hope Kenobi wouldn't be angry enough at her failure to report her to C'baoth.

A flicker from the Force was her only warning, but she reacted to it instantly. Taking a leaping step to the side, she spun around, drawing her lightsaber from her sash and igniting it.

The spinning disk gliding in through the alleyway behind her caught the sunlight as it tilted slightly, altering its direction toward her new position. Getting a two-handed grip on her lightsaber, she watched it come, wondering why anyone would bother with such a relatively slow weapon.

Half a second later she got her answer as the disk split into thirds, the top and bottom sections becoming duplicates of the original and swinging wide to approach her from different angles.

So it had become three against one. Still not a problem. She took a step backward, mentally mapping out the sequence she would use against them. They hummed their way into range; and with a quick one–two–three she slashed the glowing blade outward, slicing all three disks in half.

And as the sections of the last one clattered to the alley floor, an arm snaked around her shoulder from behind to wrap firmly around her neck.

She inhaled sharply in chagrin. So that was the reason for the simplicity of the attack. It had been nothing but a diversion, driving her into the tunnel vision of combat while Riske slipped out of concealment from one of the garbage stacks and sneaked up behind her. She shifted her grip on her lightsaber, wondering if she would have time to stab backward with it before he got another weapon into position.

"Easy, girl," a mild voice said as something hard pressed against her neck beneath her right ear. "Close it down and put it away. I just want to talk."

"About what?" she demanded.

"Put it away and I'll tell you," he said. "Come on, girl—this isn't worth getting your head blown off over."

"I'm a Jedi," she warned. "We don't respond well to threats."

"Maybe Jedi don't," Riske agreed, an almost amused edge to his voice. "But you're no Jedi—you got suckered way too easily for that." The arm around her throat tightened slightly. "Come on. Cool down and let's talk."

Lorana glared at the alley wall. Still, derision aside, if he'd wanted to kill her he probably could have done so long before now. "Fine," she said, closing down her lightsaber and sliding it back into her sash.

"There, now, that wasn't so hard, was it?" he said soothingly as he let go of her neck.

"I'm glad you're happy," Lorana said, taking a step forward and turning around to face him. "What do you want to talk about?"

"Let's start with you," Riske suggested, tucking a small hold-out blaster back into concealment in his tunic. "Why is C'baoth having you follow me?"

"Master C'baoth has nothing to do with this," she told him, stretching out to the Force and trying to get a feel for the man. He was cool and unemotional, with the alert detachment she'd often seen in professional bodyguards. But beneath the calm she could sense a certain honor, or at least a willingness to stand by his word.

And the fact that he'd put his blaster away implied he expected a certain degree of honor from her in return. That alone dictated that she at least hear him out.

"Was it the other Jedi, then?" Riske asked. "The one with you in the cantina?"

There are times when you'll wish your identity to remain unknown, C'baoth had reminded her back on Coruscant. Clearly, it hadn't worked with Riske. "He was interested in you, yes, but following you was my idea," she told him. "He was mostly surprised that a person of Magistrate Argente's stature would be handling these negotiations personally."

"I could say the same about Jedi Master C'baoth," Riske said. "Magistrate Argente was rather surprised himself when he showed up." He gestured in the direction of the cantina. "And now we have another Jedi in the game, this one trying to eavesdrop on private conversations. What exactly is the Council playing at?"

"As far as I know, the Council isn't playing at anything," Lorana said. "We're not supposed to take sides in these things."

Riske snorted. "Like you didn't take sides on Naboo?" he said pointedly. "I noticed your high-minded neutrality was surprisingly helpful to Queen Amidala and her government."

"I don't know anything about that," Lorana said. "As you've already guessed, I'm only a Padawan. But I *can* tell you that the

Council didn't send us here. It was Master C'baoth's idea, and the Council only reluctantly gave him permission."

Riske frowned. "So he came up with this all on his own?"

"Well, actually, he was responding to something Supreme Chancellor Palpatine said," Lorana amended. "But it still wasn't the Council's idea."

"Palpatine," Riske muttered, rubbing his cheek thoughtfully. "Interesting."

"My turn now," Lorana said. "What are *you* doing wandering around the city?"

"Trying to keep Magistrate Argente alive, of course," Riske said, his tone suddenly dark. "Nice talking with you, Padawan. Try and stay out of my way, all right?" With that he turned and strode away down the alley.

Lorana watched him until he disappeared out the other end into the city's pedestrian traffic. Then, with a sigh, she turned and headed back the way she'd come. Master Kenobi, she knew, was not going to be happy about this.

With no easy way to locate Lorana, and with every reason to expect they would most likely chase each other in circles if he tried, Obi-Wan had opted to wait for her on a bench in a small park across the street from the cantina.

Anakin was just finishing his tarsh maxer when she finally returned.

"Interesting," Obi-Wan said when she'd finished her story. "So Magistrate Argente's in danger, is he?"

"Or at least Riske thinks he is," Lorana said, her eyes holding the wary look of someone bracing herself for a reprimand.

In fact, as Obi-Wan gazed into those eyes, it occurred to him that they seemed to fall into that mode far too naturally. Apparently, C'baoth's teaching style was as domineering as the rest of the man's personality. "But he didn't seem to think the danger was coming from you or Master C'baoth?"

"No, though he did ask what the Council was up to," Lorana said. "But it seemed almost a perfunctory comment, as if it was just natural to assume that the Council was playing politics. I don't think he would have been so open with me if he'd really thought we were plotting against Argente."

"You call *that* being open?" Anakin demanded scornfully. "Hints and threats?"

"Telling her to stay out of his way wasn't necessarily a threat," Obi-Wan told him. "Professional bodyguards like Riske always worry about bystanders or well-meaning but amateurish helpers getting in the way."

"He thinks we're *amateurs*?"

"In certain aspects of that job, we are," Obi-Wan told him bluntly, turning back to Lorana. "So what do *you* think? *Is* Argente in danger?"

A flicker of surprise crossed her face. C'baoth, he reflected, probably didn't ask her opinion very often. "I don't know," she said. "But feelings *are* running high about the Corporate Alliance's efforts to take full possession of the mines."

"I can imagine," Obi-Wan said. "Do you know which hotel Argente is staying at?"

"The Starbright," Lorana said. "It's about a kilometer east of the city center."

"Which isn't the direction Riske was going," Obi-Wan pointed out. "But it *is* the direction to Patameene District."

"Patameene District?" Anakin asked.

"I heard the bartender mention it to him," Obi-Wan said. "It's one of the city's biggest subdivisions, straddling both some very rich and very poor areas. If we're going to nose around, that would probably be a good place to start."

"We're going to *help* him?" Anakin objected. "I thought the Corporate Alliance was trying to steal the mineral rights from the Brolfi."

"That's what the negotiations are supposed to determine," Obi-Wan reminded him. "At any rate, that's not our concern. Our job as Jedi is to protect and preserve life across the Republic."

"I don't know," Lorana said hesitantly. "Master C'baoth wasn't very happy to find you two here. He might not like us interfering in matters this way. Riske and his people seem to be on top of things—shouldn't we let them handle it?"

"Who's interfering with anything?" Obi-Wan asked blandly as he stood up. "We're going on a tour of the city, just as Master C'baoth suggested. If we happen to run into some trouble, that's hardly our fault."

It was a ten-minute walk to the nearest edge of Patameene District. Obi-Wan kept his eyes moving as they walked, hoping to spot Riske in the crowd. But having been caught once, the bodyguard was apparently too cagey to let it happen again.

"This should be the edge of the district," he said as they reached a low decorative stone wall and passed through a pedestrian archway. "Anakin, remember that we're just here to look around."

"Sure," Anakin said, his eyes already sweeping the area, his sense that of a hunting darokil straining at its leash. "Okay if I go ahead a little?"

"All right, but not too far," Obi-Wan said. "I don't want you getting lost."

"I won't." Slipping between a pair of Karfs, the boy ducked into the crowd.

"You sure he'll be all right?" Lorana asked.

"He'll be fine," Obi-Wan assured her. "He's a little reckless, but he's strong in the Force and generally behaves himself."

"You must have great confidence in him," Lorana murmured.

Obi-Wan gave her a sideways look. There'd been an odd wistfulness in her tone just then. "C'baoth doesn't have as much confidence in you, I take it?"

"Master C'baoth has had several Padawans in his lifetime of service to the Jedi Order," she said, her voice going carefully neutral. "He knows what he's doing."

"Yes, of course," Obi-Wan said. "He does have a rather overpowering personality, though, doesn't he?"

"His reputation is well earned," she said, again clearly picking her words carefully. "He's skilled and knowledgeable and intelligent. I've learned a great deal from him."

"Though he's also perhaps a little too demanding?"

"I wouldn't characterize him that way," she said, her voice going a little cooler.

"Of course you would," Obi-Wan said, giving her a reassuring smile. "I thought that about *my* Master at times. And I *know* Anakin thinks that about me."

For a moment she hesitated. Then, almost reluctantly, she smiled back. "Sometimes I wonder if I'll ever be able to please him," she admitted.

"I know the feeling," Obi-Wan said. "Just remember that this, too, will pass. And once you're a Jedi Knight, your job will no longer be a matter of pleasing a single Master or even a group of them. Your job will be to do what is right."

"That's the part that seems so hard," she confessed. "How do you ever know what is truly right?"

Obi-Wan shrugged. "When you're at peace," he said. "When you're truly attuned to the Force."

"If I ever am."

Obi-Wan grimaced. On one hand was Anakin, pushing ahead so eagerly that he was forever overstepping his limits, though he had to admit the boy succeeded more often than he failed. On the other hand was Lorana, so awed by C'baoth's presence and reputation that she was afraid to even stretch herself beyond anything she already knew.

Somewhere, there had to be a middle ground.

For another few minutes they walked together in silence, weaving their way through the other pedestrians and shoppers. Obi-Wan kept his eyes moving, watching for signs of Riske or of the trouble he apparently expected to find here and making sure to keep Anakin's bobbing head within sight.

Ahead, off to the left, was a landspeeder repair shop, with a display of shiny parts in the open-air front room and half-seen figures working in the darker repair area in back. Several Brolfi were browsing around the front room displays, most of them adults but one a teenager about Anakin's age. Obi-Wan eyed him, noting his reddish brown craftsman's vest with its multiple pockets. Most Brolfi seemed to make do without nearly that much carrying capacity; apparently, this boy was the sort who liked carrying all his little treasures with him.

He smiled to himself. Jedi, forever wandering the galaxy with most of their possessions on their backs or belts, were hardly in a position to point fingers on that one. Throwing one final look at the boy, he started to turn away.

But to his surprise, something drew his eyes back again.

Something about the youngster's posture, perhaps, or the way he was looking around him.

Or perhaps it was the subtle prompting of the Force. Frowning, he kept his attention on the boy as he and Lorana continued to weave their way through the milling crowds.

And as he watched, the young Brolf stepped close to a rack of burst thrusters, a set of cutters appearing magically in his hand. With a glance at the workers in the back room, he deftly snipped the anchor lines of two of the thrusters, catching each in turn and slipping them out of sight inside his vest. The cutters followed the thrusters, and a second later the boy wandered casually out of the shop. Turning his back to the approaching Jedi, he melted into the crowd.

Obi-Wan grabbed Lorana's upper arm. "Brolf teenager in a red-brown vest," he said in a low voice, pointing at the spot where the youth had disappeared. "Get Anakin, find him, and follow him."

"What?" Lorana asked, staring at him in bewilderment.

"Find him and follow him," Obi-Wan repeated, glancing around. To their right was a narrow alleyway cutting a path between a pair of ten-story buildings. "Go."

Still clearly puzzled, Lorana nevertheless nodded and hurried ahead. Obi-Wan caught a glimpse of her grabbing Anakin's arm; and then he was in the alley, dodging the garbage containers as he headed to the center. It was probably thirty meters to the tops of the buildings flanking him, and even with Jedi strength enhancement a leap like that was well beyond his capabilities.

But there were other ways. Glancing both directions down the alley to make sure no one was watching, he stretched out to the Force and leapt.

His boots hit the right-hand wall about four meters above the ground. Bending his knees to absorb the impact, he shoved off again before he could start falling back down, pushing himself upward and toward the wall on the left-hand side. That jump gained him another two meters, and he pushed off again toward the right, frog-hopping his way upward.

He reached the top with only minor twinges in his knees and leg muscles to mark the strain. Running to the edge of the roof, he dropped flat onto his stomach and looked down.

The streets looked just as crowded from up here as they did from down below. Pulling out his comlink, he keyed for Anakin.

"Skywalker," Anakin's voice came promptly. "What's this about a kid in a brown vest?"

"He stole a pair of burst thrusters from that shop back there," Obi-Wan explained, shading his eyes from the sun with one hand as he searched the crowd below for the young thief.

"You mean like you use in Podracers and swoops?"

"Right," Obi-Wan said. "They're also the drive system of choice for homemade missiles."

There was a gentle hiss from the comlink. "Got it," Anakin said, his voice suddenly grim. "Did you see which way he went?"

"He left the shop going west," Obi-Wan said. "But he could easily have changed—wait a minute." He leaned a little farther over the edge of the roof as a flicker of red-brown caught his eye before it passed out of sight beneath an awning. He watched the other side, and moment later it emerged. "There he is," he told Anakin. "He's headed north now."

"What street?"

"Not a clue," Obi-Wan admitted. "Where are you two?"

"Just passing a building with a big blue-and-gold sign talking about medicines," Anakin said. "Across the street is a green hanging banner—"

"Right—I've got you," Obi-Wan cut in as he spotted them. "Take the next street to your right, and you'll see him about a block ahead."

He watched Anakin and Lorana long enough to see them pick up their pace, then shifted his attention back to the thief, wishing he'd thought to bring along some macrobinoculars. Anakin had a set, but that wasn't going to do Obi-Wan any good.

"Obi-Wan?"

Obi-Wan lifted his comlink again. "Go."

"We've turned north," Anakin reported. "I think I see him ahead."

"Stay where you are," Obi-Wan ordered. A somewhat chunky Brolf had stepped from one of the storefronts and was moving to intercept the thief. "I think he's about to pass off his ill-gotten gain. Put Lorana on."

There was a moment of silence. "Yes?" Lorana's clear voice came.

"Move forward a little from where you are," Obi-Wan told her. "The thief's rendezvousing with someone—slightly overweight Brolf with a dark blue sash over a lighter blue tunic."

"I see him," Lorana confirmed. "He's moving in close . . . looks like they're talking . . ."

"Is the boy giving him the thrusters?" Obi-Wan asked. "The adult's blocking my line of sight."

"He's in mine, too," Lorana said tightly. "I can't—there they go."

"Blast," Obi-Wan muttered under his breath as the two Brolfi separated, the teen continuing north while the adult turned west. "Did he give him the thrusters?"

"I couldn't tell," Lorana said. "I'm sorry."

Obi-Wan scowled as he watched the two Brolfi heading their separate ways. The adult had certainly had the time and the opportunity to take the thrusters. Problem was, he'd also had the time to merely confirm that the grab had been made, to check for followers, or to give the boy new instructions.

And no matter which way the rendezvous had gone, the whole thing might simply be a bit of Barlok's normal criminal activity. It might have nothing to do with Passel Argente and Riske's paranoia.

But Riske had been looking for trouble out this way. Obi-Wan had found some. It was definitely worth checking out.

And here he was, stuck on a rooftop a block away.

"Then I guess we'll have to follow both of them," he decided, looking around the nearby rooftops. If he could leap to the next one over, then the one next to that, then find a stairway or turbolift to get back to street level . . .

But no. In broad daylight, in the middle of a crowded city, there was an even chance someone would spot his acrobatics and recognize him for what he was. The minute any potential attackers realized there was a Jedi on their trail, they would go to ground so fast and so deep that even a professional like Riske would have trouble rooting them out.

"I agree," Lorana said. "I'll take the adult."

Obi-Wan hesitated. Lorana was the older of the two Padawans, and thus theoretically the more capable. But he knew Anakin's capabilities and experience, and knew the boy could deal with any trouble he might run into.

Still, if there was one thing Lorana lacked in abundance, it was confidence. It wouldn't help to send her after a teenager, especially not with Anakin listening.

And after all, she would only be following the Brolf, not confronting or fighting him. That should be safe enough.

"Fine," he told her. "Take Anakin's comlink—it's linked directly to mine—and give him yours. What's your frequency?"

She gave him the number. "We're splitting up," she added. "I'll contact you when the adult comes to roost."

"Right," Obi-Wan said. "Tell Anakin I'll catch up with him as soon as I can."

Switching off the comlink, Obi-Wan pushed himself back to his feet. He took one final look over the edge of the roof, then turned and hurried toward the stairs. Yes, his Padawan could deal with any trouble he might run into.

Probably.

For a wonder, Anakin didn't get himself into any mischief in the time it took Obi-Wan to reach the street and catch up with him. The young Brolf, for his part, continued on his way, apparently oblivious to the fact he was being followed.

Obi-Wan had noted earlier that Patameene District included rich neighborhoods as well as poorer, working-class ones. The teen led them into one of the latter, finally entering one of the units in a slightly dilapidated house ring.

The house ring was a standard Brolfi urban structure, consisting of a circle of houses or apartment buildings built around a central courtyard. The courtyard was designed to be a common recreation area for the ring, but through a gap where one of the houses had collapsed Obi-Wan saw that this particular courtyard had been turned into something that more closely resembled a junkyard.

"Looks like Watto's back area," Anakin murmured, ducking

his head to peer inside. "They've got at least three projects going on in there."

"Any of them look like something that would use burn thrusters?" Obi-Wan asked.

"Hard to tell," Anakin said. "The one on the left—"

"Hold that thought," Obi-Wan cut him off quietly. There had been a flicker in the Force . . .

"Can we help you?" a suspicious voice asked from behind them.

Keeping his hands visible, Obi-Wan turned around. There were three adult Brolfi coming toward them, their simple tunics worn but neat and clean. "No thank you," he said politely. "We were just noticing all the construction work in there and wondering what they were building."

"Why would you care?" the spokesman asked.

"My young friend here used to build Podracers," Obi-Wan explained. "He's always been fascinated with that sort of thing."

"Really," one of the other Brolfi said, looking Anakin up and down. "You know anything about split-X air intakes?"

"Never used them myself," Anakin said. "But I can install them or fix them if there's a problem."

"Really." The Brolf filled his lungs. "Duefgrin!"

There was a slight pause; then the teen they'd been following appeared at the gap in the ring. "Yes, Uncle?" he called.

"Couple of humans here who say they know split-X systems," the Brolf said. "You still having trouble with yours?"

"I don't know," the teen said, eyeing Obi-Wan and Anakin doubtfully. "I just picked up a new compression controller. Maybe that'll help."

Obi-Wan suppressed a grimace. So that was what he and the adult had been doing back in the marketplace. The boy had handed over the stolen burst thrusters and gotten the controller in exchange.

Either that, or he'd stolen the controller earlier in the day. In that case, he might still have the thrusters.

"Only if the split-X doesn't have a backstability problem," Anakin said. "What kind of coupling you have on it? Binary or tertiary?"

"Binary," Duefgrin said. "I couldn't afford a tertiary."

"Let me take a look," Anakin offered, starting toward him. "If that's okay?" he added, looking at Obi-Wan.

Obi-Wan looked questioningly at the three Brolf adults. "Sure, go ahead," Duefgrin's uncle said, waving a hand. "The sooner he gets that junk heap working and out of the yard, the sooner the neighbors will quit complaining about it."

"Thanks," Obi-Wan said, mentally crossing the three adults off his suspects' list. If they were willing to let strangers wander freely through the area, they probably weren't hiding any plots. "Okay, Anakin, but make it quick."

"Sure," Anakin called back over his shoulder. Already, Obi-Wan noted, he and Duefgrin were deep into technical talk. "I'll be ready to leave when you are."

"I've heard *that* before," Obi-Wan said under his breath as he followed them into the courtyard. Still, Duefgrin himself could be involved with a group of plotters without his uncle's knowledge. It wouldn't hurt for Obi-Wan to take a leisurely turn or two around the house ring while the teenagers worked, stretching out with the Force for any signs of violent intent.

And after that, he would pry Anakin away from whatever it was Duefgrin was building and they would see what kind of luck Lorana was having.

* * *

The young Brolf thief, Lorana had noticed, had left the rendezvous at a casual walk, without any indication that he suspected he might be followed or, indeed, any indication that he even cared whether he was or not.

The adult Brolf was another kettle of Giju entirely. He was about as blatantly nervous and suspicious as it was possible to be without actually carrying a sign to that effect. Every dozen steps he threw a quick look over his shoulder, and he crossed and recrossed the street at least once a block. Every block or two he changed directions, sometimes pausing at one of the open-air shops lining the street and pretending to examine the merchandise while actually studying the pedestrians behind him.

It was so ludicrous that it was almost funny. But Lorana felt no urge to laugh. Riske was a professional, with a professional's bearing and subtlety. This Brolf was just the opposite: an amateur conspirator, with an amateur's lack of finesse or ability. And it was the amateur—uncalculating, unthinking, unpredictable—who was often the more dangerous opponent.

Fortunately, it was also the amateur who was the easier to deceive. Lorana had picked up a few tricks about tailing people during her years of Jedi training, and over the next hour she ended up using every one of them. She varied her distance from the Brolf, ducked through alleys and side streets to get ahead of him, and periodically altered her appearance by putting her robe's hood up or down or using a cord to tie her hair back instead of letting it hang free.

Eventually, the Brolf's paranoia seemed to ease, and his convoluted path straightened out as he turned northwest. Lorana stayed as far back as she could, watching the ornamentation and value of the homes and shops around her steadily diminishing as they moved farther and farther into one of the poorer areas of the district. Whereas the richer neighborhoods had waist-high walls or fences to delineate the property lines, here the boundaries were marked off by low, tightly woven hedges or simple rows of distinctive flowering plants. A fair sprinkling of the pedestrians she passed wore tunics with Mining Guild markings, she noted, and many of them paused in their activities to scrutinize her as she passed through their midst.

More than once she thought about calling Obi-Wan and asking for advice or assistance. More often than that she considered simply turning around and heading back to the safe familiarity of the city center, leaving whatever plots and counterplots to be dealt with by those with more wisdom and experience in such matters.

But each time she took a calming breath, stretched out to the Force, and continued on. A Jedi should never turn away from a path merely because it seems hard or dangerous.

She was just passing one of the low hedges when she felt a warning flicker from the Force.

She kept walking, resisting the impulse to break step. The vague sense of threat was still too diffuse, and coming to a sudden halt would only tip off her unknown foes that she was aware of them. A few more steps, a little carelessness on their part, and she should be able to switch the tables when they made their move.

Her patience was rewarded. A few meters along the sense came into sudden focus: two Brolfi, coming up quickly but silently behind her, both of them simmering with suspicion. She caught the whisper of metal rubbing against cloth—

She stopped abruptly, the sleeve of her robe catching briefly on the hedge beside her as she spun around to face them. "Yes?" she asked mildly.

The Brolfi twitched with surprise, coming to a slightly shambling halt a couple of meters away from her. The shorter of the two, Lorana saw, had an antique blaster tucked tightly against his side, as if pressing it against his leg would actually hide it from her. The larger had a less sophisticated but equally nasty weapon: a miner's quarter-pick ax. "What are you doing here?" the shorter demanded.

"Is this not a public street?" Lorana asked.

"You don't belong here," the larger growled, taking a step toward her and fingering his ax restlessly. "What are you looking for?"

"What could be here that anyone would look for?" she countered, feeling her heartbeat starting to pick up. This was it. Somehow, though she wasn't sure exactly how, she knew beyond a doubt that she'd found the threat that Riske had been trying to locate.

The question now was what she should do about it. Because these two Brolfi—or even these two plus the one she'd been following—were merely the edge of the grove. Whipping out her lightsaber would put her no closer to learning the details of the plot or who ultimately was behind it. What she really needed was for them to take her to the actual leaders.

And for them to do that, they would have to think she was harmless.

"Never mind," she said, taking as a step backward, staying close to the hedge beside her. "If you want me to go, I'll go."

"Not so fast," the smaller Brolf said, apparently emboldened by her sudden apparent nervousness. "What's your hurry?"

"No hurry," Lorana said. She took another step backward, hoping she wasn't getting too close to the end of this particular section of hedge. "I'm just ready to leave, that's all." She threw a glance to the side, wishing she knew which of the dilapidated house rings around them the two Brolfi had come out of.

Apparently, her glance was close enough. "Get her, Vissfil," the shorter Brolf snapped, swinging up his blaster and pointing it nervously. "She knows."

"I don't know anything," Lorana protested, taking a final step back as Vissfil strode toward her, his ax held high. "Please—don't hurt me." She lifted her hands toward the ax as if to ward off an expected blow.

And with Vissfil's full attention on her uplifted hands, and his body blocking his companion's view, she stretched out with the Force, sliding her lightsaber from inside her tunic and shoving it into concealment inside the hedge beside her.

"Get her comlink," the smaller Brolf ordered as Vissfil shifted his ax to one hand and pulled her robe partially open with the other.

"Yeah, yeah, I know," Vissfil growled. For all his size and gruffness, he was clearly uncomfortable as he ran his hand gingerly over her body. He found her comlink and stuffed it inside his own tunic; then, almost as an afterthought, he relieved her of her belt with its attached food and equipment pouches. "No weapons," he announced, taking a step back from her. "What do we do with her?"

"Take her to Defender, I guess," the other said. He gestured her toward the ring house she'd glanced toward earlier. "He'll know what to do. This way, human."

They were crossing the street when Lorana heard a soft tone from behind her, and glanced back to see the smaller Brolf draw a comlink from his tunic. "What?" he muttered.

She couldn't hear the voice coming from the comlink, but it was impossible to miss the sudden spike in the Brolf's tension level. "Right," he muttered, then put the instrument away. "Change of plans," he announced, stepping close to Lorana and pressing the muzzle of his blaster against her back. "We're going to that house over there." He pointed to a blue house to their left.

Lorana felt her throat tighten. The indicated house had the look of a place that had been abandoned for years. The only reason to take her there would be for a serious interrogation, or to shut her up permanently.

On the other hand, they didn't know who they had here. She could play along and wait for her opportunity, watching for the warning signs that the game was nearly over—

With the Brolf's intent masked by his overall anxiety, the stun blast that rippled across her back came as a complete surprise. Before she could even begin to run through the countermeasures she'd been trained in, the nerve-deadening wave swept over her, plunging her into darkness.

"Well?" the Brolf who called himself Patriot growled.

Doriana didn't bother to answer. Standing at the window, he watched as Vissfil and his brother worked their way up the uneven walkway toward the dilapidated blue house, carrying the unconscious form of Padawan Lorana Jinzler between them.

And the two idiots had nearly brought her here. If Doriana hadn't been watching out the window and seen them coming . . .

He waited until the group had disappeared inside. Then, slowly and deliberately, he turned to face Patriot. "If this is an example of your security," he said, measuring out each word, "it's a wonder you're not all pinioned to shame posts by now."

"There is no problem," Patriot insisted. "It's only a single human, who had no time to alert any friends she might have."

"Any weapons?"

"None," Patriot said.

Doriana frowned. "None?"

"We are not children, Defender," Patriot growled. "We know how to search someone for weapons."

"Of course you do," Doriana said, feeling his skin prickling. Jinzler must have left her lightsaber with Kenobi and Skywalker, knowing it would be a dead giveaway as to who she really was. Did that mean the other two were already nearby, waiting an opportune moment to move in?

Regardless, it was well past time to wrap this up. "Do you have the final two burst thrusters?" he asked.

"Jhompfi just arrived with them," Patriot said. "He's passed them to Migress, who's already on his way to where the missile is being prepared. They'll be installed within the hour."

"Jhompfi being the one the human female was following, I presume?"

Patriot's eyes narrowed. "I've already said she can do us no damage. We'll be leaving this house ring as soon as you fulfill your part of the bargain. All is well."

"Of course," Doriana said. All was well; except that Jinzler could identify Jhompfi by face, and had obviously seen him with the thrusters . . .

He took another calming breath, keeping his tirade to himself. Yes, Patriot and his fellow conspirators were idiots. But then, he'd known that going in.

"I still don't understand why so many thrusters are needed," Patriot said, a hint of suspicion creeping into his voice. "A normal missile would require only two."

"A normal missile would arc high over the marketplace, where Argente's security forces could destroy it at their leisure,"

Doriana pointed out. "The weapon I've designed for you is known as a slinker: a projectile that will fly at waist height directly through the archway of the administration building, find its way along the corridors to the conference room, and there explode, destroying the traitors and would-be traitors alike."

"So you claim," Patriot said, his tone still suspicious. "I've never heard of a weapon that was able to find its way through a building without a full droid control system."

"That's because no weapon you've heard of has had my special guidance system," Doriana said, pulling a data card from his pocket. "It will locate the outer archway and seek out its targets, wherever they hide."

"Without its sensor emissions being detected?" Patriot asked, taking the card carefully.

"Neither detected nor jammed," Doriana assured him. "It doesn't rely on sensor frequencies the security forces will be monitoring."

In actual fact, of course, the card didn't rely on sensors at all. It was nothing more than a geographically programmed course director that would take the missile on the precise path Doriana himself had systematically paced out on his last trip to Barlok. And far from seeking out the negotiators, if C'baoth suddenly decided to hold the meeting in a different room tomorrow morning, the missile would find itself going to the wrong place entirely. That would be embarrassing, not to mention disastrous.

But that was as unlikely as Patriot and his simple-minded conspirators realizing how thoroughly the flopbrim was being pulled over their eyes. Nothing impressed people more than the perception that they were being entrusted with exotic technology.

"Then our victory is assured," Patriot said, fingering the data card almost reverently.

"It is indeed," Doriana said. "One final matter, then. Were you planning to return to your homes when you leave here this evening?"

"Of course," Patriot said, frowning. "We'll need a good meal, and sleep—"

"And you'll get them as far from your homes as you can travel," Doriana interrupted. "From this time onward, you must stay strictly away from your families and your other friends."

Patriot's whole body jerked in stages, from his feet up to a little whiplash jerk of his head. "What are you saying?"

"I'm saying that by noon tomorrow, with Magistrate Argente and Guildmaster Gilfrome lying dead, the authorities will descend upon the homes of every member of your guild," Doriana said coldly. "You and your friends must not be there, nor can anyone know where you've gone."

"But for how long?"

"As long as necessary," Doriana said. "Make no mistake, Patriot. From now on you and the others will be fugitives, running and hiding from the very people whose lives and prosperity you will have risked your lives to protect." He lifted his eyebrows. "If you aren't strong enough to pay that price, now is the time to renounce your oath."

Patriot straightened up, the resolve in his face visibly hardening. "We do what is necessary for our guild and our people," he said firmly. "We will pay the price for all."

"Then you are a Brolf of high honor indeed," Doriana said gravely. For some people the prospect of life on the run would be grounds to take a second, harder look at what they were doing. But for Patriot and his friends, such a potentially bleak future merely added to the perceived nobility and glamour of their insane plot.

Which was why Doriana had recruited them for this mission in the first place. Stupid, angry, and malleable, they'd been the perfect pawns for his plan. The deed would be done, and Doriana himself long gone, before any of them realized what had actually happened. If indeed they ever did. "Then here and now we stand together on the path to glory and destiny," he continued. "By tomorrow noon these traitorous negotiations will lie crumbled in the dust of history, and the precious minerals of Barlok will be forever held in Brolf hands."

"And those who would betray us will know the cost of such betrayal," Patriot intoned solemnly. "The Brolf people are deeply in your debt, Defender. Someday, I swear, this debt *will* be repaid."

"And I swear in turn that I will return to collect that payment," Doriana said, though offhand he couldn't imagine anything he was less likely to do. "I have one more small adjustment to make to the missile after the burst thrusters are in place, and then will leave to prepare my own part in this redemption of the Brolf people. Be certain you place the missile at precisely the spot we agreed on. Only there will it be inside the sensor shadow that guarantees it will not be spotted." And only from there, he added to himself, would the pre-programmed path take it where it had to go.

"I will," Patriot promised. "Then to our victory, Defender."

Doriana smiled. "Yes," he said softly. "To our victory."

Car'das had noted on their first approach to Thrawn's asteroid that the base itself seemed remarkably well hidden. It was only as they approached now for the second time that he found out how the commander had pulled off that particular trick.

Instead of being built on the surface, the base was inside.

Inside, in fact, down a long, twisting tunnel, a path the *Springhawk*'s helmsman took at a far better clip than was actually necessary. "Impressive place," Car'das said aloud, trying to cover his nervousness as he watched the rocky walls shooting past. "Is this typical Chiss construction?"

"Not at all," Thrawn said, his voice sounding odd as he gazed out the bridge viewport. "Most bases are on the surface. I wanted this one to be more difficult for potential enemies to penetrate."

"Hardly an original idea," Qennto put in. His voice was casual, but Car'das could see a little tightness around his eyes as he paid close attention to the helmsman's maneuvering. "You make the approach tricky so an attacker has to come at you slowly. 'Course, that makes it just as hard to get your own ships out, but that's the price you pay."

"There are ways of minimizing that particular problem," Thrawn told him. "At the moment, the Chiss Defense Fleet is working with this same concept with another base, on a much larger and more sophisticated scale than this. Interesting."

"What?" Car'das asked.

"That pattern of colored lights woven between the approach markers," Thrawn said, pointing to the wall just ahead. "It indicates the presence of visitors."

"Is that good or bad?" Maris asked.

Thrawn shrugged. "That depends on who the visitors are."

Three minutes later they came around a final curve and the tunnel opened up into a large cavern. At the far side, the rock face was alive with the glinting lights of ranging markers and viewports, with eight ships nestled up against various docking stations. Five were the Chiss fighters Car'das had already seen in action, two were small transport-style shuttles, and the eighth was a cruiser about the size of the *Springhawk*. Unlike the smoothly contoured military ships, though, this one was all planes and corners and sharply defined angles. "Ah," Thrawn said. "Our guests are from the Fifth Ruling Family."

"How can you tell?" Maris asked.

"By the design and markings of the spacecraft," Thrawn said. "I can also tell that the visitor is of direct but peripheral family lineage."

"So is *that* good or bad?" Car'das asked.

"Mostly neutral," Thrawn said. "The Fifth Family has interests in this region, so this is most likely a routine survey. Certainly someone of higher rank, and from the First or Eighth Families, would have come to deliver a reprimand."

Car'das frowned sideways at Maris. A reprimand?

"You'll all be my guests at the welcoming ceremony, of course," Thrawn continued as the *Springhawk* made its way toward an empty docking station. "You may find it interesting."

Interesting, in Car'das's opinion, was far too mild a word.

To begin with, there was the welcoming chamber itself. At first it appeared to be nothing more than an empty, unadorned gray room just off the docking station. But at a touch of a hidden button all that changed. Colorful panels folded out from the walls, reversing and settling themselves flat again. A handful of draperies descended from hidden panels in the ceiling, along with wavy stalactite-like formations that reminded Car'das of frozen pieces of aurora borealis skyfire. The floor tiles didn't flip or reconfigure, but intricate patterns of colored lights appeared through a transparent outer surface, some of them remaining stationary or slowly pulsing while others ran sequences that gave the illusion of flowing rivers. Every color of the spectrum was represented, but yellow was definitely favored.

It was an impressive display, and the Chiss who stepped through the portal a minute later was no less impressive. He strode in flanked by a pair of young Chiss wearing dark yellow uniforms and belted handguns, his own outfit consisting of an elaborately layered gray robe with a yellow collar and generous yellow highlights. Though not much older than Thrawn, there was an air about him of nobility and pride, the bearing of someone born to rule. The movements of his escort were crisp and polished, and Car'das had the impression that they and the four black-clad warriors Thrawn had brought along were having a subtle contest as to which group could look the most professional.

Thrawn's greeting and the visitor's response were in Cheunh, of course, and once again Car'das was only able to catch occasional words. But the tone and flow of the speeches, along with the equally formalized gestures and movements, had a sense of ancient ritual that he found fascinating.

It was an attitude, unfortunately, that his fellow travelers didn't seem to share. Maris, with her philosophical disdain for the Republic's structured corruption, clearly had little patience with official ritual of any sort, and watched the proceedings with a sort of polite detachment. Qennto, for his part, merely looked bored.

The ceremony ended, the two yellow-clad Chiss moved back to flank the doorway to the ship, and with a gesture Thrawn led his visitor to where the three humans waited. "May I present

Aristocra Chaf'orm'bintrano of the Fifth Ruling Family," he said, switching from Cheunh to Sy Bisti. "These are K'rell'n traders, visitors from a far world."

Chaf'orm'bintrano said something, his tone rather sharp. "In Sy Bisti, Aristocra, if you please," Thrawn said. "They do not understand Cheunh."

Chaf'orm'bintrano snorted, again in Cheunh, and the corners of Thrawn's mouth tightened briefly. "Aristocra Chaf'orm'bintrano is not interested in communicating with you at present," he translated. "One of my warriors will show you to your quarters." His eyes flicked to Car'das. "My apologies."

"No apologies needed, Commander," Car'das assured him, feeling a tightness in his throat as he gave Chaf'orm'bintrano an abbreviated bow. "None at all."

The rooms Thrawn had ordered for them were built along the same lines as their quarters aboard the *Springhawk*, though somewhat larger. There were also two sleeping rooms this time instead of one, with a common refresher station set between them. Qennto and Maris were shown to one of the rooms, while Car'das was taken to the other. Exploring his new quarters, Car'das discovered to his mild surprise that his clothing and personal effects had already been brought from his cabin on the *Bargain Hunter* and arranged neatly in the various storage drawers. Apparently, Thrawn was planning an extended stay for them.

He paced the floor for a while, trying not to think about Chaf'orm'bintrano and his unconcealed disapproval of their presence in Chiss territory. An hour later a silent warrior arrived at his door with a meal on a tray. Car'das briefly considered checking on Qennto and Maris, decided they could come find him if they wanted his company, and ate his meal alone.

Afterward, he sat down at the computer station and tried the procedure Thrawn had taught them aboard the *Springhawk* for accessing the Cheunh vocabulary lists. The procedure worked on this computer, too, and he settled down to study.

It was five hours later, and he was dozing at the computer station, when another Chiss finally came to fetch him.

He was taken to a darkened room that was a close double of the *Springhawk*'s Forward Visual Triangulation Site. In this case the wide viewport looked out into the docking cavern outside, and Car'das could see the distant glow of drive engines as a vessel made its way toward the exit tunnel. "Good evening, Car'das," Thrawn said from one of the seats to the side of the room. "I trust you had a productive day."

"Reasonably productive, yes," Car'das said, going over and sitting down beside him. "I worked ahead a little on my language lessons."

"Yes, I know," Thrawn said. "I wanted to apologize to you for Aristocra Chaf'orm'bintrano's lack of courtesy."

"I'm sorry he took a dislike to us," Car'das said, trying to be diplomatic. "I enjoyed the welcoming ceremony, and was looking forward to seeing more of how the Chiss do things."

"It was nothing personal," Thrawn assured him. "Aristocra Chaf'orm'bintrano considers your presence here a threat to the Ascendancy."

"May I ask why?"

Thrawn shrugged fractionally. "To some people, the unknown always represents a threat."

"Sometimes they're right," Car'das conceded. "On the other hand, you Chiss seem quite capable of taking care of yourselves in a fight."

"Perhaps," Thrawn said. "There are times when I wonder.

Tell me, do you understand the concept of neutralizing a potential enemy before that enemy can launch an attack against you?"

"You mean like a preemptive strike?" Car'das asked. "Certainly."

"It's widespread among your people, then?"

"I'm not sure *widespread* is the right word," Car'das hedged. "I know there are people who consider it immoral."

"Do you?"

Car'das grimaced. He was twenty-three years old, and he worked for a smuggler who liked to tweak Hutts. What did *he* know about the universe? "I think that if you're going to do something like that, you need to make very sure they're a genuine threat," he said slowly. "I mean, you need to have evidence that they were actually planning to attack you."

"What about someone who may not plan to attack you personally, but is constantly attacking others?"

It was pretty obvious where this was going. "You mean like the Vagaari?" Car'das asked.

"Exactly," Thrawn confirmed. "As I told you, they have not yet attacked Chiss territory, and military doctrine dictates they must therefore be ignored. Do the beings they prey on have any claim on our military strength, or must we simply stand aside and watch as they are slaughtered or enslaved?"

Car'das shook his head. "You're asking questions that have been argued since civilization began." He stole a look at the commander's profile. "I take it you and Aristocra Chaf'orm'bintrano disagree on this point?"

"I and the entire Chiss species disagree on this point," Thrawn said, a note of sadness in his voice. "Or so it often seems. I'm relieved to hear that the question isn't as clear-cut for others as it is for our Ruling Families."

"Did you tell the Aristocra about the Vagaari ship?" Car'das asked. "There seemed to be plunder in there from a *lot* of different species."

"I did, and he wasn't particularly impressed," Thrawn said. "For him, the defensive-only doctrine admits to no exceptions."

"What if some of those victims were species you know?" Car'das suggested. "Friends, or even just trading partners? Would that make a difference?"

"I doubt it," Thrawn said thoughtfully. "We do little trading outside our borders. Still, it might be useful to examine the treasure in detail." He cocked his head. "Would you be interested in assisting?"

"Of course," Car'das said. "Though I don't know what help I would be."

"You might recognize some of the artifacts," Thrawn said, standing up. "If they also prey on worlds of your Republic, you may have additional data that would be useful."

"In that case, you should also invite Maris and Qennto along," Car'das said, standing up as well. "They've traveled a lot more than I have."

"A good suggestion," Thrawn said as he led the way toward the exit. "That will also give Captain Qennto a chance to choose which of the items he'll wish to keep for himself." He smiled slightly. "Which will in turn help establish the relative values of the items."

"You're not cynical at all, are you, Commander?" Car'das said.

"I merely understand how others think and react," Thrawn said, his smile fading. "Perhaps that's why I have so much difficulty with a philosophy of waiting instead of acting."

"Perhaps," Car'das said. "For whatever it's worth, I doubt

the people you'd be taking action to help would see any moral problems with it."

"True," Thrawn agreed. "Though their gratitude might be short-lived."

"Sometimes," Car'das conceded. "Not always."

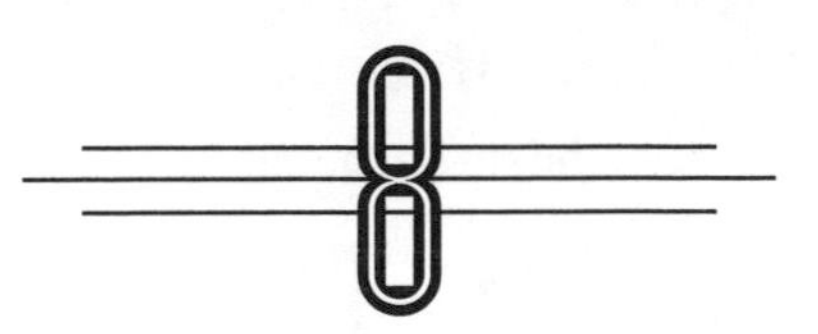

With a sigh, Obi-Wan shut off his comlink and slipped it back into his belt. "Still nothing?" Anakin asked.

"No," Obi-Wan said, throwing a look at the darkening sky. The stars were starting to appear, and all around them house lights were coming on as families settled in for the evening.

Anakin muttered something under his breath. "We should have tried calling her earlier."

"We *did* try calling her earlier," Obi-Wan told him. "You were just too busy playing with Duefgrin's swoop to notice."

"Excuse me, Master, but I was *working*, not playing," Anakin said stiffly. "The Brolf we're looking for is named Jhompfi, he lives in the Covered Brush house ring, and he's supposedly using the burst thrusters on a speeder bike he uses to smuggle rissle sticks out to the Karfs."

Obi-Wan stared at his Padawan. "When did you get all that?"

"When you were wandering around the neighborhood looking for clues," Anakin said. It was hard to sound hurt and smug at the same time, but the boy managed to pull it off. "Those were the only times he'd talk to me." He wrinkled his nose. "I don't think he trusts grown-ups very much."

"You should have said something the minute you had that information," Obi-Wan said tartly, slipping the guide card into his datapad and keying for a house ring search. "Or hadn't it occurred to you that Lorana might be in trouble?"

"No, but it occurred to me that if we left too suddenly, Duefgrin might have called Jhompfi and warned him," Anakin retorted.

"Mind your place, Padawan," Obi-Wan warned the boy. It was a warning he seemed to be delivering more and more often these days.

Anakin gave a theatrical sigh. "My apologies, Master."

A map appeared on the datapad's display, showing the way to the Covered Brush house ring. "There it is," Obi-Wan said, angling the datapad so that Anakin could see.

"That's not the direction he was going when he left Duefgrin," Anakin pointed out uneasily.

"I know," Obi-Wan said grimly. "But right now, it's all we've got. Let's go take a look."

The neighborhood where the Covered Brush house ring was located was similar to many Obi-Wan had seen in his journeys around the Republic. It was poor but clean, a place where the people worked hard for what little they had but nevertheless worked equally hard to maintain their pride and dignity.

Some Jedi, he knew, treated such places and people with disdain or condescension. For his own part, he far preferred them to Coruscant's upper-level inhabitants with their immensely greater wealth but shifting-sand ethics. Most of the people in these places were friendlier and more forthright, without hidden political agendas or the lust for position and power.

At the very least, if someone here wanted to stab someone, he used a knife and not a deceitful smile.

"Where do we start?" Anakin murmured as they stopped beside one of the hedges across the street from the building.

"You could start by staying out of my way," a voice murmured from somewhere behind them.

Obi-Wan spun around, his hand darting beneath his tunic to his lightsaber as a face rose from concealment behind a section of hedge they'd just passed.

One look was all he needed. "Hello, Riske," he said, releasing his grip on his lightsaber. "Imagine meeting you here."

"I could say the same thing," Riske said sourly, jerking his head toward his side of the hedge. "You want to step into my office a minute?"

Obi-Wan glanced around. There were only a few Brolfi still out in the gathering dusk, and none of them was looking in their direction. Tapping Anakin on the arm, he did a quick backward leap over the hedge. He landed in a crouch, Anakin right beside him.

"You're persistent, I'll give you that," Riske said as he waddled over to join them, keeping his head down. "What are you doing here?"

"We're looking for a Brolf named Jhompfi," Obi-Wan told him. "He had someone steal a pair of burst thrusters for him this afternoon. We were hoping to ask him why."

"While you're at it, you could also ask about the explosives that disappeared from a mining site one of his close friends was working at," Riske said darkly. "Or about the stabilization system another friend apparently borrowed from his boss's hobby swoop, or the alloy packing cylinders that were lifted from another work site. You seeing a pattern here?"

Obi-Wan grimaced. "Someone's building a homemade missile."

"Or two or three of them," Riske said. "And it doesn't look like either of us will be able to ask Jhompfi about it, since he and all his friends seem to have disappeared."

"Wonderful," Obi-Wan said, peering over the hedge.

"Yeah, that's the word *I* was thinking," Riske said. "So what's your interest in him?"

"Our friend—the Padawan you ran into earlier—was following him," Obi-Wan said. "She's disappeared, and I can't raise her on the comlink."

"Too bad," Riske said. "Nice kid, but not much combat savvy."

"We're not ready to give up on her quite yet," Obi-Wan growled. "You have any idea where Jhompfi might have gone to ground?"

"If I did, I wouldn't be hanging around here," Riske countered. "I've got people checking out the Mining Guild centers, but if Jhompfi's not coming home I doubt he'd be stupid enough to go to any of them."

"So what do we do?" Anakin asked.

"What *I'm* going to do is head back to the hotel and make sure we've got our security set up," Riske said. "I'm figuring it'll come tonight—the duracrete slugs always disappear just before they drop the house on you."

"Or they might try for the city administration center tomorrow," Obi-Wan suggested.

"Unlikely," Riske said. "Jhompfi's hardly going to attack a

place where his own guildmaster is busy negotiating for him. No, it's got to be the hotel, or maybe the route to the admin center in the morning."

Unfortunately, Riske's analysis made sense. "Okay," Obi-Wan said. "You tie down that end, and we'll keep looking for Lorana."

"Good luck." Riske shook his head. "You know, I almost planted a tracker on her earlier, just so I could make sure she was staying out of my way. I wish now I had."

"I wish you had, too," Obi-Wan said. "We'll just have to manage on our own."

"Jedi are supposed to be good at such things," Riske said, pulling out a data card and handing it over. "This'll give you a direct connection to my comlink, running it through one of our encryptions. Call me if you hear anything, okay?"

"I will," Obi-Wan promised, sliding the card into his comlink pouch.

Riske nodded and moved away. He reached the far end of the hedge, glanced over it, then slipped back around and headed off at a brisk walk. "Now what?" Anakin asked.

"We'd better let Master C'baoth know what happened," Obi-Wan said reluctantly. "He and Lorana may be close enough for him to be able to detect her Force-signature."

"Maybe," Anakin said doubtfully as they returned to the end of the hedge and back onto the walkway. "You know, maybe we *all* should carry trackers."

Obi-Wan looked sideways at him. "I can think of at least *one* person who ought to have one," he muttered under his breath.

"What was that?"

Obi-Wan shook his head. "Never mind."

* * *

C'baoth, when they finally raised him on the comlink, wasn't at all happy about being disturbed. He was even less happy when he heard their story. "For the moment we'll pass over the fact that you involved yourself with the Barlok situation against my direct order," the Jedi Master rumbled, and Obi-Wan could imagine his eyes flashing from beneath his bushy eyebrows. "The important point right now is that you've put my Padawan at risk."

"I understand your anger, Master C'baoth—" Obi-Wan began.

"Anger?" C'baoth cut him off. "There is no anger, Master Kenobi. Not for a Jedi."

"My apologies," Obi-Wan said, trying hard to suppress some annoyance of his own. A situation like this, and all the man could do was recite Jedi canon? "It was an improper choice of words."

"Better," C'baoth rumbled. "What about you, Padawan Skywalker? Have you any thoughts?"

Obi-Wan angled the comlink toward the boy. "Not really, Master C'baoth," Anakin said. "Mostly, I'm concerned about Lorana's safety. I'm worried that she may have been killed."

For a moment C'baoth didn't answer. "No, she's not dead," he said at last. "I would have felt such a disturbance in the Force."

"Then you can locate her?" Anakin asked hopefully.

"The one does not necessarily follow from the other," C'baoth told him. "Unfortunately, I can't pick up her Force-signature at the moment. Master Kenobi, you said you'd spoken to the boy who obtained the boosters. He might know where Jhompfi's favorite hiding spots are."

"I don't think so," Anakin said. "He doesn't seem to be a part of the actual conspiracy."

"Yet he knows Jhompfi, and may have seen something in the past that will point the way."

"I doubt he'd be willing to discuss it," Obi-Wan said. "At least not with strangers."

"Did I *ask* if he would be willing?"

Obi-Wan felt his throat tighten. "Are you suggesting I force his mind?"

"No, of course not," C'baoth assured him. But the words, Obi-Wan knew, were for Anakin's benefit. That was, in fact, exactly what C'baoth had been suggesting. "We're the protectors of the weak, not their oppressors. At the same time, a crime has been perpetrated against a Jedi. Such a thing cannot be allowed to go unchallenged. Even if Padawan Jinzler chose not to fight in her own defense," he added darkly.

Obi-Wan frowned. "What do you mean?"

"There have been no reports of lightsabers being seen in the city, Master Kenobi," C'baoth said patiently. "Nor has news of multiple severed limbs reached my ears. Lorana Jinzler is only a Padawan, but I have certainly instructed her in combat better than *that.*"

"Of course," Obi-Wan said, a sudden idea striking him. If C'baoth was right about Lorana going quietly with her kidnappers . . . "Thank you for your time, Master C'baoth."

"I will expect my Padawan to be at my side when I meet Magistrate Argente and Guildmaster Gilfrome in the morning," C'baoth warned.

"Understood," Obi-Wan said. Breaking the connection, he slid the comlink back into his belt.

"So how are we going to find her?" Anakin asked.

"Master C'baoth gave us the hint himself," Obi-Wan told

him. "He's right: if Lorana had fought against her attackers, we certainly would have heard of it. Therefore, she didn't."

"Okay," Anakin said. "And that means what?"

"It means that she must have decided that surrendering quietly would gain her more than fighting," Obi-Wan said. "She probably hoped she'd be taken into the center of the conspiracy where she could meet the people in charge. *But.*"

He let the word hang expectantly in the air, hoping Anakin would pick up the train of logic. "But they'd be crazy to bring a Jedi to their leaders," the boy said slowly. "Even a Padawan."

"Exactly," Obi-Wan said. "And what's the fastest way to tell if someone like Lorana is a Jedi?"

"If you catch her carrying a lightsaber," Anakin said, his voice suddenly picking up on Obi-Wan's own cautious hope. "So she had to get rid of it!"

"Right," Obi-Wan confirmed. "And she probably got rid of it on the spur of the moment, someplace near where she was kidnapped."

"Someplace close enough for us to be able to sense its Ilum crystal," Anakin finished excitedly. "But we'll still have to get pretty close, won't we?"

"True, but at least out in the street we'll be *able* to get that close," Obi-Wan pointed out. "If she and her lightsaber were both inside a house, we probably wouldn't be able to spot the crystal, at least not from outside." He gestured down the street, darkened now except for the faint glow of streetlights. "We'll start here in the Covered Brush area. Jhompfi was smart enough to stay away from his own house, but he may have been stupid enough to go to a nearby friend's. If we don't find anything, we'll start going through the poorer neighborhoods of Patameene District."

"Because that's the sort of neighborhood Jhompfi's used to?"

"No, because that's where they use hedges instead of walls to mark the land boundaries," Obi-Wan said. "You're not going to bury a lightsaber inside a stone wall without somebody noticing. If we don't find her there, we'll move on to the wealthier areas, then move on to other districts."

Anakin took a deep breath. "All right. I'm game if you are."

"Good," Obi-Wan said. "Then clear your mind, my young Padawan. It's likely to be a long night."

They'd been tramping the streets for hours when Obi-Wan finally felt the tingle he'd been waiting for.

The Ilum crystal in Lorana's lightsaber was close at hand.

He looked sideways at Anakin, waiting for the boy to sense it as well. Even in the middle of a serious situation, training exercises were part of a Padawan's life.

They got three more steps before Anakin's steady footsteps suddenly faltered. "There," the boy said. "Just ahead, on the left."

"Very good," Obi-Wan said approvingly, letting his eyes drift around the neighborhood. It was still a good two hours till dawn, and the houses around them were dark and silent, their inhabitants fast asleep.

Or at least, most of them were. The particular inhabitants they were interested in would be very much awake. "No, don't go to it," he told Anakin, catching the boy's arm as he started toward the hedge where Lorana's lightsaber lay hidden. "Here, around on the other side—quickly, now."

Together they moved around the end of the hedge and ducked down out of sight. "Is someone watching us?" Anakin murmured as Obi-Wan led them in a crouch to within a few meters of the lightsaber.

"We'll find out in a moment," Obi-Wan said. "Tell me, what would you do if you were guarding a prisoner in the middle of the night and suddenly something strange happened outside your window?"

"I don't know," Anakin said, frowning in thought. "I suppose it would depend on how strange it was."

"Let's find out." Stretching out to the Force, Obi-Wan reached his mind across the distance and triggered Lorana's lightsaber.

With a muted *snap-hiss* the green blade lanced out, startlingly bright in the nighttime darkness. A few small leaves showered down where they'd been cut loose from their branches, but the handle was wedged solidly in place and stayed where it was. "Now, let's see who in the neighborhood is still awake," he commented.

They didn't have long to wait. Less than a minute later a door in one of the houses across the street opened, and a lone Brolf peered anxiously out, his eyes darting around. Seeing no one, he lumbered across the street to the blazing lightsaber.

For a moment he stared at it uncertainly. Then, gingerly, he reached into the mesh of branches and pulled the weapon free. Holding it at arm's length, he turned it carefully in his hand, clearly trying to figure out how to shut it off.

"Allow me," Obi-Wan spoke up, rising to his full height behind the hedge. Reaching out with the Force, he closed down the lightsaber.

The Brolf was fast, all right. Almost before the blade had vanished he leapt into action, jumping sideways and hurling the lightsaber straight at Obi-Wan's face as he hauled a blaster out of his tunic.

Fast, but stupid. Obi-Wan was a Jedi, with Jedi reflexes, and he had his own lightsaber ready in his hand before the Brolf even started his leap. Reaching up with his free hand, he caught Lorana's weapon and then ignited his own, casually catching the Brolf's shot on his blade and sending it ricocheting off into the night sky.

Stubbornly, the Brolf kept at it, firing again and again with the single-minded foolhardiness of a battle droid. Obi-Wan settled into battle mode, his attention focused inward as he let the Force guide his hands, deflecting the shots as he strode toward his attacker.

And then, through his tunnel vision, he dimly sensed something happening across the street. The Brolf heard or saw it, too, and for a split second his attention wavered as his eyes darted that direction.

It was all the opening Obi-Wan needed. Taking an extra-long step forward, he gave a short, controlled slash that sliced the Brolf's blaster neatly in half.

The Brolf had been quick to attack. Now, with equal speed, he dropped the remaining half of his blaster and took off down the street as fast as his stubby legs could carry him. Obi-Wan considered chasing him down, decided against it, and turned toward the house the other had emerged from.

It was only then that he realized Anakin was no longer with him.

"Blast!" he bit out under his breath, breaking into a run. There was a diffuse blue light flickering from somewhere inside the house, and as he headed up the walkway to the open door he heard the familiar hum of his Padawan's lightsaber. Picking up his pace, he charged inside.

He found Anakin in one of the inner rooms, standing over Lorana's limp form, his lightsaber held in guard position toward a pair of Brolfi cowering in the corner. A third Brolf lay motionlessly on the floor, the remains of a blaster beside him. "Master," Anakin said, clearly trying to sound casual but not entirely succeeding. "I found her."

"So I see," Obi-Wan said, closing down his lightsaber and kneeling down beside the young woman. Her breathing and pulse were slow but steady. "What did you use on her?" he demanded, turning toward the Brolfi in the corner.

Neither answered. "I didn't see anything when I came in," Anakin offered.

"Then they must have it on them," Obi-Wan said. Stepping past Anakin, he ignited his lightsaber and started deliberately toward them.

As with the Brolf he'd dealt with outside, neither of these two was interested in being a hero. "He's got it," one of them spoke up hastily, digging a thumb into his partner's side.

"Yeah, here it is," the other agreed, digging a hypo from inside his tunic and lobbing it at Obi-Wan's feet.

"Thank you," Obi-Wan said politely. "Let's add your comlinks to the pile, shall we? And any weapons, of course."

A moment later two comlinks and a pair of long knives had joined the hypo. "What do we do with them?" Anakin asked.

"That depends on what they've been dosing her with," Obi-Wan said ominously, closing down his lightsaber again and picking up the hypo. It was unlabeled, of course. Running through his Jedi sensory enhancement techniques, he squirted a small drop of the liquid onto his sleeve and held it up to his nose.

One sniff was all it took. "It's okay," he assured Anakin as he let the enhancement fade away. "It's a strong sedative, not a poison. She'll be all right once it wears off."

He gestured toward the two Brolfi. "Which means they won't be facing any murder charges." He cocked his head. "At least, not until their homemade missile goes off."

Both of the prisoners jerked noticeably at the word *missile.* "We had nothing to do with that," one of them insisted. "It was all Filvian's idea. His, and the human's."

Obi-Wan frowned. There was a human mixed up in this? "What human?" he demanded. "What's his name?"

"He calls himself Defender," the Brolf said. "That's all I know."

"What does he look like?"

The Brolf looked helplessly at his companion. "Like a human," the second Brolf said, waving a hand vaguely.

"Do they need more persuasion, Master?" Anakin asked, letting his voice harden.

Obi-Wan suppressed a smile. In his experience, threats from fourteen-year-olds were seldom very convincing.

His eyes dropped to the dead Brolf on the floor. On second thought, in this case maybe they were. "Don't bother," he told Anakin. "They probably really *don't* know how to describe him."

"I'll bet Riske could get something out of them," Anakin suggested.

For a long moment Obi-Wan was tempted. After all, the assassination plot *was* directed against Magistrate Argente. It would be only fitting for them to be turned over to Argente's people for interrogation.

But that wasn't the way Jedi were supposed to do things. "We'll turn them over to the city police," he told Anakin, pulling out his comlink. "Then I guess we'll just have to wait for Lorana to wake up. Maybe she can tell us more."

"We going to wait here?" Anakin asked, frowning.

"Of course," Obi-Wan said, smiling tightly. "After all, Jhompfi or Filvian or Defender might drop by."

"Right," Anakin murmured understandingly. "If we're lucky."

The Vagaari ship had been anchored to the outside of the Crustai asteroid base a quarter of the circumference around from the entrance tunnel. With a Chiss warrior at the controls, Thrawn and the three humans took one of the transports out from the base and docked with it.

To Car'das's private dismay, the alien bodies were still there, lying crumpled right where they'd fallen.

Qennto was apparently not thrilled by that fact, either. "You *are* planning to clean up this place eventually, aren't you?" he asked distastefully as they picked their way through the corridor toward the treasure room.

"Eventually," Thrawn assured him. "First we need to learn what we can of the enemy's strategy and tactics, and for that we need to know where each combatant was and how he was positioned when he died."

"Shouldn't you have put the ship somewhere out of sight?" Maris asked. She was clinging tightly to Qennto's arm as they walked, Car'das noted, apparently not doing nearly as well this time around as she had on their last visit. It made him feel better, somehow.

"Eventually, we'll move it inside the base," Thrawn said. "But we need to first establish that there are no dangerous instabilities in its engines or weaponry."

The treasure room, like the corridors, looked exactly the same as it had just after the ship's capture, except that now there were a pair of Chiss moving along the stacks, apparently making sensor records of the various items. "Spread out," Thrawn ordered the humans. "See if you can find anything of a familiar style."

"You mean like different kinds of money?" Qennto asked as he looked around the room.

"Or are you talking about the gemstones?" Maris added.

"I was speaking mainly of the artwork," Thrawn said. "We can learn more from that than we can from currency or gems."

Qennto snorted. "You expecting there to be sales receipts?"

"I was thinking more of the art's origins." Thrawn gestured toward a set of nested tressles. "Those, for instance, were probably created by beings with an extra joint between wrist and elbow, who see largely in the blue-ultraviolet part of the spectrum."

Qennto and Maris exchanged looks. "The Frunchies, you think?" Maris suggested.

"Yeah, right," Qennto said with a grunt. He eyed Thrawn suspiciously, then unhooked Maris's arm from his and strode over to the tressles.

"What are Frunchies?" Car'das asked.

"The Frunchettan-sai," Maris explained. "They have a couple of colony worlds in the Outer Rim. Rak calls them Frunchies because—"

"I'll be broggled," Qennto said, cutting her off as he leaned over the tressles with his head cocked to the side.

"What?" Maris said.

"He's right," Qennto said, sounding stunned. "It's signed with formal Frunchy script." He turned back to Thrawn, a strange expression on his face. "I thought you said you hadn't made it to Republic space."

"To the best of my knowledge, we haven't," Thrawn said. "But the artist's physical characteristics are obvious simply from looking at his work."

"Maybe to *you* it's obvious," Qennto growled, looking back at the tressles. "It sure isn't to me."

"Or me," Maris seconded.

Thrawn raised his eyebrows at Car'das. "Car'das?"

Car'das peered at the artwork, trying to spot whatever these subtle cues were that Thrawn had seen. But he couldn't. "Sorry."

"Maybe it was just luck," Qennto said, abandoning the tressles and kneeling down beside an elaborate blue-and-white sculpt. "Let me see here . . . yeah, I thought so." He looked over his shoulder at Thrawn. "How about *this* one?"

For a moment Thrawn studied the sculpt in silence, his eyes occasionally flicking around the rest of the room as if seeking inspiration. "The artist is humanoid," he said at last. "Proportioned differently from humans and Chiss, with either a wider torso or longer arms." His eyes narrowed slightly. "There's something of a distance to his emotional state, too. I would say his people are both drawn to and yet repulsed by or fearful of the physical objects they live among."

Qennto's breath went out in a huff. "I don't believe this," he said. "That's the Pashvi, all right."

"I don't think I know them," Maris said.

"They've got a system on the edge of Wild Space," Qennto said. "I've been there a few times—there's a small but stable market for their art, mostly in the Corporate Sector."

"What did Commander Thrawn mean about fear of physical objects?" Car'das asked.

"Their world is sprinkled with thousands of rock pillars," Qennto said. "Most of the best food plants grow on the tops. Unfortunately, so does a nasty predator avian. It makes for—well, for pretty much just what he said."

"And you got all that from a single sculpt?" Maris asked, gazing at Thrawn with a strange look on her face.

"Actually, no," the Chiss assured her. "There are—let me see—twelve more examples of their artwork." He pointed to two other areas of the room.

"You sure?" Car'das asked, frowning at the indicated sculpts and flats. "They don't look at all alike to me."

"They were created by different artists," Thrawn said. "But the species is the same."

"This is really weird," Qennto said, shaking his head. "Like some crazy Jedi thing."

"Jedi?" Thrawn asked.

"They're the guardians of the peace in the Republic," Maris told him. "Probably the only reason we've held together as long as we have. They're very powerful, very noble people."

Qennto caught Car'das's eye, his nose wrinkling slightly. His opinion of Jedi, Car'das knew, was considerably lower than his girlfriend's.

"They sound intriguing." Thrawn nodded toward the sculpt. "I presume these Pashvi won't have put up much resistance to Vagaari raids?"

"Hardly," Qennto confirmed grimly. "They're a pretty agreeable people. Lousy at fighting."

"And your Republic and these Jedi don't protect them?"

"The Jedi are spread way too thin," Car'das said. "Anyway, Wild Space isn't actually part of the Republic."

"Even if it were, the government is too busy with its own intrigues to bother with little things like life-and-death situations," Maris said, a bitter edge to her voice.

"I see," Thrawn said. "Well. Let us continue our survey, and please inform me if you find anything else from your region of space."

He looked at Maris. "And as we search, perhaps you'll tell me more about these Jedi."

Guildmaster Gilfrome's here," Anakin's voice said softly from Obi-Wan's comlink. "Just coming up the steps to the east door."

"Magistrate Argente's here, too," Obi-Wan told him, gazing down from the administration building's west door as Argente climbed up the stairs on that side, his people pressed protectively around him. "And I see Master C'baoth and Lorana approaching through the marketplace."

"So that's it?" Anakin asked.

Obi-Wan scratched his cheek thoughtfully. The expected attack on Magistrate Argente hadn't come during the night, nor had it been launched on the trip here to the conference room. Now, with the miners' representative on the scene, the conspirators' last chance was gone, at least until the negotiators broke for lunch. "It is for now, anyway," he told Anakin. "But stay alert."

Argente and his people reached the top of the stairs, and Obi-Wan bowed in greeting. The group brushed past without a single acknowledging glance and disappeared inside. Suppressing a flicker of annoyance, Obi-Wan turned his attention to C'baoth and Lorana as they started up the stairs. Lorana, he noted, was a bit pale, her steps a little tentative. But her expression was determined, and as they reached the top of the steps she smiled a bit awkwardly at him. "Master Kenobi," she said, nodding. "I never had a chance to properly thank you for what you and Anakin did for me yesterday."

"And this is also not the time," C'baoth put in. Nevertheless, there was a flicker of approval in his eyes as the two Jedi exchanged nods. "There is still danger, both to the negotiators and the negotiations themselves. Stay here with Master Kenobi and watch the crowd for familiar faces."

"Yes, Master C'baoth," Lorana said.

With another nod at Obi-Wan, C'baoth strode past through the doorway, leaving the two of them alone. "How do you feel?" Obi-Wan asked.

"Much better, thank you," Lorana said. "I really don't know how much good I can do here, though," she added, turning toward the marketplace spread out before them at the bottom of the steps. "I only saw three of the conspirators."

"That's three more than the rest of us have," Obi-Wan pointed out. "Not counting the ones already in custody, of course."

"Maybe their arrest scared off the others."

"It may have scared them away from a missile attack, but they're not going to just give up and go away," Obi-Wan said. "They seem obsessed with what they see as the Corporate Alliance's attempt to steal their planet's wealth, and once a person's obsessed he or she doesn't listen to logic anymore. Sheer momentum will carry them the rest of the way through this."

Lorana shook her head. "I'm afraid I don't understand that kind of thinking."

"You need to learn to understand it," Obi-Wan told her. "Obsession is something that can happen to even the strongest person, and for the best of motives." He gestured. "Still, with you and me at this door, Anakin and Riske at the other, and the police and the Corporate Alliance's security watching the sky, we should be able to stop whatever they throw at us."

"I hope you're right," Lorana murmured. "If not, Master C'baoth will never let us hear the end of it."

Seated on his hotel room balcony, Doriana smiled down at the scene below him. The players had assembled, and it was time for the performance to begin.

Picking up his comlink, he keyed it on and punched in the proper activation code. Then, setting the comlink aside, he settled down to watch.

Even stretched out to the Force, Lorana's only warning was a burst of commotion at the leftmost edge of the marketplace, a sudden movement of shoppers as they scattered away from one of the booths. "Something's happening," she warned, pointing.

The words were barely out of her mouth when the booth erupted in a flash of light and a burst of smoke. "Watch out!" Obi-Wan barked, the *snap-hiss* of his lightsaber sounding behind her.

Lorana yanked out her own lightsaber, igniting it as she tried to pierce the expanding smoke cloud. As far as she could tell, nothing else seemed to be happening. "To the right!" Obi-Wan warned.

Lorana turned; and to her horror she saw a silvery cylinder streak out of another of the booths, flying a bare meter above the ground.

Coming straight toward them.

"I've got it," she said, jumping into its path and lifting her lightsaber into attack-3 position. Defense against incoming remotes was an exercise C'baoth had drilled her in for hour after wearying hour. Behind her, she sensed Obi-Wan moving back and to her right into backstop position. She settled her breathing, watching the missile approach, trying not to think about what would happen if her attack detonated the warhead . . .

It was nearly to her when, without warning, the front of the nose cone erupted into a cloud of sparkling smoke, and a cone of roiling black liquid sprayed out at her.

She squeezed her eyes tightly shut, instinctively flinching to the side as she did so. She sensed the missile start to pass, and swung her lightsaber as hard as she could in that direction.

But her sidestep had put her off balance, and even as her blade sliced through the air she knew she was too late. Behind her, she heard the pitch of Obi-Wan's lightsaber change as he took his own shot at it. But the missile's roar changed as fresh thrusters kicked in, and as the heat of the missile's exhaust swept across her she could tell that he, too, had missed.

"Come on!" he shouted. A hand grabbed her arm, and suddenly they were running through the heat and dissipating smoke in the missile's wake. She blinked her eyes open, ignoring the sting as the black liquid dribbled into them, to see the missile jinking back and forth down the wide central corridor like a droid seeking a target. Across the building at the far door she saw Anakin and Riske charging in from the other door, Anakin's lightsaber blazing in his hand, Riske's blaster firing uselessly. Letting go of Lorana's arm, Obi-Wan locked his lightsaber on and hurled it at the missile.

But even as the spinning green blade closed on it, the missile's nose dipped and it made a hard turn to the left. She could sense Obi-Wan stretching to the Force, trying to bring his lightsaber back on target. But she could also sense that he wouldn't be in time.

Which left only one thing they could do. Closing her eyes, she stretched out to the Force, turning her thoughts to her Master. *Master C'baoth,* she sent urgently toward the room beyond the archway. *Danger. Danger. Danger.* The missile disappeared through the archway, and she joined with the others in racing down the corridor after it. She caught up with Obi-Wan just as he reached the opening, and turned the corner with him.

And found herself confronted by an extraordinary sight.

Seated at opposite ends of the table, the mining and Corporate Alliance representatives had turned in their chairs to stare with a mixture of surprise, fascination, and terror at the missile that had intruded into their solemn proceedings. Between them, half risen from his own chair, C'baoth was holding a hand palm outward toward the missile, his eyes blazing.

But the missile was no longer moving. It was frozen in midair, halfway between the archway and the table, its thrusters spitting fire uselessly as they tried to drive it forward against C'baoth's Force grip.

"Don't be concerned," the Jedi Master intoned, his voice resonating with power and authority. "So certain parties believe that they know best what is right and just for Barlok, do they?

That killing us will bring them their desire? That the influence of violence supersedes the authority of justice?"

The thrusters gave a final sputter and fell silent, and still the missile hung in midair. "Thank you, Master C'baoth—" Obi-Wan said, starting toward the missile.

"Stand fast, Master Kenobi," C'baoth ordered sharply. "*That* is what our attackers believe, Magistrate Argente; Guild-master Gilfrome," he said, sending a hard look at each end of the table. "Do *you* believe it, as well?"

Argente found his voice first. "No, of course not," he said, his voice quavering, his eyes locked on the missile that had nearly brought a sudden and violent death to them all.

"Then why do you persist in eroding the legitimate rights of the people of Barlok?" C'baoth demanded. "And *you,*" he added, turning back to Gilfrome's end of the table. "Why do *you* persist in denying the time and expense the Corporate Alliance has spent in developing resources that would otherwise have forever lain uselessly beneath the soil of your world?"

Gilfrome bristled. "Now, see here, Master C'baoth—"

"No, *you* see," C'baoth cut in, looking again at Argente. "*Both* of you see. I have listened to your arguments and your positions and your selfish pettiness. It ends here."

Deliberately, he closed his outstretched hand. With a raucous crackling of stressed metal, the body of the missile crumpled in on itself. "The people of Barlok demand a fair and just decision," he said, more quietly now as he gestured Obi-Wan forward. "I will tell you what that decision is going to be."

The room was silent as Obi-Wan stepped to the mutilated weapon, stretching out his hand to take its weight from C'baoth. Holding it in a Force grip in front of him, he turned and headed back toward the archway. Lorana looked a question at C'baoth, got a microscopic nod in return, and turned to go with Obi-Wan.

It was only then that she noticed Anakin standing beneath the archway, his eyes filled with admiration as he gazed across the room at C'baoth. "That's telling them," he murmured as she and Obi-Wan reached him.

"Come on," Obi-Wan said, his forehead wrinkling slightly as he looked at the boy. "Let's get this thing to the police disposal team."

"Report," the gravelly voice of Darth Sidious ordered, his hooded face hovering above the holoprojector.

"The Barlok operation has been a complete success, my lord," Doriana told him. "Both sides of the negotiations were so shaken by the attack that C'baoth was able to force them into an agreement."

"And is of course taking full credit for it?"

"Knowing C'baoth, there was never any doubt on that score," Doriana said. "Fortunately, the whole planet seems quite happy to let him have it. Another day or two, and he'll be the hero of the entire sector. Give him a week, and he'll probably be organizing his own victory parade through midlevel Coruscant."

"You have done well," Sidious said. "And what of the unanticipated interference from Kenobi and Skywalker?"

"Negligible," Doriana said, wondering again at the speed and breadth of the Sith Lord's knowledge. He hadn't even mentioned Kenobi's unwelcome arrival on Barlok, yet Sidious apparently knew all about it. Clearly, he had excellent sources of information. "All I had to do was add a shroud-liquid sprayer to the missile to make sure they wouldn't be able to stop it until it reached the conference chamber where C'baoth could make his dramatic grandstand play."

"And neither he nor Kenobi suspect your manipulation of the events?"

"Not at all, my lord," Doriana said. "My sources tell me the police analysts could tell the sprayer was a last-minute add-on, but they've concluded that it was added in response to C'baoth's appearance on the scene, not Kenobi's."

"I don't want Kenobi taking any of the credit," Sidious warned. "He cannot be permitted to blunt C'baoth's triumph and prestige."

"He won't," Doriana assured him. "Kenobi isn't the type to seek public recognition. C'baoth certainly isn't the type to offer him a share."

"Then all continues to go according to my plan," Sidious concluded with satisfaction. "Opposition in the Senate and the Jedi Council to C'baoth's pet project will melt away now before the fire of his newly enhanced stature."

"And if not, I have other contingency plans for raising it even higher," Doriana said. "The right word in Palpatine's ear is all it will take."

"Yes," Sidious said. "Speaking of Palpatine, you'd best leave Barlok and return to your official business. I also want you to find a way to make yourself the Supreme Chancellor's personal liaison to Outbound Flight's final preparations."

"Easily done, my lord," Doriana assured him. "Palpatine is so tied up with other matters that he'll welcome the chance to pass this one onto my shoulders."

"Excellent," Sidious said. "You have done well, my friend. Contact me when you return to Coruscant, and we'll discuss the final details."

The image vanished, and Doriana keyed off the connection. A simpler man, he reflected, even a master of the Dark Side like Lord Tyranus, might have tried to eliminate C'baoth directly through a genuine assassination, utilizing a more potent attack from more competent conspirators.

But as Sidious himself had pointed out, Doriana was more subtle than that. After all, why simply dispose of a powerful troublemaker like Jorus C'baoth when you could dispose of him *and* as many other Jedi as he could talk into accompanying him on Outbound Flight?

Smiling to himself, Doriana began to disassemble his holoprojector. Jorus C'baoth, Jedi Master and potential threat to Darth Sidious's plan for the Republic, was dead.

He just didn't know it yet.

It had been a long, frustrating day at the Preparation Center, one more of an endless series of them stretching back to the beginning of time, and as Chas Uliar keyed open his apartment door he wondered yet again if all of this was ever going to be worth it.

He'd been fresh out of school when he'd been approached by Outbound Flight's recruiters, and in the excitement and optimism of youth had instantly signed up to go along. But now, after two years of ever-slowing preparations and ever-lengthening delays, the shine had begun to fade. The latest rumor was that the Senate Appropriations Committee had decided to scratch all the families off the voyage, which would essentially turn Outbound Flight into little more than an extended military reconnaissance mission.

Which would, of course, take away the one thing which had made this whole project unique. But then, what did the corrupt bureaucrats of Coruscant care about anything as trivial as history or glory or even a vision for the Republic's future?

The glowplates in the common room were off, but as he switched them on he spotted a sliver of light coming from beneath the doors of both sleeping rooms. At least two of his three roommates were home, then. The planners had deliberately packed the recruits tightly together this way to simulate the close quarters that would exist aboard the six Dreadnaughts once Outbound Flight set off on its mission. Some people, mostly those from the more sparsely settled Mid Rim worlds, hadn't been able to handle the lack of privacy and had dropped out, but Uliar himself hadn't had any problems.

Though if all the families were tossed out like the Senate wanted, he thought sourly, he would probably get a suite this size all to himself.

He was looking through the pantry, trying to decide what to have for dinner, when one of the doors opened behind him. "Hey, Chas," Brace Tarkosa called from behind him. "You hear the news?"

Uliar shook his head. "I've been on D-Five all day trying to run down a fuel line problem," he said, turning around. "Let me guess: the Senate's decided to close us down completely?"

"You've got it backward," Tarkosa said, grinning. He was a strongly built man, two years older than Uliar, and allegedly one of the first hundred people to have signed up with the project. "Not only are they not closing us down, they've restored full funding *and* authorized the final assembly of the Dreadnaughts *and* reversed themselves on dropping the families."

Uliar stared at him. "You're kidding," he said. "Did someone on Coruscant have spoiled shellfish for lunch and start hearing voices?"

Tarkosa shook his head. "Rumor has it that it's all Jedi Master C'baoth's doing. He came roaring back from some negotiation session two days ago with enough momentum to crush-roll this whole thing straight through committee." He lifted a finger. "*And* it looks like we're going to get some more Jedi, too."

"How many?"

"Don't know," Tarkosa said. "As many as C'baoth wants, apparently."

"Wouldn't that be nice," Uliar murmured, a faint wisp of hope tugging at him. Rumors around here were as cheap as hardware problems, and he certainly wasn't ready to take any of this at face value. But if the Jedi *had* genuinely signed on to the project, maybe things would finally start to turn around. After all, a solar wind drove all wisp-sails, and everyone knew that Jedi always got the best of everything. "So when is this all supposed to happen?"

"Any day now," Tarkosa assured him. He grinned lopsidedly. "Hey, have a little faith. Come on—let's go get Keely and hit the tapcaf for dinner."

"You go ahead," Uliar told him, turning back to the pantry and pulling out a packaged ship's ration. "I'll save my celebrating until the Jedi are actually here."

"*Six* of them?" Obi-Wan repeated disbelievingly.

"Including C'baoth himself, yes," Windu confirmed, his back rigid as he stared out the Council Chamber window at the evening Coruscant skyline. "And eleven Jedi Knights have signed on to go along, as well."

Obi-Wan grimaced. Six Jedi Masters, plus eleven Jedi Knights, was not an insignificant number in these increasingly dark days. "I thought you and Master Yoda told him he could have no more than two other Jedi."

"That was before Barlok," Windu said ruefully, turning to face him. "*After* Barlok . . . well, let's just say that not even the Council is completely immune to pressure."

"Yes, I heard some of it," Obi-Wan said, nodding. "He was pushing his arguments to anyone who would listen."

"And he can be highly persuasive when he wants to be," Windu said. "I just wasn't expecting so many to get caught up in his excitement."

Obi-Wan felt a frown crease his forehead. Jedi Master Mace Windu, as closely attuned with the Force as any Jedi in the Republic . . . and yet he hadn't foreseen something this dramatic? "Couldn't you refuse them permission?"

"Of course we could," Windu said. "But I'm afraid that at the moment that would just cause more dissension. We can't afford that, not in these times of turmoil. And to be honest, there *are* good arguments to have a strong Jedi presence aboard Outbound Flight." He paused, studying Obi-Wan's face. "Tell me, did the investigators on Barlok ever locate or identify the human whom the Brolf conspirators claimed had helped with their missile attack?"

"Not as of when Anakin and I left," Obi-Wan said. "I haven't heard anything since then, either. Why?"

"It just bothers me somehow," Windu said. "We have a human help to launch a missile, which is then stopped in the nick of time by another human. Coincidence?"

Obi-Wan felt his eyebrows creeping up his forehead. "Are you suggesting C'baoth might have set the whole thing up *himself*?"

"No, of course not," Windu said. But he didn't sound entirely certain. "Only a Jedi who'd turned to the dark side would be capable of such cold-blooded manipulation. I can't believe he'd do that, not even for something he believes in this strongly."

"On the other hand, we suspect there may be a Sith out there somewhere," Obi-Wan pointed out. "Maybe . . . no. No, I can't believe it, either."

"Still, we can't afford to take chances," Windu said. "That's why I asked you here tonight. I want you and Anakin to find C'baoth and ask to go along with him. Not all the way to the next galaxy," he hastened to add as Obi-Wan felt his jaw drop. "Just through the Unknown Regions part of the exploration."

"That could take months," Obi-Wan protested. "I have work to do on Sulorine."

"Sometimes a Jedi's most important duty is to stand and wait," Windu countered mildly. "I presume you've mentioned that to Anakin on occasion?"

Obi-Wan grimaced. "Not more than twice a day," he conceded. "Did you have any suggestions on how to convince C'baoth to turn around when we reach the edge of the galaxy and take us back?"

"That would be an interesting conversation to sit in on," Windu said drily. "But no, my thought was to put a Delta-Twelve Skysprite aboard one of the Dreadnaughts for you. It's a bigger, two-seat version of the Delta-Seven Aethersprite you've been training on, only with the weapons packs stripped off. Kuat Systems is hoping to put them on the civilian market sometime in the next few months."

"No internal hyperdrive, I take it?"

Windu shook his head. "It uses the same TransGalMeg hyperdrive ring as the Aethersprite."

"I don't know," Obi-Wan said doubtfully, running the numbers in his head. "We're talking an awful lot of distance for something that size. Especially with two people aboard."

"It would be tight, but doable," Windu assured him. "Especially since both you and Anakin can use Jedi hibernation to stretch out the supplies of air and food."

Obi-Wan spread his hands. "If that's what the Council wishes, Anakin and I stand ready to obey. *If* C'baoth will have us, that is."

"Just find a way aboard," Windu said, his eyes darkening. "However you have to do it."

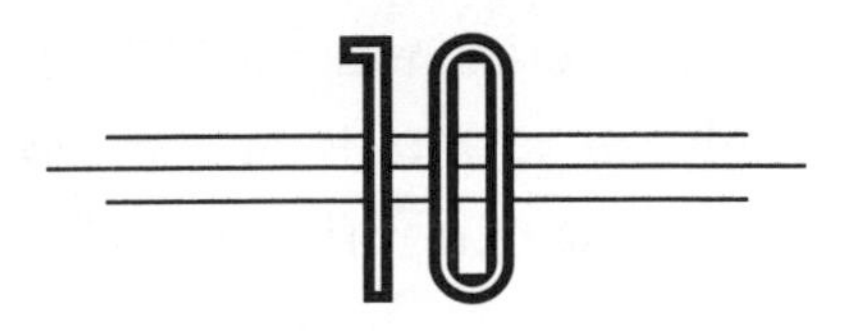

What is your profession?" Thrawn asked in Cheunh.

"I am a merchant trader," Car'das said carefully in the same language, forcing the odd sounds through unwilling tongue and lips.

Thrawn lifted his eyebrows politely. "You are a fishing boat?" he asked, switching to Basic.

Car'das looked at Maris. "That's what you said," she confirmed, an amused smile on her face.

He lifted his hand slightly, let it fall back into his lap. "I am a merchant trader," he said, giving up and switching over to the Minnisiat trade language.

"Ah," Thrawn said in the same language. "You're a merchant trader?"

"Yes." Car'das shook his head. "I really said I was a fishing boat?"

"Pohskapforian; Pohskapforian," Thrawn pronounced. "Can you hear the difference?"

Car'das nodded. He could hear the difference between the aspirated and unaspirated *p* sounds in the second syllable, all right. He just couldn't make the difference with his own mouth. "And I practiced that all evening, too," he grumbled.

"I warned you Cheunh would most likely be beyond your physical capabilities," Thrawn reminded him. "Still, your increase in comprehension level has been quite amazing, especially after only five weeks. And your progress with Minnisiat over the same period has been nothing less than remarkable. I'm impressed." His glowing eyes shifted to Maris. "With both of you," he added.

"Thank you, Commander," Car'das said. "To have impressed you is high praise indeed."

"Now you flatter me," Thrawn warned with a smile. "Is that the correct word? *Flatter*?"

"The word is correct," Car'das confirmed. Whatever progress he and Maris might have made with their studies, Thrawn's own work on Basic had far surpassed them, a feat rendered all the more remarkable given how much less time he'd had to devote to language studies. "But I would argue with the usage," he added. "*Flattery* implies exaggeration or even falsehood. My statement was the truth."

Thrawn inclined his head. "Then I accept the tribute as given." He turned to Maris. "And now, Ferasi, I'm ready with your special request."

Car'das frowned. "Special request?"

"Ferasi asked me to create a description of one of the artworks aboard the Vagaari pirate vessel," Thrawn told him.

Car'das looked at her. "Oh?"

"I wanted some extra practice with abstract terms and adjectives," she said, meeting his eyes coolly.

"Okay, sure," Car'das said hastily. "I was just wondering."

She held his gaze a fraction of a second longer, then turned back to Thrawn. "May I ask which piece you've chosen?"

"Certainly not," he admonished her with a smile. "You'll have to deduce that from my description."

"Oh," she said, sounding momentarily nonplussed. She glanced at Car'das, then set her jaw firmly. "All right. I'm ready."

Thrawn's eyes seemed to defocus as he gazed across the room. "The changing of colors is like a rainbow's edge melding into a sunlit waterfall . . ."

Car'das listened to the melodious flow of Cheunh words, struggling to keep up as he studied Maris out of the corner of his eye. She was struggling a little, too, he could see, her lips occasionally moving as she worked through some of the more complex terms. But behind the concentration he thought he could see something else in her eyes as she looked at Thrawn.

Only it wasn't the kind of look a language student should be giving her teacher. It most certainly wasn't a look a captive should be giving her captor.

An unpleasant sensation began to drift into his gut. She couldn't actually be falling for Thrawn, could she? Surely she wouldn't let herself be drawn in by his intelligence and courtesy and sophistication.

Because she wasn't just Qennto's partner and copilot, after all. And while Car'das had never seen Qennto in a fit of jealousy, he was pretty sure he didn't want to.

". . . with a deep sense of disconnection and strife between the artist and his people."

"Beautiful," Maris murmured, her eyes shining even more as she gazed at Thrawn. "That was the flat with the carved edging, wasn't it? The landscape with the darkness growing upward from the lower corner?"

"Correct," Thrawn confirmed. He looked at Car'das. "Were you also able to identify it?"

"I—no," Car'das admitted. "I was mostly concentrating on understanding the words."

"One can concentrate so closely on the words of a sentence that one thereby misses the meaning," Thrawn pointed out. "As can happen in any area of life. You must never lose focus on the larger landscape." He looked over at a series of lights on the wall above the door and stood up. "Today's lesson is over. I must see to my guest."

"Guest?" Maris asked as she and Car'das also stood up.

"An admiral of the Chiss Defense Fleet is on her way to take possession of the Vagaari vessel," Thrawn said as they all headed to the door. "Nothing you need concern yourselves with."

"May we observe the welcoming ceremony with you?" Car'das asked. "This time we should be able to understand what's being said."

"I believe that will be permissible," Thrawn said. "Admiral Ar'alani will certainly have heard of your presence from Aristocra Chaf'orm'bintrano and will want to see you for herself."

"Are they both from the same family?" Maris asked.

Thrawn shook his head. "Senior officers of the Defense Fleet belong to no family," he said. "They're stripped of family name and privilege and made part of the Defense Hierarchy in order that they may serve all Chiss without deference or prejudice."

"So military command is merit-based, and not something that comes from Family connections?" Maris asked.

"Exactly," Thrawn confirmed. "Officers are taken into the Hierarchy once they've proven themselves, just as the Ruling Families themselves select merit adoptives."

"What are merit adoptives?" Car'das asked.

"Chiss brought in from outside a Family's bloodlines to enrich or diversify or invigorate," Thrawn told him. "All warriors are made merit adoptives when they're accepted into either the Defense Fleet or the Expansionary Fleet." He tapped the burgundy patch on his shoulder. "That's why every warrior wears the color of one of the Families."

"Which one is yours?" Maris asked.

"The Eighth," Thrawn said. "My position is actually different from that of most warriors, as I've been named a Trial-born of the family. Most warriors' positions automatically cease when they leave the military, but mine carries the possibility that I will be deemed worthy and matched permanently to the Family. I may even be granted the position of ranking distant, which will tie my descendants and bloodline into that of the Family."

"Sounds complicated," Car'das commented.

"Sounds smart," Maris countered. "The Republic could use a lot more of that, instead of always going with straight bloodlines, or the highest bidder."

"Mm," Car'das said noncommittally. This was not the time to get into a discussion about Republic politics. "And you said there are nine of these Ruling Families?"

"There are nine at present," Thrawn said. "The number fluctuates with events and political fortunes. At various times over the centuries there have been as many as twelve and as few as three."

They reached the welcoming chamber to find it had already been configured for the new arrival. The wall and ceiling hangings were totally different from those featured for Aristocra Chaf'orm'bintrano's arrival, and to Car'das's eye the arrangement seemed less elaborate. Perhaps even a senior military officer didn't rank as highly as a distant relative of one of the Ruling Families.

"The ceremony will be considerably shorter and less formal than the last one you witnessed," Thrawn said as he gestured them into positions flanking him but two paces back. "You should be able to follow." He seemed to consider, then favored them with a small smile. "The admiral's appearance may surprise you a bit, as well," he added. "I'll look forward to hearing your thoughts later."

He turned toward the door and nodded to one of the warriors. With a melodious chiming that reminded Car'das of a water carillon, the door slid open and four black-clad Chiss warriors came through, taking up flanking positions on either side. Wondering what Thrawn had meant by their guest's appearance, Car'das straightened into his best approximation of military attention as a tall female Chiss stepped into view.

Only instead of the normal black uniform, she was dressed from collar to boots in dazzling white.

Car'das blinked in surprise as she strode past her escort into the welcoming chamber. Every Chiss warrior he'd seen up to now had invariably worn black, except for the clearly family-based guards who had accompanied Chaf'orm'bintrano. Was it because she was connected to the Defense Fleet instead of the Expansionary Fleet?

The admiral stepped to the center of the room and stopped. "In the name of all who serve the Chiss, I greet you, Admiral Ar'alani," Thrawn intoned, taking a step toward her.

"I accept your greeting, and greet you in return, Commander Mitth'raw'nuruodo," the admiral responded. Her words were to Thrawn, but Car'das could tell that her eyes were on the two humans standing behind him. "Do you guarantee my safety, and the safety of my crew?"

"I guarantee your safety with my life and the lives of those of my command," Thrawn said, bowing his head low. "Enter in peace, and with trust."

Ar'alani bowed in return. "Who are these who stand behind you?" she asked, her tone subtly changed.

And with that, apparently, the ceremony was over. "Visitors from a distant world," Thrawn told her, half turning to gesture them forward. "Car'das and Ferasi, may I present Admiral Ar'alani."

"We are honored, Admiral," Car'das said in Cheunh, trying to duplicate the bow he'd just seen Thrawn make.

Ar'alani seemed to draw back. "Aristocra Chaf'orm'bintrano didn't tell me they spoke Cheunh," she said, an unpleasant edge to her tone.

"Aristocra Chaf'orm'bintrano didn't know," Thrawn countered politely. "He spent little time here, and showed no interest in learning about my guests."

Ar'alani's eyes flicked to him, came back to Car'das. "The report said there were three of them."

"The third is otherwise occupied," Thrawn said. "I can summon him if you wish."

Ar'alani lifted her eyebrows. "He is allowed to roam freely through an installation of the Chiss Expansionary Fleet?"

Thrawn shook his head. "All three are under constant surveillance."

"You are studying them, then?"

"Of course," Thrawn said, as if that was obvious.

Car'das suppressed a grimace. He'd known from the start that this was one of Thrawn's reasons for keeping him and the others around. But it was nevertheless a little discomfiting to hear it stated aloud.

"And what have you learned?" Ar'alani asked.

"A great deal," Thrawn assured her. "But this is neither the time nor the place to discuss it."

Ar'alani's eyes flicked to Thrawn's warriors, still standing at attention against the welcoming chamber walls. "Agreed," she said.

"I presume you'll wish to tour the captured vessel before you take it in tow," Thrawn went on. "I have a shuttle waiting."

"Good," Ar'alani said, reaching to her belt and touching the smoothly curved shape of a Chiss comlink fastened there. "Let me summon my passenger, and we'll go."

Thrawn's eyes narrowed, and for the first time Car'das sensed a flicker of surprise in his face. "No passengers were mentioned."

"His presence is not officially sanctioned by the Defense Fleet," Ar'alani said. "I brought him here as a favor to the Eighth Ruling Family." Behind her, a young Chiss male stepped into view, his short robe and tall boots composed of a patchwork pattern of gray and burgundy, a slight smile on his face.

Thrawn stiffened. "Thrass!" he breathed. He stepped toward the other as he entered the chamber, meeting him halfway. Reaching out his right hand, he grasped the other's right arm at the elbow as the other gripped his in return. "Welcome," he said, smiling. "This is a surprise indeed."

"An achievement I have rarely achieved," the other said, inclining his head. He was still smiling, but Car'das could see hints of tension lines around his eyes as his gaze shifted over Thrawn's shoulder.

Thrawn obviously noticed the shift. "My guests," he said, releasing the other's arm and gesturing at the humans. "Car'das and Ferasi, K'rell'n traders from the Galactic Republic."

"Aristocra Chaf'orm'bintrano's description didn't do them justice," Thrass commented, looking them up and down. "Particularly the clothing."

"Their regular shipments of style-design from Csilla must have been delayed," Thrawn said drily. "Car'das and Ferasi: this is Syndic Mitth'ras'safis of the Eighth Ruling Family." He smiled a little wider. "My brother."

"Your *brother*?" Maris breathed.

"*And* they speak Cheunh?" Mitth'ras'safis said, his tone darkening a little.

"After a fashion," Thrawn said. "Admiral Ar'alani and I were on our way to visit the captured pirate vessel. Would you care to accompany us?"

"That's the main reason I'm here," Mitth'ras'safis said.

"The *main* reason?" Thrawn asked.

The other's lip twitched. "There are others."

"I see," Thrawn said. "But we'll speak of them later. If you'll come this way, Admiral?"

For the most part, the trip around the side of the asteroid was made in silence. Thrawn occasionally mentioned something technical in the pirate ship's design as they approached, but neither the admiral nor Mitth'ras'safis seemed interested enough to respond with anything more than grunted monosyllabic comments or an occasional question. The admiral's escort, as befit proper warriors, said nothing at all.

Once or twice along the way Car'das noticed Mitth'ras'safis

frowning at him and Maris, as if wondering why Thrawn had brought non-Chiss along for the ride. But he never asked for an explanation, and Thrawn never offered one.

The alien bodies had long since been removed from the ship, but there were many other details and deductions that Thrawn was able to point out as the group passed down the corridors, everything from the probable physical characteristics of no fewer than three different species of Vagaari slaves all the way to the equipment their masters had probably permitted them to use.

Car'das hadn't heard any of this analysis, and listened in fascination to the commander's monologue. Again, Ar'alani and Mitth'ras'safis absorbed the information in silence.

Until, that is, they reached the treasure room.

"Ah—there you are," Qennto's deep voice boomed from one of the back corners, waving with one hand as he clutched what looked like an ancient decorated battle shield with the other.

"What's this alien doing here?" Ar'alani demanded.

"He's helping catalog the items for me," Thrawn replied. "Some of the systems plundered by the Vagaari are in Republic territory, and he has some knowledge of their origin and value."

"What did he say?" Qennto called, looking at Maris.

She looked questioningly at Thrawn. "In Sy Bisti, if you please," the commander said, switching to that language. "We don't want to leave the admiral and syndic out of the conversation."

"Yes, Commander." She turned back to Qennto and translated Thrawn's last comment.

"Oh, I'm helping catalog, all right," Qennto said, eyeing the newcomers suspiciously. "I'm also picking out the items I'll be taking home with me."

"What items are these?" Ar'alani asked in Cheunh, her glowing eyes narrowing. "Commander?"

"In Sy Bisti, if you please, Admiral," Thrawn reminded her.

"This is not an interspecies conversation circle," Ar'alani countered tartly, ignoring the request. "What exactly have you promised these aliens?"

"They're merchants and traders," Thrawn reminded her, his own voice going a little stiff. "I've offered them some of the items as compensation for their weeks of service."

"What service?" Ar'alani demanded, shifting her glare to Car'das and Maris and then to Qennto. "You've provided them with food and living quarters, taught them Cheunh—and for this *they* deserve compensation?"

"We're also teaching the commander our language," Maris offered.

"You will not speak to an admiral of the Chiss unless first spoken to," Ar'alani told her brusquely.

Maris reddened. "My apologies."

"There's plenty here for both our visitors and the Ascendancy," Thrawn said. "If you'll come this way, there are some details of the engine room I'd like to show you." He took a step toward the door

"A moment," Ar'alani said, her eyes back on Qennto and the shield he was still defiantly gripping. "Who will decide which items your humans will be permitted to take?"

"My intent was to leave that decision largely to Captain Qennto," Thrawn said. "He's been working on this inventory for some weeks now and has an extensive knowledge of the contents. I can provide you with a copy of the complete listing before you leave."

"A listing of what's in here now?" Ar'alani asked. "Or a listing of what was here *before* he removed his chosen items?"

"Both lists will be available," Thrawn assured her, taking another step toward the door. "And my spot checks have shown the lists and descriptions are accurate enough. At any rate, you'll have time on the voyage home to examine both the lists and the treasures themselves."

"Or I could examine them right now," Ar'alani said, gesturing to one of her two warriors. "You—get the listing. I think, Commander, that I'd prefer to take my own inventory."

"As you wish, Admiral," Thrawn said. "Unfortunately, I'll be unable to assist you in that task. There are administrative matters that require my attention."

"I can make do without your assistance," Ar'alani said. From the tone of her voice, Car'das had the feeling that she would just as soon *not* have him looking over her shoulder. "Make sure I have a shuttle with which to return to my ship when I'm finished." Her eyes flicked to Thrawn's brother. "And I think it would be wise if Syndic Mitth'ras'safis remained with me. With the syndic's permission, of course."

"I have no objections," Mitth'ras'safis assured her. To Car'das's eye, his face looked a bit troubled.

"Then I'll look forward to conversing again with you at your convenience," Thrawn said. Catching Car'das's eye, he nodded toward the door.

They were twenty meters down the corridor before Car'das dared to speak. "You don't really have any administrative work to deal with, do you?" he asked Thrawn, keeping his voice low. "You just wanted to get away from the admiral for a while."

"A harsh accusation," Thrawn said mildly. "You'll tarnish Ferasi's high opinion of me."

Ferasi's—? Car'das looked behind him, to discover that Maris had indeed followed them out of the treasure room. "Oh. Hi," he said lamely.

"I think you missed the point, Jorj," she said. "Commander Thrawn didn't duck out on the admiral. He maneuvered her into deciding on her own to stay behind."

"What leads you to that conclusion?" Thrawn asked.

"The fact that this is the first I've heard about Rak spending weeks taking inventory of the treasure," she said. "He would certainly have mentioned something like that to me."

"Yet he didn't deny it," Thrawn pointed out.

"Because that part of the conversation was in Cheunh," Car'das said, finally catching on. "Which he doesn't understand."

"Excellent," Thrawn said, nodding. "Both of you."

"So what exactly is going on?" Maris asked.

They rounded a corner, and Thrawn abruptly picked up his pace. "I've had a report of another Vagaari attack, this one still in progress," he said. "I'm going to take a look."

"How far away is it?" Car'das asked. "I mean, the treasure room's not going to hold their attention *that* long."

"It's approximately six standard hours away," Thrawn said. "And I fully expect Admiral Ar'alani to deliver a severe reprimand when I return, assuming she delays her departure until then. For now, though, all I need is for her to be distracted long enough for us to slip away."

Car'das's stomach tightened. "You're not just going there to observe, are you?"

"The purpose of the trip is to evaluate the situation," Thrawn said evenly. "But if I judge there's a reasonable chance of eliminating this threat to the Chiss Ascendancy . . ." He left the sentence unfinished, but there was no doubt as to his intentions. He was going to attack.

And from the way he'd pulled Car'das out of the treasure room, it was clear he expected his language tutor to come along for the ride.

Car'das took a deep breath. He'd already been through more space battles than he liked, and going up against a fully armed Vagaari raiding party was *not* something he really wanted to do. But maybe there was still a chance of gracefully backing out. "I'm sure you'll do whatever is right," he said diplomatically. "Good luck, and—"

"May I go with you?" Maris interrupted him.

Car'das threw her a startled look. Her eyes flicked to his, a hard-edged warning in her expression. "It might be good to have a witness along," she continued. "Especially someone who has no connection to any of the Ruling Families."

"I agree," Thrawn said. "That's why I'm taking Car'das."

Car'das winced. So much for a graceful exit. "Commander, I appreciate the offer—"

"Two witnesses would be better," Maris said.

"Actually, Qennto would be a better choice than either Maris or me," Car'das tried again. "He's the one—"

"In theory, yes," Thrawn agreed, his eyes on Maris. "But no matter how carefully planned or executed, a battle always entails risks."

"He's the one who really likes this kind of excitement—"

"So does flying with Rak," Maris countered. "I'm willing to take my chances."

"I could go get him out of the treasure room—"

"I'm not sure *I* am," Thrawn countered in the same tone.

"Should you be injured or killed, I wouldn't want to be the one to bring that news to your captain."

"If we're on the bridge together, you won't have to," Maris pointed out. "If I die, you probably will, too, and someone else would get stuck with that job." She jerked a thumb at Car'das. "It sounds like Jorj would rather stay behind anyway. He can do it."

"Forget it," Car'das said firmly, his mind suddenly made up for him. He'd seen Thrawn's combat abilities, and he'd seen Qennto's temper, and he knew which one sounded safer. "If Maris goes, we both go."

"I'm honored by your trust," Thrawn said as they reached the shuttle bay. "Come then. May warriors' fortune smile on our efforts."

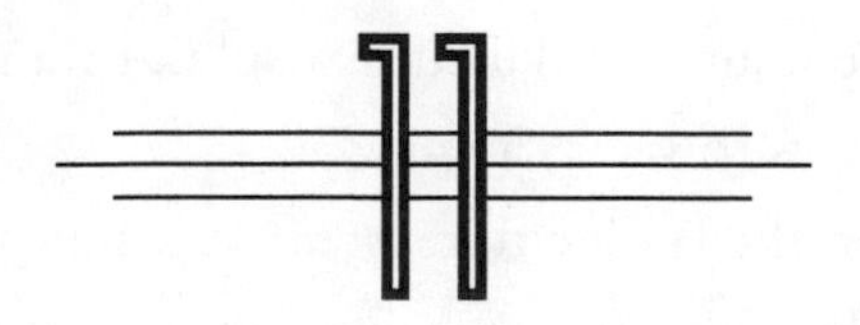

One minute to breakout," the helmsman called.

"Acknowledged," Thrawn replied. "Warriors, stand ready."

Standing behind the commander's chair, Car'das stole a look at Maris. Her face looked a little pale above the wide collar of her vac suit, but her eyes were clear and her jaw firmly set. Probably looking forward to Thrawn being all noble and honorable, he thought sourly. Waiting for him to bolster her already stratospheric opinion of him. Women.

So what in blazes was *he* doing here?

"If the reports are accurate, we'll arrive in a safe area a short way beyond the outer edge of the battle zone," Thrawn said, his eyes dropping to the helmets gripped in their hands. "Still, it would be wise for you to have your helmets already in place."

"We can get them on fast enough if we need to," Maris assured him.

Thrawn hesitated, then nodded. "Very well. Then stand ready."

He swiveled back to face forward. Car'das watched the countdown timer, his mouth feeling uncomfortably dry; and as it hit zero the starlines appeared out of the hyperspace sky and collapsed into stars.

And through the canopy he found himself staring at the most horrific sight he'd ever witnessed.

It wasn't the simple pirate attack he'd expected, with three or four Vagaari marauders preying on a freighter or starliner. Stretched out before them, writhing against the backdrop of a cloud-flecked blue-green world, were at least two hundred ships of various sizes locked in battle, linked together in twos or threes or groups by savage exchanges of laser- and missile fire. In the distance, on the far side of the planet, he could see the glittering points of a hundred more ships, silently waiting their turn.

And through the swirling combat drifted the debris and bodies and dead hulks of perhaps twenty more ships.

This wasn't a pirate attack. This was a war.

"Interesting," Thrawn murmured. "I seem to have miscalculated."

"No kidding," Car'das said, the words coming out like an amphibian's croak. He wanted to tear his eyes away from the carnage but found himself unable to do so. "Let's get out of here before someone sees us."

"No, you misunderstand," Thrawn said. "I knew the battle would be of this scale. What I hadn't realized was the Vagaari's true nature." He pointed through the canopy at the distant cluster of ships. "You see those other vessels?"

"The ones waiting their turn to fight?"

"They're not here to fight," Thrawn corrected him. "Those are the civilians."

"Civilians?" Car'das peered out at the distant points of light. "How can you tell?"

"By the way they're grouped in defensive posture, with true war vessels set in screening positions around them," Thrawn said. "The error I spoke of was that the Vagaari aren't simply a strong, well-organized pirate force. They're a completely nomadic species."

"Is that a problem?" Maris asked. She was gazing calmly at the panorama, Car'das noted with a touch of resentment, almost as calmly as she'd faced the piles of bodies aboard the Vagaari treasure ship.

"Very much so," Thrawn told her, his voice grim. "Because it implies in turn that all their construction, support, and maintenance facilities are completely mobile."

"So?" Car'das asked.

"So it will do us no good to capture one of the attackers and use its navigational system to locate their homeworld," Thrawn said patiently. "There *is* no homeworld." He gestured out at the battle. "Unless we can destroy all of their war vessels at once, they will simply melt away into the vastness of interstellar space and regroup."

Car'das looked at Maris, feeling a fresh wave of tension ripple through him. A bare handful of ships at his disposal, and he was talking about destroying an entire alien war machine? "Uh, Commander . . ."

"Calm yourself, Car'das," Thrawn said soothingly. "I don't propose to destroy them here and now. Interesting." He pointed out into the melee. "Those two damaged defenders, the ones trying to escape. You see them?"

"No," Car'das said, looking around. As far as he could tell, no part of the battle area looked any different from any other part.

"Over there," Maris said. Pulling him close to her, she stretched out her arm for him to sight along. "Those two ships heading to starboard with a triangle of fighters behind them."

"Okay, right," Car'das said as he finally spotted them. "What about them?"

"Why haven't they jumped to hyperspace?" Thrawn asked. "Their engines and hyperdrives appear intact."

"Maybe they feel it would be dishonorable to abandon their world," Maris suggested.

"Then why run at all?" Car'das said, frowning at the scenario. The fighters were rapidly closing, and the escapers were already far enough outside the planet's gravitational field to make the jump to lightspeed. There was no reason he could see how further delay would gain them anything.

"Car'das is correct," Thrawn said. "I wonder . . . there!"

Abruptly, with a flicker of pseudomotion, the lead ship had made the jump to safety. A moment later, the second also flickered and vanished.

"I don't get it," Car'das said, frowning as the pursuing fighters broke off and curved back toward the main part of the battle. "What were they waiting for? Clearance?"

"In a sense, yes," Thrawn said. "Clearance from the laws of physics."

"But they were already clear of the planet's gravity field."

"From the *planet's* field, yes," Thrawn said. "But not from the Vagaari's."

He looked up at them again, a glitter in his glowing eyes. "It appears the Vagaari have learned how to create a pseudograv-field."

Car'das felt his jaw drop. "I didn't even know that was possible."

"The theory's been around for years," Maris said, her voice suddenly thoughtful. "We used to talk about it at school. But it's always required too much energy and too big a generator configuration to be practical."

"It would seem the Vagaari have solved both problems," Thrawn said.

Car'das gave him a sideways look. There was something in the commander's voice and expression that he didn't care for at all. "And this means what to us?" he asked cautiously.

Thrawn gestured at the canopy. "The Vagaari are obviously using it to keep their prey from escaping until they can be obliterated. I think perhaps I could find more interesting uses for such a device."

Car'das felt his stomach tighten. "No. Oh, no. You *wouldn't.*"

"Why not?" Thrawn countered, his eyes sweeping methodically across the battle scene. "Their main attention is clearly elsewhere, and whatever defenses they have around their gravity projectors will be arrayed against a possible sortie from their victims."

"You assume."

"I saw how they defended their treasure ship," Thrawn reminded him. "I believe I have a good sense for their tactics."

Which, translated, meant that Car'das had zero chance of talking him out of this lunatic scheme. "Maris?"

"Don't look at me," she said. "Besides, he's right. If we want to grab a projector, this is the time to do it."

Something cold settled into the pit of Car'das's stomach. *We?* Was Maris starting to actually identify herself with these aliens?

"There," Thrawn said abruptly, pointing. "That large spherical gridwork."

"I see it," Car'das said with a sigh of resignation. The sphere was near the Chiss edge of the battle, where they could get to it without having to charge halfway through the fighting. There were three large warships hovering protectively between it and the main combat area, but only a handful of Vagaari fighters actually within combat range of it.

A tempting, practically undefended target. Of course Thrawn was going to go for it. "I'd just like to remind everyone that all we have is the *Springhawk* and six heavy fighters," he pointed out.

"*And* Commander Mitth'raw'nuruodo," Maris murmured.

Thrawn inclined his head to her, then swiveled around toward the port side of the bridge. "Tactical analysis?"

"We've located five more of the projectors, Commander," the Chiss at the sensor station reported. "All are at the edges of the battle area, all more or less equally well defended."

"Analysis of the projector layout and the jump pattern of the escaped vessels indicates the gravity shadow is roughly cone-shaped," another added.

"Are the three defending war vessels within the cone?" Thrawn asked.

"Yes, sir." The Chiss touched a key and an overlay appeared on the canopy, showing a wide, pale blue cone stretching outward from the gridwork sphere into the battle zone.

"As you see, the three main defenders are inside the cone, which limits their options," Thrawn pointed out to Car'das and Maris. "And all three vessels are positioned with their main drives pointing toward the projector. Years of success with this technique has apparently made them overconfident."

"Though those close-in fighters *are* dipping in and out of the cone," Car'das pointed out.

"They won't be a problem," Thrawn said. "Does the projector itself appear collapsible?"

"Unable to obtain design details at this distance without using active sensors," the Chiss at the sensor station reported.

"Then we'll need a closer look," Thrawn concluded. "Signal the fighters to prepare for combat; hyperspace course setting of zero-zero-four by zero-five-seven."

"*Hyperspace* setting?" Car'das echoed, frowning. Back at their first tangle with the Vagaari, Thrawn had successfully pulled off a fractional-minute microjump. But their target sphere was way too close for that trick to work now.

And then, beside him, he heard Maris's sudden chuckle. "Brilliant," she murmured.

"What's brilliant?" Car'das demanded.

"The course setting," she said, pointing. "He's sending them to the edge of the gravity cone, the edge right by the projector."

"Ah," Car'das said, grimacing. Of course there was no need for an impossibly short microjump here. The fighters could head into hyperspace as if they intended to make it their permanent home, relying on the field itself to snap them out again at precisely the spot where Thrawn wanted them.

"Once in place, they're to clear out the enemy fighters and create a defensive perimeter between the projector and the war vessels," Thrawn continued. "The *Springhawk* will follow and attempt to retrieve the sphere."

Car'das squeezed his hands into fists. Very straightforward . . . unless they missed the edge of the cone they were aiming for and got pulled out somewhere in the middle of the battle instead. Or unless such a short jump fried all their hyperdrives, which would lead to the same result.

"Assault Teams One and Two are to prepare for out-hull operation," Thrawn said. "There will most likely be an operational crew aboard the projector; they're to locate and neutralize with minimal damage to the projector itself. They'll be joined by Chief Engineer Yal'avi'kema and three of his crew, who will either find a way to collapse the projector to a size we can take aboard or else attach it as is to our hull for transport. All groups are to signal when ready."

The minutes crept by. Car'das watched the battle, wincing at each defender that flared and died under the merciless assault and wondering how long Thrawn's own luck would hold out. Certainly the Chiss ships had proved their exceptional stealth capabilities back when they'd sneaked up on both the *Bargain Hunter* and Progga's ship. But even so, sooner or later someone on the Vagaari side was bound to notice them sitting quietly out here.

Fortunately, Thrawn's crew also recognized the need for haste. Three minutes later, the fighters and assault teams had all signaled their readiness.

"Stand by, fighters," Thrawn said, his eyes on the battle. "Fighters attack . . . *now*." In the distance there was a flicker of pseudomotion, and the six Chiss fighters appeared in a loose line just off the projector's starboard side. "Helm: prepare to follow."

Thrawn had called the enemy's defense setup overconfident, but there was nothing sloppy about their response to this unexpected threat. Even as the Chiss fighters swung into their attack the Vagaari ships began to spread out, trying to deprive the intruders of clustered targets as they returned fire with lasers and missiles.

Unfortunately for them, their attackers' commander had already seen Vagaari fighter tactics in action. The enemy ships got off perhaps two shots each before the Chiss settled into their own counterattack and the Vagaari fighters began exploding. Less than a minute after their sudden arrival, the Chiss held the field alone.

Alone, but not unnoticed. In the near distance, the three larger warships were beginning to respond, their aft batteries opening fire as they began ponderously turning around.

"Fighters: take defensive positions," Thrawn ordered. "Helm: go."

Car'das set his teeth. The stars began their usual stretch into starlines; then with a horrible-sounding thud from somewhere aft, the stars were back.

"Assault One to projector's starboard side," Thrawn called. "Assault Two to port. Chief Yal'avi'kema, you have five minutes."

"Question is, do *we* have five minutes?" Car'das muttered, eyeing the shots starting to sizzle past the *Springhawk*'s canopy.

"I think so," Thrawn said. "They'll need to be much closer before they can attack in earnest. Otherwise, they risk overshooting us and destroying their own projector."

"So?" Car'das countered. "Isn't that what they probably think *we're* trying to do to it?"

"Actually, I suspect they're rather confused about our intentions at the moment," Thrawn said. "An attacker whose sole purpose was destruction would hardly have had to move in this close." He gestured toward the battle. "But whatever they perceive our plan to be, they still must allow the projector to remain functional as long as possible. Once the gravity shadow vanishes, the defenders inside its cone will be free to escape and possibly regroup. They thus cannot risk overshooting us and *must* come in closer."

Car'das grimaced. Certainly the logic made sense. But that was no guarantee the Vagaari wouldn't do something stupid or panicky instead.

The enemy warships had made it halfway around now, allowing them to bring their flank laser batteries into play. Still, so far they did seem to be concentrating most of their fire on the Chiss fighters arrayed against them.

And then, as the light of the distant sun played across the warships' sides, Car'das spotted something he hadn't noticed before. "Hey, look," he said, pointing. "They have the same bubbles all over their hulls that we saw on the treasure ship."

"Get me a close-up," Thrawn ordered, his eyes narrowing. On the main monitor display the running series of tactical data vanished and was replaced by a hazy telescopic view of the bubble pattern.

Car'das felt his throat suddenly tighten as, beside him, he heard Maris's sharp intake of breath. "Oh, no," she whispered.

The bubbles weren't observation ports, as Qennto had once speculated. Nor were they navigational sensors.

They were prisons. Each one contained a living alien being, all of them of the same species as the mangled bodies Car'das could see floating among the battle debris. Some of the hostages were cowering against the walls of their cells, while others had curled up with their backs to the plastic, while still others gazed out at the battle with the dull resignation of those who have already given up hope.

Even as they watched, a stray missile exploded a glancing blow at the edge of the telescope display's view. When the flash and debris cleared away, Car'das saw that three of the bubbles had been shattered, their inhabitants blown into space or turned into unrecognizable shreds of torn flesh. The metal behind the broken bubbles, clearly the main hull, was dented in places but appeared to be intact.

"Living shields," Thrawn murmured, his voice as cold and as deadly as Car'das had ever heard it.

"Can your fighters use their Connor nets?" Car'das asked urgently. "You know—those things you used on us?"

"They're still too far away," Thrawn said. "At any rate, shock nets would be of little use against the electronic compartmentalization of war vessels that size."

"Can't they shoot *between* the bubbles?" Maris asked, her voice starting to shake. "There's room there. Can't they blast the hull without hitting the prisoners?"

"Again, not at their distance," Thrawn said. "I'm sorry."

"Then you have to call them back," Maris insisted. "If they keep firing, they'll be killing innocent people."

"Those people are already dead," Thrawn replied, his voice suddenly harsh.

Maris flinched back from his unexpected anger. "But—"

"Please," Thrawn said, holding up a hand. His voice was calm again, but there was still an undercurrent of anger simmering beneath it. "Understand the reality of the situation. The Vagaari have killed them, all of them, if not in this battle then in battles to come. There's nothing we can do to help them. All we can do is focus our resources toward the Vagaari's ultimate destruction, so that others may live."

Car'das took a deep breath. "He's right, Maris," he told her, taking her arm.

Angrily, she shook it off and turned away. Car'das looked at

Thrawn, but the other's attention was already back on the approaching warships and the six Chiss fighters standing in their path.

"Assault One reports Vagaari crew has been eliminated," one of the crewers called. "Chief Yal'avi'kema reports that they've located the projector's collapse points and are folding it for transport. Assault Two is assisting."

"Order Assault One to assist, as well," Thrawn said. "I thought there would be some sort of quick-set arrangement," he added to Car'das. "The Vagaari wouldn't want to hold position for hours as they assembled their gravity projectors in full view of their intended victims." He looked back at the Vagaari warships, their turns now nearly completed, and his mouth briefly tightened. "Stand ready to fire on the war vessels."

Car'das looked at Maris, but her back was to him, her shoulders hunched rigidly beneath her vac suit.

"Weapons ready."

"Fire full missile bursts on my command," Thrawn said. His eyes flicked to Maris— "And instruct the fighters to fire shock nets at the war vessels' bridge and command sections at the moment of minimum visibility."

"Acknowledged."

"Fire missiles," Thrawn ordered. "Chief Yal'avi'kema, you now have two minutes."

"Chief Yal'avi'kema acknowledges, and estimates the projector will be collapsed on schedule." Across by the distant warships, there were multiple flashes of light as the Chiss missiles struck—

"Helmets!" someone barked.

Car'das reacted instantly, snatching up his helmet and throwing it over his head, peripherally aware that everyone on the bridge was doing the same. He had locked the helmet onto its collar and was looking for the source of the threat when there was a sudden burst of light and fire and the portside section of the canopy disintegrated.

Through the deck he felt the thud of airtight doors slamming shut, and for a fraction of a second he heard the wail of warning alarms before the sudden decompression robbed them of any conducting medium. Blinking against the dark purple afterimage of the flash, he peered through the still swirling debris at the impact point.

It was as bad as he'd feared. The three Chiss who'd been closest to the blast were lying twisted and crumpled on the deck. Other Chiss had also been thrown from their chairs, though most of them appeared to still be alive. Here and there he could see crewers struggling with torn suits or cracked helmets as they or fellow crewers fastened emergency patches in place. The control boards in the area of the blast had been turned into mangled, sharp-edged twistings of metal and tangled wiring, while elsewhere the rest of the panels appeared dead.

He was still assessing the damage when Maris suddenly shoved past him, nearly knocking him off his feet, and dropped to her knees beside the command chair.

It was only then that he saw that Thrawn, too, was lying on the deck, his glowing eyes closed, a violently fluttering tear in the chest of his vac suit leaking away his air.

"Commander!" he snapped, dropping to the deck beside Maris and fumbling in his suit pocket for a sealant patch. "Medic!"

"I've got one," Maris said, a patch already in hand. Ripping off the protective backing, she slapped it against the torn fabric. For a moment it bulged with the remaining air pressure from inside the suit; and then, to Car'das's horror, one edge began to come loose. "It won't bond to this material," Maris bit out, glancing around her. "Help me find something to hold it."

Frantically, Car'das looked around. But there was nothing. He looked up at the walls, knowing the Chiss must surely have medpacs scattered around their warships. But he couldn't focus enough of his mind on the Cheunh lettering to read the markings.

"Never mind," Maris gritted. She pushed down the edges of the patch again; and then, with just a second of hesitation, she leaned over to lie chest-to-chest across his torso, pressing her stomach against the wound. "Go get help," she ordered, wrapping her arms tightly around Thrawn's back to hold herself in place. "Come on—this can't be doing his injuries any good."

Breaking free of his paralysis, Car'das turned toward the door.

And once again was nearly bowled over as two Chiss pushed past him, dropping to their knees on either side of their unconscious commander and the human lying across him. "Prepare to move," one of them snapped, a large patch gripped between his hands. ". . . *move.*"

Maris rolled away. Almost before she had cleared the wound area the Chiss had his patch in place, completely covering the one Maris had tried to use. She pushed herself completely away, and Car'das saw thin tendrils of smoke drift up from the edges of the new patch. "Seal good," the Chiss confirmed.

The second crewer was ready, jabbing the hose of a hand-sized air tank into a valve built into the helmet collar. "Pressure stabilizing," he reported, peering at a row of indicator lights beside the valve.

"Can we help?" Maris asked.

"You've already done so," the first Chiss said. "We'll handle it from here."

They had lifted Thrawn between them and were heading for the airtight door when the stars outside the canopy abruptly flashed into starlines.

For the first two hours the medics worked behind sealed doors, with no news coming out and only fresh supplies and more injured going in. Car'das hung around the medbay area, trying to stay out of the way, occasionally being pressed into service to run errands for the staff. He didn't know at first what had happened to Maris, but from bits of overheard conversation he eventually learned she was helping clear debris from the bridge.

They were still four hours from home when the two of them were finally summoned into medbay.

They found Thrawn half lying, half sitting on a narrow bed inside a set of biosensor rings that wrapped around him from neck to knees like the ribs of a giant snake. "Car'das; Ferasi," he greeted them. His face was drawn, but his voice was clear and calm. "I'm told I owe you my life. Thank you."

"It was mostly Maris, actually," Car'das said, not wanting to accept credit he didn't deserve. "She's faster in emergency situations than I am."

"Comes of spending time with Rak on the *Bargain Hunter*," Maris said, trying a smile that didn't reach all the way to her eyes. "How are you feeling?"

"Not well, but apparently out of danger," Thrawn said, studying her face. "I'm also told you've been assisting with the task of clearing the bridge."

She shrugged self-consciously. "I wanted to help."

"Even after I launched missiles against the Vagaari's living shields?"

She lowered her eyes. "I'm sorry I . . . well, that I complained about that," she said. "I realize you didn't have any choice."

"Which doesn't necessarily make it easier to accept," Thrawn said. "It is, unfortunately, the sort of decision all warriors must make."

"Did we get the gravity projector, by the way?" Car'das asked. "I never heard one way or the other."

Thrawn nodded. "It was collapsed and spark-welded to the outside of the hull just before we made our jump. All six of the fighters escaped, as well."

Car'das shook his head. "We were lucky."

"We had a good leader," Maris corrected. "The Vagaari are going to be very unhappy about this."

"Good," Thrawn said evenly. "Perhaps they'll be angry enough to make an overt move against the Chiss Ascendancy."

Car'das frowned. "Are you saying you were *trying* to goad them into an attack?"

"I was trying to obtain a gravity projector," Thrawn said. "Other consequences will be dealt with if and when they occur."

Car'das looked sideways at the medics and assistants working on the other casualties. "Of course," he murmured.

"Meanwhile, our focus must be to return to Crustai with all possible speed," Thrawn continued. "We need more complete medical assistance for our wounded, and to begin repairs to our vessels."

"And in the meantime, you probably need some more rest," Maris added, touching Car'das's arm and nodding toward the door. "We'll see you later, Commander."

"Yes," Thrawn said, his eyes turning to glowing red slits behind sagging eyelids. "And I'm sure you were right, Car'das. I imagine Qennto will be sorry he missed all the excitement."

They arrived at the base to discover that Qennto had far more pressing matters on his mind than missed adventures.

"I'll kill her," the big man promised blackly as he glared at Maris and Car'das through the slotted plastic door of his cell. "I ever get her alone, I *swear* I'll kill her."

"Just calm down," Maris soothed, her tone a mixture of patience and understanding. It was a combination she seemed to use a lot with Qennto. "Tell us what happened."

"She tried to rob me—*that's* what happened," Qennto bit out. "You were both there. Thrawn *specifically* told us we could pick some of the loot from the pirate ship in payment for language lessons. Right?"

"More or less," Maris agreed cautiously. "Unfortunately, Admiral Ar'alani outranks him."

"I don't care if she's the local deity," Qennto shot back. "That stuff I picked out was *ours*. She had no business trying to take it away."

"And of course, you told her so," Car'das murmured.

"I'd watch my mouth if I were you, kid," Qennto warned, glaring at him. "You may be teacher's pet *here,* but it's a long way back to civilization."

"So what happened to your collection?" Maris asked.

"She *was* going to take all of it with her," Qennto said, letting his glare linger on Car'das a couple of seconds longer before turning back to Maris. "Luckily for me, that other Chiss—that Syndic Mitth-whatever—"

"Thrawn's brother," Maris interjected.

Qennto's eyes widened. "No kidding? Anyway, he decided he needed to hear Thrawn's version first, so he made her leave it behind. But then *she* insisted it be put under prescribed seal, whatever the frizz that means."

"So bottom line is . . . ?" Car'das asked.

"Bottom line is that it's locked away somewhere," Qennto growled. "And according to Syndic Mitth-whatever, even Thrawn can't get it out."

"We'll check with him," Maris promised. "Incidentally, it's not *Syndic Mitth-whatever.* It's Syndic Mitthrassafis."

"Yeah, sure," Qennto said. "So go talk to Thrawn, already. While you're at it, see if you can get me out of here."

"Sure," Maris said. "Come on, Jorj. Let's see if the commander's accepting company."

At first the guard outside Thrawn's quarters was reluctant to even inquire as to whether the commander would see them. But Maris eventually persuaded him to ask, and a minute later they were standing at his bedside.

"Yes, I saw Thrass's report," he said when Maris had outlined the situation. He still looked weak, but definitely stronger than he had back aboard the *Springhawk*. "Captain Qennto needs to learn how to control his temper."

"Captain Qennto needs to learn how to control more that that," Maris said ruefully. "But being locked up has never done him any good before, and it's not likely to do anything now. Can you get him released?"

"Yes, if you'll warn him about disrespecting Chiss command officers," Thrawn said. "Perhaps we should simply lock him up whenever one is on the base."

"Wouldn't be a bad idea," Maris agreed. "Thank you."

"What about the items your brother had sealed away?"

Car'das asked. "Qennto will be impossible to live with until he gets them back."

"Then it's time he began developing patience," Thrawn said. "A syndic of the Eighth Ruling Family has declared it sealed against a command officer's claim of possession. It cannot be unsealed until Admiral Ar'alani returns to present her arguments."

"When will that be?" Car'das asked.

"Whenever she so chooses, but probably not until the Vagaari treasure ship has been examined and its systems and equipment analyzed. She'll want to be present for that."

"But that could take months," Car'das protested. "We can't stay here that long."

"And we can't go back without the extra goods to placate our clients," Maris added.

"I understand," Thrawn said. "But it truly is out of my hands."

Behind Car'das, the door slid open. He turned, expecting to see one of the medics—

"So warriors' fortune has finally failed you," Syndic Mitth'ras'safis said as he strode into the room.

"Welcome," Thrawn said, beckoning him in. "Please; come in."

"We need to speak, Thrawn," Mitth'ras'safis said, eyeing Car'das and Maris as he stepped to the other side of his brother's bed. "Alone."

"You need not fear their presence," Thrawn assured him. "Nothing said will be repeated outside this room."

"That's not the point," Mitth'ras'safis said. "We have Chiss business to discuss, which is none of their concern."

"Perhaps not now," Thrawn said. "But in the future, who knows?"

Mitth'ras'safis eyes narrowed. "Meaning . . . ?"

Thrawn shook his head. "You're gifted in many ways, my brother," he said. "But you have yet to develop the farsightedness you will need to survive the intrigues and conflicts of political life." He gestured toward Car'das and Maris. "We have been granted a rare opportunity: the chance to meet and interact with members of a vast but hitherto unknown political entity, people with insights and thoughts different from our own."

"Is that why you insist on bringing them along even when giving an admiral an official tour?" Mitth'ras'safis asked, eyeing Car'das doubtfully. "You think their thoughts will be of value?"

"All thoughts are worth listening to, whether later judged to be of value or not," Thrawn said. "But equally important are the social and intellectual bonds we are building between us. Someday, our Ascendancy and their Republic will make contact, and the friends and potential allies we create now may well define what direction that contact will take."

He looked at Car'das and Maris in turn. "I imagine both of them have already come to that same conclusion, though of course from their own point of view."

Car'das looked at Maris. Her slightly twisted lip was all the answer he needed. "Yes, actually, we have," he admitted.

"You see?" Thrawn said. "Already we understand each other, at least to a small extent."

"Maybe," Mitth'ras'safis said doubtfully.

"But you came here with specific business to discuss," Thrawn reminded him. "May my guests call you Thrass, by the way?"

"Absolutely not," Mitth'ras'safis said stiffly. He looked at Maris, and his expression softened a little. "Though I understand you saved my brother's life," he added reluctantly.

"I was glad I could help, Syndic Mitthrassafis," Maris said in Cheunh.

Mitth'ras'safis snorted and looked at Thrawn, and the hint of a wry smile finally touched his lips. "They really *aren't* very good at it, are they?"

"You could try Minnisiat," Thrawn offered. "They speak that better than they do Cheunh. Or you could use Sy Bisti, which I believe you also know."

"Yes," Mitth'ras'safis said, switching to an oddly accented Sy Bisti. "If that would be easier."

"Actually, we'd prefer you stick with Cheunh, if you don't mind," Car'das said in that language. "We could use the practice."

"That you could," Mitth'ras'safis said. He hesitated, then inclined his head. "And since you were both instrumental in saving my brother's life . . . I suppose it would be all right for you to call me Thrass."

Maris bowed her head. "Thank you. We're honored by your acceptance."

"I just don't want to keep hearing my name mispronounced." Thrass turned back to Thrawn. "Now," he said, his tone hardening again. "What exactly do you think you're doing?"

"The job for which I was commissioned," Thrawn replied. "I'm protecting the Ascendancy from its enemies."

"Its *enemies,*" Thrass said, leaning on the word. "Not *potential* enemies. Do you hear the difference?"

"Yes," Thrawn said. "And no."

Thrass lifted a hand, let it slap against his thigh. "Let me be honest, Thrawn," he said. "The Eighth Ruling Family is not happy with you."

"They sent you all the way here to tell me that?"

"This isn't a joking matter," Thrass bit out. "That pirate treasure ship was bad enough. But this last escapade was far and away over all the lines. And right under an admiral's nose, too."

"The Vagaari aren't pirates, Thrass," Thrawn said, his voice low and earnest. "They're a completely nomadic species—hundreds of thousands of them, perhaps millions. And sooner or later, they *will* reach the Ascendancy's borders."

"Fine," Thrass said. "When they do, we'll destroy them."

"But why wait until then?" Thrawn pressed. "Why leave our backs turned while millions of other beings are forced to suffer?"

"The philosophical answer is that *we* don't force anyone to suffer," Thrass countered. "The practical answer is that we can't defend the entire galaxy."

"I'm not asking to defend the entire galaxy."

"Really? And where would you have us stop?" Thrass gestured toward the wall. "Ten light-years beyond our borders? A hundred? A thousand?"

"I agree we can't protect the entire galaxy," Thrawn said. "But it's foolhardy to always permit our enemies to choose the time and place of battle."

Thrass sighed. "Thrawn, you can't continue to push the lines this way," he said. "Peaceful watchfulness is the Chiss way, and the Nine Ruling Families won't stand by forever while you ignore basic military doctrine. More to the point, the Eighth Family has made it clear that they'll release you before they permit your actions to damage their standing."

"We were both born as commoners," Thrawn reminded him. "I can live that way again if I have to." His lips tightened briefly. "But I'll do what I can to assure that the Eighth Family doesn't release or rematch you on my account."

"I'm not worried about my own position," Thrass said stiffly.

"I'm trying to keep my brother from throwing away a fine and honorable career for nothing."

Thrawn's eyes took on a distant look. "If I do throw it away," he said quietly, "I guarantee that it *won't* be for nothing."

For a long moment the two brothers gazed at each other in silence. Then Thrass sighed. "I don't understand you, Thrawn," he said. "I'm not sure I ever have."

"Then just trust me," Thrawn suggested.

Thrass shook his head. "I can trust you only as far as the Nine Ruling Families do," he said. "And that trust is strained to the breaking point. This latest incident . . ." He shook his head again.

"Do you have to tell them?" Maris spoke up.

"With four warriors dead?" Thrass countered, turning his glowing eyes on her. "How do I keep that a secret?"

"It was a reconnaissance mission that got out of hand," Maris said. "Commander Thrawn didn't go there with any intention of fighting."

"Any mission to that region would have been pushing the lines," Thrass told her heavily. "Still, I can try to frame it in those terms." He looked back at Thrawn. "But it may be that nothing I say will make any difference. Action was taken, and deaths ensued. That may be all the Ruling Families will care about."

"I know you'll do what you can," Thrawn said

"But is what I *can* do the same as what I *should* do?" Thrass asked. "It would seem that protecting you from the consequences of self-destructive decisions merely gives you freedom to make more of them. Is that really the best way to serve my brother and my family?"

"I know what *my* answer would be," Thrawn said. "But you must find the answer for yourself."

"Perhaps someday," Thrass said. "In the meantime, I have a report to prepare." He gave Thrawn a resigned look. "And a brother to protect."

"You must do what you feel right," Thrawn said. "But you don't know these Vagaari. I do. And I *will* defeat them, no matter what the cost."

Thrass shook his head and went back to the door. There he stopped, his hand over the control "Has it ever occurred to you," he said, not turning around, "that attacks like yours might actually *provoke* beings like the Vagaari to move against us? That if we simply left them alone, they might never become any threat to the Ascendancy at all?"

"No, I've never had any such thoughts," Thrawn replied evenly.

Thrass sighed. "I didn't think so. Good night, Thrawn." Tapping the control to open the door, he left the room.

There," C'baoth said, pointing through the viewport as their transport came around the curve of Yaga Minor. "You see it?"

"Yes," Lorana said as she gazed at the massive object hanging in low orbit over the planet. Six of the brand-new Dreadnaught warships, arranged in a hexagon pattern around a central storage core, the whole thing tied together by a series of massive turbolift pylons. "It's quite impressive."

"It's more than just impressive," C'baoth said gravely. "Therein lies the future of the galaxy."

Lorana stole a furtive glance at him. For the past three weeks, ever since her official elevation from Padawan to full Jedi Knight, C'baoth had been showing a marked change in attitude. He spoke with her more often and at greater length, asking her opinion on politics and other matters, opening up to her as if to a full equal.

It was gratifying, even flattering. But at the same time, it stirred some uncomfortable feelings. Just as he'd expected so much of her as his Padawan, it seemed that he now expected her to suddenly have all the wisdom, experience, and power of a seasoned, experienced Jedi.

This trip to Yaga Minor was just one more example. Out of the clear and cloudless sky he'd invited her to come along with him to observe the final stages of preparation. It would have been more fitting, in her opinion, for him to invite Master Yoda or one of the other Council members to see him off on his historic journey.

But instead he'd chosen her.

"The crew and families are already aboard, stowing their gear and making final preparations," C'baoth continued. "So are most of the Jedi who'll be accompanying us, though two or three are still on their way. You'll want to meet them all before we leave, of course."

"Of course," Lorana said automatically, feeling her muscles tense as a horrible thought suddenly occurred to her. "When you say *we,* Master C'baoth, who exactly—I mean—"

"Don't flounder, Jedi Jinzler," C'baoth reproved her mildly. "A Jedi's words, like a Jedi's thoughts, must always be clear and confident. If you have a question, ask it."

"Yes, Master C'baoth." Lorana braced herself. "When you say, *we* . . . are you expecting me to come with you on Outbound Flight?"

"Of course," he said, frowning at her. "Why else do you think I recommended your elevation to Jedi Knighthood so soon?"

A familiar tightness wrapped itself around Lorana's chest. "I thought it was because I was ready."

"Obviously, you were," C'baoth said. "But you still have much to learn. Here, aboard Outbound Flight, I'll have the necessary time to teach you."

"But I can't go," Lorana protested, her brain skittering around desperately for something to say. She didn't want to leave the Republic and the galaxy. Certainly not with so much work here to be done. "I haven't made any preparations, I haven't asked permission from the Jedi Council—"

"The Council has granted me whatever I need," C'baoth cut in tartly. "As for preparations, what sort of preparations does a Jedi need?"

Lorana clamped her teeth firmly together. How could he have made such a decision without even consulting her? "Master C'baoth, I appreciate your offer. But I'm not sure—"

"It's not an offer, Jedi Jinzler," C'baoth interrupted. "You're a Jedi now. You go wherever the Council chooses to send you."

"Anywhere in the Republic, yes," Lorana said. "But this is different."

"Only different in your mind," C'baoth said firmly. "But you're young. You'll grow." He pointed at the approaching collection of ships. "Once you see what we've done and meet the other Jedi you'll be more enthusiastic about the destiny that awaits us."

"What about this one?" Tarkosa asked, tapping his fingers on a rack of negative couplings. "Chas?"

"Just a second, just a second," Uliar growled, scanning the racks already in place as he silently cursed the crowd of tech assistants the Supreme Chancellor's Office had sent from Coruscant to help with the loading. For the most part, they'd proven themselves completely useless: dropping delicate components, sorting others into the wrong storage areas, and more often than not doubling up on one rack of spares while the proper set was left buried somewhere in the bowels of the storage core far beneath them. "It goes there," he told Tarkosa, pointing to a spot next to a rack of cooling-pump parts.

"What in the *worlds*?" a deep voice said from behind him.

Uliar turned to see a balding middle-age man in a plain tan robe standing in the doorway. "Who are you?" he demanded.

"Jedi Master Justyn Ma'Ning," the other said, his forehead creasing as he surveyed the chaos in the room. "This equipment should have been stowed two days ago."

"It was," Uliar said. "Very badly. We're trying to fix it."

"Ah," Ma'Ning said, a wryly knowing look on his face. Apparently, he'd met the Coruscant tech assistants, too. "Better speed it up. Master C'baoth is arriving today, and he won't be happy if he sees things this way." With a nod, he turned and headed off down the corridor.

"Like Jedi happiness is our problem," Uliar muttered under his breath at the empty doorway. He turned back to the storage racks; and as he did so, a repeater diagnostic display suddenly flickered on.

"That got it?" a voice called, and a young man popped his head into view through an open floor access panel.

"Hang on." Uliar stepped to the display and ran through its options list. "Looks perfect," he confirmed. Coruscant's tech assistants might be worthless, but the few actual techs who'd come with them were another story completely. "Thanks."

"No problem," the other said, setting his toolbox on the floor beside the panel and pulling himself out. "You still having trouble with the repeater in the aft reactor bay?"

"Unless what you just did fixed that one, too," Tarkosa said.

"Probably not," the young man said as he maneuvered the

access panel back into place. "These things are hooked parallel, but I doubt the circuit extends that far. I'll try to get to it when I get back from D-One."

"Why not do it now?" Uliar suggested. "D-One's all the way over on the far side of the hexagon. Why go all the way there and then have to come all the way back?"

"Because D-One's also the command ship," the tech reminded him. "Mon Cals might look like pushovers, but when Captain Pakmillu says he want something fixed, he means *now.*"

Tarkosa snorted. "What's he going to do, bust all of us to civilian?"

"Don't know what he'd do to *you,*" the tech said drily, "but *I'd* still like to have a job once you fly off into the wild black. It won't take long, I promise."

"We'll hold you to that," Uliar said. "You sure we can't persuade you to come along? You're light-years ahead of most of our regular techs."

A muscle twitched in the other's cheek. "I doubt that, but thanks anyway," he said. "I'm not ready to leave civilization just yet."

"You'd better hope civilization doesn't leave *you,*" Tarkosa warned. "The way things are going on Coruscant, I wouldn't bet on it."

"Maybe," the tech said, picking up his toolbox. "See you later."

"Okay," Uliar said. "Thanks again."

The other smiled and left the room. "Good man," Tarkosa commented. "You ever get his name?"

Uliar shook his head. "Dean something, I think. Doesn't matter—it's not like we'll ever see him again after tomorrow.

Okay, that rack of shock capacitors goes next to the negative couplings."

"The entire system can be run from here," Captain Pakmillu said, waving a flippered hand around the vast Combined Operations Center. "That means that if there's an emergency or disaster on any of the ships, countermeasures can be instituted immediately without the need to physically send people to those sites."

"Impressive," Obi-Wan said, looking around. Situated just aft of the cross-corridor behind the bridge/monitor room complex, the ComOps Center stretched probably thirty meters aft and filled the entire space between the Dreadnaught's two main bow corridors. It was currently a hive of activity, with dozens of humans and aliens bustling around and half the access panels and consoles open for last-minute checks or adjustment.

"What's that thing?" Anakin asked, pointing to a low console two rows over from where they were standing. "It looks like a Podracer control and monitor system."

"You have sharp eyes, young one," Pakmillu said, his own large eyes rolling toward the boy. "Yes, it is. We use it to control our fleet of speeders and swoops."

"You're joking," Obi-Wan said, frowning at the console. "You run *swoops* through these corridors?"

"Outbound Flight is a huge place, Master Kenobi," Pakmillu reminded him. "While each Dreadnaught is linked by the pylon turbolifts to its neighbors and the core, there's still a great deal of travel involved where the turbolifts do not go. Speeders are vital for moving crewers back and forth in both emergency and nonemergency situations."

"Yes, but *swoops*?" Obi-Wan persisted. "Wouldn't a more extensive turbolift system have been safer and more efficient?"

"Certainly," Pakmillu rumbled. "Unfortunately, it would also have been more expensive. The original Dreadnaughts did not include such a system, and the Senate did not wish to pay the costs of retrofitting."

"These control systems really are pretty good, though," Anakin assured him. "Some of the Podracers on Tatooine use them when they're trying out a new course."

"There aren't fifty thousand people wandering in and out of a Podracing course where they could be run over," Obi-Wan pointed out.

"But there *are* plenty of animals on the courses," Anakin countered, a little too tartly. "You know, like dewbacks and banthas?"

"Anakin—" Obi-Wan began warningly.

"We have already tried the system, Master Kenobi," Pakmillu put in quickly. "As Padawan Skywalker said, it works quite well."

"I'll take your word for it," Obi-Wan said, eyeing Anakin darkly. The boy had developed a bad habit of disrespect lately, especially in public where he perhaps thought that his master would be reluctant to reprimand him. It was partly his age, Obi-Wan knew, but even so it was unacceptable.

But Anakin also knew just how far he could push it. In response to Obi-Wan's reproving look, he dropped his gaze, his expression indicating at least outward contrition.

And with that, this particular incident was apparently over. Making a mental note to have yet another talk with the boy the next time they were alone, Obi-Wan turned back to Pakmillu. "I understand you'll be making a short tour through Republic space before you enter the Unknown Regions."

"A sort of shakedown cruise, yes," Pakmillu said. "We must confirm that our equipment is functioning properly before we go beyond reach of repair facilities."

He stepped to a nearby navigational console and touched a key, and a holo of the galaxy appeared overhead. "From here we go to Lonnaw in Droma sector," he said, pointing. "After that, we'll cut through the edge of Glythe sector to Argai in Haldeen sector. Then we'll travel through Kokash and Mondress sectors, with a final stop possible in Albanin sector if it seems necessary."

"That's a lot of stops," Obi-Wan said.

"Most will just be flybys," Pakmillu assured him. "We won't actually stop unless there are problems."

"What happens then?" Anakin asked.

"If all goes well, three weeks from now we'll formally enter Unknown Space," Pakmillu said. "At a point approximately two hundred thirty light-years from the edge of Wild Space we'll stop for a final navigational calibration"—his mouth tendrils wiggled as he shut down the holo—"and we'll then begin our journey in earnest. Through the Unknown Regions, and to the next galaxy."

Anakin whistled softly. "How long before you'll get back?"

"Several years at least," Pakmillu told him. "But the storage core has supplies enough for ten years, and we expect to be able to supplement its stores of foodstuffs and water along the way. In addition, our numbers may well diminish if we find hospitable worlds to colonize."

"You're not just going to leave people behind in the Unknown Regions, are you?" Anakin asked, frowning.

"If we do, it will be with enough food and equipment to get settled," Pakmillu assured him. "We would also leave one of the Dreadnaughts behind for defense and transport. As you can see from Outbound Flight's design, it will be relatively easy to detach a single ship from the rest of the complex."

Anakin shook his head. "Still sounds dangerous."

"We are well prepared," Pakmillu reminded him. "And of course, we have eighteen Jedi aboard. It will be safe."

"Or at least as safe as one can be anywhere in these times," Obi-Wan murmured.

"And it will be a glorious adventure, as well," Pakmillu continued, eyeing Anakin. "A pity you will not be joining us."

"There are still a lot of things I want to do here," Anakin said, an unexpected flicker of emotion coloring his voice and sense. He looked sideways at Obi-Wan, and the emotion vanished beneath a more proper Jedi composure. "Besides, I can't leave my master until my training is complete."

"With six Jedi Masters aboard you would have several choices of a teacher," Pakmillu pointed out.

"That's not really how it works," Obi-Wan told him. It amazed him sometimes how people who had no idea whatsoever of the inner workings of Jedi methodology nevertheless had equally few qualms about expressing that ignorance. "You said Master C'baoth will be arriving soon?"

"He is in fact here," C'baoth's voice boomed from across the room.

Obi-Wan turned. There, just entering the room, were C'baoth and Lorana Jinzler. "This is a surprise, Master Kenobi," C'baoth continued as he strode casually through the bustle of activity. No one actually had to move to let him pass, Obi-Wan noticed, but there were quite a few near misses. Fortunately, most of the techs were too preoccupied to even notice his passage. Lorana picked her way through the crowd more carefully, looking distinctly uncomfortable. "I thought you'd be on your way back to Sulorine by now."

"I was relieved of that assignment," Obi-Wan said. "There's something I need to discuss with you, Master C'baoth."

C'baoth nodded. "Certainly. Go ahead."

Obi-Wan braced himself. Between C'baoth and Anakin, this was likely to be unpleasant. "Anakin and I would like to join the expedition."

Out of the corner of his eye he saw Anakin turn to him in astonishment. "We *would*?" the boy asked.

"We would," Obi-Wan said firmly. "At least to the edge of the galaxy."

C'baoth's lip quirked. "So Master Yoda finally concedes that I might indeed find Vergere?"

"Who's Vergere?" Lorana asked.

"A missing Jedi," C'baoth said, his eyes still on Obi-Wan's face. "Master Kenobi tried once to find her and failed."

"There was nothing in the voyage mandate about a search and rescue mission," Pakmillu said, his voice suddenly wary.

"That's because it's Jedi business, Captain, and none of your concern," C'baoth told him. "Don't worry, it won't interfere with our schedule." He lifted his eyebrows toward Obi-Wan. "I hope you didn't ask to come along in the hope of assuaging any feelings of guilt."

"I didn't *ask* to come at all," Obi-Wan said. "I simply do as the Council directs me."

"As do we all," C'baoth said, an edge of irony in his voice as he shifted his eyes to Anakin. "What about you, young Skywalker? You seem unhappy with this change in your plans."

Obi-Wan held his breath. There were several reasons he

hadn't told Anakin in advance about Windu's mandate, not the least of them being the fact that the boy still obviously held C'baoth in high esteem. If he'd told Anakin they were coming to Yaga Minor to keep an eye on the man, he would have pressed for further explanation. It wouldn't have done to disillusion him with Windu's concerns about C'baoth's possible involvement with the Barlok incident.

Fortunately, it was quickly evident that the decision to keep the boy in the dark had been the right one. "I'm not unhappy at all, Master C'baoth," Anakin said with a clear voice and sense of complete honesty. "I was just surprised. Master Obi-Wan hadn't told me about it."

"But you *do* want to come see the Unknown Regions with me?"

Anakin hesitated. "I don't want to leave the Republic forever," he said. "But I was impressed by how you handled things on Barlok, ending the deadlock and all. I think I'd learn a lot just by watching you in your daily activities."

C'baoth smiled wryly at Obi-Wan. "One thing at least you've given the lad, Master Kenobi: a smooth tongue."

"I would hope I've given him more than that," Obi-Wan said evenly. "Still, he's right about how much he could learn from you." He nodded to Lorana. "As I'm sure Padawan Jinzler would agree."

"Indeed," C'baoth said. "And it's *Jedi* Jinzler now. She was elevated to Jedi Knighthood three weeks ago."

"Really," Obi-Wan said, carefully hiding his surprise. From the way she'd been talking on Barlok, he would have guessed that event to be years in the future. "My apologies, Jedi Jinzler, and my congratulations. Do I take it you'll also be traveling aboard Outbound Flight with Master C'baoth?"

"Of course she will," C'baoth said before Lorana could answer. "She's one of the chosen, one of the few among even the Jedi whom I trust completely."

"You don't trust even Jedi?" Anakin asked, sounding surprised.

"I said I trust her *completely,*" C'baoth told him gravely. "Certainly there are others I trust. But only to a degree."

"Oh," Anakin said, clearly taken aback.

"Fortunately, you and your instructor are among that somewhat larger group," C'baoth said, a small smile touching his lips. "Very well, Master Kenobi. You and your Padawan may accompany me to the edge of the galaxy, provided you make your own arrangements for returning to the Republic."

"Thank you," Obi-Wan said. "The Delta-Twelve Skysprite we'll be using for our return is on the surface, ready to be brought up and loaded aboard."

"Good," C'baoth said. "You'll stay here aboard Dreadnaught-One. Captain, you'll arrange quarters for them."

"Yes, Master C'baoth," Pakmillu rumbled. "I'll have the quartermaster—"

"*You* will arrange quarters for them," C'baoth repeated, a subtle but unmistakable emphasis on the first word. "These are Jedi. They will be treated accordingly."

Pakmillu's mouth tendrils twitched. "Yes, Master C'baoth." He stepped to one of the consoles and tapped at the keys with his flippered hands. "And Jedi Jinzler?"

"I've already reserved her quarters near my own," C'baoth told him. "Deck Three, Suite A-Four."

"Very well," Pakmillu said, peering at the display. "Master Kenobi, you and Master Skywalker will have Suite A-Eight on Deck Five. I trust that will be acceptable."

"It will," C'baoth said before Obi-Wan could answer. "You may now assign someone to escort them to their quarters."

From behind them came a sudden crinkling sound of tearing metal. Obi-Wan spun around to see that a large sheet of secondary conductive grid had come loose from the wall and was hanging precariously over a bank of control consoles. He stretched out with the Force—

C'baoth got there first, catching the sheet in a Force grip even as it came the rest of the way loose. "Jedi Jinzler: assist them," he ordered.

"Yes, Master C'baoth," Lorana said, hurrying off.

"Captain Pakmillu, you were going to find an escort for our new passengers?" C'baoth continued in a conversational tone, even as he continued to hold the grid floating in midair.

"That won't be necessary," Obi-Wan said. "I studied Dreadnaught deck plans on the trip here. We can find our own way."

C'baoth frowned slightly, and for a second Obi-Wan thought he was going to insist on an escort anyway, as befit proper Jedi treatment. But then the wrinkles smoothed and he nodded. "Very well," he said. "Captain Pakmillu is hosting a First Night dinner in the senior officers' wardroom at seven. My fellow Jedi Masters will be there. You'll attend, as well."

"We'll be honored," Obi-Wan said.

"And you'll need to stop by the Dreadnaught-One medcenter," Pakmillu added. "The Supreme Chancellor's representative has instructed that all personnel be given a complete examination, including the taking of analysis-grade blood and tissue samples for shipment to Coruscant. Apparently, there's some concern about hive viruses or potential epidemics."

"We'll get ourselves checked out," Obi-Wan promised. "Until tonight, then."

He nudged Anakin, and together they made their way across the room. "Master C'baoth certainly seems to know what he wants, doesn't he?" he commented.

"Nothing wrong with that," Anakin said firmly. "If Master Yoda or Master Windu talked that way to the Chancellor and Senate once in a while, maybe more things would get done."

"Yes," Obi-Wan murmured. "Maybe."

The grid was heavy, and flexible enough to be difficult to get a grip on. Fortunately, that wasn't a problem for a Jedi. Stretching out with the Force, Lorana lifted it back into position, holding it in place while the techs hurriedly worked at its fastenings.

"Thanks," the overseer puffed when it was finally secured. "Those things are a real fl—I mean, they're a real pain when they get loose like that."

"No problem," Lorana assured him. "I was glad I could help."

"Me, too," he grunted. "Did I hear someone say your name was Jinzler?"

"Yes," she confirmed. "Why?"

" 'Cause we've got a Jinzler on our work team," he said, fumbling out a comlink and punching in a code. "Guy named Dean. Relative of yours?"

"I don't know," Lorana said. "I was only ten months old when I entered the Jedi Temple. I don't know anything about my family."

"What, they never came to see you?"

"Families aren't allowed to visit," Lorana told him.

"Oh," the other said, sounding surprised. A tone sounded, and he lifted the comlink to his lips. "Jinzler? Brooks. Where are you? . . . Okay, find a stopping place and hop on over to the messroom . . . 'Cause I want to see you, that's why."

He keyed off and returned the comlink to his belt. "This way, Jedi Jinzler," he said, gesturing toward one of the ComOps Center's starboard doors.

"But I already said I don't know him," Lorana protested as she followed.

"Yeah, but maybe he'll know you," Brooks said. They stepped through the door into the corridor and he turned toward the nearest turbolift. "Worth checking out anyway, isn't it?"

Lorana felt her throat tighten. "I suppose."

They took the turbolift three levels down from the command deck and along a narrow corridor to a large table-filled room with a full-length serving counter stretching across one end. A dozen humans and aliens were scattered in twos and threes around the various tables, conversing in low tones over multicolored liquids, while three serving droids busied themselves behind the counter. "There he is," Brooks said, pointing at a table along the back wall. A lone, dark-haired man sat there, his back to the rest of the room, cradling a steaming mug between his hands. "Come on, I'll introduce you."

He set off across the room, exchanging nods and greetings with some of the others as he passed. Lorana followed, her quiet misgivings growing steadily stronger . . . and as they got within three meters of the man he half turned, and she got her first look at his profile.

It was the man she'd seen so many times back on Coruscant.

She stopped short, her whole body going taut. Brooks didn't notice, but continued the rest of the way to the table. "Hey, Jinzler," he said, gesturing toward her. "Want to introduce you to someone."

The young man turned the rest of the way around in his chair. "No need," he said, his voice steady but edged with an unpleasant mixture of tension and bitterness. "Jedi Lorana Jinzler, I presume."

With an effort, Lorana found her voice. "Yes," she said. The word came out calmer than she had expected it to. "Dean Jinzler, I presume."

"You two know each other?" Brooks asked, frowning back and forth between them.

"Hardly," Jinzler said. "She's only my sister."

"Your—?" Brooks stared at him, then at Lorana. "But I thought—"

"Thank you," Lorana said, catching his eye and nodding microscopically toward the door.

"Uh . . . yeah." Still staring at them in confusion, Brooks backed away between the tables, his hands groping behind him for obstacles. He reached the door and escaped from the room.

"I suppose you're going to want to sit down," Jinzler said, an edge of challenge in his voice.

Lorana turned her attention back to him. He was gazing up at her with the same bitterness she'd noted at their other near encounters. His eyes, contrary to her expectations, weren't dark but were instead the same odd shade of gray as hers. "Yes," she said, circling to a chair at the far side of the table. Gathering her robes around her, she eased down into it.

"I suppose I should congratulate you on passing the trials," Jinzler said. "You're a real Jedi now."

"Thank you," Lorana said, searching his face. There *was* a family resemblance there, she could see. Strange that she'd never noticed it before. "You keep up on such things?"

"My parents do." His mouth tightened. "*Our* parents do," he corrected himself.

"Yes," she murmured. "I'm afraid I don't know anything about them. Or about you."

"No, of course not," he said. "But *I* know everything about *you. Everything,* from your youngling training, to your apprenticeship to Jorus C'baoth, to your first lightsaber, to your elevation to Jedi Knighthood."

"I'm impressed," Lorana said, trying a hesitant smile.

"Don't be," he said, not returning the smile. "I only know because my parents had a friend who still worked inside the Temple. They rammed your every accomplishment down my throat. They loved you, you know." He snorted gently. "No. Of course you don't. You never bothered to find out."

He dropped his eyes from her face and took a sip from his mug. Lorana gazed at him, wincing at the anger and bitterness flowing toward her like the steam from his drink. What had she done to make him so angry? "We weren't allowed as Padawans to know anything about our families," she said into the silence. "Even now that I'm a Jedi, it's still frowned on."

"Yeah," he said. "Sure."

"And there are good reasons for it," she continued doggedly. "There are many worlds in the Republic where family connections and position are the most important parts of their culture. A Jedi who knew which family she'd come from might find it impossible to deal impartially in any of her people's disputes."

"Doesn't stop the family from finding *you,* though, does it?" he shot back. "Because mine sure did. Even after your precious Jedi got them fired, they still managed to keep tabs on you—"

"Wait a minute," Lorana interrupted him. "What do you mean, they got them fired? Who got them fired?"

"You Jedi have hearing problems?" he demanded. "I already told you: one of your high and mighty Jedi. Mom and Dad were civilian workers at the Temple, handling electronics maintenance and repair in the public areas. They were good at it, too. Only after you were taken, they got fired. Your Jedi didn't want them even in the same building with you, I guess."

Lorana felt her stomach tighten. She wasn't familiar with this particular incident, though there had been others she'd heard of. But it was clear that it would do no good to give her brother the rationale behind the Temple's strict isolation policy. "Were they able to find other jobs?"

"No, we all starved to death," he retorted. "Of course they found other jobs. Lower-paying jobs, of course, jobs where they had to scramble to get us packed and moved because no one had even bothered to tell them they couldn't stay on at the Temple once you were there. But that's not the point."

"Then what *is* the point?"

For a long minute he just stared at her, his turmoil surging like the ocean's edge in a winter storm. "You Jedi think you're perfect," he said at last. "You think you know what's right for everyone and everything. Well, you're not, and you don't."

Lorana felt her throat tighten. "What happened to you, Dean?" she asked gently.

"Oh, so now it's *Dean,* is it?" he said scornfully. "*Now* you want to pretend you're my loving big sister? You think you can wave your hand or your precious lightsaber and make it all up to me?"

"Make *what* up to you?" Lorana persisted. "Please. I want to know."

"I thought you Jedi knew everything."

Lorana sighed. "No, of course not."

"Well, you'd never know that by listening to our parents," he bit out. "You were the perfect one, the one all the rest of us were measured against. Lorana would have done this, Lorana would have done that; Lorana would have said this, Lorana would *never* had said that. It was like living with a minor deity. And so completely absurd—they couldn't possibly have the slightest idea what you might actually do or say in some situation. You could barely even *walk* when they sent you away."

His eyes hardened even further. "But of course, you *were* away, weren't you? That's what made the whole thing work. You were never around to make mistakes or lose your temper or drop dinner all over the floor. They could set up their little shrine to you without ever having to see anything that might burst the bubble of perfection they'd built around you."

He scooped up his mug, but set it down again without drinking. "But *I* know," he growled, staring into it. "I've been watching you. You're not perfect. You're not even close to perfect."

Lorana thought back across the wearying years of her training, and C'baoth's constant criticism. "No," she murmured. "I'm not."

"You're not very observant, either." He gestured at her. "Let me see that fancy weapon of yours."

"My lightsaber?" Frowning, she slid it out of her belt and set it on the table.

"Yeah, that's the one," he said, making no move to touch it. "That's an amethyst, right?"

"Yes," she said, focusing on the activation stud. "It was a gift from some people Master C'baoth and I helped in one of Coruscant's midlevels."

Jinzler shook his head. "No, it was a gift from your parents.

They knew the people, and asked them to give it to you." His mouth twisted. "And you couldn't even figure *that* out, could you?"

"No, of course not," Lorana said, her frustration with this man and his anger threatening to bubble over into anger of her own. "How could I?"

"Because you're a Jedi," he shot back. "You're supposed to know everything. I'll bet your Master C'baoth knew where it came from."

Lorana took a careful breath. "What do you want from me, Dean?"

"Hey, *you're* the one who came looking for me just now, not the other way around," he countered. "What do *you* want?"

For a moment she gazed into his eyes. What *did* she want from him? "I want you to accept what is," she told him. "The past is gone. Neither of us can change it."

"You want me to *not* change the past?" he said scornfully. "Yeah, okay, I think I can handle that."

"I want you to accept that, whatever your feelings about your—about our—parents, your value isn't defined by their opinions or judgments," she continued, ignoring the sarcasm.

He snorted. "Sorry, but you already said not to change the past," he said. "Anything else?"

She looked him straight in the eye. "I want you to stop hating," she said quietly. "To stop hating yourself . . . and to stop hating me."

She saw the muscles work briefly in his neck. "I don't hate," he said, his voice steady. "Hate is an emotion, and Jedi don't have emotions. Right?"

"You're not a Jedi."

"And that's the *real* problem, isn't it?" he said bitterly.

"That's what Mom and Dad wanted: Jedi. And I'm not one, am I? But don't worry, I can still play the game. *There is no emotion; there is peace. Jedi serve others rather than ruling over them, for the good of the galaxy. Jedi respect all life, in any form.* See?"

Abruptly, Lorana had had enough. "I'm sorry, Dean," she said, standing up. "I'm sorry for your pain, which I can't heal. I'm sorry for your perceived loss, which I can't give back to you." She forced herself to lock gazes with him. "And I'm sorry you're on your way to wasting your life, a decision that only you can change."

"Nice," he said. "The one thing no one can top Jedi at is making speeches. Especially farewell speeches." He raised his eyebrows. "That *was* a farewell speech, wasn't it?"

Lorana glanced around the room, belatedly remembering where she was. Outbound Flight . . . "I haven't made up my mind."

He lifted his eyebrows. "You actually have a *mind*?" he said. "I thought the Jedi Council made all your decisions for you."

"I hope you'll find your way, Dean," Lorana said, picking up her lightsaber and sliding it back into her belt. "I hope you'll find your healing."

"Well, you can spend the next few years worrying about it," he said. "Hurry back. We have so much more to talk about. Sister." Picking up his mug, he shifted around in his seat to put his back to her.

Lorana stared at the back of his head, the acid taste of defeat in her mouth. "I'll talk to you later," she said. "My . . . brother."

He didn't reply. Blinking back tears, Lorana fled from the room.

For a long time she wandered the maze of corridors, maneuvering mechanically around the techs and droids as she tried to work through the pain darkening her eyes and mind. It was therefore with a certain sense of distant shock that her eyes cleared to show she was back in the Dreadnaught's ComOps Center.

C'baoth and Pakmillu were still there, holding a discussion over one of the navigation consoles. "Ah—Jedi Jinzler," C'baoth said, gesturing her over. "I trust your quarters are satisfactory?"

"Actually, I haven't seen them yet," Lorana admitted.

"But you *will* be joining us, will you not?" Pakmillu added in his gravelly voice. "I understand there is some confusion on this point."

"There's no confusion," C'baoth insisted. "She *is* coming with us."

Pakmillu's large eyes were steady on her. "Jedi Jinzler?" he invited.

Lorana took a deep breath, her brother's face floating in front of her. The face that from this point on would forever hover at the edges of her life. "Master C'baoth is correct," she told the captain. "I'll be honored to travel with you aboard Outbound Flight."

And, she added bitterly to herself, the sooner they were gone, the better.

. . . And the final crew and passenger list," Captain Pakmillu said, handing over the last data card.

"Thank you," Doriana said, accepting the card and tucking the entire stack away inside his coat. "And there's nothing else you need?"

"Nothing that I or fifty thousand other people have been able to think of," Pakmillu said with typically dry Mon Cal humor. "I believe Outbound Flight is ready to fly."

"Excellent," Doriana said. "Supreme Chancellor Palpatine will be pleased to hear it."

"We couldn't have done it without his help," Pakmillu said gravely. "Please extend our gratitude one final time to him for all his efforts on our behalf."

"I certainly will," Doriana promised. A final time it would be, too. "Then that's that. I'll see you in—what? Five years? Ten?"

"However long it takes," Pakmillu said, looking around his Dreadnaught-1 command bridge. "But we *will* be back."

"I'll look forward to your return," Doriana said with all the false sincerity he could conjure up. "In the meantime, a safe voyage to you. And don't forget, if you *do* discover anything else you need, the Supreme Chancellor's Office stands ready to assist. You still have three weeks before you leave Republic space—plenty of time for emergency supplies or equipment to be assembled and transported to you."

"I will remember," Pakmillu said, bowing his head. "May I escort you back to your transport?"

"No need," Doriana assured him. "I know you must have a hundred matters yet to deal with before you leave Yaga Minor. Fly safely, and may the Force be with you."

"With nineteen Jedi aboard, I'm sure it will," Pakmillu assured him. "Rather, nineteen and a half."

"Most definitely," Doriana agreed, keeping his smile in place as he frowned behind it. Nineteen Jedi? And a *half*? "Good-bye, Captain."

He waited until the pilot had maneuvered the transport out of Dreadnaught-1's forward hangar bay and had them skimming smoothly across the outer fringes of Yaga Minor's atmosphere before he pulled out Pakmillu's passenger list and plugged it into his datapad. The last Jedi numbers he'd heard had put the total at seventeen, not nineteen. Had there been a sudden change in plans? And what in blazes was half a Jedi, anyway? The rumors about how Darth Maul had died flashed unpleasantly to mind . . .

He pulled up the Jedi list and ran his eye down it. The names were very familiar, most of them potential troublemakers whom he himself had subtly nudged C'baoth into inviting aboard his grand expedition. The first addition to the list, Lorana Jinzler, wasn't really a surprise; Doriana had always thought it likely that C'baoth's former Padawan would decide to stay with him awhile longer. The other two were Obi-Wan Kenobi and his Padawan, Anakin Skywalker.

Doriana smiled to himself. So Skywalker was Pakmillu's half Jedi. Cute; and an unexpected bonus for all his hard work, as well. Ever since Kenobi and the boy had nearly scuttled the Barlok operation, he'd had an uncomfortable feeling about the pair. Their deaths aboard Outbound Flight would be nicely convenient.

Outbound Flight had disentangled itself from the last of its docking and support equipment now and was making its ponderous way out of Yaga Minor's gravity well toward deep space. A minute later, as Doriana continued to watch through the transport's canopy, it flickered and vanished into hyperspace.

He looked back down at his datapad. Still, bonus or not, he'd better check with Sidious and let him know that Kenobi and Skywalker were aboard, just to make sure that fit in with the Sith Lord's plans.

And he'd better check *before* Outbound Flight meandered its way out of the Republic. Forever.

The shuttle took him to the Yavvitiri Spaceport, a few kilometers from the Preparation Center where all the preliminary work on Outbound Flight had taken place. Palpatine and the Senate had tried to keep a low profile on the project, perhaps fearing a backlash about all the money they were spending, and for the most part they'd succeeded. In his various official and unofficial travels over the past six weeks, Doriana had found virtually no one who had even heard of it.

Still, here at the very center of the project, it could hardly have been ignored. But to his mild surprise, he didn't hear a single word about Outbound Flight's departure as he walked through the spaceport's corridors. True, the work had for the most part moved up to the Dreadnaughts themselves four weeks ago, taking the project out of the public's day-to-day view. But he still would have expected *someone* to have raised his head out of the mud long enough to take note of such a historic event.

Perhaps in these days of growing political and social turmoil, he mused, even historic events were soon forgotten. In this particular case, it was just as well.

He'd left his own ship berthed on the far side of the spaceport, in the restricted zone reserved for diplomats and high governmental officials. Passing through security, he headed through the maze of corridors to his docking bay. He keyed open the hatch and went inside, locking it again behind him, then made his way to the cockpit. Seating himself in the pilot's seat, he punched for the tower. "This is Kinman Doriana of Supreme Chancellor Palpatine's Office," he identified himself when the controller answered. "Requesting a lift slot in thirty minutes."

"Acknowledged, Doriana," the other said. "Thirty-minute lift slot confirmed."

"Thank you." Shutting off the comm, Doriana keyed for full-ship start-up, watching the displays closely as the systems began coming online.

"You are late, Commander Stratis."

Doriana gave the displays one more leisurely look. Then, just as leisurely, he turned around.

The Neimoidian was wedged half hidden in the holo alcove off the cockpit's aft bulkhead, glowering at him from beneath his short, five-cornered hat. "Vicelord Siv Kav," Doriana greeted him. "May I say how very uncomfortable you look."

"Very amusing," Kav growled. Working his shoulders back and forth, he managed to extricate himself and his elaborately layered robes from the alcove. "You should have been here an hour ago."

"Why?" Doriana countered calmly. "Isn't your fleet ready?"

"Of course it is."

"And Outbound Flight only just now left," Doriana said. "Plenty of time to set up our ambush." He cocked his head slightly. "Or are you simply annoyed that I made you hide there in your little hole longer than you expected?"

"I was *not* hiding," the Neimoidian insisted stiffly. "I simply did not wish to be seen if someone from the Spaceport Authority came in unexpectedly."

"You could have accomplished that by waiting in the guest cabin as I'd instructed," Doriana pointed out. "But of course, in there you wouldn't have been able to eavesdrop on my clearance request to the tower. Tell me: was the knowledge of my true name and position worth the wait?"

Kav's large eyes studied his face. "We were betrayed once by your Master," he said, his voice darkening. "Darth Sidious promised that Naboo would be ours, that we would have the foothold we needed there. But the battle turned, and he abandoned us."

"The reversal of battle was not his fault," Doriana countered. "You want to blame someone, blame Amidala. And you have hardly been abandoned."

"Is Naboo ours, then?" Kav said sarcastically. "I must have missed that fact."

"Naboo is nothing," Doriana said. "The continued existence and functioning of your Trade Federation is infinitely more valuable. Or did you also miss the fact that it has yet to be punished for its excesses?"

"The lack of punishment is not Sidious's doing," Kav insisted. "That is the doing of the judiciary, at the cost of far too many expensive legal representatives."

Doriana smiled thinly. "Do you really think the judiciary wouldn't have bowed to Senate pressure by now without someone operating behind the scenes on your behalf?"

A hint of uncertainty crossed Kav's face. "You?" he suggested.

Doriana shrugged. "Lord Sidious has many servants."

"Yet this particular servant resides in the Supreme Chancellor's Office," Kav said, gesturing toward him. "That must be very useful for him."

Doriana let his face harden. "Yes, it is," he said softly. "And from this point on you will forget you've ever heard that name and that position. Forever. Is that clear?"

Kav started to sniff in contempt, took another look at Doriana's face. "It is clear, Master Stratis," he said instead.

"Good." Doriana gestured toward the cockpit door. "Then if you'll return to your cabin, I have a ship to fly. You have the fleet's coordinates for me?"

"Yes." Kav's long fingers dipped into a recess of his robe and emerged with a data card. "It will take no more than two days to reach them."

"Good," Doriana said. "That should give us time to finalize our attack strategy."

"*I* am the one trained in battle tactics," the other said stiffly. "The attack strategy will be mine."

"Of course," Doriana said, suppressing a sigh. "I meant only that I'd be available to assist you. Now if you'll return to your cabin, we'll be on our way."

The Neimoidian drew himself up and, with his pride at least momentarily appeased, strode from the room.

Shaking his head, Doriana crossed to the holo alcove. *Neimoidians.* If they didn't control one of the best collections of military hardware in the Republic, he would have recommended dumping the whole species down the refresher long ago. He just hoped Sidious was working on finding someone more competent to replace them.

Positioning himself in the alcove, he keyed for a HoloNet relay. The lights winked on, and he signaled for his Master.

The wait was longer than usual, and more than once he considered taking a quick trip forward to check again on the status boards. But each time he resisted the temptation. If Sidious came on and had to wait, he would not be happy.

At last the familiar hooded figure appeared. "Report."

"Outbound Flight is on its way, Lord Sidious," Doriana said. "I have Vicelord Kav aboard, and will be heading for the rendezvous within the hour."

"Excellent," Sidious said. "And you know precisely where in the Unknown Regions Outbound Flight will be stopping?"

"Yes, my lord," Doriana said. "Captain Pakmillu has two separate navigational checks planned for the first eight hundred light-years beyond Republic space. I have the coordinates of both."

"Be sure you take the first one," Sidious warned. "It may be that C'baoth in his impatience will order the second to be canceled."

"That is indeed my plan, my lord," Doriana confirmed. "One final matter. I have Pakmillu's final passenger listing, and three more Jedi have been added."

"One of them being Lorana Jinzler, no doubt," Sidious said. "C'baoth had earlier informed the Senate she would be accompanying him." The drooping corners of his mouth turned briefly upward in a sardonic smile. "Though I don't believe he had mentioned it to the woman herself."

"Yes, she's one of them," Doriana confirmed. "The others are Obi-Wan Kenobi and his Padawan, Anakin Skywalker."

Sidious's smile vanished. *"Skywalker?"* he hissed. "Who authorized this?"

"I don't know, my lord," Doriana said, feeling his heart starting to thud in his chest. The last time he'd seen Sidious like this, someone had died. Violently. "It must have been C'baoth—"

"He cannot go on that ship," Sidious cut in sharply. "He must remain here. You will see to it."

"Understood, my lord," Doriana said quickly. "Don't worry, I'll get him off."

He reached for the cutoff switch, his mind whirling as he tried to sort through the options. Outbound Flight's first scheduled stop was at Lonnaw system. If he headed there immediately—

But he couldn't, not with Vicelord Kav aboard. Too much risk that someone would see the Neimoidian and make a connection they couldn't afford. He would first have to drop Kav with the attack force, then go after Outbound Flight. That meant the Lonnaw connection wouldn't work, which meant he would have to try for their next stop, Argai, all the way over in Haldeen sector. If he missed them there—

"Wait."

Doriana paused, his hand hovering over the control. Sidious's lips had tightened, and Doriana had the sense that the Sith Lord was running through the same logic chain he himself had just been working out.

And apparently had come to the same conclusion. "No, you continue with the plan," he said, his voice calm again. "*I* will remove Skywalker from Outbound Flight."

"Yes, my lord," Doriana said, wilting a little with relief. He didn't have the foggiest idea how Sidious was going to pull that one off, especially with C'baoth and five other Jedi Masters on hand to oppose him. But that was the Sith Lord's problem. Doriana was off the hook, and that was the important thing. "I'll contact you again when the mission has been accomplished."

"Do that, Doriana," Sidious said. His eyes, as always, were hidden by his hood; just the same, Doriana could almost see them burning a hole through the long light-years separating the two men before the image flickered and vanished.

For a few seconds Doriana remained where he was, taking deep breaths as he worked out the tension still quivering through his body. Once again, the game had nearly proved fatal. Once again, he had made it through unscathed.

One of these times, perhaps, he wouldn't.

But that future was a long way away. Right now he had a fleet to find, and an ambush to prepare.

And eighteen Jedi to kill.

Shutting down the holoprojector, he went back to the pilot's chair and plugged Kav's data card into the reader slot. Time to find out exactly where they were going.

The pylon turbolift car door opened into yet another spacious lobby area. "Okay," Anakin said, leaning out for a look. "And this one is"—he threw a not quite surreptitious look at the marking on the side—"Dreadnaught-Four?"

"Correct," C'baoth said, putting a hand on the boy's shoulder and pressing him forward out of the car. "We're now at the farthest side of Outbound Flight from the command ship, Dreadnaught One."

"Rather like Tatooine in that respect," Obi-Wan added drily.

"Right," Anakin said. "Only cooler and less sandy."

"Tatooine?" C'baoth asked.

"A small planet where Anakin grew up," Obi-Wan explained. "The locals like to say that it's the farthest point from the center of the universe, like Dreadnaught-Four's the farthest from Dreadnaught-One's command areas."

C'baoth nodded. "Ah."

Dreadnaught-Four's architecture and equipment, Obi-Wan

noted, were identical to those of the other ships they'd visited on C'baoth's tour. Not really surprising, considering how the expedition had been put together. Also as in the other Dreadnaughts, the people passing through the corridors around them all seemed to be moving with a brisk, business-like step, their expressions cheerful, confident, and determined.

Small wonder. Against steep odds their grand adventure had finally begun, and the warm glow of that accomplishment was still with them.

"Jedi Master Justyn Ma'Ning is in charge of this particular Dreadnaught," C'baoth said as they headed aft. "I believe you spoke with him at the First Night dinner."

"Yes, we chatted for a few minutes," Obi-Wan said. "I thought Commander Omano was in charge of Dreadnaught-Four."

"I meant that Master Ma'Ning oversees Jedi operations and activities," C'baoth said. "He should be back in Conference Room Five with his two Jedi Knights and a select group of families. Let's go see how they're doing."

"What were these families selected for?" Obi-Wan asked.

"The highest honor possible," C'baoth said. "Over the next few days, one of each family's children will be starting Jedi training."

Obi-Wan stared at him. "*Jedi* training?"

"Indeed," C'baoth confirmed. "You see, along with their basic technical skills, prospective colonists were also screened for the presence of Force-sensitive children. Those families with the most promise were given preferential status, though of course we kept that a secret up until now. We have eleven candidates in all, including the three here in Dreadnaught-Four."

"How old are these children?" Obi-Wan asked.

"They range in age from four to ten," C'baoth said. He cocked an eyebrow at Anakin. "Which is, I believe, the same age Master Skywalker was when you took him as your Padawan."

"It is," Obi-Wan confirmed, feeling his lip twist. For centuries standard Temple policy had been to accept only infants into Jedi training, and C'baoth knew it. Unfortunately, Anakin was a glaring exception to that rule, an exception C'baoth clearly intended to use as his justification for this. "What about their parents?"

"What about them?"

"They've all given their permission for this training?"

"They will," C'baoth assured him. "As I said, giving a child to the Jedi is the highest honor possible."

"So you haven't actually asked them yet?"

"Of course not," C'baoth said, an edge of puzzlement creeping into his tone. "What parent wouldn't be proud to have a Jedi son or daughter?"

Obi-Wan braced himself. "But if for some reason they don't see it that way—"

"Later," C'baoth interrupted, gesturing to a door to their right. "We're here."

The conference room was one of many midsize meeting areas scattered around a typical Dreadnaught. At the far end, standing beside a podium, was Jedi Master Ma'Ning, listening intently to a question from a woman in the front row. Flanking him, dressed in Jedi robes, were a pair of Duros.

And seated in the rows of chairs in front of them, nearly packing the available space, were perhaps forty men, women, and children. Far more than the three families C'baoth had implied would be here.

C'baoth was clearly surprised, too. "What in the . . . ?" he rumbled under his breath, his eyes flashing as he looked around.

"Maybe they brought their friends?" Anakin suggested hesitantly.

"Friends were not invited," C'baoth growled. He started to move forward, then seemed to think better of it. Instead, he gave an impatient gesture to his right. Turning that direction, Obi-Wan saw Lorana Jinzler detach herself from the back wall where she'd been standing and walk over to them.

She nodded in greeting as she reached them. "Master C'baoth," she said quietly. "Master Ma'Ning said you might drop in on us."

"And it's fortunate that I did," C'baoth said. His voice was low, but Obi-Wan could see a few of the people in the back row starting to look around to see what was going on. "What are all these people doing here?"

"Master Ma'Ning invited all the secondaries and their families, as well," Lorana told him.

"Secondaries?" Obi-Wan asked.

"Those with a small amount of latent Force sensitivity, too small for them to ever become Jedi," C'baoth said, glowering across the room at Ma'Ning. "What about *you,* Jedi Jinzler? Why aren't you attending to your duties on Dreadnaught-One?"

"Master Ma'Ning asked me to come," she said, her voice a little strained.

C'baoth rumbled deep in his throat. "I see," he said darkly.

They waited in silence as Ma'Ning answered the question he'd been asked—something about ration redistribution for those whose children would be undergoing the training—and called for more questions. There were none, and with a final word of thanks he called the meeting to a close.

And as the audience began to gather themselves together,

C'baoth strode down the aisle toward the front. Obi-Wan followed, Anakin and Lorana at his sides. As near as Obi-Wan could tell from the snatches of conversation he could hear, most of the people did indeed seem pleased or even excited by the fact that they had future Jedi in their families.

Most of them. But not all.

Ma'Ning nodded in greeting as the group approached. "Master C'baoth," he said. "Master Kenobi; Young Sky—"

"What do you mean by bringing the secondaries to this meeting?" C'baoth demanded.

"I thought it would be useful to let everyone know at once why they'd been selected to fly on Outbound Flight," Ma'Ning said. His voice was calm, but Obi-Wan could see tension lines at the corners of his eyes. "Since the secondaries are the ones most likely to produce Jedi offspring in the future, I thought they should know what to expect."

"That could have been dealt with if and when it happened," C'baoth growled. "This is not how it should have been."

"*None* of it is as it should be," Ma'Ning countered. "Children this age—*and* taking them from their families by force—"

"By force?" Obi-Wan put in.

"I don't expect force to be necessary," C'baoth insisted, glaring at Obi-Wan and Ma'Ning in turn. "The few parents who have doubts will undoubtedly come around. Certainly the children themselves will be thrilled to begin their training."

"The question remains why we're even doing this," Ma'Ning said.

"We're doing this because we're setting off on a long and dangerous trip," C'baoth told him. "We'll need all the Jedi we can get, far more than Master Yoda would permit me to invite.

Very well; so we will raise them up by ourselves. And please don't quote me that learned nonsense about how young a Jedi candidate has to be, because that's all it is: nonsense."

"Master Yoda would disagree with you," Ma'Ning said.

"Then Master Yoda would be wrong," C'baoth said flatly. "We don't train children or adults because we choose not to. That's the *only* reason." He gestured at Anakin. "Padawan Skywalker is proof that older children are trainable."

Ma'Ning's lip twitched. "Perhaps," he conceded. "But there are other reasons for accepting only infants."

"What other reasons?" C'baoth asked. "Tradition? Politics? There's certainly nothing in the Code itself that specifically speaks to the issue."

"Actually, that's not true," Obi-Wan put in. "The writings of Master Simikarty are very clear on the subject."

"Master Simikarty's writings are his interpretations of the Code, not part of the Code itself," C'baoth said. "More tradition, under a different name."

"You do not approve of tradition?" one of the Duros asked.

"I don't approve of simply and blindly accepting it as truth," C'baoth told him. "Nor can we afford to do so. The lists of Jedi are shrinking all across the Republic. If we're to continue our role as the guardians of peace and justice, we *must* find ways to increase our numbers."

"By forcibly taking trainees from their parents?" Ma'Ning asked. "Especially considering the fact that none of these parents had wanted their children to become Jedi in the first place?"

"What makes you think that?" C'baoth asked.

"The fact that if they had, they'd have taken them for testing when they were infants," Ma'Ning said.

"Perhaps there were other reasons," C'baoth rumbled. "But

all right, yes, the parents have always made the decision whether or not their children would be trained. More tradition. But what about the child's wishes? Wouldn't it be more ethical to allow him or her to make that decision?"

"But as Master Ma'Ning says, there *are* good reasons for accepting only infants," Obi-Wan said.

"Most of which don't apply here," C'baoth said firmly. "There are no deep-rooted family hierarchies aboard Outbound Flight to deal with. Nor will the children be going hundreds or thousands of light-years away to the Temple on Coruscant where their families will never see them again." Beside C'baoth, Lorana stirred but remained silent. "No, here they'll be merely a turbolift ride away in the storage core," C'baoth continued. "After some initial training, we might even consider allowing them occasional evenings with their families."

"You're putting them in the *storage core*?" Ma'Ning asked, frowning.

"I want the training center as far away from noise and mental confusion as possible," C'baoth told him. "There's plenty of room down there."

Ma'Ning shook his head. "I still don't like this, Master C'baoth."

"New ideas are always discomfiting, as are new ways of doing things," C'baoth said, looking at each of the others in turn. "In many ways all of Outbound Flight is a grand experiment. And remember that if we're successful, we may return to the Republic with the key to a complete reinvigoration of the entire Jedi Order."

"And if we *don't* succeed?" Obi-Wan asked.

"Then we fail," C'baoth said stiffly. "But we won't."

Obi-Wan looked at Ma'Ning. The other still didn't look

happy, but it was clear he didn't have any fresh arguments to offer.

Besides, C'baoth was right. Something new had to be tried if the Jedi Order was going to survive.

And once upon a time, according to the histories, the Jedi *had* been willing to take risks.

"All right," Ma'Ning said at last. "We'll try this grand experiment of yours. But move carefully, Master C'baoth. Move very carefully."

"Of course," C'baoth said, as if there were no doubt. "Then all that remains is to prepare the training center." He turned to Lorana. "Since you're here, Jedi Jinzler, you will see to that."

Lorana bowed her head. "Yes, Master C'baoth."

"And in the future," C'baoth added, looking back at Ma'Ning, "you'll check with me before you take any of my Jedi from their assigned duties."

Ma'Ning's lip twisted slightly, but he, too, bowed his head. "As you wish, Master C'baoth."

C'baoth held his eyes a moment longer, then turned to Obi-Wan and Anakin. "And now, we'll continue our tour," he said, gesturing toward the door.

He strode down the aisle toward the rear, ignoring the small clusters of crewers still conversing quietly among themselves, and out into the corridor. "You mentioned Jedi duties," Obi-Wan said as they turned aft. "What exactly will you be wanting us to do?"

"At the moment, the sorts of things you've always done," C'baoth said. "Patrolling Outbound Flight and assisting where you're needed. Later, I'll want you to assist with the training of our prospective Jedi. And, of course, we'll be needed to maintain order aboard the ships."

"I hadn't noticed a great deal of disorder," Obi-Wan pointed out.

"There will be," C'baoth said grimly. "This many people can't live this closely together without friction. Even before we leave the Unknown Regions, I fully expect we'll be regularly called upon to resolve disputes among passengers, as well as organizing proper rules of conduct."

Rules of conduct? "Wouldn't that sort of thing be Captain Pakmillu's responsibility?" Obi-Wan asked carefully.

"Captain Pakmillu will have his hands full with the physical requirements of running Outbound Flight," C'baoth said. "Besides, we're the best qualified for such tasks."

"As long as we remember that our role is to advise and mediate," Obi-Wan cautioned. " 'Jedi serve others rather than ruling over them, for the good of the galaxy.' "

"I said nothing about ruling over anyone."

"But if we take over Captain Pakmillu's job of keeping order, isn't that essentially what we're doing?" Obi-Wan asked. "Mediation offered with the underlying threat of compulsion hardly qualifies as mediation."

"As I threatened the two sides on Barlok?" C'baoth asked pointedly.

Obi-Wan hesitated. He remembered feeling uncomfortable with the tone C'baoth had used to the two sides in the aftermath of the abortive missile attack. *Had* he in fact overstepped his bounds by forcing them to accept his terms? Or had the compulsion merely come from the attack itself, coupled with their sudden and sobering recognition that the negotiations were no longer purely matters of charts and abstract numbers?

And what *was* C'baoth's connection, if any, to that attack? That was a question he was still no closer to answering.

"They *did* need someone to tell them what to do," Anakin offered into his thoughts. "And we're supposed to have wisdom and insight that non-Jedi don't have."

"Sometimes wisdom requires us to stand by and do nothing," Obi-Wan said, Windu's words back at the Temple echoing through his mind. Still, if the Council had reprimanded C'baoth for his actions, Windu hadn't mentioned it. "Otherwise people might never learn how to handle problems by themselves."

"And such wisdom comes only through a close understanding of the Force," C'baoth said, his tone indicating the discussion was over. "As you will learn, young Skywalker." He gestured ahead. "Now, down here we have the central weapons and shield cluster . . ."

C'baoth and the others disappeared through the conference room door. Lorana watched them go, sighing with tiredness and frustration.

Why had Ma'Ning asked her here, anyway? Because she presumably knew C'baoth better than anyone else aboard? If so, she certainly hadn't been of much use during the discussion. Was she supposed to have joined the others in objecting to his Jedi training plan, then? Well, she'd failed on that account, too.

"Is he always this overbearing?"

Lorana turned back around. The two Duros had wandered away and were talking quietly together, but Ma'Ning was still standing there, eyeing her thoughtfully. "He didn't seem particularly overbearing to me," she said, automatically rising to her Master's defense.

"Perhaps it's just his personality," Ma'Ning said. But there was a knowing look on his face. Maybe he'd seen other Jedi come to C'baoth's defense before, for the same reasons Lorana had. Whatever those reasons were. "Tell me, what do you think of this scheme of his?"

"You mean the training of older children?" She shrugged helplessly. "I don't know. It's all new to me."

"He hasn't talked about this before?"

"No," she said. "At least, not to me."

"Mm," Ma'Ning said, pursing his lips. "It's an interesting concept, certainly. And he's right: there *have* been exceptions in the past, most of whom have worked out fine."

"Like Anakin?"

"Perhaps," Ma'Ning said cautiously. "Though until a Padawan actually achieves Jedi Knighthood, there's always the danger he or she might fall away. I'm not expecting that of Skywalker, of course."

"No," Lorana agreed. "If you'll excuse me, Master Ma'Ning, I need to find some crewers to help me start organizing the new training center."

"Certainly," Ma'Ning said, nodding. "I'll speak with you later."

He stepped over to the two Duros, joining in their conversation. Three Jedi, holding a private discussion among themselves.

With Lorana on the outside. As if she were still just a Padawan.

Still, she *had* said she was leaving. Maybe that was all it was. Taking a deep breath, putting such thoughts from her mind, she headed down the aisle toward the door.

She was nearly there when a man stepped partway into her path. "Your pardon, Jedi," he said tentatively. "A word, if I may?"

"Certainly," Lorana said, focusing on him for the first time. He was a typical crewer, young and bright-eyed, with short dark hair and a hint of greasy dirt on the collar of his jumpsuit. Summoned directly from his shift to Ma'Ning's meeting, probably. Behind him stood a young woman with a sleeping infant in one arm and a boy of five or six standing close beside her. Her free hand was resting on the boy's shoulder. "How can I help you?"

"My name's Dillian Pressor," the man said, gesturing back to the others. "My son, Jorad, has a question."

"All right," Lorana said, stepping over to the boy, noting that as she approached the woman seemed to tighten her grip on her son's shoulder. "Hello, Jorad," she said cheerfully, dropping to one knee in front of him.

He gazed at her, his expression a mix of uncertainty and awe. "Are you really a Jedi?" he asked.

"Yes, indeed," she assured him. "I'm Jedi Jinzler. Can you say that?"

He pursed his lips uncertainly. "Jedi Jisser?"

"Jinzler," his father said. *"Jinzler."*

"Jedi Jissler," the boy tried again.

"Or we could just make it Jedi Lorana," Lorana suggested. "You have a question for me?"

The boy threw an uncertain look up at his mother's face. Then, steeling himself, he looked back at Lorana. "Master Ma'Ning said only the people he called were going to be Jedi," he said. "I wanted to know if I could be one, too."

Lorana glanced up at the woman, noting the tight lines in her face. "I'm afraid it's not something any of us has a say in," she said. "If you aren't born with Force sensitivity, we can't train you to be a Jedi. I'm sorry."

"Well, what if I got better?" Jorad persisted. "He said the rest of us were close, and it's been a long time since they tested us. Maybe I got better."

"Maybe you did," Lorana said. In theory, of course, he couldn't. Force sensitivity could be nurtured, but not created.

On the other hand, C'baoth *had* said these were the families who had low but non-negligible sensitivity. It was at least theoretically possible that the boy's testing had been inaccurate. "I tell you what," she said. "I'll talk to Master Ma'Ning about having you tested again, all right? If you've gotten better, we'll see if we can get you into the program."

Jorad's eyes lit up. "Okay," he said. "When can I do it?"

"I'll talk to Master Ma'Ning," she repeated, wondering if she'd already promised more than she could deliver. "He'll set it up with your father."

"Jorad?" the boy's mother prompted.

"Thank you," Jorad said dutifully.

"You're welcome," Lorana said, standing up and looking at the baby in her mother's arm. "Is this your sister?"

"Yes, that's Katarin," Jorad said. "She mostly just cries a lot."

"That's what babies do best," Lorana agreed, looking at the mother and then Dillian. "Thank you all for coming."

"No problem," Dillian said, taking his son's hand and stepping to the door. It opened, and he ushered the boy out into the corridor. "Thank you again, Jedi Jinzler."

"Jedi Lorana," Jorad corrected him.

Almost unwillingly, Dillian smiled. "Jedi Lorana," he amended. Holding out a hand to his wife, he led her out behind Jorad—

"*There* you are," an irritated voice called down the corridor.

Lorana stepped out into the corridor behind the others. Striding toward them was a young man with dirtwater-colored hair, his mouth set in a thin line as he glared at Dillian. "What the brix are you doing here, Pressor?"

"It was a special meeting," Dillian said, gesturing toward Lorana. "This is Jedi Lorana Jinzler—"

"Since when do you skip out in the middle of a duty shift for a meeting?" the man cut in. "In case you've forgotten, it's a little difficult to do a hyperdrive reactor communication deep-check without the hyperdrive man actually being there."

"I know," Pressor said, giving Jorad's hand to his mother. "Sorry—I thought we'd be done sooner than this."

"Well, you weren't." The man shifted his glare to Lorana. "Is this going to be a regular occurrence around here, Jedi Jinzler?"

"What do you mean, ah . . . ?"

"Chas Uliar," the man said shortly. "I mean you Jedi coming in and messing with our work schedules."

"I'm not sure what you mean," Lorana said.

"Two days ago Master Ma'Ning pulled everyone off systems control for a coolant-leak drill," Uliar said. "Never mind that we've already done five of them in the past month. Now you're calling special bounce-of-the-moment meetings that pull people off important duty stations. What's on line for tomorrow? Escape pod practice?"

"Is there a problem, Uliar?" Ma'Ning's voice came from behind them.

Lorana turned as Ma'Ning stepped out into the corridor. "I just want to get my day's work done in peace so that I can sleep the sleep of the virtuous," Uliar said with a hint of sarcasm. "Or do I need to make a formal requisition for that?"

"Not at all," Ma'Ning assured him. "Pressor, you're free to return to your station."

"Thank you," Pressor said.

"And in the future we'll try to be more considerate of the various work schedules," Ma'Ning added to Uliar.

"Fine," Uliar said, a little less truculently. "Come on, Pressor. Let's try to get this done before the next shift comes on."

He headed back down the corridor at a fast walk. "See you later," Pressor said, touching his wife's arm and then hurrying after him.

"Good-bye, Jedi Lorana," Jorad said gravely, looking up at her. "I hope we'll see you again."

"I'm sure you will, Jorad," Lorana said, smiling at the boy. "You take good care of your little sister, okay?"

"I will." Holding his mother's hand tightly, he headed the other direction down the corridor.

"Sounds like an irritable sort," Lorana commented to Ma'Ning.

"Who, Uliar?" The Master shrugged. "A bit. Still, he's got a point about us changing things around with no notice. You might want to speak to Master C'baoth about that."

"I thought he said *you'd* called for the coolant-leak drill."

"Under Master C'baoth's orders." Ma'Ning smiled wryly. "And he's right—we *do* have an escape pod drill scheduled for later this week."

Lorana nodded. "I'll talk to him," she promised.

They were six standard days out of Yaga Minor and had stopped for a routine navigational check in Lonnaw system when the trouble started.

A crowd had already gathered in the Dreadnaught-2 aft passenger section when Obi-Wan arrived. "Let me through, please," he said, starting to ease his way through the mass of people.

"Look—there's another one," a Rodian voice muttered.

"Another one what?" Obi-Wan asked, turning in that direction.

"Another Jedi," the Rodian said, looking him square in the face.

"Easy, Feeven," a man nearby cautioned. "Don't start pointing blame."

"Can you tell me what happened?" Obi-Wan asked.

"What happened is thieves in the night," the Rodian bit out. "Thieves with robes and lightsabers."

"Feeven, shut *up*," the man said. He looked at Obi-Wan, lowered his eyes. "They came for someone's kid, that's all."

"In the middle of the night," Feeven insisted.

"What night?" the man scoffed. "This is space. It's always night here."

"The family was sleeping," Feeven countered. "That makes it night."

"Thank you," Obi-Wan said, easing away from them and continuing on through the crowd. Middle of ship's night or not, perhaps he ought to give C'baoth a call.

There was no need. He reached the open area in the center of the crowd to find that C'baoth was already there. "Master C'baoth," he said, taking in the rest of the scene with a glance. Standing in the doorway to one of the rooms was a hulking figure of a man, his hands gripping the sides of the doorway as if daring anyone to pass. Behind him in the room was a frantic-eyed woman kneeling on the floor clutching a young boy tightly to her. The child himself looked frightened but also oddly intent.

C'baoth half turned to frown at him. "What are you doing here?" he demanded. "You should be sleeping."

"I heard there was some commotion," Obi-Wan said, crossing to the doorway. "Hello," he said to the man.

"You're not taking him," the other said flatly. "I don't care how many of you there are, you're not taking him."

"You have no choice," C'baoth said flatly. "As Jedi Master Evrios explained to you nearly a week ago. Your son is a potential Jedi, and he's agreed to enter training. That means he comes with us."

"Says who?" the man retorted. "Ship's law says decisions about children are made by their parents. I looked it up."

"Ship's law wasn't written to cover this situation," C'baoth said. "It therefore doesn't apply."

"So now you just throw out the law when it doesn't suit you?"

"Of course we don't throw it out," C'baoth said. "We merely rewrite it."

"Who does?" the man demanded. "You Jedi?"

"Captain Pakmillu is the final legal authority aboard Outbound Flight," Obi-Wan put in. "We'll call him and ask—"

"He *may* be the final legal authority," C'baoth said, cutting him off with a warning glare. "That remains to be seen."

Obi-Wan felt an uncomfortable tingling across his skin. "What do you mean?"

"Outbound Flight is first and foremost a Jedi project," C'baoth reminded him. "Jedi requirements therefore supersede all other authority."

Obi-Wan took a careful breath, suddenly aware of the people silently pressing around them. "May I see you for a moment, Master C'baoth? In private?"

"Later," C'baoth said, craning his neck over the crowd. "Captain Pakmillu has arrived."

Obi-Wan turned to see the crowd opening up to let Pakmillu

through. Even dragged out of bed as he must have been, the Mon Cal's uniform was still immaculate. "Master C'baoth," he said, his voice even more gravelly than usual. "Master Kenobi. What is the problem?"

"They want to take my son away from me," the man in the door bit out.

"The boy is to enter Jedi training," C'baoth said calmly. "His father seeks to deny him that right."

"What right?" the man snapped. "His right? Our right? *Your* right?"

"The Jedi are the guardians of peace," C'baoth reminded him. "As such—"

"Maybe in the *Republic* you are," the man cut in. "But that's why we're leaving the Republic, isn't it? To get away from arbitrary rules and capricious justice and—"

"Perhaps we should wait until morning to discuss this," Obi-Wan interrupted. "I think we'll all be calmer and clearer of mind then."

"There's no need for that," C'baoth insisted.

"Master Kenobi speaks wisdom," Pakmillu said. "We'll meet tomorrow after morning meal in Dreadnaught-Two's forward command conference room." His eyes rolled to first the man and then C'baoth. "There you'll both have an opportunity to present your arguments, as well as relevant articles of Republic law."

C'baoth exhaled loudly. "Very well, Captain," he said. "Until tomorrow." With a final look at the man and boy, he strode off, the crowd opening up even faster for him than it had for Pakmillu. Obi-Wan followed, making it through the gap before it closed again.

For the first hundred meters they walked in silence. Obi-Wan was starting to wonder if C'baoth even knew he had tagged along when the other finally spoke. "You shouldn't have done that, Master Kenobi," C'baoth rumbled. "Jedi should never argue in public."

"I was unaware that trying to clarify a situation qualified as arguing," Obi-Wan said, stretching to the Force for patience. "Though if it comes to that, a Jedi should never deliberately antagonize the people he's supposed to be serving, either."

"Taking a child into Jedi training is not antagonism."

"Doing so in the middle of the night is," Obi-Wan countered. "There's no reason that couldn't have waited until morning." He paused. "Unless, of course, you were deliberately trying to force the issue of control."

He'd hoped the other would instantly and hotly deny it. But C'baoth merely looked sideways at him. "And why would I do that?"

"I don't know," Obi-Wan said. "Particularly since the Code specifically forbids Jedi to rule over others."

"Does it? Does it really?"

Obi-Wan felt a tingling at the back of his neck. "We've already had this discussion," he reminded the other.

"And my position remains the same as it was then," C'baoth said. "The Jedi Order has accumulated many rules over the centuries that are clearly erroneous. Why should this not be one of them?"

"Because Jedi aren't equipped to rule," Obi-Wan said. "Because seeking power is the dark side."

"How do you know?" C'baoth demanded. "When was the last time we were ever given the opportunity to try?"

"I know because the Code says so," Obi-Wan said flatly. "We're here to guide, not become dictators."

"And what is the purpose of rules and regulations if not to

guide people into the behavior that will best serve them and their society?" C'baoth countered.

"Now you're playing with semantics."

"No, I'm speaking of intent," C'baoth corrected. "Rule is of the dark side because it seeks personal gain and the satisfaction of one's own desires over the rights and desires of others. Guidance, in any form, seeks the other person's best interests."

"Is that truly what you're seeking here?"

"That's what all of us seek," C'baoth said. "Come now, Master Kenobi. Can you truly say that Master Yoda and Master Windu couldn't run the Republic with more wisdom and efficiency than Palpatine and the government bureaucrats?"

"If they could resist the pull of the dark side, yes," Obi-Wan said. "But that pull would always be there."

"As it is in whatever we do," C'baoth said. "That's why we seek the guidance of the Force for ourselves as well as for those we serve."

Obi-Wan shook his head. "It's a dangerous course, Master C'baoth," he warned. "You risk bringing chaos and confusion."

"The confusion will be minimal, and it will end," C'baoth promised. "Whatever authority we're granted, rest assured that it will be with the support of the people." He lifted a finger. "But never forget why most of them are here in the first place. You heard that man: they joined Outbound Flight to escape the corruption of the worlds we're leaving behind. Why *shouldn't* we offer something better?"

"Because this is skirting perilously close to the edge," Obi-Wan said. "I can't believe that the Code could be as wrong as you seem to believe."

"Not wrong, but merely misinterpreted," C'baoth said. "Perhaps you should focus your meditation on this question. As of course I will myself," he added. "Together, I'm sure we'll obtain the insight to find the proper path."

"Perhaps," Obi-Wan said. "I'd like to come to the meeting tomorrow morning."

"No need," C'baoth said. "Jedi Master Evrios and I will handle things. Besides, I believe you're scheduled to help with the shielding of Dreadnaught-One's new auxiliary navigation room at that time."

"I'm sure that could wait."

"And now you'll want to return to your rest," C'baoth said as they reached the pylon turbolift lobby. "You have a busy day tomorrow."

"As do we all," Obi-Wan said with a sigh. "And you?"

C'baoth gazed thoughtfully down the corridor. "I believe I'll wait for Captain Pakmillu," he said. "Sleep well, Master Kenobi. I'll see you tomorrow."

At the meeting the next morning, after all the various arguments had been presented and the discussion had wound down, Captain Pakmillu sided with C'baoth.

"They took the boy away three hours later," Uliar said, scowling across the table at his friends.

"What do you expect?" Tarkosa asked reasonably from across the table. "Jedi are as rare as dewback feathers. I can understand why they wouldn't want anyone with the talent to slip through their fingers."

"But before it was always just infants," Jobe Keely reminded him, his face puckered with uncertainty. "Kids who don't even know they're alive yet, much less knowing who Mom and Dad are. These kids have all been much older."

"But they've all been willing to go, haven't they?" Tarkosa

countered. "Even the boy this morning. He was scared, sure, but he was also pretty excited. Face it, Jobe: most kids think it would be really cool to be a Jedi."

"*My* question is what they're going to do with all of them," Uliar put in. "They going to throw everyone off one of the Dreadnaughts and build their own little Jedi Temple there?"

"I'm sure C'baoth has some ideas," Tarkosa said firmly. "Seems to me he's pretty much on top of things."

"Yeah," Uliar grunted. "Right."

For a few minutes none of them spoke. Uliar let his eyes drift around the number three messroom, as sterile and military looking as everything else aboard Outbound Flight. The people eating their dinners looked sterile and military, too, in their jumpsuits and other operational garb.

What the place needed was some character, he decided. Maybe he should get some people together and see if Commander Omano would let them redecorate the messrooms with different themes. Maybe a nice upscale Coruscant dinner club for one, a MidRim tapcaf for another, something really sleazy looking for a third, with people encouraged to dress the parts when they went to eat or drink—

"What do you know?" Keely said into his thoughts, nodding behind Uliar. "There's one now."

Uliar turned. Sure enough, there was that Jinzler woman who'd dragged Dillian Pressor to a meeting when the man was supposed to be working. She was standing just inside the messroom doorway, her head moving slowly as she scanned the occupants. A couple of the diners looked up at her, but most didn't even seem to notice she was there. "Trolling for more Jedi?" he suggested.

"Don't seem to be many kids here," Keely pointed out, looking around. "You suppose they're going to go after the adults next?"

"Maybe C'baoth's given them a quota to fill," Uliar said. "You know, like CorSec and traffic tickets."

"CorSec patrollers don't have quotas," Tarkosa said scornfully. "That's a myth."

"Well, if she's got one, she's not going to fill it tonight," Keely commented as Jinzler turned and left the room. "C'baoth's not going to be happy with *her*."

"If you ask me, I don't think C'baoth's ever happy with anything," Uliar said, picking up his mug. "I've never met anyone so full of himself."

"I had an instructor at the institute just like him," Tarkosa said. "Once night some of the students sneaked into his office, disassembled his desk, and reassembled it in the refresher station down the hall. I thought he was going to pop every blood vessel in his face when he saw it."

"But I'll bet it didn't solve anything," Keely commented. "People like that never learn." He turned to Uliar. "Speaking of solving things, Chas, did you ever figure out that line fluctuation problem you were having yesterday? We had to shut down the whole portside turbolaser system."

"Oh, yeah, we got it sorted it out," Uliar told him, dragging his mind away from Jedi and dull dining rooms. "This'll kill you. You know b'Crevnis, that big terminally cheerful Pho Ph'eahian who's supposed to be in charge of fluid-flow maintenance? It seems he managed to mislabel one of his own gauges . . ."

It took until the fourth D-4 messroom she visited, but Lorana finally found the Pressor family. "Hello," she said, smiling as she walked up to their table. "How are you all doing tonight?"

"We're fine," Pressor said, his eyes suddenly wary as he looked up at her. "Is anything wrong?"

"That depends on how you look at it," Lorana said, kneeling down between Jorad and his mother. "I wanted to tell you, Jorad, that your retest again came up negative. I'm sorry."

The boy made a face. "That's okay," he said, clearly disappointed. "Mom and Dad said it probably wouldn't change."

"Moms and dads are smart that way," Lorana said. "I hope you're not too disappointed."

"I'm sure he'll get over it," the boy's mother said, a note of relief in her voice. "There are lots of other things he can do with his life."

"Yes," Lorana murmured, her brother's face flickering across her memory. "We all have to accept our strengths and talents, and go on from there."

"Though sometimes with a little push," Pressor said grimly. "I hear you Jedi had some sort of standoff over on D-Two yesterday."

"I heard something about that," Lorana confirmed. "I wasn't there, so I can't say whether it was a standoff or not. I understand it was resolved peaceably, though."

"*I* heard the boy was hustled off to Jedi school," Pressor countered.

"Yet if that's his birthright, how can anyone deny it to him?" Lorana asked. "The life of a Jedi can be hard—and, yes, it requires sacrifice, from the parents as well as from the child. But anything that's worthwhile does."

"I suppose," Pressor said, clearly not convinced.

"Well, I'll let you get back to your meal now," Lorana said, getting to her feet again. "Thank you for your time."

"Thank you for stopping by," Pressor said.

"Good-bye, Jedi Lorana," Jorad added. For a moment his eyes seemed to linger on her lightsaber before he returned to his meal.

Lorana made her way back through the messroom, trying to get a sense of the people around her. Most of those along her path looked up casually as she passed, then turned back to their food and conversations without any detectable change in their mood. Most of the ones seated farther away didn't even notice her. Everyone seemed more or less content, aside from the inevitable few working through annoyances from their shift work. If there was any growing resentment toward the Jedi, she couldn't detect it.

So perhaps her fears were for nothing. After all, they would all be aboard Outbound Flight for a long time yet, and even those who were upset at the way the children had been taken would eventually realize that more Jedi translated into a smoother and safer voyage.

But for now, it was time to get back to work. Some of the last-minute equipment that had been packed into the storage core needed to be shifted around to other areas. The crewers had enough hands and lifters for the job, but there was always the chance that one of the stacks of crates would shift unexpectedly, and it would be safer if a Jedi was present to keep that from happening. There would undoubtedly be injuries and deaths along the way, but Lorana had no intention of letting such incidents begin this soon. Not if she could help it.

Stepping out into the corridor, she headed toward the aft pylon turbolift. One of these days, she promised herself, she would see about getting ahold of one of those swoops Captain Pakmillu had said were aboard.

. . . And this is the engine compartment," Thrawn said, stepping aside to let Thrass look through the access hatchway into the *Bargain Hunter*'s engine room. "You'll notice it has a radically differently layout from those of Chiss vessels this size."

"Yes," Thrass said. He peered inside a moment, then turned to Car'das. "What's the vessel's sublight range?"

"I'm not sure," Car'das said, looking over at Qennto. The other was standing off to one side with Maris, who was whispering a running translation to him. "Rak?" he invited in Basic.

"Why?" Qennto growled. "Is he looking to take it for a test run or something?"

"Come on, Rak," Car'das cajoled, carefully avoiding Thrawn's eyes. Qennto hadn't been happy about letting Thrawn give his brother this private tour of his ship, and he'd been wearing that annoyance on his sleeve ever since they'd arrived.

The problem was that either he didn't remember that Thrawn could now understand Basic, or else he just didn't care.

So far the commander hadn't responded to Qennto's snide comments, but that restraint was bound to have a limit. If he got tired enough of this and tossed Qennto back in the brig, even Maris might not be able to sweet-talk him out again.

Qennto rolled his eyes. "We can do six hundred hours of sublight before refueling," he said grudgingly. "Six fifty if we're careful with our acceleration."

"Thank you." Switching back to Minnisiat, Car'das translated for Thrass.

"Impressive," the syndic said, taking another look at the engine compartment. "Their fuel efficiency must be slightly better than ours."

"Yes, but their hyperdrives appear to be more fragile," Thrawn said. "Our shock net attacks disabled both theirs and their attackers' without difficulty."

"Weaponry?"

"Simple but adequate," Thrawn told him. "The equipment is difficult to get to, but my experts have studied it at length. Their energy weapons and missiles are less sophisticated than ours, and they don't carry any shock nets or other disabling equipment. On the other hand, bear in mind that this *is* merely a small private freighter."

"True." Thrass looked at Car'das. "Your people *do* have war vessels, I presume?"

"The Republic has no army of its own," Car'das said, choosing his words carefully. Peaceful watchfulness might be the Chiss way, but he still didn't want to make these people nervous. "Of course, most of our member systems have their own defense forces."

"Which can also be used for attack?"

"That does happen sometimes," Car'das conceded. "But the

Supreme Chancellor can call on member systems to help stop an aggressor, and that usually ends things pretty quickly. Mediation by the Jedi can sometimes stop trouble before it gets that far."

"Jedi?"

"A class of beings unknown to us," Thrawn told him. "Ferasi has been trying to explain them to me."

Car'das looked at Maris in surprise. He hadn't realized she'd been having private chats with the commander. Her eyes met his, ducked guiltily away, and for the first time since the session began her running translation faltered.

Qennto didn't miss any of it. His eyes narrowed, flicking to Maris, then Car'das, then back to Maris, and finally to the two Chiss.

"They appear able to access some unknown energy field," Thrawn continued to his brother. If he'd caught the interplay, he didn't show it. "It can be used for sensory enhancement, insight into others' motivations and thoughts, or as a direct weapon."

"But only for defense," Maris put in. "Jedi never attack first."

"You talking about Jedi?" Qennto put in. "Car'das? Did she say *Jedi*?"

"She's trying to describe the Jedi for him," Car'das said. "The Chiss apparently don't have anything like them."

"Good," Qennto grunted. "At least we top them in *something*. So what's she saying?"

"They were just talking about Jedi powers," Car'das said, looking at the two Chiss. Thrawn's face was expressionless, while Thrass was clearly annoyed with this side conversation in a language he didn't understand. "But we can talk about this later," he added.

"Yeah," Qennto said. "Sure."

They finished the rest of the tour and returned to the base. Car'das still couldn't tell what Thrass thought of it all, but he found himself wilting with relief as he and the others were released to go back to their quarters. He'd half expected the syndic to order them all into the brig.

The relief was premature. Even as he started to pass Qennto and Maris's quarters and head toward his own, Qennto took his arm and hauled him bodily through the door. "What—?"

"Shut up," Qennto said, pulling him the rest of the way through and letting the door close behind him. Giving him a shove toward Maris, he put his back to the door and folded his arms defiantly across his chest. "Okay," he said. "Let's hear it."

"Let's hear what?" Car'das asked, his heartbeat starting to pound again.

"The story about you and Maris and Thrawn," Qennto said coldly. "Specifically, these private chats he and Maris have been having."

Car'das caught his breath, and instantly cursed himself for his reaction. If Qennto had requested a guilty reaction in writing, he could hardly have delivered him a better one. "What do you mean?" he asked, stalling for time.

"Don't you mean, how do I know?" Qennto snorted. "What, you think that just because I don't come to your little language school I've just been sitting around staring at the walls?" He nodded at the computer across the room. "Maris was kind enough to let me watch her set up the pathway to the vocabulary lists."

Car'das felt his stomach tighten. "So you understand Cheunh?"

"I understand enough of it." Qennto looked at Maris. "I also know how to read women."

"You don't understand," Maris said, her voice low and soothing.

"Fine," he said. "Explain it to me."

She took a deep breath. "I admire Commander Thrawn," she said. Her voice was still soothing, but Car'das could hear cracks starting to form in it. She knew Qennto's temper even better than he did. "He's intelligent and noble, with an artistic sensitivity I haven't seen since I left school."

Qennto snorted. "You mean since you left those shallow needle-headed idiots you used to hang out with?"

"Yes, most of them *were* idiots," she agreed without embarrassment. "Comes of being young, I suppose."

"But Thrawn is different?"

"Thrawn is a grown-up version," she said. "His artistic sense is coupled with maturity and wisdom. I enjoy spending time talking with him." Her eyes flashed. "*Just* talking with him, if that matters."

"Not really," Qennto growled. But as Car'das watched some of the tension go out of him, he could tell that it did. "So if these meetings are so innocent, why have you been hiding them?"

A muscle in Maris's cheek twitched. "Because I knew you'd react exactly like this."

"And this secrecy was all your idea, huh?"

She hesitated. "Actually, I believe Thrawn suggested it."

Qennto grunted. "Thought so."

"And what's *that* supposed to mean?" Maris asked, her eyes narrowing ominously.

"It means he's playing you for a fool," Qennto said bluntly. "I may not be cultured or artistic, but I've been around a little. I know his type, and he's not what he seems. They never are."

"Maybe he's the exception."

"You can believe that if you want," Qennto said. "I'm just telling you that somewhere along the line this little pyramid of cards you've build around him is going to fall apart. Bet on it."

"I will," she said, her eyes blazing openly now. "You be sure to point it out when it happens." Turning her back on him, she stalked over to the computer and dropped into the chair.

Qennto watched her go, then turned to Car'das. "You have anything to say?" he challenged.

"No," Car'das said quickly. "Nothing."

"Then get out," Qennto said, moving away from the door. "And remember what I said. Don't you trust him, either."

"Sure." Sidling carefully past him, Car'das escaped out into the corridor and back to his quarters.

Through the row of viewports on the bridge of the Trade Federation battleship *Darkvenge* the starlines faded once again into stars. "We have arrived," Vicelord Kav announced from his throne-like command chair.

"Mm," Doriana murmured noncommittally from his seat on the observers' couch curving out beside the other. In general, the Neimoidians had excellent navigational systems. But systems were only as good as their operators, and in the *Darkvenge*'s case that was open to question. Sidious had insisted the crews of all the task force's ships be kept to a bare minimum, retaining only those who could be trusted to keep their mouths closed and bringing in droids to take up the slack.

More than once, Doriana had wondered whether Sidious's ultimate plan was to kill any survivors of the mission to make doubly sure that none of this ever leaked out. If so, the low crew numbers would certainly make that easier.

"Your concerns are needless," Kav said haughtily, completely missing the direction Doriana's thoughts had taken. "We are double-checking the location now."

"Thank you," Doriana said, inclining his head politely. The skeleton crew would not, of course, affect their attack capabilities to any great degree. That would be handled by droid starfighters, and that system was largely automated.

He looked around the bridge at the Neimoidians and droids working busily in the various sunken control pits, then turned his attention to the tactical board. The task force was arranging itself into a typical Neimoidian defense structure: the two huge Trade Federation split-ring battleships in the center where they would be best protected, the six armed Techno Union *Hardcell*-class transports forming a pyramid-point defensive shell around them, and the seven Trade Federation escort cruisers arrayed in a patrol cloud beyond that.

It was an awesome collection of firepower, possibly the largest assembled in one place since the fiasco at Naboo. Against even the weaponry of six brand-new Dreadnaughts, they should have no trouble carrying the day.

Assuming, of course, that Kav's navigators had indeed brought them to the right part of the right system. If they missed Outbound Flight here, they would have to hurry another six hundred light-years ahead in order to catch it at its second navigational stop.

"Our position is confirmed," Kav said with satisfaction. His nictitating membranes blinked at Doriana. "*If* the coordinates you have brought us are correct."

"They are," Doriana said. "If Outbound Flight is on schedule, they'll arrive in a little over eleven days. Until then, we'll run training exercises to make sure your people and equipment will be ready."

"They are more than ready," Kav insisted stiffly. "The combat programs for the droid starfighters are the very best, and between our two battleships we have nearly three thousand of them. No matter how strong Outbound Flight's defenses, no matter how skilled their gunners, we will destroy them with ease."

That's what you said at Naboo. With an effort, Doriana kept the comment to himself. "I'm sure you're right," he said instead. "We'll still spend the next few days running my drills."

Kav made a noise deep in his chest. "As you wish," he said with strained patience. "But the extra expenditure of fuel and energy will be upon your responsibility. When do you wish to begin?"

Doriana looked out at the stars. "There's no time like the present," he said. "We launch starfighters in ten minutes."

"And this," C'baoth said as he led the way into the unusually low-ceilinged room, "is the control room for Weapons Blister Number One. You'll notice the ceiling is low, to make extra room for the turbolaser charging equipment above us."

"Lucky we don't have any Gungans aboard," Obi-Wan commented, ducking his head a little as he stepped in. The room was equipped with a large wraparound control board in the center, with auxiliary and support consoles along the walls. From the number of chairs arranged at the various stations, it looked like the normal complement would be fifteen people, including the three actual gunners.

"Gungans wouldn't have been allowed anywhere near these

stations even if there were any aboard," C'baoth said flatly. "Weapons specialists need far more sophistication and intelligence than that."

"In my experience, those two don't necessarily go together," Obi-Wan commented. "And there are four of these blisters on each Dreadnaught?"

"Correct," C'baoth said, crossing to the main firing console and resting his hand on the headrest of one of the chairs. "Come and sit down, Master Skywalker."

Anakin glanced at Obi-Wan, then walked over and lowered himself gingerly into the seat. "Looks complicated," he commented.

"Not really," C'baoth said, pointing over his shoulder at the various sections of the board. "Here are the actual firing controls. Note that you can aim and fire both the forward and aft turbolasers from here as well as your own starboard-side weaponry. Over here is the sensor-lock monitor; this is the secondary fire control; this is the weapons status board; this is the comm; this is the tactical display system. All quite straightforward."

"Still pretty complicated," Anakin said. "I'll bet I could design a better layout."

"I'm sure you could," C'baoth said, throwing Obi-Wan an amused smile. "Unfortunately, Rendili StarDrive didn't think to consult any Jedi during production. Still, you'll learn it quickly enough. We'll start with an overall tutorial and then a simple simulation. You access both over here—"

"Wait a minute," Obi-Wan said, frowning as he stepped to Anakin's other side. "What are you doing?"

"I'm teaching Master Skywalker how to handle Dreadnaught-One's weaponry, of course," C'baoth said.

"Doesn't Captain Pakmillu already have experienced crewers for that job?"

"Experience is not always the most important aspect of combat," C'baoth pointed out. "Timing and coordination are also key, and no amount of experience can give ordinary gunners the edge that we already possess. Tell me, Master Skywalker, has Master Kenobi ever spoken to you of the Jedi meld?"

"I don't think so," Anakin said. "What does it do?"

"It permits a group of Jedi to connect their minds so closely as to act as a single person," C'baoth told him.

"It can also be very dangerous," Obi-Wan warned. "It takes a Jedi Master of great power and depth in the Force to create such a state without killing or destroying the minds of everyone involved."

"A Jedi Master such as myself," C'baoth said calmly. "I've successfully performed such a meld on four separate occasions."

Obi-Wan stared at him. *"Four?"*

"Three were training exercises, of course," C'baoth conceded. "But the fourth was under serious field conditions, with five other Jedi in the meld. As you can see, we came through it successfully."

"That was with six of you," Obi-Wan pointed out. "There are nineteen of us aboard Outbound Flight."

"Twenty, including Master Skywalker," C'baoth corrected, laying a hand on Anakin's shoulder. "Certainly we'll need to proceed with caution. I'll be discussing the procedure with each of my Jedi, and we'll be carrying out a number of practice sessions before we leave Republic space. Still, once we're all comfortable with the technique, we'll become an awesome fighting force indeed. With Jedi working as one at the weapons systems of all six Dreadnaughts, Outbound Flight will be virtually unbeatable."

Obi-Wan looked down at Anakin. The boy was taking in all of this eagerly, with apparently no qualms whatsoever. "I don't know, Master C'baoth. Weapons control, large-scale combat—that's not the Jedi way."

"It will be," C'baoth said grimly, his eyes taking on a faraway look. "The time is coming when all Jedi will be forced to take up arms against a great threat to the Republic. I have foreseen it."

Obi-Wan felt a shiver tingle his spine. C'baoth always seemed so proud and confident, often to the point of arrogance. But there was something dark and uncertain in the other's sense now, something almost fearful. "Have you told Master Yoda about this?" he asked.

C'baoth's eyes came back to focus and he snorted. "Master Yoda keeps his own counsel, and listens to no other," he said with a touch of scorn. "But why do you think I worked so hard to bring Outbound Flight to fruition? Why do you think I was so insistent that as many Jedi as possible should accompany us?" He shook his head. "Dark days are coming, Master Kenobi. It may be that we of Outbound Flight will be all who will be left to breathe life back into the ashes of the universe we once knew."

"Perhaps," Obi-Wan said. "But the future is never certain, and each of us has the power to affect what is to be." He looked at Anakin again. "Sometimes without even knowing what it is we do."

"I agree," C'baoth said. "Outbound Flight is *my* way of affecting the future. And now, young Skywalker—"

He broke off as the comlink at his belt gave an insistent twitter. "One moment," he said, pulling it free and clicking it on. "Jedi Master C'baoth."

The voice on the other end was too faint for Obi-Wan to

make out the words, but he could hear the urgency in the tone. He could also see the exasperation settling into C'baoth's face. "Keep them both there," he ordered. "I'm on my way."

Shutting off the comlink, he reached over and tapped a pair of switches on the board. "Here's the tutorial," he told Anakin. "Start learning where everything is and how it works." He threw Obi-Wan a hard look. "Stay here, Master Kenobi. I'll be back shortly."

With his robes billowing behind him, he left the room. "Master?" Anakin asked tentatively.

"Yes, go ahead," Obi-Wan confirmed. Setting his jaw, he headed after C'baoth.

The other had already made good progress down the corridor, striding along with his usual indifference toward those who had to scramble to get out of his way. Obi-Wan followed at a discreet distance, trying not to run over anyone himself.

A few minutes later, they arrived at a knot of people gathered in the middle of the corridor. "Move aside," C'baoth ordered.

The crowd opened, and Obi-Wan saw a man half lying, half sitting against the corridor wall, his face twisted with silent pain as he gripped his right shoulder. A few paces away a second man stood beside one of Dreadnaught-1's single-seat speeders, his hands working nervously at his sides. "What happened?" C'baoth demanded, kneeling beside the injured man.

"He ran right into me," the man said, his face twisting even more with the effort of talking. "Rammed right into my shoulder."

"He jumped in front of me," the man by the speeder protested. "I couldn't stop in time."

"If you hadn't been riding so *fast*—"

"Enough." C'baoth ran his hands gently across the other's injured shoulder. "It's merely a dislocation." His hand twitched as he stretched out to the Force—

"Aaahhh!" the man gasped, his whole body surging violently before sagging back against the wall. "Aahh," he breathed more quietly.

C'baoth straightened up and picked two people out of the crowd with his eyes. "You and you: accompany him to the mid-line medcenter."

"Yes, Master C'baoth," one of them said. Crouching beside the injured man, they helped him to his feet.

"As for you," C'baoth continued, turning toward the speeder's driver as the others made their way out of the crowd, "you were clearly driving recklessly."

"But I wasn't," the other protested. "It's not my fault. These things are set at way too high a speed."

"Really?" C'baoth said coolly. "Then how do you explain that in twelve days, among nearly two hundred speeders and swoops aboard six Dreadnaughts, this is the first accident that's happened? I've ridden them four times myself without any problems."

"You're a Jedi," the man said sourly. "You never have problems like that."

"That is as it may be," C'baoth said. "Nevertheless, for your role in this accident, you are hereby docked one day's pay."

The man's eyes widened. "I'm *what*? But that's—"

"You are also forbidden to use Outbound Flight's speeder system for one week," C'baoth interrupted.

"Now, wait a frizzing minute," the man said, consternation starting to edge into his shock. "You can't do that."

"I just did," C'baoth said calmly. He looked around the

crowd, as if daring anyone to argue the point, then brought his eyes to rest on a Rodian in a maintenance jumpsuit. "You: take this speeder back to its parking area. The rest of you, return to your jobs."

Reluctantly, Obi-Wan thought, the crowd began to disperse. C'baoth waited long enough to see the Rodian ride away with the speeder, then turned and headed back the way he'd come, his mouth twitching as he spotted Obi-Wan. "I told you to remain with Padawan Skywalker," he said as he approached.

"I know." Obi-Wan gestured toward the dissipating crowd. "What exactly was that?"

"It was justice," C'baoth said, passing Obi-Wan without breaking stride.

"Without a hearing?" Obi-Wan asked, hurrying to catch up with him. "Without even an investigation?"

"Of course there was an investigation," C'baoth said. "You were there; you heard it."

"A couple of questions to the participants hardly qualifies as an investigation," Obi-Wan said stiffly. "What about a call for witnesses, or an examination of the speeder itself?"

"What about the Force?" C'baoth countered. "Don't we as Jedi have an insight that permits us to make these decisions more quickly than others?"

"In theory, perhaps," Obi-Wan said. "But that doesn't mean we should ignore the other resources available to us."

"And what would you do with these resources?" C'baoth asked. "Impanel a committee and spend hours in interviews and examinations? Do you think expending all that time and effort would lead to a different outcome?"

"Probably not," Obi-Wan had to admit. "But you passed judgment without even consulting the captain or ship's law."

"Bah," C'baoth snorted, waving a hand in dismissal. "A pittance of money in punishment, plus a temporary and perfectly reasonable restriction on his movements. Would you really have me waste Captain Pakmillu's time—and my own—with something so trivial?"

"The captain still needs to be informed."

"He will be," C'baoth promised, eyeing him thoughtfully. "Your attitude surprises me, Master Kenobi. Isn't this sort of mediation and conflict resolution precisely the sort of thing Jedi throughout the Republic do every day?"

Obi-Wan glared at the corridor ahead. "Usually one party or the other specifically asks for Jedi assistance. Here, neither of them did."

"Yet is not a Jedi who sees such a problem honor-bound to lend his aid?" C'baoth pointed out. "But now to more important things. Your Padawan should have finished with the tutorial by now. Let us see how quickly he takes to this form of combat."

Car'das started awake to find a pair of glowing red eyes hovering above him in the darkness. "Who is it?" he asked anxiously.

"Thrawn," the commander's voice came back. "Get dressed."

"What's happened?" Car'das asked as he pushed off the blanket and swung his legs over the edge of the bed.

"One of my scouts has reported a group of unidentified vessels in the area," Thrawn said. "Quickly, now—we leave in thirty minutes."

Forty-five minutes later, the *Springhawk* cleared the asteroid tunnel and made the jump to lightspeed.

And not just the *Springhawk*. Before they made the jump Car'das counted no fewer than eleven other ships forming up around and behind them, including two more *Springhawk*-size cruisers. "Is this more Vagaari?" he asked as the starlines melted into the hyperspace sky.

"It doesn't appear to be," Thrawn said. "The ship designs

are entirely different. I wanted you aboard to see if you can identify them."

"You might have done better to bring Qennto instead," Car'das warned. "He's a lot more knowledgeable about those things than I am."

"I thought it best to leave both him and Ferasi behind," Thrawn said. "I've sensed certain . . . problems there."

Car'das winced. "You're right," he had to admit. "So where exactly are these invaders?"

"Why do you call them invaders?"

"Well, I—" Car'das floundered. "I just assumed they were in Chiss space, after that talk you had with your brother." He frowned. "They *are* in Chiss space, aren't they?"

"The charter of the Expansionary Defense Fleet is to observe and explore the region around the Chiss Ascendancy," Thrawn said. "That's all we intend to do today."

Which was pretty much exactly what he'd said about the Vagaari attack. Terrific. "How long until we get there?"

"Approximately four hours," Thrawn said. "In the meantime, I've had a combat suit prepared for you, one with more armoring and self-sealant capabilities than your suit from the *Bargain Hunter.* Go below and put it on. The armorer will assist you."

It took Car'das and the armorer most of the first three hours to get the suit fitted correctly, with the fourth hour spent in checking him out on its features. Once that was finished, though, he found the suit quite comfortable to wear, though noticeably heavier than the simple vac suits he was used to.

He returned to the bridge to find that in his absence Thrawn and the rest of the bridge crew had also donned their combat suits. "Welcome back," the commander greeted him, running an eye over his suit. "We're nearly there."

Car'das nodded and moved to his usual place beside the other's command chair. Listening to the clipped comments of the bridge crew, he let his eyes roam the displays and status boards and waited. The time count went to zero, and they were once again back among the stars.

"Where are they?" he asked, peering through the viewports at the stars and a very distant sun.

"There," Thrawn said, pointing a few degrees off the starboard bow. "Sensors: magnify." The main display rippled and steadied . . .

Car'das caught his breath, his chest suddenly squeezing tightly against his heart. In the center of the display was a horrible, terrifying, impossible sight: a pair of Trade Federation battleships.

"You recognize them?"

For a moment Thrawn's question didn't register. Car'das continued to stare at the image, his eyes tracing along the curved split-ring configuration of the ships and up the antenna towers that distinguished Trade Federation battleships from simple freighters. Then his brain seemed to catch, and he tore his eyes away from the sight.

To find the commander gazing up at him, a hard and knowing expression on his face . . . and once again, Car'das knew it would be fatal to lie. "Yes, I do," he said, marveling at how calm his voice sounded. "They're battleships from a group called the Trade Federation."

"Members of your Republic?"

Car'das hesitated. "Technically speaking, yes," he said. "But these days they seem to be largely ignoring our laws and directives." He forced himself to meet Thrawn's gaze. "But you already knew where they were from, didn't you?"

"The hull markings follow a similar pattern to those on the *Bargain Hunter*," Thrawn said. "I thought there was a reasonable chance they were from your Republic."

"But they don't represent the Republic itself," Car'das added hastily. "The Republic doesn't have any army of its own."

"So you've told me," Thrawn said, his voice suddenly cold. "You also told me the Republic doesn't condone slavery."

"That's right, we don't," Car'das agreed cautiously.

"Then why did I find evidence of slavery aboard the ship that was pursuing you?"

The rings of tension around Car'das's chest tightened a few more turns. He'd forgotten all about Progga. "I also told you there were some cultures in our area that *do* keep slaves," he said, fighting to keep his voice steady. "The Hutts are one of them."

"And the Trade Federation?"

"No," Car'das said. "Well, not that I've ever heard, anyway. They're so heavily into droids they probably wouldn't know what to do with slaves if they had them." Car'das nodded toward the display. "Which could be a serious problem for us right now. Each of those battleships carries over a thousand droid starfighters, not to mention a few thousand battle droids and the landers and carriers to move them around."

"Then this *is* an invasion force?"

Car'das winced. "I don't know," he said. "I don't think so, not with only two of them."

"But they *could* be here to attack us."

"I don't know why they're here," Car'das insisted, sweat

gathering around his collar. It was one thing to listen to Thrawn talk about preemptive strikes against vicious conquerors like the Vagaari. It was something else entirely to stand here and see him mentally lumping the Trade Federation or even the entire Republic into that same category. "Why don't you ask them?"

A faint smile creased Thrawn's face. "Yes. Why don't we?"

He swiveled around. "Communications: identify their main command frequency and create a channel," he ordered. "These people speak Basic, I presume?"

"Yes," Car'das said, frowning. Surely the commander wasn't going to try something this potentially tricky in a language he'd barely learned, was he? "But they'll also have protocol droids aboard that can translate Sy Bisti."

"Thank you, but I'd prefer to see their reaction when they're hailed in the language of the Republic," Thrawn said.

"Ready, Commander," the comm officer called.

Thrawn tapped a key on his board. "This is Commander Mitth'raw'nuruodo of the Chiss Expansionary Defense Fleet," he said. "Please identify yourselves and state your intentions."

Doriana was still fumbling with his tunic belt as he hurried through the open blast doors onto the bridge. "What's this about an attack?" he asked as he crossed the walkways to where Kav stood in front of his command chair.

"Soothe yourself, Commander Stratis," Kav said. "It is not as serious as was first thought."

"This is Commander Mitth'raw'nuruodo of the Chiss Expansionary Defense Fleet," a voice said from the comm speaker beside the vicelord's chair. "Please identify yourselves and state your intentions."

"He has been repeating that message for ten minutes," Kav said contemptuously. "But then, what else can he do?"

"Explain," Doriana growled. After being hauled out of bed, he was in no mood to put up with Neimoidian smugness. "You can start by telling me who he is."

"How should I know?" Kav said scornfully. "But he is a braggart beyond anything I have yet seen."

He seated himself in his chair and touched a control, and a tactical overlay appeared on the main display. "Behold," he said, waving his long fingers. "He dares to threaten us with three small cruisers and nine fighters. Most likely they are pirates with a sense of bluff as large as a Dug's pride."

The message repeated. "I hear no threat in that message, Vicelord," Doriana pointed out, trying to suppress his growing annoyance. He'd been dragged out of bed for *this*? "All I hear is a local asking what we're doing in his territory."

"The threat is implied, Commander Stratis," Kav countered. "It is built into all warships, as much a part of them as weapons and shields."

Doriana looked at the tactical, then at the corresponding telescope display. Even knowing where the ships were, it was incredibly hard to pick them out of the starfield behind them. Superb stealthing, which meant that Kav was right. They were warships, all right. "Maybe he's got more firepower hanging back in reserve."

"No," Kav assured him. "We have done a complete sensor scan of the entire area. Those twelve ships are all there are."

"This is Commander Mitth'raw'nuruodo—"

"Shall we consider this an unscheduled drill?" Kav added as the message continued to play in the background.

"Let's try talking first," Doriana suggested, sitting down on the couch beside the other. The fact that this Mitth'raw'nuruodo spoke Basic might very well mean he was a pirate with some familiarity with some of the outer reaches of the Republic.

But it could also mean this was a trick by person or persons unknown to smoke out the truth about the *Darkvenge*'s mission. "Open a hailing channel," he ordered.

"Open."

Doriana reached over to Kav's station and keyed the control. "I greet you, Commander Mitth'raw'nuruodo," he said, stumbling a bit over the unusual glottals at the section breaks. "This is Stratis, commanding Special Task Force One."

"My greetings in return, Commander Stratis," Mitth'raw'nuruodo's voice came back. "Please explain to me the purpose of your task force."

"We intend no harm to you or your people," Doriana said. "But I'm afraid the details of our mission must remain confidential."

"I'm afraid in turn that your reassurances are insufficient," Mitth'raw'nuruodo said.

Beside Doriana, Kav muttered something. "I'm sorry, Commander," Doriana said, throwing a warning look at the Neimoidian. "Unfortunately, I'm under orders."

"Why do you waste time this way?" Kav demanded.

Cursing under his breath, Doriana lunged for the mute control. "With all due respect, Vicelord, what do you think you're doing?"

"What do you think *you* are doing?" Kav countered. "They are no more than a parasite fly fluttering against a window. Let us destroy them and be done with it."

"If you don't mind, I'd first like to find out who they are and where they come from," Doriana said, summoning every bit of patience he could muster.

"We can learn that from their charred remains," Kav said, drawing himself up to his full height. "And *you* are not in command of this fleet, Stratis. *I* am."

"Yes, of course," Doriana said, shifting quickly to a more soothing tone.

But it was too late. The vicelord had decided to take offense at the unintentional slight, and had also concluded this was a quick and easy victory ripe for the plucking. With a Neimoidian, that was a bad combination. "The time for talk is over," Kav announced. With a decisive jab of his finger, he cut off the comm channel. "Order the *Keeper* to launch half its droid starfighters," he called across the bridge, gesturing toward the second Trade Federation battleship. "Three groups will attack the intruders, the rest forming a defense screen around the task force. And order a transfer of command; I will control all the starfighters from here."

"Yes, Vicelord," one of the Neimoidians said. "Do we launch our starfighters, as well?"

"We will hold them in reserve." Kav looked at Doriana. "In case they have reinforcements on the way," he added almost grudgingly.

Doriana sighed silently to himself. He would have liked to find out more about this Mitth'raw'nuruodo and his Chiss before they were slaughtered. He could only hope there would be enough wreckage left to examine.

"Here they come," Car'das said, pointing at the display. "Droid starfighters—you see them?"

"Yes, of course," Thrawn said calmly. "All vessels, pull back.

Car'das, you said droids can think and act on their own. Do these droid starfighters also have that capability?"

"I don't think so," Car'das said, trying to unfreeze his mind and think as the *Springhawk* began moving backward. The sight of this many incoming Trade Federation starfighters was enough to rattle anyone. "No, I'm sure they don't. They're remotely controlled in groups from one of the battleships."

"Comm?" Thrawn called. "Have you located and identified their control frequencies?"

"Yes, Commander," the comm officer reported. "The control appears to be secured with a rolling encryption system. I estimate maximum range to be ten thousand *visvia*."

"Pull us back to eleven thousand," Thrawn ordered, turning back to Car'das. "Ten thousand *visvia* is approximately sixteen thousand of your kilometers. Does that sound like the correct operating range?"

Car'das spread his hands helplessly. "I'm sorry, but I don't know."

"No apologies needed," Thrawn assured him. "At any rate, we'll know soon enough."

"Enemy fighters still approaching," one of the crewers warned. "Main group is holding back."

"Interesting," Thrawn said thoughtfully. "The main body appears to be forming a defensive screen around the larger vessels. Considering his numerical advantage, this Commander Stratis seems unusually cautious."

"That's typical of the Neimoidians who build and run these things," Car'das told him, feeling a frown creasing his forehead. Now that he thought about it, though, Stratis's voice had sounded human, not Neimoidian. Could the Trade Federation have started selling or leasing their battleships?

"Attackers pulling back," the sensor officer called. "Re-forming into an outer screen between us and the fleet."

"Apparently, we were correct about the ten-thousand-*visvia* range," Thrawn concluded. "Excellent."

"So what do we do now?" Car'das asked, eyeing the swarming starfighters uneasily.

For a moment Thrawn sat silently, his eyes narrowed as he gazed at the displays. "We try an experiment," he said at last. "*Whirlwind:* move to deployment position. Fighter Four: probe attack, course one-one-five by three-eight-one."

There were two acknowledgments, and Car'das watched as one of the other two *Springhawk*-size ships broke away from the group, heading to starboard, while one of the nine fighters headed off the opposite direction. "What kind of experiment?" he asked.

"With so many fighters to control, I suspect the system designers didn't have room to be overly clever," Thrawn said. "Let's see just how clever they were."

"Incoming!" one of the Neimoidians in the control pits called sharply. "Single fighter, vector zero-four-two by zero-eight-eight."

"The fool," Kav said with a snort. "Does he think us inattentive? Outer group: intercept and destroy."

Doriana watched the displays as the three groups of droid starfighters re-formed from their outer picket screen and swung to intercept the lone alien fighter. But they had barely settled into their attack vector when the intruder broke off, swinging around in a tight curve and hurrying back to the safety of distance. "Return them to patrol," Kav ordered. "Does this Mitthrawdo not realize how badly he is outmatched?"

"Maybe all he wants is to sit back there out of range and watch us," Doriana pointed out. "I don't need to remind you that we can't afford to have witnesses around when Outbound Flight gets here."

"Do you suggest they are Senate spies?"

"Or they might be from the Jedi, or from Palpatine, or from someone else," Doriana said. "All I know is that no one this far from the Republic should be speaking Basic."

"He comes at us again, Vicelord," the Neimoidian at the sensors called. "Same fighter, same vector."

"Same response, then," Kav called back, leaning forward to study the displays. "Perhaps he is trying to judge exactly how far our control extends."

"Be careful," Doriana warned. "If they figure out how to jam the signal, those starfighters will go dormant."

"And will self-destruct a few minutes later," Kav said impatiently. "Thank you, Commander Stratis; I *am* familiar with my own weaponry. See—again he pulls back, no wiser than he was before."

"Unless he's a decoy," Doriana said, searching the other displays. "Don't forget the cruiser that detached itself from the group the same time the fighter did."

"I have not forgotten," Kav assured him. "But that one has merely traveled along our flank, and has made no attempt to attack or move closer."

Doriana shook his head. "He's up to something, Vicelord."

"Whatever it is, it will gain him nothing," Kav said. "Outbound Flight is not due for another nine days. That is more than enough time to choose how we will deal with this annoyance."

On the display the retreating fighter suddenly flipped over and again charged in. "Vicelord—" a Neimoidian began.

"Same response," Kav cut in. But this time there was a note of satisfaction in his voice. "I see now his plan, Commander Stratis. He hopes to drain the starfighters of their fuel and then drive in unopposed. What he does not realize is that I still have all the *Darkvenge*'s starfighters in reserve, plus half of the *Seeker*'s."

"Maybe," Doriana murmured, his vague sense of uneasiness deepening as he watched the same scenario play itself out for a third time. Surely Mitth'raw'nuruodo could come up with something better than to just run the same simple-minded attack over and over.

And always on exactly the same vector. Was he trying to find a weakness in the droid starfighters' attack formation?

Once again the starfighters chased the intruder away. Once again, the alien ship flew out of range and flipped over for another run. The show repeated twice more, and Doriana was just checking the chrono to see how close the starfighters were to their twenty-five-minute fuel time limit when Kav abruptly slammed his fist on the arm of his chair. "I weary of this game," he said. "You—order the *Keeper* to move toward the aliens."

"Careful, Vicelord," Doriana cautioned as the comm operator turned to his board. "Let's not be too quick to split up the fleet."

"I have been more than patient," Kav countered. "It is time to end this. Signal the *Keeper* to advance, and to launch the rest of its starfighters into shield configuration—"

"Hold it," Doriana cut in. Suddenly the scenario had changed. The fighter was again retreating with starfighters in pursuit, but this time the rest of the alien force had leapt forward, driving hard toward the gap that had opened up between them and the main task force.

"And so they make their final mistake," Kav said with satisfaction. "Signal the starfighters to attack." The Neimoidian acknowledged and tapped at his board.

But to Doriana's disbelief the droids didn't respond. Instead, they continued in pursuit of the retreating fighter.

"Order them to attack!" Kav snapped again. "What are you doing? Call them to the attack!"

"They do not respond," the other Neimoidian called back.

"Impossible," Kav insisted. "They cannot possibly be jamming our signal."

"They're not," Doriana said grimly. "If the starfighters weren't getting a signal, they'd have shut down and gone dormant. But they're still flying at full power."

"But they are flying *away* from us. How can this be?" Kav demanded in clear bewilderment.

"Never mind the *how*," Doriana spat. "Here they come."

"I don't believe it," Car'das murmured as he watched the droid starfighters ignore the incoming Chiss ships completely as they headed mindlessly toward deep space. "How did you get them to do *that*?"

"The command signal uses a rolling encryption," Thrawn explained as the *Springhawk* shot forward past the now vanished outer defense screen. "But with so many fighters requiring signals, I knew the rotation would have to be a limited one. It turns out that there are only three separate encryption patterns for this group. I simply recorded the version the droids would be expecting next, then broadcast it to them with enough power to override whatever their masters in the battleship were trying to send."

"But how could you figure out—oh," Car'das interrupted himself as it finally clicked. "With your fighter always going in on the same vector, and the droids' command always the same come-out-of-this-formation-and-attack-the-enemy-on-this-vector code, the only part that ever changed was the encryption pattern itself."

"Which allowed us to isolate the command we wanted and duplicate it," Thrawn confirmed. "The secret to successful analysis, Car'das: whenever possible, reduce matters to a single variable."

Ahead, the nearest starfighters in the inner screen were starting to shift positions, moving from their general defense pattern onto intercept vectors. "I don't think that's going to work on the rest of them, though," Car'das warned. "They're coming from different initial formations, and there are probably entirely different codes and encryptions for them."

"That doesn't matter," Thrawn assured him. "All I needed was to get past the outer group and into closer range." He tapped a key on his board. "All vessels: attack pattern *d'moporai*."

"Here they come," Doriana muttered, his fingers digging tensely into the couch cushion beside him. On the face of it, there was still no way Mitth'raw'nuruodo's pitiful collection of patrol ships could do anything against the combined might of the Trade Federation task force. No way at all.

But the alien commander had just gotten past three groups of droid starfighters without firing a shot, and that was supposed to be impossible, too. Whatever Mitth'raw'nuruodo had in mind for his next trick, Doriana had a strong suspicion he wasn't going to like it.

Yet even through his apprehension, a small detached part of him was looking forward to seeing what that trick would be.

He didn't have long to wait. The incoming aliens were

widening their formation now, sacrificing the protection of overlapping shields to gain extra maneuvering room. Swarms of starfighters from the nearer parts of the defense screen were breaking their own formation in response, sweeping in over a wide, three-dimensional wavefront toward the intruders. The two groups were nearly within laser range of each other . . .

And then each of the alien fighters launched a single missile.

There was a subtle flicker in the indicator lights of the *Darkvenge*'s computer command board as the starfighters' sensor information was collected, compiled, and analyzed, and the proper response formulated. The response was translated into a hundred updated commands, which were then sorted, encrypted, and transmitted back to the primitive droid brains riding in their armored casings. A sliver of a second later the starfighters responded to those commands with a rain of concentrated laserfire that blew all nine missiles into shrapnel. "A foolish waste of effort," Kav commented. "The range was clearly too great for—"

"Hold it," Doriana said, frowning at the displays. There was something still moving along the shattered missiles' lines of flight, filmy spots of nearly invisible haze that seemed to be growing larger as they sped toward the incoming starfighters. "Call them back," he told Kav urgently.

But it was too late. Even as the alien attack formation abruptly came apart, with all eleven ships shooting off in all different directions, the hazy spots intersected their target starfighter groups. There were multiple flashes of subdued light—

"They do not respond!" one of the Neimoidians called from the computer board. "Nine groups of droids have gone silent!"

"Connor nets," Doriana snarled, digging his fingers even harder into the cushion. Nine groups of starfighters, neatly and efficiently knocked out of action.

Out of action, but not out of the fight. Their momentum was still carrying them onward . . . and as he watched in helpless fascination, they slammed squarely into other groups that had shifted their own vectors to chase the dispersing aliens. There were more multiple flashes, this cluster much brighter than the last.

And suddenly the gaping hole in the task force's defensive screen no longer had any starfighters left to fill it. "This is impossible," Kav said, his five-cornered hat bobbing as he swung his head back and forth around the bridge. "How can he *do* this?"

"Get the rest of the starfighters into space," Doriana ground out. *"Now."*

Kav didn't need any prompting. "Order *Keeper* to activate all remaining droid starfighters," he called. "They will launch when ready. And move all those already launched to intercept."

"Wait a minute," Doriana objected. "You can't leave our other flanks unguarded."

"Against what?" Kav retorted. "*This* is the battlefront. If we do not defend it, there will be no other flanks left to guard." He gestured across the bridge. "Obey my order."

"Here they come," Car'das murmured, wondering if Thrawn had finally sliced off more than he could serve. The Chiss had dispatched those first few groups of droid starfighters with relative ease, but tricks like that only worked once against a given opponent.

And now all the rest of those hundreds of starfighters were sweeping around the flanks of the Trade Federation fleet, heading straight toward them.

Unless that was exactly what Thrawn had been waiting for.

Car'das shifted his eyes across the displays, looking for the cruiser that had slipped away from them just before the fighting started. If the main Chiss force was merely a diversion . . .

But the *Whirlwind* wasn't charging in from the side for a sucker-punch attack. It was still sitting quietly in space, apparently being held in reserve.

He looked back at the incoming starfighters. "I hope you've got one Great Father of a shock net up your sleeve," he warned.

"We'll certainly have to consider creating such a device if we begin facing opponents like this on a regular basis," Thrawn said drily. "Tell me, what happens to these droids if their communication signals are cut off?"

"If the—? Are you talking about *jamming*?"

"You disapprove?"

"No, of course not," Car'das said. "But Trade Federation command signals are supposed to be unjammable. They can change frequencies and command patterns instantly—the minute you block off one part of the spectrum they just shift to another."

"And if you block the entire spectrum at once?"

Car'das stared at him. The man was serious. "You can't blanket the whole area, Commander," he ground out between clenched teeth. "It's too big. The minute you start, they'll know what you're doing and send a set of contingency orders to everything outside your jamming. Those droid starfighters may not be smart, but they're certainly capable of downloading enough general commands to keep them functioning until they've pounded us to dust."

"Only if there are any starfighters still outside the jamming," Thrawn pointed out. "But it seems our opponent has taken care of that problem for us." He pointed. "Even as we close the distance, he is converging all his starfighters into this one small area."

Car'das stared at the displays. Thrawn was right—the Trade Federation commander had abandoned the rest of his picket area to bring all his starfighters to the attack. Didn't he realize the possible implications of what he was doing? "What about your own communications?" he asked. "If you jam the whole spectrum, you'll be out of touch with your people, too."

"Fortunately, my warriors are capable of more than simply downloading general commands," Thrawn said. "Let's see which side's battle philosophy proves the more versatile." Leaning forward, he took a deep breath. "Full-spectrum jamming: now."

For a long, horrifying second the *Darkvenge*'s bridge was filled with a screech like something from the restless undead of ancient Coruscant legend. Then the Neimoidian at the comm slapped at the switch, cutting off the wail and leaving only a distant ringing in Doriana's ears. "What in the name of—?"

"Vicelord—we are being jammed!" the Neimoidian called, staring at his board in obvious disbelief. "All starfighters have gone dormant!"

Doriana stared out the viewports, his stomach tightening into a hard knot. The starfighters had indeed locked down, each of them now flying mindlessly in whatever direction it had last been pointed.

And swerving with ease through the drifting obstacle course, blasting away at the helpless starfighters as they went, Mitth'raw'nuruodo's alien ships were headed straight for them, the fighters in screening formation ahead of the two cruisers. "Get our starfighters back online," Kav ordered tautly, jabbing a hand toward the Neimoidians at the command board. "Get them *back*."

"We are trying," one of them called. "We have opened laser communications to as many as we can."

But those comm lasers were line of sight, Doriana knew, and with a sinking feeling he realized that this limitation was growing ever tighter as expanding clouds of dust and debris from the shattered starfighters began to block even this last-gasp communication method. A few of the starfighters were coming back to life, but they were targeted and destroyed by the aliens before they could organize into an effective fighting force. "What about the other ships?" he demanded. "Why aren't they attacking?"

"There!" someone called, and Doriana saw an arm point upward from one of the pits. "The Hardcells have launched their missiles."

"About time," Doriana muttered, feeling a cautious hope rising within him as five clusters of three missiles each shot toward the attackers.

The attackers reacted instantly, five of the fighters abandoning their thrust toward the battleships and curving toward the outside of the Trade Federation formation. The missiles, locking in on the movement, followed. "Good," Kav said with satisfaction. "The next salvo will draw the rest of the fighters away and leave the cruisers undefended. Then our own quad laser batteries can destroy them with ease."

"Maybe," Doriana said cautiously, following the fleeing alien craft with his eyes. They were cutting in and out through the masses of drifting starfighters, clearly trying to throw off the pursuing missiles' homing locks.

But to no avail. Techno Union hardware was among the best in the Republic, and the missiles maneuvered their own way through the clutter with ease as they continued to close the gap. The aliens reached the edge of the starfighter cloud and curved tightly back into it again, driving inward toward the main ships. Again, the missiles matched the maneuver. The fighters straightened out; and then, in near unison, each dropped a small object aft toward its pursuers.

And Doriana stiffened as a well-remembered hazy cloud erupted from each of them, unfolding directly in the path of the incoming missile clusters. "More Connor nets!" he snapped.

But there was nothing the onlookers could do. The nets enveloped the missile clusters and flashed their killing jolts of high-voltage current, destroying homing electronics and drive systems alike and leaving the missiles as dead as the drifting starfighters around them.

Only once again, Mitth'raw'nuruodo hadn't been content to merely protect his own ships from attack. Even as Doriana's hands curled into helpless fists, their inertia sent the missiles slamming into the Techno Union ships. There were multiple blasts as sections of hull metal shattered outward into space—

And then, like a minor sun going off at close range, one of the ships exploded completely.

"What—?" Kav gasped. "No! Not from a single missile cluster. This is impossible!"

"Everything Mitth'raw'nuruodo *does* is impossible," Doriana retorted bitterly. "The missiles must have hit a weak spot."

"What kind? Where could it be?"

Doriana snorted. "Just watch his ships. They'll be targeting the same spot on all the rest of them."

He was right. Within minutes the alien fighters and cruisers had successfully dodged the desperate flurry of missiles the Techno Union ships were now throwing at them and had efficiently destroyed every one of them. The spot, Doriana noted with morbid fascination, was the line junction to the massive external fuel cells.

"We must escape," Kav said, his voice shaking. "Helm—prepare to jump to lightspeed."

"Wait a minute," Doriana protested, grabbing at his arm. The specter of defeat loomed before him, along with the fate of all those who failed Darth Sidious. "You can't just abandon the fleet."

"What fleet?" Kav snarled. "Look around you, Stratis. *What* fleet?"

Doriana felt his throat tighten. He was right, of course. All six of the Techno Union Hardcells were gone, half of them destroyed by their own missiles. The seven escort cruisers, never intended to operate against such enemies without capital ship support, were being systematically hunted down and eliminated. Only the two Trade Federation battleships were still in any condition to fight or run.

But with their communications still blocked, there was no way to order a general retreat. If the *Darkvenge* left, it would be leaving alone.

"Jump calculated," the helmsman called.

"Make the jump," Kav ordered, glaring at Doriana as if daring him to argue. "Do you hear me? *Now.*"

"The hyperdrive does not respond!" the helmsman said, his voice bubbling with sudden panic. "It claims we are too close to a planetary mass."

Doriana twisted around to look at the row of status boards. That was what the readings said, all right.

But there were no planetary masses nearby, or even any sizable asteroids. "Malfunction?"

"No malfunction," Kav murmured, his voice dull and fatalistic. "Merely more Chiss wizardry."

A fresh flicker of light caught Doriana's eye, and he looked back out the viewports. Across the field of carnage, droid starfighters were starting to explode as too many minutes without communication passed and they began to activate their self-destruct mechanisms. Through the scattered bursts of fire, Doriana saw the *Keeper* suddenly lurch as the upper surface of its starboard ring half erupted in a hundred small explosions. "Vicelord!" someone called.

"I know," Kav said with a tired sigh. "The starfighters I ordered prepped are exploding."

Doriana nodded, his own bitterness long since faded into a deep sense of the inevitable. The reinforcements would have been flying through the hangar bays when Mitth'raw'nuruodo's jamming began and they went dormant. Tumbling helplessly at high speed down a curved corridor, they would have slammed into bulkheads or storage racks or other equipment. There they'd lain, tangled and broken, while they waited for their own self-destruct chronos to run down.

"Then it is over," Kav said quietly. Lifting his hands, he carefully removed his five-cornered hat and set it with equal care on the floor in front of him. "We are all dead."

"It would seem so," Doriana agreed mechanically, feeling his forehead creasing as a strange fact suddenly struck him.

With all the death and debris and charred hulks of ships floating all around them, the *Darkvenge* itself had yet to be so much as scratched.

He took another, longer look at the status boards. Except for the inexplicably dormant hyperdrive, everything else seemed perfectly functional. "Or maybe not," he added. "I think Mitth'raw'nuruodo has something else in mind for us."

Kav snorted derisively. "And what precisely gave you that impression?"

Puzzled, Doriana turned back—

To find that one of the alien cruisers had suddenly appeared outside the viewports. It was hovering bare meters away from the transparisteel, its missile racks pointing in to the bridge in silent warning and clear command. "Close down the midline quad laser batteries, Vicelord," Doriana said quietly. "Then seal the main hangar exits and shut down all the droid starfighters." He took a careful breath. "And then," he said, "prepare for company."

The final turbolift door slid open, and twenty meters down the corridor Car'das saw at last the open blast doors of the battleship's bridge.

Twenty meters of corridor lined on both sides with armed, tense-looking battle droids.

Thrawn didn't even hesitate. He strode forward calmly, his two warriors equally sedate as they walked at his sides. Swallowing hard, not wanting to walk that gauntlet but even less willing to cower in the turbolift car all alone, Car'das forced himself to follow.

There were dozens of droids on duty on the bridge, most of them service and monitor units seated or plugged into the various stations in the control pits. Standing in the center of the quiet activity were just two actual beings, waiting together beside the vacant helm chair: a tall Neimoidian in elaborate robes, and a more sedately dressed human male. Again, Thrawn didn't pause, but headed down the walkway toward them. He stopped three meters away, and for a moment seemed to size them up. Then, deliberately, he swiveled to face the human. "Commander Stratis," he said, nodding his head in greeting. "I am Commander Mitth'raw'nuruodo."

"Stratis does not command this vessel," the Neimoidian said stiffly before Stratis could answer. "I am Vicelord Kav of the Trade Federation. And *you,* Commander Mitthrawdo, have committed an act of war."

"Vicelord, please," Stratis said. His voice was calm, but there was a warning edge to it. "Recriminations will serve no useful purpose."

"Do not think you have gained anything with your audacity," Kav continued, ignoring him. "Even now, I could destroy you where you stand."

He gestured, and from behind them came a sudden metallic racket. Car'das spun around, his heart freezing as a pair of droideka destroyer droids rolled into view and came to a halt just inside the bridge blast doors. They unfolded into their tripod stance, and a second later Car'das found himself staring down the barrels of four pairs of high-energy blasters.

"Vicelord, you *fool,*" Stratis bit out urgently. "What do you think—?"

"Calm yourself, Commander," Thrawn soothed him. "We're in no danger."

Carefully, hardly daring to breathe, Car'das turned his head. Stratis's eyes had gone wide, his throat muscles tight as he gripped the Neimoidian's arm. But Thrawn merely stood quietly, his face expressionless as he studied the droidekas. The Chiss warriors had their hands on their weapons, but following their commander's lead hadn't drawn them. "Interesting design," Thrawn went on. "That shimmering sphere—a small force shield?"

"Uh . . . yes," Stratis said cautiously. "I assure you, Commander—"

"Thank you for the demonstration, Vicelord," Thrawn interrupted, turning his glowing red eyes back to Kav. "But now you will send them away."

For a long, terrible moment Car'das thought the Neimoidian was going to defy Thrawn's order the way he'd ignored Stratis's rebuke. The Chiss and Neimoidian locked eyes, and for half a dozen heartbeats the bridge was silent.

And then Kav's entire body seemed to wilt, his eyes dropping away from Thrawn's stare as he half lifted a hand toward the droidekas. Looking back over his shoulder, Car'das watched in relief as the destroyers folded up again and rolled their way off the bridge.

"Thank you," Thrawn said. "Now. As I asked you before: please state your intentions and those of your task force."

"A task force that no longer exists," Kav put in, his voice hovering between anger and dejection.

"That loss was your doing," Thrawn countered. "All I wished was a civilized answer." He turned to Car'das. "Is that correct? *Civilized*?"

"Or just *civil*," Car'das told him, feeling his face warming at being suddenly dragged into the middle of the conversation. "Or *polite*."

"Civil," Thrawn said, as if testing the word against some unknown set of guidelines. "Yes. All I wished, Commander, was a civil answer."

"Yes, I know," Stratis said, his eyes on Car'das. "May I ask your companion's name and origin?"

"I'm just a visitor," Car'das said quickly. The last thing he wanted was for these people to know his name. "That's all."

"Not quite," Thrawn corrected. "Car'das *was* simply a visitor. Now he's my translator." His expression hardened. "And my prisoner."

Car'das felt his mouth drop open, and for the second time in two minutes felt his heart freeze. "I'm *what*?"

"You arrived uninvited in Chiss space," Thrawn reminded him darkly. "Now, less than three months later, an invasion fleet from your people has appeared. Coincidence?"

"I had nothing to do with this," Car'das protested.

"And we're not an invasion fleet," Stratis added.

"Make me believe that," Thrawn said, his voice darkening even further. "Both of you."

Car'das looked at Stratis. Suddenly, in the wink of an eye, this whole side trip had taken on a very bad taste. "Commander?" he entreated.

Stratis's eyes flicked to him, then back to Thrawn, a thoughtful expression suddenly appearing on his face. "Very well," he said, gesturing toward the side of the bridge. "There's an office back there where we'll have more privacy."

Thrawn inclined his head slightly. "Lead the way."

Doriana led them to Kav's command office, his skin prickling with anticipation and the stirrings of fresh hope. An hour ago it had been all over, the mission a failure, Doriana himself among the walking dead. Even if their attackers allowed them to return to the Republic, he knew the payment Darth Sidious would demand for his failure.

But now, suddenly, all that had changed. Maybe.

"Please make yourselves comfortable," Doriana invited, gesturing his guests to seats facing the desk as he circled around the massive carved-wood structure and sat down in Kav's equally elaborate chair. Out of the corner of his eye he saw the vicelord glowering at him, but he had no time now for petty Neimoidian pride. "May I offer you some refreshment?"

"No thank you," Mitth'raw'nuruodo said as he and Car'das sat down. The two Chiss guards, as Doriana had expected, remained standing in the doorway where they could watch everyone in the room as well as keep an eye on what might be happening on the bridge proper.

"All right," Doriana said, focusing his full intellect on the task at hand. This was it. "Let me tell you about a project called Outbound Flight."

He started at the beginning, describing the project's origin and its mission and making sure to emphasize the Dreadnaughts' size and weaponry. "Interesting," Mitth'raw'nuruodo said when he'd finished. "What does this have to do with us?"

"The fact that Outbound Flight is a danger to both the Republic and your own people," Doriana told him. "You remember my mentioning a group aboard called the Jedi? These are beings of great power, but who are also dangerous troublemakers."

"In what way?"

"They have very rigid ideas of how people should act and what they should think and do," Doriana said, watching Car'das out of the corner of his eye. This would have been easier without the presence of someone who actually knew something about Jedi, but Mitth'raw'nuruodo would have been instantly suspicious if Doriana had asked that the young man be left out of the conversation. Now he was going to have to walk a narrow line between making the Jedi look dangerous to Mitth'raw'nuruodo and at the same time not saying anything Car'das would know was an outright lie.

And Car'das did indeed seem a bit surprised by Doriana's assertions. But at the same time, he could also see a growing uncertainty in the young man's face. The Jedi's arrogance, coupled with their inability to do anything about the growing chaos and stagnation, had people all across the Republic wondering if perhaps their alleged guardians of the peace were more noise and bluster than genuine effectiveness. "They feel they have all the answers," he continued, "and that everyone else should submit to their concept of justice."

"Yet you say they are traveling to another galaxy," Mitth'raw'nuruodo reminded him. "Again, how then does this affect the Chiss?"

"Because before they leave they intend to explore some of the unknown parts of our own galaxy," Doriana said, wishing the Chiss were as easy to read as Car'das. So far, he didn't have a clue as to what kind of impression this was making on him. "If they arrive in Chiss space, they'll certainly attempt to impose their will upon your people."

"*Attempt* is the correct word," Mitth'raw'nuruodo said, his face hardening. "The Chiss do not simply accept alien concepts without careful consideration. We *certainly* do not submit to domination. By anyone."

"Of course not," Doriana said, his cautious hope glowing a little brighter. So species and professional pride were the hooks into Mitth'raw'nuruodo's heart. Excellent. "But I warn you not to underestimate them. The Jedi are ruthless and subtle, and I daresay their power is beyond anything you've ever encountered."

"You may be surprised at what we've encountered," Mitth'raw'nuruodo said, his voice grim. Abruptly, he stood up. "But we will discuss such matters later. Right now, there is other business that requires my attention."

"Of course," Doriana said, rising to his feet as well. "What do you wish us to do in your absence?"

"For the present, you will both remain on this bridge," Mitth'raw'nuruodo said. "I will send for you when I wish to see you again. In the meantime I will send aboard a team to examine your vessel and its equipment."

"Never!" Kav snapped. "This ship is the property of the Trade Federation—"

"Quiet," Doriana cut him off, glaring at him. Didn't the fool understand *anything*? "We will, of course, render any and all assistance they may require."

"Thank you," Mitth'raw'nuruodo said. "They will have new orders for you when they are finished. You will obey those orders."

Doriana nodded. "As you wish."

Mitth'raw'nuruodo looked at Kav, and Doriana could sense the tension between them. But the Neimoidian remained silent, and after a moment Mitth'raw'nuruodo turned to Car'das. "Come."

They left the room, the Chiss guards falling into step behind them. Doriana watched until they had disappeared through the bridge blast doors, then turned to Kav. "With all due respect, Vicelord, what in the name of your grub mother do you think you're doing?"

"That is *my* question for *you,*" Kav countered. "Do you simply turn your back downward and give over our lives and property to this primitive backworld alien?"

"Look around you, Vicelord," Doriana said grimly. "This primitive alien just wrecked our entire task force. And unless I missed it, he didn't lose a single ship of his own in the process."

"And you wish to make him even stronger by offering him access to Trade Federation secrets?"

Doriana took a deep breath. "Listen to me," he said, enunciating his words carefully. It was as if he were back on Barlok, trying to walk those idiot Brolfi through a simple assassination scheme. "We've failed our mission. Even if Mitth'raw'nuruodo turned tail right now and left us in peace, there's no way in the universe our single battleship could take on Outbound Flight's six Dreadnaughts. We would have no choice but to return to the Republic and face Darth Sidious's anger . . . and I can *assure* you that you would wish you had died today, torn apart in agony by the Chiss fighters." He lifted a finger. *"Unless."*

He let the word hang in the air. "Unless?" Kav asked, his voice subdued.

"Unless," Doriana said, "we can persuade Mitth'raw'nuruodo to destroy Outbound Flight for us."

For a long minute the room was silent. "I see," Kav said at last. "Do you think you can do that? And if you can, do you think *he* can achieve that victory?"

"I don't know," Doriana had to admit. "He's no fool, and he surely knows my description of Outbound Flight and the Jedi was horribly slanted. Odds are he cut off the talks so he could go off and get Car'das's take on the whole thing."

"But why would he listen to a human he believes to be a spy?" Kav objected.

"He doesn't," Doriana said, smiling tightly. "If he did, he certainly wouldn't have said so right in front of the man. I think he just wants us to believe that so that we *won't* think he'll listen to Car'das advice."

Kav shook his head. "This is too complicated for me."

"Yes, I know," Doriana said. "That's why you have to leave everything to me. *Everything.*"

Kav rumbled something under his breath. "Very well," he growled. "For now. But I *will* be watching you."

"You do that," Doriana said. "Just keep in mind that your life is worth a lot more than your pride."

"Perhaps," Kav said. "But you say Mitthrawdo does not believe your warnings about the Jedi. How then will you convince him to destroy Outbound Flight?"

"I have more in my persuasive arsenal than just lies about the Jedi," Doriana said. "Trust me."

"Very well." Kav inclined his head. "For now."

Car'das had been sitting alone at the computer desk in his *Springhawk* quarters for three hours, struggling through pages and pages of technical Cheunh text and scans, when Thrawn finally arrived.

"My apologies for my long absence," the commander said as the door slid shut behind him. "I trust you've kept yourself occupied?"

"I've been studying the tech teams' reports as you requested," Car'das said stiffly, turning back to the computer. It was rude, he knew, but he wasn't in a very hospitable mood right now.

"And?"

"And what?"

"Your assessment of the Trade Federation's capabilities?" Thrawn asked patiently.

Car'das sighed, feeling like a ship with a misfiring gyro. Right before the battle Thrawn had accused him of lying about widespread Republic slavery; and then, right *after* the battle, he'd accused him of being a spy for the Federation. Now he wanted a military assessment from him? "Those droid starfighters are top-line weapons," he growled. "I read a report a few months ago speculating that the only reason they didn't completely wipe out their attackers at Naboo was that having to control all those ground troops at the same time overloaded the computer systems and made the starfighter control more sluggish than it should have been. Here, they weren't running any ground troops. In my humble civilian's opinion, if you hadn't knocked out their communications the way you did, they'd have cut us to ribbons."

"Agreed," Thrawn said. "Fortunately, Expansionary Fleet vessels are equipped with more powerful transmitters than those of the regular Defense Fleet forces, since we seldom have a normal colony system's network of boosters and repeaters to draw on. What about Vicelord Kav and Commander Stratis personally?"

"Why are you even asking me this?" Car'das demanded, giving up and swiveling around to face him. "I thought you didn't trust me."

Thrawn shook his head. "Not at all," he said. "If you and your companions were spies, you'd have used your access to the base's computer to study our technology and learn the locations of our worlds. Instead, you've merely worked on improving your language skills. May I sit down?"

"Yes, of course," Car'das said, scrambling out of his chair and extending a hand. Preoccupied with his own uncertainty and bruised pride, he hadn't even noticed the utter weariness in Thrawn's face and posture. "Are you all right?"

"I'm fine," Thrawn assured him, waving off the proffered hand as he stepped over to the bunk and sank down onto it. "It's simply been a very long day."

"You look more than just tired," Car'das commented, peering at him closely. "Is something wrong?"

"Nothing serious," Thrawn said. "I just received word that Admiral Ar'alani is on her way back."

Car'das frowned. It had been barely five weeks since Ar'alani had taken the captured freighter away with her. "They're finished studying the Vagaari ship already?"

"I believe she's cut short her role in the examination," Thrawn said. "That was why I made a point of accusing you of espionage in front of my warriors. After today's events she will undoubtedly be questioning them, and I wished to have a plausible reason on record as to why you and the others were still in Chiss space. My apologies for any distress that may have caused you."

"Don't worry about it," Car'das said, frowning. "You think Ar'alani's suspicious of you?"

"I have no doubt," Thrawn said. "Particularly given the reports she's been receiving from Crustai."

"But who at your base would have—" Car'das broke off as a horrible thought struck him. "*Thrass*? Your *brother*?"

"Who else would have felt it necessary to keep her informed?"

"Are you saying your own *brother* is trying to sink you?" Car'das demanded, still not believing it.

"My brother cares deeply about his blood family, including me," Thrawn said, his voice tinged with sadness. "But he's disturbed by what he sees as my self-destructive behavior . . . and as a syndic of the Eighth Ruling Family, his duty is to protect that family's honor and position."

"So he calls an *admiral* down on you?"

"If Admiral Ar'alani is here to reverse my orders, I'll be unable to do anything that will lead to further trouble," Thrawn pointed out. "Or so he reasons. With a single course of action he thus protects both me and the Eighth Family."

Car'das thought about the Vagaari attack they'd witnessed, and the people pinned helplessly under fire in their hull bubbles. "And meanwhile, people like the Vagaari will be free to go their way."

"Indeed." Thrawn pressed the palm of his hand against his forehead. "Still, until the admiral arrives, command remains mine. What's your impression of Vicelord Kav and Commander Stratis?"

With an effort, Car'das dragged his mind away from the images of the Vagaari's living shields. "For starters, I don't think Stratis is really in command. I just can't see the Neimoidians handing their own ships over to a human that way."

"Unless the human is somehow higher in authority than they are," Thrawn pointed out. "Or if the human is an agent for such a person. *Stratis* itself is of course an assumed name."

"Could be," Car'das agreed. "I *do* think that they're telling the truth about not being an invasion force, though. Even if their storage rings are packed to the shock webbing with battle droids, they can't possibly have enough for a planetary occupation."

"Then you conclude their mission is indeed to ambush this Outbound Flight?"

"I might, if I knew what Outbound Flight was," Car'das said. "But I've never heard of it, and I don't necessarily trust Stratis's opinions."

Thrawn nodded. "Perhaps Qennto or Ferasi will have more information."

"Maybe," Car'das said. "We're heading back to Crustai, then?"

"I need to be there to welcome Admiral Ar'alani," Thrawn reminded him. "My people here can finish the examination without us."

"What if Kav and Stratis decide to kill all of them and make a run for it?"

"They won't," Thrawn assured him. "First of all, they can't simply jump to hyperspace, no matter how much the vicelord might like to. Not with the *Whirlwind* pinning them in place."

"Ah-*ha*," Car'das said, his face warming with embarrassment. With everything else that had happened, he'd completely forgotten the cruiser Thrawn had sent off to the side before the battle began. Apparently, the Chiss techs had figured out a way to tuck the Vagaari grav projector inside a ship's hull.

"But even if they could escape, I don't think they would," Thrawn continued. "Stratis very much wants me to destroy Outbound Flight for him."

Car'das felt his eyes widen. "Is *that* where this is going?"

"What did you think all that talk of weaponry and dangerous Jedi was all about?" Thrawn countered.

"I just—I mean, I thought he was trying to get you to let them go," Car'das said, stumbling over his own tongue. "You aren't thinking—?"

"I will do whatever necessary to protect those who depend on me," Thrawn said, his voice carefully precise. "No more. But no less."

He stood up. "But that isn't your concern," he said. "Once again, I thank you for your assistance."

"No problem," Car'das said, standing up as well. Was it his imagination, or had the commander staggered slightly as he got back to his feet? "You'd better get some rest. It won't be fun for anyone if you collapse from exhaustion before Ar'alani even has a chance to throw you in the brig."

"Thank you for your concern," Thrawn said drily. "I'll try not to disappoint her."

"One last question, if I may," Car'das added as the commander stepped to the door. "How were you so sure that those droidekas wouldn't gun us down?"

"Those—? Oh, the rolling droid fighters," Thrawn said. "It wasn't difficult. Everything about the bridge design spoke of a people who would never willingly put themselves at more risk than absolutely necessary."

"That's Neimoidians, all right," Car'das agreed. "You could get that just from the bridge design?"

"Architecture is merely another form of art," Thrawn reminded him. "But even without those indications, the triple blast doors we passed through would have told me these Neimoidians are not warriors."

"Which is why they have battle droids to fight for them," Car'das said. "But isn't gunning us down exactly what cowards like that would do?"

Thrawn shook his head. "Vicelord Kav was too close to the line of fire. He would never have ordered the droidekas to attack."

Car'das grimaced. "A bluff."

"Or he was making a point," Thrawn said. "These combat droids are a new concept to me, but one worth careful thought." He grimaced. "I sincerely hope the Vagaari haven't visited a world where they might have picked up such weapons."

"Probably not," Car'das said. "The Neimoidians keep them pretty close to home."

"We shall see." Thrawn touched the control, and the door slid open. "Sleep well, Car'das."

For a few minutes Car'das gazed at the closed door. So Thrawn had now assured him that he didn't really suspect him of spying. That was reassuring . . . except that he'd stated exactly the opposite in front of witnesses, and with exactly the same degree of apparent sincerity.

So what *was* the truth? Were he and Qennto and Maris just pawns in some sort of political game? And if so, what was the game?

Maris, Car'das knew, trusted Thrawn's honor. Qennto just as strongly distrusted his alienness and the fact that he was a military officer. Car'das himself no longer knew what to think.

But one thing he knew. Things were heating up out here, and he had the uncomfortable feeling that the *Bargain Hunter*'s crew had overstayed their welcome. Somehow they had to find a way out.

And they had to find it soon.

The first Uliar knew of the trouble was when he rounded the corner to find the other two members of his watch shift standing outside the monitor room door. "What's going on?" he asked as he came up to them.

"Got a special tour going on," Sivv, the senior officer, told him. "Ma'Ning and some sprouts."

"Some *what*?"

"Some of his junior Jedi," Algrann said scornfully. "They swept in ten minutes before Grassling's shift ended and threw everyone out."

"And we're not allowed in?" Uliar asked, not believing it.

Sivv shrugged. "He told Grassling he'd let him know when they could come back in," he said. "I haven't actually asked my-self."

Uliar glowered at the door. Jedi. Again. "Mind if I try?"

Sivv waved a hand. "Help yourself."

Stepping to the door, Uliar slapped the release. It slid open, and he stepped inside.

Jedi Master Ma'Ning was standing to the side of the main board, in the middle of a discussion about how the monitors and control systems worked. His eyes turned questioningly to Uliar as he came in, but he didn't miss a beat of his lecture. Seated at the board itself were four children, the two shortest having to kneel on the seats in order to see.

It was like a scene out of a second-tier classroom, except that this wasn't a scribble board or even a training mock-up. This was the real, actual control system for one of the reactors that kept power flowing to Dreadnaught-4.

Ma'Ning finished the sentence he'd been on and lifted his eyebrows toward Uliar. "Yes, Uliar?" he asked.

"No offense, Master Ma'Ning," Uliar said, coming closer to the others, "but what in blazes are you doing?"

The lines around Ma'Ning's eyes might have tightened a lit-tle. "I'm instructing the young Padawans in the basics of reactor operation."

Uliar took another look at the children. Ages five to eight, he guessed, all of them with the bright eyes and bouncy curiosity of children everywhere.

But there was something more there, he saw now. An under-lying layer of seriousness that was definitely *not* characteristic of children that age. Some Jedi thing? "Much as I appreciate their desire to learn, this is no place for children," he said. "And if I may say so, you're hardly the one to be instructing *anyone* in the subtleties of reactor operation."

"I'm simply giving them an overview," Ma'Ning assured him.

"You shouldn't be giving them *anything*," Uliar countered. "Where high-energy equipment is concerned, a little knowledge is worse than useless, and dangerous on top of it. Whose stupid idea was this, anyway?"

Ma'Ning's lips tightened slightly. "Master C'baoth has decided all Jedi and Padawans need to learn how to control Outbound Flight's critical systems."

Uliar stared at him. "You're joking."

"Not at all," Ma'Ning assured him. "Don't worry, we'll be out of your way in another half hour."

"You'll be out of our way a lot sooner than that," Uliar growled, reaching between two of the children to the comm control. "Bridge; Reactor Control Three. Commander Omano, please."

"One moment."

Uliar looked over at Ma'Ning, wondering if the other would try to stop this. But the Jedi was just standing there, his eyes lowered in a sort of half-meditation look.

"Commander Omano."

"Reactor Tech Four Uliar, Commander," Uliar identified himself. "There are unauthorized personnel in our control room who refuse to leave."

Omano's sigh was a faint hiss in the comm speaker. "Jedi?"

Uliar had the sudden sense of the floor preparing to drop out from beneath him. "One of them is a Jedi, yes," he said carefully. "They're still not authorized to—"

"Unfortunately, they are," Omano cut him off. "Master C'baoth has requested that his people be given full access to all areas and systems aboard Outbound Flight."

Even though he'd suspected what was coming, the words were still like a cold-water slap across the face. "With all due respect, Commander, that's both absurd *and* dangerous," Uliar said. "Having children in the—"

"You have your orders, Tech Uliar," Omano again cut him off. "If you don't like it, you're welcome to take it up with Master C'baoth. Omano out." There was a click, and the comm went dead.

Uliar looked up to find Ma'Ning's eyes on him. "Fine," he said, meeting the Jedi's gaze head-on. If they thought he was going to bow and scrape just because they wore those affected peasant robes and carried lightsabers, they had an extra bonus think coming. "Where do I find Master C'baoth?"

"He's down in the Jedi training center," Ma'Ning said. "Storage core, section one twenty-four."

Uliar stared at him. "Your school's in the *storage core*? What's wrong with the Dreadnaughts?"

Ma'Ning's lip twitched. "Master C'baoth thought it would be best if we were as far away from distractions as possible."

Distractions like parents and family and normal people? Probably. Deep inside him, Uliar's annoyance was starting to turn into a genuine simmering anger. "Fine," he said. "I'll be back."

"Well?" Algrann asked when he emerged into the corridor.

"Omano's knuckled under," Uliar told him tartly. "I'm going to go talk to the Big Clouf himself and see if I can talk some sense into him."

"Captain Pakmillu?"

"Pakmillu doesn't seem to be running the show anymore," Uliar growled. "I'm going to see C'baoth. Either of you want to come along?"

They exchanged glances, and Uliar could almost see them shrinking back behind their faces. "We'd better stay here," Sivv answered. "Whenever Ma'Ning finishes, we *are* supposed to be on duty."

"Sure," Uliar said, feeling his lip twist with contempt. Why did everyone go instantly spineless whenever Jedi were involved? "See you later."

He took a turbolift down to Dreadnaught-4's lowest level, then made his way forward until he reached one of the massive pylons that attached the Dreadnaughts to the storage core beneath them. Four of the six turbolift cars that ran through the pylon were off somewhere else, but the other two were waiting, and a few minutes later he arrived in the storage core.

The core was arranged in a series of large rooms, each nearly filled with stacks of crates held in place by multiple wrappings of crash webbing. A relatively narrow section at the front of each room was empty, providing a walkway and work area for sorting the crates. At each end of the walkway were a pair of doors leading into the rooms forward and aft of it: one of the doors person-sized, the other the much larger access panel required for transfer carts.

The turbolift let him out in section 120, Uliar saw from the small plaque attached to the crash webbing. Ma'Ning had said the Jedi school was in 124, and he headed aft.

Neither of the doors into 124 was marked with any special notice of its new classroom status. Steeling himself, trying not to think about all the legends about Jedi power, he walked up to the smaller door and touched the control.

Nothing happened. He tried again; still nothing. He moved to the larger cargo door, only to find that it, too, was sealed. Stepping back to the smaller door, he curled his right hand into a fist and pounded gently on the metal.

There was no answer. He knocked again, gradually increasing the volume level. Were they *all* out making nuisances of themselves?

"What do you want?"

He jumped, turning to a comm display that had been set up to his left just inside the cargo netting. C'baoth's face was framed there, glowering at him. "I need to talk to you about your students and their teachers," Uliar said, feeling his resolve starting to erode beneath that intimidating gaze. "They're in a reactor control and monitor room where they have no business—"

"Thank you for your interest," C'baoth interrupted. "But there's no need for concern."

"Excuse me, Master C'baoth, but there's *every* need for concern," Uliar insisted. "Some of those systems are very delicate. It took me four *years* to learn how to handle them properly."

"Your ways are not the Jedi ways," C'baoth pointed out.

"That's a nice slogan," Uliar growled. His anger, which had faded somewhat during the trip down here, was starting to bubble again. "But devotion to platitudes is no substitute for tech school."

C'baoth's dark look went a little darker. "Your lack of faith is both thoughtless and insulting," he said. "You will go now, and you will not return."

"Not until those children are out of my reactor room," Uliar said doggedly.

"I said *go*," C'baoth repeated.

And suddenly an invisible hand was pressing against Uliar's

chest, pushing him inexorably away from the locked door and back toward the other end of the section. "Wait!" Uliar protested, batting uselessly at the pressure against his chest. He'd never realized Jedi could do this through a comm display, without actually being there in person. "What about the children?"

C'baoth didn't answer, his image following Uliar with his eyes until he was nearly to the far door. Then, simultaneously, the display image and the pressure on Uliar's chest vanished.

For a long minute Uliar stood where he was, his heart pounding with tension and dissipating adrenaline, trying to decide whether he should go back across the room and try again. But there was obviously no point in doing so. Taking a deep breath, he turned and made his way back up to Dreadnaught-4 and the reactor room.

Ma'Ning and the children were gone when he arrived, and Sivv and Algrann were at their stations. "Well?" Sivv asked as Uliar silently took his seat.

"He told me to go away and mind my own business," Uliar told him.

"This *is* our business."

"Don't tell *me*," Uliar said tartly. "Go tell *him*."

"Maybe we should talk to Pakmillu," Algrann suggested hesitantly.

"What for?" Uliar growled. "Looks to me like the Jedi are the ones running the show now."

Algrann cursed under his breath. "Terrific. We leave a tyranny run by bureaucrats and corrupt politicians, only to end up in one run by Jedi."

"It's not a tyranny," Sivv disagreed.

"No," Algrann said tightly. "Not yet."

"Outbound Flight," Qennto repeated, frowning off into space as he slowly shook his head. "Nope. Never heard of it."

"Me, neither," Maris seconded. "And you say this Kav and Stratis want to *destroy* it?"

"Kav and whoever," Car'das said. "Thrawn thinks *Stratis* is an alias."

"Fine; Kav and Master No One," Qennto said impatiently. "So why do they want to destroy it?"

Car'das shrugged. "Stratis spun a big loop pastry about how dangerous the Jedi are and how they want to take over and make everyone to do things their way. But that has to be a lie."

"Not necessarily," Qennto said. "A lot of people out there are starting to wonder about the Jedi."

"They're certainly helping to prop up the Coruscant bureaucracy," Maris pointed out. "Anyone who wants genuine government reform will have to persuade the Jedi to change sides."

"Or else kill them," Qennto said.

Maris shivered. "I can't believe it would ever come to that."

"Well, Stratis sure wasn't talking about persuasion," Car'das said. "What about these Dreadnaughts? You ever hear of *them*?"

"Yeah, they're Rendili StarDrive's latest gift to the militarily obsessed," Qennto said. "Six hundred meters long, with heavy shields and a whole bunch of upgraded turbolaser cannons, most of them clustered in four midline bubbles where they can deliver a terrific broadside volley. Normal crew runs around sixteen thousand, with room for another two or three thousand troops. I hear the Corporate Sector's been buying them up like Transland Day souvenirs, and some of the bigger Core Worlds aren't far behind."

"Has Coruscant been doing any of the buying?" Maris asked.

Qennto shrugged. "There's been talk lately about the Republic finally getting its own army and a genuine battle fleet. But they've been talking that way for years, and nothing's ever come of it."

"So with six Dreadnaughts, we're talking up to a hundred thousand people aboard Outbound Flight?" Car'das asked.

"Probably no more than half that," Qennto said. "A lot of the standard jobs would be duplicated among the ships. Besides that, you want to build in extra elbow room on a long-term colony ship."

"That's still a lot of people to kill if all they want is to get at a few Jedi," Maris pointed out.

"Don't worry, I'm sure your noble-minded Commander Thrawn won't fall for it," Qennto said sourly.

"But even if Thrawn doesn't cooperate, Stratis still has an intact Trade Federation battleship on hand," Car'das reminded them. "That's a lot of firepower, and they might have more of them on the way."

"So what do we do?" Maris asked.

"*We* do nothing," Qennto said firmly. "It's not *our* job to look out for this Outbound Flight."

"But we can't just sit here and do nothing," Maris protested.

"No, we can run like scalded hawk-bats," Qennto retorted. "And I'm thinking this would be a real good time to do just that."

"But—"

"Maris," Qennto said, cutting her off with an uplifted hand. "It's not our problem. You hear me? It's *not our problem.* If the Jedi are going to go flying off into the Unknown Regions, it's up to *them* to figure out how to protect themselves. It's up to *us* to figure out how to get ourselves out of here. That is, if you think you can drag yourself away from all this nobility and culture."

"That's not fair," Maris protested, her eyes hard even as a touch of pink colored her cheeks.

"Whatever." Qennto turned back to Car'das. "You're his confidant these days, kid. You think you can sweet-talk him into letting us have that Vagaari loot his brother locked away?" He jerked a thumb at Maris. "Or should I ask Maris to do it?"

"Rak—" Maris began.

"I don't think sweet talk is going to be the issue," Car'das said hastily. The tension between Qennto and Maris was starting to drift into the red zone again. "He can't give it to us unless his brother and Admiral Ar'alani both let him."

"So how do we get Ar'alani back here?" Maris asked.

"We don't have to," Car'das said grimly, glancing at his chrono. "As a matter of fact, Thrawn's probably welcoming her onto the base right now."

"Great," Qennto said, brightening. "Let's get our hearing, get our loot, and get out of here."

"I don't think so," Car'das said. "She's here to see whether or not Thrawn should be relieved of command."

There was a moment of stunned silence. "That's insane," Maris said at last. "He's a *good* commander. He's a good *man*."

"And when did either of those ever matter?" Qennto muttered. "Oh, boy. And she was already dead set against giving us the Vagaari stuff. This is not good."

"Can't you for one minute forget about your loot?" Maris asked crossly. "This is Thrawn's career and life we're talking about."

"No, I *can't* forget about the loot," Qennto countered. "In case you've forgotten, sweetheart, we're already two and a half months late getting Drixo her furs and firegems. The *only* thing that's going to keep us alive when we finally show up is if we have something extra to calm her down with."

Maris grimaced. "I know," she murmured.

"So what do we do?" Car'das asked.

"What *you're* going to do is convince them to hand it over," Qennto said. "And don't ask how," he added as Car'das opened his mouth. "Beg, cajole, bribe—whatever it takes."

"You're the only one who can do it," Maris agreed soberly. "Anytime Rak or I even step outside our quarters, we have an escort following us around."

Car'das sighed. "I'll do what I can."

"And don't forget this is a limited-time window," Qennto warned. "Right now, we have at least half an ally in Thrawn. If he gets the boot, we won't have even that much."

Briefly, Car'das wondered what they would say if he told them Thrawn had publicly accused all three of them of espionage. But there was no point in worrying them any more than they were already. "I'll do what I can," he said again, getting to his feet. "See you later."

He left their quarters and started down the corridor.

Ar'alani's welcoming ceremony was probably over, but she and Thrawn were most likely still together. Probably talking about Thrass's accusations; Ar'alani hadn't struck him as the sort who would waste any more time with ceremonial niceties than necessary. Maybe he could leave word with one of Thrawn's officers that he wanted to see the commander at his earliest convenience.

"So you *do* have free run of the base."

Car'das turned. Thrass was coming up behind him, his expression giving no hint as to what was going on behind those glowing eyes. "Syndic Mitth'ras'safis," Car'das greeted him, fighting to get his brain online again. "Forgive my surprise; I assumed you'd be with your brother and the admiral."

Thrass inclined his head. "Come with me, please." He turned and strode off down the corridor. With his pulse pounding uncomfortably in his throat, Car'das followed.

Thrass led the way to the upper level of the base, where Thrawn and the senior officers had their quarters. They passed a few warriors along the way, none of whom gave either the syndic or the human so much as a curious glance, and finally arrived at a door marked with Cheunh symbols that Car'das couldn't quite decipher. "In here," Thrass said, opening the door and gesturing inside. Bracing himself, Car'das stepped past him into the room.

He found himself in a small conference room with half a dozen computer-equipped chairs arranged in a circle around a central hologrammic display. Seated on the far side of the circle, resplendent in her white uniform, was Admiral Ar'alani. "Be seated, Car'das," she said in Cheunh as Thrass stepped into the room behind him.

"Thank you, Admiral," Car'das said in the same language as he took the seat directly across from her. "Welcome back."

She nodded acknowledgment, studying him thoughtfully as

Thrass sat down in the chair to her right. "Your proficiency in Cheunh has improved," she commented. "My compliments."

"Thank you," Car'das said again. "It's a beautiful language to listen to. I only regret that I'll never speak it as well as a Chiss."

"No, you won't," Ar'alani agreed. "I understand you were with Commander Mitth'raw'nuruodo on this latest military venture. Tell us what happened."

Car'das glanced at Thrass, back at Ar'alani. "Forgive my impertinence, but shouldn't you ask Commander Mitth'raw'nuruodo about this instead of me?"

"We will," Ar'alani assured him darkly. "Right now, we're asking *you*. Tell us about this latest act of aggression."

Car'das took a deep breath. "First of all, it wasn't really an act of aggression," he said, picking his words carefully. "It was an expedition to investigate unknown warships that had been reported in the area."

"Vessels that wouldn't have been reported at all if Mitth'raw'nuruodo wasn't already inclined to premature military action," Ar'alani pointed out.

Beside her, Thrass stirred in his seat. "The Expansionary Fleet's charter does require observation and exploration in the regions around the Chiss Ascendancy," he said.

"Observation and exploration," Ar'alani countered. "*Not* unprovoked military action." She lifted her eyebrows. "Or do you deny military action was taken and Chiss casualties sustained?"

Car'das frowned. Thrawn hadn't mentioned anything about casualties. "I was unaware that any Chiss warriors had been lost."

"The *Whirlwind* did not return from the battle," Ar'alani said.

"Oh," Car'das said, breathing a little easier. Of course; the missing cruiser was still at the battle scene, keeping the *Darkvenge* pinned down with the Vagaari grav projector. But he obviously couldn't tell Ar'alani that. "I still maintain that Commander Mitth'raw'nuruodo fought only in self-defense."

"Did the unknown enemy fire first?"

"The firing of weapons isn't always the first act of aggression," Car'das hedged, once again feeling as if he were walking a narrow board over a pit of gundarks. "The Trade Federation battleships launched a massive force of droid starfighters. I've read reports of battles in which these weapons were used, and if Commander Mitth'raw'nuruodo hadn't acted to neutralize them, his force would quickly have been overwhelmed."

"Perhaps," Ar'alani said. "We'll know better once you've shown us around the battle zone."

Car'das felt his mouth go suddenly dry. "Around the . . . ?"

"You object?" Ar'alani demanded.

"Well, for starters, I don't even know where it is," Car'das said, stalling for time as he thought furiously. If Ar'alani found the *Darkvenge* sitting out there—

"The location isn't a problem," Ar'alani assured him, holding up a slender cylinder tapered at both ends. "I have the last two months' worth of the *Springhawk*'s navigational data."

Car'das fought back a grimace. Terrific. "All right," he said. "But shouldn't we check first with Commander Mitth'raw'nuruodo?"

"We're going now precisely because I *don't* want Commander Mitth'raw'nuruodo to know about it," Ar'alani said. "I've sent him on a security sweep of the nearby systems, which should give us time to examine the battle zone and return." Her eyes glittered. "And only *then* will we ask for his version of the battle."

* * *

"Preparing for first target," C'baoth said, his deep voice sounding strained as it resonated from the low ceiling of the weapons blister. "Firing now." His hands moved in an almost dream-like way over the controls, and there was a flicker of indicator lights as one of Dreadnaught-1's sets of turbolasers delivered a massive broadside blast.

Standing near the blister's doorway, Obi-Wan stretched out to the Force. On the other side of the Dreadnaught, he could sense Lorana Jinzler also firing her turbolasers, while all the way on the far side of Outbound Flight on Dreadnaught-4 Ma'Ning and the two Duros Jedi did the same.

"Whoa," Anakin muttered at his side. "That's . . . intense."

"Yes," Obi-Wan agreed, eyeing C'baoth closely. This was the Jedi Master's third meld today, and the strain of the procedure had to be getting to him. But if it was, Obi-Wan couldn't detect it in the other's face or sense.

He'd always assumed that at least part of C'baoth's unshakable confidence in himself was either an act or else a vast overestimation of his actual abilities. Now, for the first time, he began to wonder if the man might actually be as strong in the Force as he claimed.

"Spotter control: all test-one volleys on target," a voice reported from the comm panel.

"Pretty good," Anakin muttered.

"*Very* good, you mean," Obi-Wan said. "Can you sense any of Master C'baoth's commands, or just the presence of the meld itself?"

"I don't know," Anakin said, and Obi-Wan could sense the boy tightening his concentration.

"Preparing for second target," C'baoth announced.

"Spotter control ready."

"Firing now," C'baoth said.

Again, the indicators flickered. "Target two hit," the spotter reported. "One flier."

"What's a flier?" Anakin asked.

"It means one of the shots missed the target," Obi-Wan told him, frowning. There'd been something odd on that last shot, something he couldn't quite put his finger on. Stretching out again to the Force, this time focusing on the edges of the meld instead of on its center, he tried to track it down.

"Preparing for third target," C'baoth said. "Firing now."

And this time, as the indicators once again flickered, Obi-Wan saw it.

C'baoth had set up a total of six targets in this exercise. Obi-Wan forced himself to wait until all six had been destroyed, the last four with as impressive an accuracy quotient as the first two.

The spotter delivered his final report, and with a shaking jerk of his head C'baoth broke the meld. For a few seconds he just sat there, blinking rapidly as the last tendrils of connection between him and his fellow Jedi dissolved completely away. Then, taking a deep breath, he exhaled a long sigh and turned to Obi-Wan and Anakin. "What did you think, Young Skywalker?"

"Very intense," Anakin said. "I've ever seen anything like it before. When can I try it?"

"Not until after you've completed your training," C'baoth said. "This isn't something Padawans should be fooling around with."

"But I could handle it," Anakin insisted. "I'm very strong in the Force—you can ask Obi-Wan—"

"*When* you're a Jedi," C'baoth said firmly, his forehead wrinkling slightly as he shifted his eyes to Obi-Wan. "You have a question, Master Kenobi?"

"If you have a moment, yes," Obi-Wan said, trying to keep his voice casual. "Anakin, why don't you head back to Reactor Two and see if they're ready for us to help with that cooling-rod bundle yet. I'll be there in a few minutes."

"Okay," Anakin said, his forehead wrinkling briefly as he left the room.

"Well?" C'baoth asked, making the word a challenge.

"You had D-Four's Padawans in the weapons blisters with Master Ma'Ning just now, didn't you?" Obi-Wan asked.

"Yes, I did," C'baoth said evenly. "Is there a problem with that?"

"You just finished telling Anakin that this was way beyond a Padawan's abilities."

C'baoth smiled thinly. "Calm yourself, Master Kenobi," he said. "Of course they weren't actually participating in the meld."

"Then why were they there at all?"

"For the same reason your Padawan was here," C'baoth said, an edge of impatience creeping into his voice. "So that they could get an idea of what a Jedi meld is like."

"What kind of idea could they get?" Obi-Wan asked. "They've barely even begun their training. They could hardly see any more than any other non-Jedi could."

"Again, is that a problem?" C'baoth asked.

Obi-Wan took a careful breath. "It is if the lure of such advanced techniques goads them into pressing ahead too quickly and too impatiently."

C'baoth's eyes narrowed. "Speak carefully, Master Kenobi," he warned. "Such impatience is the mark of the dark side. I will not have you accuse me of walking that path, nor of guiding others along it."

"I don't accuse you of anything," Obi-Wan said stiffly. "Except perhaps of having overly high expectations of those under your tutelage."

C'baoth snorted. "Better expectations too high for Padawans to ever quite reach than ones so low they never need to stretch beyond what is already known."

"Better still high but realistic goals that allow for the satisfaction and confidence of achievement," Obi-Wan countered.

Abruptly, C'baoth stood up. "I will not have my teaching philosophy dissected as if it were an interesting biological specimen," he growled. "Particularly not by one as young as you."

"Age isn't necessarily the best indicator of knowledge in the Force," Obi-Wan pointed out, struggling for calm.

"No, but experience *is*," C'baoth shot back. "When you've trained as many Jedi as I have, we'll discuss this further. Until then, I believe your Padawan is waiting for you in Reactor Two."

Obi-Wan took a careful breath. "Very well, Master C'baoth," he said. "Until later."

He stalked out into the corridor, drawing on the Force for calm. He hadn't really wanted to come aboard Outbound Flight, despite his and Windu's concerns about C'baoth. Not even with the possibility of finding Vergere as extra incentive.

Now, though, he was glad he'd come. In fact, when they reached the Roxuli system in four days, their final stop in Republic space, he might consider contacting Windu to ask permission for him and Anakin to stay aboard Outbound Flight for the entire duration of its mission.

Because one of the other reasons for taking only infants into the Temple was to catch them before they could develop preconceived ideas of what a Jedi's life was like and how quickly they could achieve that goal. If all of C'baoth's Padawans had been cautious types like Lorana Jinzler, that was an issue he'd probably never even had to consider.

But inexperienced though Obi-Wan might be at training future Jedi, this was one problem he knew all about.

And if the eagerness he'd sensed in the children watching the meld was any indication, Outbound Flight's Jedi were going to have their hands full keeping their new Padawans from impatiently pushing their boundaries, possibly right over the line into the dark side.

Somehow, whether C'baoth wanted to hear it or not, he had to get that message through to him. Before it was too late.

The starlines cleared away, and a small and distant red sun appeared in the *Darkvenge*'s bridge viewports. "So?" Kav growled.

"Patience, Vicelord," Doriana advised, watching the blue-skinned alien standing beside the helm peering at the small device in his hand. Mitth'raw'nuruodo had left the technician behind to guide them to the location the Chiss commander had specified. A moment later the tech gave a small nod and murmured a few words to the silvery TC-18 translator droid at his side. "He says, 'We're here,' Vicelord Kav," the droid reported in its melodic voice.

Kav sniffed. "Wherever *here* is."

"*Here* is wherever Commander Mitth'raw'nuruodo wants us to be," Doriana said, not bothering to conceal his disgust with the other. Kav had had plenty of time to come to grips with his task force's destruction, but he was just as angry and irritable as ever.

And if he didn't watch his tongue and his temper, he was going to get the rest of them killed, too.

"Then where *is* he?" Kav demanded.

"Two incoming vessels," the Neimoidian at the sensors called. "One Chiss cruiser, one smaller vessel."

The Chiss tech spoke again in the Sy Bisti trade language. " 'They are the *Springhawk* and a long-range shuttle,' " the TC droid announced primly. " 'Commander Mitth'raw'nuruodo will wish to board immediately.' "

"Tell the commander his usual docking port has been prepared for him," Doriana said.

A few minutes later, Mitth'raw'nuruodo strode through the blast doors onto the bridge, a pair of Chiss warriors trailing behind him. "Welcome aboard, Commander," Doriana said, rising from the couch.

"Thank you," Mitth'raw'nuruodo said, his eyes flicking briefly to Kav's stiff face and posture. "I appreciate your swift compliance with my instructions."

"As I told you earlier, we wish to be fully cooperative," Doriana reminded him.

"Excellent," Mitth'raw'nuruodo said. "I wish you to begin unloading your droid starfighters."

Kav jerked like he'd been kicked. "What do you say?" he breathed, his eyes bugging even more than usual.

"Your droid starfighters are to be transported to that asteroid." Mitth'raw'nuruodo pointed out the viewports at a small, irregularly shaped crescent of faint light against the stars. "After that, I will require the services of those who program their combat movements."

Kav gurgled under his breath, and for once Doriana could

sympathize with him. The main strength of a Trade Federation battleship lay in its starfighters, the retrofitted quad laser batteries along the split-ring midline more of an afterthought than serious defensive armament. Removing its starfighters would leave the *Darkvenge* as helpless as the freighter it had once been. "This is outrageous," the Neimoidian protested. "I will not consent to—"

"Be silent," Doriana cut in, his eyes on Mitth'raw'nuruodo. Either he wanted the *Darkvenge* to be helpless, or— "You have a plan for dealing with Outbound Flight, don't you?"

"I have a plan," Mitth'raw'nuruodo confirmed. "Whether or not I activate it depends on whether or not you're ready to tell me the truth."

An uncomfortable lump formed in Doriana's throat. "Explain, please."

"Your name is not Stratis," Mitth'raw'nuruodo said. "You're not your own master, but answer to another. And the social threat posed by these Jedi is not the true reason you seek Outbound Flight's destruction." He lifted his eyebrows. "If, indeed, you genuinely *do* seek its destruction."

"What other reason would we have to be here?" Doriana asked.

"Perhaps your intent was to rendezvous with them," Mitth'raw'nuruodo suggested. "If Outbound Flight is filled with warriors instead of colonists, together your combined forces would have had both the firepower and the personnel necessary to launch an effective bridgehead invasion."

"I've already told you we're not here for conquest."

"I know what you told me," Mitth'raw'nuruodo said, his face expressionless. "Now you must persuade me to believe it."

"Of course," Doriana said. This was going to be risky, he knew, but he'd suspected from the beginning that Mitth'raw'nuruodo would eventually come to this conclusion. It was time to give him the rest of the truth. "I believe I can answer all of your questions together. If you'll come with me, I'd like to introduce you to my superior." Deliberately, he looked at Kav. "You, Vicelord, will remain here."

He didn't wait for Kav's inevitable protest, but set off across the bridge, leading Mitth'raw'nuruodo back to the office where they'd first conferred two days earlier. He ushered the Chiss inside and sealed the door, noting with no real surprise that Mitth'raw'nuruodo had also left his warrior escort behind. The commander was supremely confident in his abilities, and had clearly deduced that Doriana himself was no threat to him.

At least, not yet.

Doriana's special holoprojector was already hooked into the *Darkvenge*'s comm system. Punching in the access code, he gestured Mitth'raw'nuruodo to the desk chair. "Your first point is absolutely correct," he began, mentally crossing his fingers that the battleship's huge transmitter would be able to punch a signal back to the Republic's HoloNet system. "My true name is Kinman Doriana, an identity I've taken care to keep secret from Vicelord Kav's crew and other associates."

"You play mutually opposing roles, then?"

Doriana stared. "How did you know that?"

"It was obvious," Mitth'raw'nuruodo said. "Who are your two masters?"

"My official, public master is Supreme Chancellor Palpatine, the head of the Republic government," Doriana said, the words echoing strangely in his ears. He hardly dared even think such things in the privacy of his own mind. To be saying them aloud, and to an unknown alien, was virtually unthinkable. "My true Master is a Sith Lord named Darth Sidious."

"A Sith Lord is . . . ?"

"A being who stands against the Jedi and their control over the Republic," Doriana explained.

"Ah," Mitth'raw'nuruodo said, a faint smile touching the corners of his mouth. "A power struggle."

"In a way," Doriana conceded. "But on a plane far different from the one where beings like you and I exist. What's important right now is that Lord Sidious has access to information sources that the Jedi don't have."

"And what do these sources tell him?"

Doriana braced himself. "There's an invasion coming," he said. "A massive assault force of dark ships, shadowy figures, and weapons of great power, based on organic technology of a sort we've never seen before. We believe these Far Outsiders, as we call them, already have a foothold at the far edge of the galaxy, and even now have scouting parties seeking information on worlds and peoples to conquer."

"Stories of mysterious invaders are both convenient and difficult to disprove," Mitth'raw'nuruodo pointed out. "Why do you only now tell me this?"

Doriana nodded toward the door. "Because Vicelord Kav and his associates don't know," he said. "Neither does anyone else in the Republic. Not yet."

"When will Darth Sidious tell them?"

"When he's turned the Republic's chaos into order," Doriana said. "When we've built an army and a fleet capable of dealing with the threat. To announce it before then would do nothing but create panic and leave us open to disaster."

"How does Outbound Flight fit into all this?"

"As I said, we believe the Far Outsiders are currently still gathering information," Doriana said. "So far, there's no indication that they even know about the Republic." He felt his throat tighten. "Actually, that's not entirely true," he corrected himself reluctantly. "One of the Jedi, a being named Vergere, disappeared in that region some time ago. That's one of Outbound Flight's private agendas, in fact: to try to learn what happened to her."

"I see," Mitth'raw'nuruodo said, nodding slowly. "And while a single prisoner can give only hints of his or her origin, an entire shipful of them can provide all that would be needed for a successful invasion."

"Exactly," Doriana said. "Not to mention all the data files and technology they would be able to examine. If Outbound Flight blunders into their bridgehead, we could find ourselves facing an attack long before we're ready."

"And the Jedi do not understand this?"

"The Jedi think of themselves as the masters of the galaxy," Doriana said bitterly. "Especially the chief Jedi Master aboard Outbound Flight, Jorus C'baoth. Even if he knew about the Far Outsiders, I doubt it would make any difference to him."

Above the holoprojector, the familiar hooded figure shimmered into view. The hologram was a bit more ragged than usual, Doriana noted, but the connection itself seemed more solid than he'd feared it would be. Sidious was evidently somewhere much closer than his usual haunts on Coruscant. "Report," the Sith Lord ordered. His unseen eyes seemed to catch sight of Mitth'raw'nuruodo, and the drooping corners of his mouth drooped a little farther. "Who is this?" he demanded.

"This is Commander Mitth'raw'nuruodo of the Chiss Expansionary Defense Fleet, Lord Sidious," Doriana said, stepping behind Mitth'raw'nuruodo where he would be in view. "I'm afraid we've had a slight setback in our mission."

"I don't wish to hear about setbacks, Master Doriana," the Sith Lord said, his gravelly voice taking on a menacing edge.

"Yes, my lord," Doriana said, trying to stay calm. Even hundreds of light-years away, he could practically feel Sidious's Force grip resting against his throat. "Let me explain."

He gave Sidious a summary of the one-sided battle with the Chiss. Somewhere during the explanation, Sidious's face turned from staring at him to staring at Mitth'raw'nuruodo. "Impressive," he said when Doriana finished. "And only one of your ships survives?"

Doriana nodded. "And only because Commander Mitth'raw'nuruodo chose to leave it intact."

"Most impressive," Sidious said. "Tell me, Commander Mitth'raw'nuruodo, are you typical of your species?"

"I have no way of answering that question, Lord Sidious," Mitth'raw'nuruodo said calmly. "I can only point out that I'm the youngest of my people to ever hold the position of Force Commander."

"I can see why," Sidious said, a slight smile finally lightening some of his brooding darkness. "I take it from your presence here that Doriana has explained the need to stop Outbound Flight before it passes beyond your territory?"

"He has," Mitth'raw'nuruodo confirmed. "Have you proof of this impending alien threat?"

"I have reports," Sidious said. If he was insulted that Mitth'raw'nuruodo would dare to question his word, he didn't show it. "Doriana will detail them for you if you wish. Assuming you're convinced, what will be your response?"

Mitth'raw'nuruodo's eyes flicked to Doriana. "Assuming I'm convinced, I'll agree to Doriana's request to intercept and stop Outbound Flight."

"Excellent," Sidious said. "But be warned. The Jedi will not accept defeat lightly, and they have the power to reach across great distances to touch and manipulate the minds of others. You cannot allow them knowledge of your attack before it is launched."

"I understand," Mitth'raw'nuruodo said. "Tell me: does this ability to touch others' minds also work the opposite direction? If I, for example, am impressed enough with the need for them to return home, would my urgency influence their thoughts and decisions?"

"They will indeed sense your urgency," Sidious said, the corners of his mouth drooping again. "But don't expect them to act on it. Master C'baoth will not under any circumstances return to the Republic. To even offer him that possibility would rob you of your only chance for a surprise attack."

"Perhaps," Mitth'raw'nuruodo said. "Though to those who can touch others' minds the concept of surprise may be limited at best."

"Which is why Doriana proposed to use droid starfighters as the main thrust of his attack," Sidious pointed out. "Still, with all power comes a corresponding weakness. Amid the clutter of the thousands of minds aboard Outbound Flight, even Jedi sensitivity will be blunted. And once those same thousands of people begin to die in battle—" His lip twitched. "—that handicap will increase all the more."

"I understand," Mitth'raw'nuruodo said again. "Thank you for your time, Lord Sidious."

"I look forward to hearing the report of your victory," Sidious said, inclining his head. He sent a final look at Doriana, and with a flicker the image was gone.

For a long moment Mitth'raw'nuruodo sat without speaking, his glowing eyes glittering with thought. "I'll need a full technical readout on Outbound Flight and its component Dreadnaughts," he said at last. "I trust you have current information?"

"Up to and including even the final passenger listings," Doriana assured him. "Now that you know about Jedi power against living gunners, shall I cancel your order to remove our droid starfighters?"

"Of course not," Mitth'raw'nuruodo said, sounding mildly surprised. "And I'll expect the off-loading to be completed by the end of the day. I'll also need two of your droidekas and four of your battle droids to be packed and loaded aboard my long-range shuttle for transport to my base. I presume that six droids can be controlled by something more portable than this vessel's computer?"

"Yes, there are localized datapad systems that can handle up to two hundred droids each," Doriana said, suppressing a grimace. Kav was upset enough at him for simply handing over his starfighters for the Chiss to pick apart. He wasn't going to be any happier about losing his combat droids. "I'll pack one in with the droidekas."

"Good," Mitth'raw'nuruodo said. "I take it only the droidekas come with those built-in force shields?"

"Correct," Doriana said. "But if you're thinking about adapting the shields for use by your warriors, I'd advise against it. There's a fairly dense radiation quotient involved, plus high-twist magnetic fields that turn out to be fairly nasty for living beings."

"Thank you for your concern," Mitth'raw'nuruodo said, inclining his head slightly. "As it happens, we're somewhat familiar with such devices, though they were generally used with reversed polarity."

"Reversed polarity?" Doriana frowned. "You mean with the deflection field facing *inward*?"

"They were used as intruder traps," Mitth'raw'nuruodo explained. "Many an unwary robber incinerated himself as he tried to shoot a guard or homeowner from the inside."

Doriana winced. "Ah."

"But as you say, they proved too dangerous to bystanders and innocents who were accidentally caught," the commander went on. "Their use was discontinued many decades ago." He stood up. "I must leave now. I'll return later to confirm that my orders have been carried out."

19

"Fourteen vessels," Admiral Ar'alani declared, her glowing eyes sweeping the field of debris stretched out before them. "Possibly thirteen, if the two sections of wreckage to the right belonged to a single vessel that broke apart before exploding."

"Is that the correct number, Car'das?" Thrass asked.

"Yes, that's sounds about right," Car'das agreed, his muscles wilting a little with relief. The fifteenth ship, the intact Trade Federation battleship, was nowhere to be seen. He just hoped that it was Thrawn who'd moved it, and that it hadn't managed to skip out on its own. "Of course, I was just an observer," he reminded them. "I didn't have access to the sensor information."

"Plus there were a considerable number of those," Ar'alani continued, pointing at the charred sections of two droid starfighters floating past the bridge canopy. "Too small to be staffed."

"They're mechanical devices called droids," Car'das said. "These in particular are called droid starfighters."

Thrass grunted. "If the field of battle is any indication of their combat abilities, I would say they're misnamed."

"Don't be misled by your brother's skill at warfare, Syndic Mitth'ras'safis," Ar'alani warned. "If these droids were as useless as you imply, no one would take the time and effort to build them."

"I've seen reports of them in combat," Car'das confirmed. "Against most opponents, they're quite formidable."

"Yet I still see no evidence that these weapons or their masters attacked first," Ar'alani pointed out.

"I can only repeat what I said earlier, Admiral," Car'das told her. "The mere act of launching the starfighters was an overt act of aggression. Commander Mitth'raw'nuruodo responded in the only way he could to protect his forces."

"Perhaps," Ar'alani said. "That will be for a military tribunal to decide."

Car'das felt his stomach tighten. "You're bringing him up on charges?"

"That will also be for the tribunal to decide," Thrass said. "But we'll first need to examine the records of the battle and interview the warriors who were present."

"At this battle as well as the earlier raid against the Vagaari," Ar'alani added.

"I understand," Car'das said, his heart starting to beat a little faster. Here was the opening he'd been looking for. "Speaking of the Vagaari, my colleagues and I were hoping we could settle the question soon about the treasure we were promised, so that we could be on our way."

Ar'alani's eyebrows arched. "Now, suddenly, you're in a hurry to return home?"

"We're merchants," Car'das reminded her. "This has been an interesting and productive side trip, but the cargo in our hold is way overdue for delivery."

"A cargo you would very much like to supplement with stolen pirate plunder."

"Yes, but only because our customers will demand late-delivery penalties," Car'das explained. "There's no way for us to pay those without the items Captain Qennto has requested."

"You should have thought about that before deciding to stay," Thrass said. "At any rate, the matter of the treasure will have to wait until the tribunal has made its decision. If my brother is found to have violated Chiss military doctrine, he'll have no standing to argue your side of the question."

"I understand," Car'das said heavily. "How long is this hearing likely to take?"

"That depends on how quickly I can collect the details of the two battles," Ar'alani said. "Once I've done so, I'll request that a tribunal be seated."

Weeks, in other words. Possibly even months. "And what will Commander Mitth'raw'nuruodo's status be until then?"

"I'll be supervising his operations and overseeing all of his orders," Ar'alani said. She nodded fractionally at Thrass. "At Syndic Mitth'ras'safis's request."

Car'das looked at Thrass, a prickling sensation on the back of his neck. Once again, Thrawn's analysis had proved right on the mark. "You'd do this to your own brother?"

The muscles in Thrass's cheeks tightened; but it was Ar'alani who answered. "Neither Syndic Mitth'ras'safis nor I is unsympathetic toward Commander Mitth'raw'nuruodo," she said evenly. "We wish only to protect him from his own excesses of zeal and ability."

"From his excess of *ability*?" Car'das snorted. "*That's* a new one."

"He's a gifted tactician and commander," Ar'alani said. "But without proper restraint he'll eventually go too far and end his days in exile. What good will those gifts do anyone then?"

"And meanwhile, the Vagaari are free to destroy and kill?"

Ar'alani looked away. "The lives of other beings are not ours to interfere with, for good or for ill," she said. "We cannot and will not trust in whatever feelings of sympathy we might have for the victims of tyranny."

"Then trust in Mitth'raw'nuruodo," Car'das urged. "You both agree he's a gifted tactician; and *he's* convinced that the Vagaari are a threat you'll eventually have to face. The longer you wait—the more alien technology and weaponry you let them steal—the stronger they'll be."

"Then that is what we'll face," Thrass said firmly. "And as a syndic of the Eighth Ruling Family I cannot listen to any more of this." He jabbed a finger at the carnage outside the viewport. "Now. Describe this battle for us."

It was half an hour past the shift change, and D-4's number three messroom was crowded as Lorana came in. Taking a long step to the side out of the doorway and the people moving in and out, she scanned the crowd for Jedi Master Ma'Ning.

But he was nowhere to be found. Giving the room one final sweep, she started to turn toward the door.

"Hey!" a child's voice called over the hum of background conversation. "Hey! Jedi Lorana!"

It was Jorad Pressor, waving his fork over his head to get her attention. His parents, in contrast, had their eyes firmly fixed on their plates as they continued to eat. Deliberately ignoring her—

and it wasn't hard to guess why. Two days ago Master Ma'Ning had briefly taken over Pressor's hyperdrive maintenance bay to show to some of the young Jedi candidates, and one of the children had managed to dump a container of inverse couplings all over the floor. Pressor had had words with Ma'Ning about that, to the point where C'baoth had intervened and docked Pressor two days' pay.

Best if she left them alone until they got over it, Lorana decided. Waving and smiling back at Jorad, she turned to leave.

And nearly ran into Chas Uliar as he came into the messroom. "Slumming, are we?" he asked, making no attempt to hide his own coolness.

"I'm looking for Master Ma'Ning," she said, determined not to respond in kind to his open unfriendliness. C'baoth had wanted Uliar thrown in D-4's brig for his attempt to push his way into the Jedi school a few days ago, and it was only with the greatest of tact and diplomacy that Captain Pakmillu had managed to talk him out of it. "Have you seen him?"

"Oh, he never comes *here,*" Uliar said. "The officers and other important people eat in one of the *nicer* messrooms."

Lorana's eyes flicked back into the messroom, focusing this time on the décor. It looked fine to her.

"Oh, I'm sure it's just like the ones you have over on D-One," Uliar went on. "But it could have been a lot more interesting if you Jedi had a cubic centimeter of style and creativity among you."

"What does our style or creativity have to do with this?" Lorana asked.

For a moment Uliar's eyes searched her face as if looking for a lie. Then his lip twitched. "I guess you really *don't* know," he said grudgingly. "We wanted to decorate this room like one of the Coruscant underlevels—you know, kind of sleazy in an over-the-top sort of way. The folks stationed forward have already done up their messrooms in theme styles."

"And?"

"And your stiff-as-permacrete Master Ma'Ning wouldn't let us," Uliar said acidly. "Some nonsense about a low-culture look promoting rebellious attitudes."

Lorana winced. Now that he mentioned it, she *had* heard about this debate. It hadn't made much sense to her, either. "Let me talk to him," she offered. "Maybe I can get him to change his mind. Any idea where he might be?"

"You might try the senior officers' conference room," Uliar said, and she thought she could sense a small crack in his animosity. "I hear he spends a lot of time in there when it's not being used."

"Thank you," Lorana said. "I'll get back to you on the decorating."

She found Ma'Ning alone in the conference room, seated in one of the chairs as he gazed out the small viewport at the hyperspace sky flowing past. "Master Ma'Ning?" she called tentatively as the door slid shut behind her.

"Jedi Jinzler," he said without turning around. "What brings you to D-Four?"

"You weren't answering your comlink," she said. "Master C'baoth asked me to come find you."

"I was meditating," he explained. "I always turn off my comlink at such times."

"I see," Lorana said, studying him closely as she stepped to his side. His face and manner seemed oddly tense. "Are you all right?"

"I'm not sure," he said. "Tell me, what do you think of what Master C'baoth is doing?"

The question caught her by surprise. "What do you mean?"

"Did you know he's suspended the authority of the Commander's Court to rule on grievances?"

"No, I didn't," she said. "What system is he planning on using instead?"

"Us," Ma'Ning said. "As best I can figure, he essentially wants us to take over supervision of every aspect of life aboard Outbound Flight."

"Such as how the people decorate their messrooms?"

Ma'Ning grimaced. "You've been talking to Chas Uliar and his committee."

"I talked to Uliar," Lorana confirmed, frowning. "I didn't know he had a committee."

"Oh, it's just a group of people who don't like others telling them what to do," Ma'Ning said, waving a hand in dismissal. "Mostly reactor complex techs and support people. Their complaints are mostly trivial, like this whole messroom thing."

"With all due respect, Master Ma'Ning, for us to even get involved with Outbound Flight's décor seems a little ridiculous," Lorana offered.

"No argument from me," Ma'Ning admitted. "But Master C'baoth was adamant—said the idea of decorating the place like a criminals' den would encourage antisocial attitudes we can't afford in such a close-knit community. The point is that I'm sensing a growing resentment toward us from the people in general. I'm worried that Master C'baoth may be taking these so-called reforms of his too far."

"Still, it's hard to argue with his basic premise," Lorana said, feeling distinctly uncomfortable with talking about C'baoth behind his back this way. "People attuned to the Force *should* be more capable of dispensing justice and maintaining integrity than those who aren't. But it's also hard to see what that has to do with how people decorate their own messrooms."

"Exactly," Ma'Ning agreed. "But I can't seem to get that distinction through to him. Do you think you could make him understand?"

Lorana grimaced. First Uliar had asked her to talk to Ma'Ning, and now Ma'Ning was asking her to talk to C'baoth. Had someone appointed her official mediator of the Jedi Order when she wasn't looking? "I doubt he'll pay any more attention to me than he would to you," she warned. "But I can try."

"That's all I ask," Ma'Ning said, sounding relieved. "And don't mark yourself short. There's a special bond between Master and Padawan, a bond that can run far deeper than any other relationship. You may be the only person aboard Outbound Flight he *will* listen to."

"I'm not sure about that," she said. "But I'll do what I can."

"Thank you," Ma'Ning said. "You said Master C'baoth was trying to reach me?"

Lorana nodded. "He wants all the Jedi Masters at a meeting tonight at eight in the D-One senior officers' conference room."

"More reforms, no doubt," Ma'Ning grumbled as he stood up. "Talk to him soon, will you?"

"If I can slow him down long enough," Lorana said. "In the meantime, what do I tell Uliar?"

Ma'Ning sighed. "Tell him I'll think about it. Maybe Master C'baoth will eventually load himself up with so many other matters that he won't even notice how Outbound Flight is decorated."

Lorana looked out at the hyperspace sky. "Somehow, I don't think so."

Ma'Ning shook his head heavily. "No. Neither do I."

It had been a long and tiring day, but the last group of droid starfighters had finally been unloaded and deployed across the asteroid's uneven landscape. Now, his growling stomach reminding Doriana of the lateness of the hour, he made his way to the *Darkvenge*'s Supreme Officers' dining room to get something to eat.

Kav was already there, seated alone at one of the corner tables, his expression daring anyone to interrupt him. Doriana took the hint and directed the serving droid to one of the tables on the opposite side of the room. The vicelord had been in a thunderous mood all day, which was almost funny in a species as cowardly as the Neimoidians. But no one else aboard had dared to laugh, and Doriana wasn't going to try it, either. Even cowards could be pushed too far.

He was halfway through his dinner when Kav suddenly stood up and made his way across the room. "This Mitthrawdo," he said without preamble as he sat down across from Doriana. "You think him a genius, do you?"

"I consider him a highly effective military commander and tactician," Doriana said, eyeing the other. Where was *this* suddenly coming from? "His abilities at art or philosophy I can't vouch for."

"Amusing," Kav growled. "But he is not even a good tactician. He is, instead, a fool." Pulling a datapad from inside his robes, he dropped it on the table in front of Doriana. "See the reprogramming he has ordered for my starfighters."

Doriana glanced at the datapad's display, covered with droid-language symbolics. "I don't read tech," he said. "How about giving it to me in plain Basic?"

Kav snorted contemptuously. "He has programmed the starfighters for close-approach attacks."

Doriana frowned back at the datapad. "How close?"

"I believe the term is *hull skimming,*" Kav said, tapping the display. "The chief programmer informs me the attack is set for no more than five meters above the hull."

Doriana rubbed his cheek thoughtfully. Tactically, it made good sense to cut in that close to an enemy's ships. It put the attacker inside the defender's point-defense weaponry, as well as permitting the kind of targeting accuracy that made for efficient destruction of vulnerable equipment and hull-plate connection lines.

The catch, of course, was that it was enormously difficult to get inside those point defenses in the first place. "I don't suppose anyone thought to mention to him that Dreadnaughts come with a very good point defense system?"

"The programmers did not think it their place to speak out of turn."

"And neither did you?"

"I?" Kav feigned innocence. "You, of all people, should know better than to question the orders of a military genius."

Doriana took a deep breath. "Vicelord, I strongly suggest you remember our ultimate objective here. We've been sent to destroy Outbound Flight. Without Mitth'raw'nuruodo's aid, we have no chance of doing that."

"Yet a being of his genius is certainly capable of grasping technical readouts," Kav said blandly. "Perhaps his plan is to throw our starfighters against Outbound Flight in an awesome display of disintegrating metal that will frighten Captain Pakmillu into submission."

Doriana let his gaze harden, utterly disgusted by this pathetic excuse of a military commander. "So in the end all you care about is your pride," he said. "You don't even care if Darth Sidious executes us both as long as you can find some small point where you can feel superior to Mitth'raw'nuruodo."

"Calm yourself," Kav said, resettling himself comfortably in his chair. "There is no reason why my pride and my victory cannot coexist."

"Explain."

"I have not told Mitthrawdo of the flaw in his plan," the vicelord said with spiteful satisfaction. "But I *have* instructed the chief programmer to create a secondary attack pattern for the starfighters, which has been overlaid across Mitthrawdo's primary pattern. Once he has wasted the first wave in his foolish close-approach attack, I will take command and switch to a more effective line of attack."

Doriana thought it over. That *would* probably work, he decided. "It still loses us a full attack wave," he reminded Kav. "Not to mention the element of surprise."

"What surprise?" Kav scoffed. "As soon as they see the *Darkvenge* they will know to prepare for droid starfighters."

Doriana pressed his fingertips together. Surely even a Neimoidian vicelord couldn't be *this* dense. "I don't suppose it's occurred to you that Mitth'raw'nuruodo might have off-loaded the starfighters precisely because he *doesn't* intend to let Captain Pakmillu see the *Darkvenge*?" he suggested. "That, in fact, he doesn't intend for the *Darkvenge* to participate in the battle at all?"

Apparently, it *hadn't* occurred to Kav. "That is ridiculous," he protested, his eyes widening. "No military commander would refuse to bring a battleship of our might into his fleet."

"Except maybe a commander who's already seen how easily they can be destroyed?" Doriana couldn't resist asking.

Kav's whole body stiffened. "I perceive that you have come under Mitthrawdo's spell, Commander," he said evenly. "But do not be swayed by his learned manner and cultured voice. He is still a primitive savage . . . and no matter what the outcome, in the end he will have to die."

Doriana sighed. Unfortunately, he had already reached that same conclusion. Mitth'raw'nuruodo had come into contact with Car'das and his shipmates, and he might easily touch the edge of the Republic again. Until all the witnesses to Darth Sidious's betrayal of Outbound Flight had been silenced, the mission would not be complete. "Regardless, for the moment we still need him alive," he said. "How have you arranged for us to reach this second programming level?"

"I will have a relay control," Kav said. "Once Mitthrawdo's failure is apparent, I will bring the starfighters back under my control, and will complete our mission." He cocked his head. "Unless you have further objections?"

Doriana shook his head. "Though we'll have to make sure we're on his bridge when the battle begins."

"I leave that to you," Kav said. "He is a fool in other areas, as well. Did you know he has taken twenty of my starfighters and linked them together by twos with a spare fuel tank between them?"

"What good does that do?" Doriana asked, frowning. "Those starfighters run on solid-fuel slugs."

"I imagine he was inspired by Outbound Flight's design,"

Kav said contemptuously. "He is probably regretful that his tanks are too small to fit six starfighters around each."

"You're sure they're *fuel* tanks?"

"What else could they be?" Kav countered, getting to his feet. "A pleasant evening to you, Commander."

The Neimoidian walked away, and Doriana returned to his meal. Somehow, the food didn't taste as good as it had five minutes earlier.

"There," Captain Pakmillu said, pointing a flippered hand at the planet visible through D-1's bridge viewports. "Roxuli, our last stop in known space. From this point on, we enter territory never before seen throughout all the ages of Republic star travel."

"It's indeed a historic moment," Obi-Wan agreed. "With your permission, Captain, I'd like to send a signal to Coruscant through Roxuli's HoloNet connection."

"Certainly," Pakmillu said, gesturing aft. "The secure comm room will be at your disposal as soon as our guest is finished."

Obi-Wan frowned. Less than an hour since Outbound Flight had made orbit, and already they had a guest? "One of the local officials?"

"Hardly," Pakmillu said drily, his eyes swiveling toward the aft blast doors. "Ah."

Obi-Wan turned, and felt his mouth drop open. Local official, nothing. Their visitor was none other than Supreme Chancellor Palpatine himself.

"Master Kenobi," Palpatine called as he crossed the bridge toward them. "Just the man I need."

"This is an unexpected honor, Chancellor Palpatine," Obi-Wan said, scrambling to find his voice. "May I ask what brings you to this edge of the Republic?"

"The same thing that moves all of us across the stars these days," Palpatine replied with a wan smile. "Politics, of course. In this case, trouble between the Roxuli central government and the system's asteroid mining colonies."

"It must be serious if you had to come out personally," Obi-Wan commented.

"Actually, they don't want me at all," Palpatine said drily. "All they want from me is to obtain for them the services of the hero of the Barlok negotiations, Master Jorus C'baoth himself."

Obi-Wan looked at Pakmillu. "I'm not sure Master C'baoth will be interested in the job," he warned Palpatine.

"As a matter or fact, he isn't," the Supreme Chancellor confirmed. "I've already spoken with him, and he flatly refuses to leave Outbound Flight."

"We could delay our departure until his negotiations have finished," Pakmillu offered. "There's no reason we couldn't spend a few days here."

"No, I've already suggested that option," Palpatine said, shaking his head. "He will not change Outbound Flight's schedule. Or leave Outbound Flight at all, for that matter." He looked back at Obi-Wan. "But there *is* another alternative. Perhaps *you* would be willing to mediate in his place."

Obi-Wan blinked in surprise. "With all due respect, Chancellor Palpatine, I don't think that's a substitution that would satisfy them."

"On the contrary," Palpatine said. "I've just spoken with them, and they would be most gratified if you would lend your assistance." He smiled again. "After all, there were other heroes at Barlok besides Master C'baoth."

Obi-Wan grimaced. Under other circumstances, he would have been only too happy to help out. But with all that was happening aboard Outbound Flight, he'd decided to ask the Council for permission to extend his tour. Now, suddenly, that decision was being cut out from under him.

Because if C'baoth wasn't willing to postpone Outbound Flight's departure for himself, he certainly wouldn't do so for Obi-Wan. If he and Anakin left now, they wouldn't be getting back aboard. "How serious is this problem?" he asked.

"Serious enough," Palpatine said, the lines in his face deepening as his small attempt at levity faded away. "If violence erupts, vital ore shipments to half the systems in this sector will be cut off. Depending on how much damage the mines sustain, the scarcity could last for years."

"I'd have to consult the Council," Obi-Wan pointed out.

"With time becoming critical, I've already taken the liberty of doing so," Palpatine said. "Master Yoda has given his permission for you to leave Outbound Flight here instead of continuing on."

And even with it couched in terms of permission, Obi-Wan nevertheless knew an order when he heard one. "Very well," he said with a sigh. "I presume I'll be bringing my Padawan, as well?"

"You can hardly let him go running off to the next galaxy without you," Palpatine agreed, the lines smoothing out a bit, and Obi-Wan could sense his relief. "I'll take the two of you down in my ship. After that, I'm afraid I must return to Coruscant, but I'll leave one of my guard and his escort ship to bring you back when you're finished."

"Thank you," Obi-Wan said, wondering briefly if he and Anakin should instead take the Delta-12 Skysprite that Windu had set up for them in D-3's hangar. But it would take time to activate and prep, and time seemed to be of the essence here. Besides, one of Palpatine's escort ships would undoubtedly be more spacious and comfortable, even if it did mean putting up with one of those humorless men Palpatine always seemed to be hiring as his guards these days. "I'll have Anakin start packing. We'll be ready to go within the hour."

"Thank you, Master Kenobi," Palpatine said, his voice low and earnest. "You may never know how much this means to me."

"My pleasure, Chancellor," Obi-Wan said, feeling a twinge of regret as he pulled out his comlink. "We Jedi live only to serve."

"There it goes," Anakin murmured as Palpatine's shuttle dropped toward the hazy atmosphere of the planet below them.

Obi-Wan looked up, but where Outbound Flight had been there was no longer anything but empty space. "They have a schedule to keep," he said.

"I suppose," the boy said, and Obi-Wan could hear some of his own unhappiness echoed in the other's voice. "I wish we could have gone a little farther with him."

"Who, Captain Pakmillu?" Palpatine asked.

"No, Master C'baoth," Anakin said. "He's a really good leader—always seems to get things done. Cuts straight through the clutter and finds a way to make everyone do what's best for them."

"He does indeed have that gift," Palpatine agreed. "There are so few like him in these troubled times. Still, our loss is Outbound Flight's gain."

"I'm sure they're pleased to have him aboard," Obi-Wan murmured.

"But he has his task before him, and we have ours," Palpatine continued, handing Obi-Wan a data card. "Here's all I have on the Roxuli dispute. You'd best familiarize yourself with it before we land."

"Thank you," Obi-Wan said, taking the card and slipping it into his datapad. "No doubt the complainants themselves will provide any details you've missed."

"No doubt," Palpatine said drily. "Settle yourself in, Master Kenobi. It's likely to be a very long and weary day."

Ar'alani's inspection group returned to Crustai from the Trade Federation battle site nearly two hours before Thrawn made it back from the inspection tour the admiral had sent him on. His report, not surprisingly, went quickly, and he was back with Car'das and Maris for a quick language session less than an hour later. If he realized something significant had happened in his absence, Car'das couldn't find it in his face or voice.

The next two days went by slowly. Ar'alani spent most of her time in her quarters studying the data she'd collected from the battle site, emerging only for meals or to roam the base looking for warriors to question. So far she didn't seem to have run into the two who'd heard Thrawn announce his suspicions about the *Bargain Hunter*'s crew, but Car'das knew it was only a matter of time before she did.

Thrawn himself was in and out quite a bit over those two days, apparently taking Ar'alani's phony inspection order very seriously. Car'das had only a single real conversation with the commander during that time, a long late-night talk in Car'das's quarters right after Ar'alani's battle-site survey. Thrawn's fatigue and tension were evident, and when he finally left Car'das pondered long and hard as to whether the commander might have finally overstretched himself.

During those days Car'das also tried to spend more time with

Qennto and Maris. But their conversations were even more depressing. Qennto was beginning to act like a caged animal, his broodings peppered with wild plans involving raids on the armory and storage room followed by a daring escape in the *Bargain Hunter.* Maris, for her part, still professed confidence in Thrawn's honor, but even she was clearly starting to have private doubts about his ability to protect them against Ar'alani.

Something had to be done. And it was Car'das who would have to do it.

There were few preparations he could make. The *Bargain Hunter* was too well guarded, and anyway he had no intention of trying to fly the ungainly freighter through the entrance tunnel with Thrawn's fighters in pursuit. But at the far end of the docking area was a long-range shuttle the Chiss seemed mostly to be ignoring. A few hours spent in the piloting tutorials of the base's computer system, combined with his previous training in reading Cheunh symbols, and he had learned the rudiments of flying it. Later, he managed to slip aboard the shuttle without being seen and spent an hour in the pilot's seat, mentally running through the lessons and checklists and making sure he knew where everything was located. When the time came, he didn't want Admiral Ar'alani charging into the shuttle to find him fumbling with the wrong controls.

Getting ahold of Ar'alani's copy of the *Springhawk*'s navigational download was somewhat more problematic. Thrawn himself provided the opening for that one, inviting Ar'alani and Thrass to a formal dinner on the second night. The cylinder the admiral had shown him was mixed in with a batch of similar tubes carrying the data she'd recorded at the battle site, and it took him several tense minutes to locate the correct one.

And with that, his preparations were finished.

He went to bed early that night, but it didn't do him any good. He spent most of the night thinking and worrying, his sleep coming in short, nightmare-filled dozings. Like the eerie calm before the bursting of a massive storm, he knew the quiet of the past couple of days was about to end.

Midmorning on that third day, it did.

"No," Car'das said firmly, meeting Ar'alani's glowing eyes as calmly as he could. "We're not spies. Not for the Republic, not for anyone else."

"Then what precisely did Commander Mitth'raw'nuruodo mean by his accusation?" the admiral countered. "And don't deny he said it. I have the sworn statements of the two warriors who were present at the time."

"I don't deny it," Car'das said, his eyes flicking to Thrass. The syndic was standing silently a few steps behind Ar'alani, his expression harder even than the admiral's. Perhaps he knew better than she did what a charge of harboring spies would mean to his brother's career. "But I also can't explain it. Maybe he was trying to confuse the Trade Federation commanders."

"Commanders who have apparently vanished," Ar'alani said pointedly. "Along with an apparently intact alien warship."

"I don't know anything about that, either," Car'das insisted. "All I know is what I've already told you: we're merchants who had a hyperdrive accident and lost our way. Ask the rest of my crew if you don't believe me."

"Oh, I will," Ar'alani assured him. "In the meantime, you're confined to your quarters. Dismissed."

For a moment Car'das was tempted to remind her that he was still under Thrawn's authority, not hers, and that she couldn't simply order him around. But only for a moment. Turning, he stalked out of the room.

But he didn't go to his quarters. The Chiss warriors were used to seeing him roaming freely around the base, and it hadn't sounded like Ar'alani would make any official pronouncements to the contrary until after she'd interrogated Qennto and Maris.

He had that long to make his escape.

The shuttle was still parked where it had been the previous day. There were a few Chiss working in the area, but the time for subterfuge was long past. Striding along like he owned the place, Car'das stepped through the hatchway into the shuttle, sealed it, and headed forward.

The vessel was a civilian model, with a simpler and quicker start up procedure than a military ship would have had. Within five minutes he had the systems up and running. Five minutes more, and he had disengaged from the docking clamps and was making his way carefully down the tunnel.

No one followed him out. He looked around as he reached open space, half expecting to see the intact Trade Federation battleship lurking in the shadow of one of the other asteroids. But it was nowhere to be seen.

Not that it mattered. He knew where he was going, and there was no one now who could stop him. Turning the shuttle onto the proper vector, he hit the hyperdrive control and made the jump to lightspeed. The next stop, assuming he'd properly programmed in the *Springhawk*'s nav data, would be the alien system where he, Thrawn, and Maris had witnessed the Vagaari attack five weeks ago. With luck, that campaign would be over.

With even more luck, the Vagaari would still be there.

* * *

Six hours later, he emerged from hyperspace to find that the battle was indeed over.

The defenders had put up a spirited defense, he saw as he eased the shuttle carefully through the debris. Blackened hulks were everywhere, floating amid bits of hull and hatch and engine. There were bodies, too. Far too many bodies.

Not that their sacrifice had done them any good. There were dozens of Vagaari ships orbiting the planet, nestled up to it like carrion avians around a fresh corpse. Most were the bubble-hulled warships they'd seen in the battle, but there were also a number of the civilian transports that had been waiting for the fighting to end. A steady stream of smaller ships were moving in and out of the atmosphere, no doubt bringing plunder and slaves up to the orbiting ships and then heading down for a fresh load. Briefly, an image flashed into Car'das's mind of streams of hive insects zeroing in on a dropped bit of rovvel picnic salad . . .

A floating body bounced gently off the shuttle's canopy, jarring him back to reality. If he had any brains, he knew, he would turn the shuttle around right now and head back to Crustai to take his chances with Admiral Ar'alani. Or else he should abandon Qennto and Maris completely and make a run for Republic space.

Swearing gently under his breath, he turned toward the largest of the orbiting warships and headed in.

Even with most of their attention on their looting, the Vagaari were cautious enough to protect their backs. The half a dozen roving fighters intercepted him before he'd covered even a quarter of the distance, and suddenly his comm crackled with melodious but evil-sounding alien speech. "I don't understand your language," Car'das replied in Sy Bisti. "Do you speak Sy Bisti?"

The only response was more alien speech. "How about Minnisiat?" he asked, switching to his newest trade language. "Can anyone there understand Minnisiat?"

There was a short pause. "State your name, your species, and your intentions," the alien voice came back, mouthing the trade language with some difficulty.

"My name is Jorj Car'das," Car'das told him. "I'm a human from a world called Corellia." He took a deep breath. "I'm here to offer you a deal."

The fighters escorted him to one of the smaller warships, directing him to a starboard docking bay. A group of heavily armed and armored guards was waiting there for him: short bipeds with large hands, their features hidden by faceplates lavishly decorated to look like fright masks. They took him to a small room loaded with sensor equipment, where he was stripped, searched, and scanned multiple times, his clothing taken away presumably for similar scrutiny. The shuttle, he had no doubt, was undergoing a similar examination. Afterward, he was taken to another room, this one bare of everything except a cot, and left there alone.

He spent most of the next two hours either trying to rest or else giving up the effort and pacing back and forth across his cell. If the Vagaari were smart, the thought kept running along the back of his mind, they would simply kill him and go on with their looting. *An avian in the hand,* after all, was a pretty universal maxim.

But maybe, just maybe, they would be greedy as well as smart. Greedy, and curious.

Two hours after he'd been tossed into his cell, the guards returned with his clothing. They watched him dress, then marched him out and along a corridor to a hatch marked with alien symbols. Beyond the hatch, to his relief, was a shuttle and not simply a quick death by spacing. They nudged him inside and piled in behind him, and a minute later they were off. The shuttle had no viewports, giving him no clue as to where they were going, but when the hatch opened again it was to a double row of Vagaari soldiers in fancier uniform armor than his captors. Apparently, someone in authority had decided to see him.

He'd expected to be taken someplace small and cramped and anonymous, as befit a proper interrogation. It was therefore a shock when the final blast door opened into a large chamber that rivaled the most elaborate groundside throne rooms he'd ever seen. Against the back wall was a raised dais with an exquisitely decorated chair in the center, occupied by a Vagaari clad in a heavy-looking multicolored robe with sunburst shoulder and ankle guards, a serrated cloak back, and no fewer than four separate belts around his waist. Flanking him were a pair of Vagaari in only slightly less gaudy robes—advisers or other underlings, probably. All three wore tall wraparound face masks that reached from cheekbones to probably a dozen centimeters above the tops of their heads, decorated in the same fearsome pattern as the soldiers' combat faceplates. A cynical thought flickered through Car'das's mind, that the height of the masks was probably designed to compensate for the species' natural shortness and make them look more dangerous to their enemies. Lining the walls were other Vagaari, some in soldiers' armor, others in what seemed to be civilian clothing and simple face paint. All of them were gazing silently at the prisoner being brought before the throne.

Car'das waited until the guards had positioned him three meters back from the throne, then bowed low. "I greet the great and mighty Vagaari—" he began in Minnisiat.

And was slammed to his hands and knees by a sharp blow across his shoulders. "You do not speak in the presence of the Miskara until spoken to," one of the guards reproved him.

Car'das opened his mouth to apologize, caught his near error just in time, and remained silent instead.

For a long minute the rest of the room was quiet, too. Car'das wondered if they were waiting for him to get up, but with his shoulder blades throbbing from that blow it seemed a better idea to stay where he was until otherwise instructed.

Apparently, it was the right decision. "Very good," a deep voice came from the dais at last. "You may rise."

Carefully, tensing for another blow, Car'das stood up. To his relief, the blow didn't come. "I am the Miskara of the Vagaari people," the Vagaari seated on the throne announced. "You will address me as *Your Eminence*. I'm told you have the insolence to demand that I bargain with you."

"I make no demands of any sort, Your Eminence," Car'das hastened to assure him. "Rather, I'm in terrible difficulty and came here hoping the great and mighty Vagaari people might be willing to come to my assistance. In return for your aid, I hope to offer something you might find of equal value."

The Miskara regarded him coolly. "Tell me of this difficulty."

"My companions and I are merchants from a distant realm," Car'das told him. "Nearly three months ago we lost our way and were taken captive by a race of beings known as the Chiss. We've been their prisoners ever since."

A twitter of muted conversation ran around the room. "Prisoners, you say," the Miskara repeated. The visible part of his face had seemed to harden at the mention of the Chiss, but his voice wasn't giving anything away. "I see no chains of captivity about your neck."

"My apparent freedom is an illusion, Your Eminence," Car'das said. "My companions are still in Chiss hands, as is our ship. Of equal importance, the Chiss now refuse to release to us some of the spoils of one of their raids, spoils that we were promised and that we need to pay off the late fees our customers will demand. Without that treasure, we will face certain death when we reach home."

"Where are your companions being held?"

"At a small base built deep inside an asteroid, Your Eminence," Car'das said. "The navigational data necessary to locate it is contained in the computer of the vessel in which I arrived."

"And how did you know how and where to find *us*?"

Car'das braced himself. *I will do whatever necessary,* Thrawn had once told him, *to protect those who depend on me.* "Because, Your Eminence," he said, "I was present aboard the Chiss attack cruiser that raided your forces here during your battle of conquest five weeks ago."

A deadly silence settled over the room. Car'das waited, painfully aware of the armed soldiers standing all around him. "You stole one of our ship nets," the Miskara said at last.

"The commander of the Chiss force did that, yes," Car'das said. "As I say, I was his prisoner, and took no part in the attack."

"Where is this commander now?"

"I don't know exactly," Car'das said. "But the base where my ship and companions are being held is under his command. Wherever he might travel, he will always return there."

The Miskara smiled thinly. "So you offer to trade your companions and some of our own treasure for nothing more than a chance at revenge?"

That was not, Car'das thought uneasily, a very auspicious way of phrasing it. "You'd get your ship net back, too," he offered.

"No," the Miskara said firmly. "The offering is insufficient."

Car'das felt his throat tighten. "Your Eminence, I beg you—"

"Do not beg!" the Miskara snapped. "Grubs beg. Inferiors beg. *Not* beings who would speak and bargain with the Vagaari. If you wish us to help you and your companions, you must find more to offer me."

"But I have nothing more, Your Eminence," Car'das protested, his voice starting to tremble. No—this couldn't happen. The Vagaari *had* to agree to the deal. "I swear to you."

"Not even those?" the Miskara demanded, pointing over Car'das's shoulder.

Car'das turned. Sometime during the conversation someone had brought in four large crates, two of them a head taller than him, the others coming only up to his waist. "I don't understand," he said, frowning. "What are those?"

"They were aboard your transport," the Miskara said suspiciously. "Do you claim ignorance of them?"

"I do, Your Eminence," Car'das insisted, completely lost now. What in the worlds could Thrawn have had stashed aboard the shuttle? "I stole the vessel solely to come ask for your help. I never looked to see if there was anything aboard."

"Then look now," the Miskara ordered. "Open the crates and tell me what you see."

Carefully, half expecting to be shot in the back, Car'das made his way back to the crates. The Vagaari had already opened all of them, of course, merely setting the front panels loosely back into place. Stepping to one of the smaller boxes, he got a grip on the panel and pulled it off.

And caught his breath. Inside, folded up neatly with their arms wrapped around their knees, were a pair of Trade Federation battle droids.

"Do you recognize them?" the Miskara asked.

"Yes, Your Eminence," Car'das confirmed. Suddenly it all made sense. "They're battle droids of a sort used by one of the species in our region of space. The commander also raided a force of those people; this must be part of the spoil of that raid."

"What are droids?"

"Mechanical servants," Car'das said. So Thrawn had been right: apparently no one out here knew anything about droids. At least, no one the Vagaari had run into. "Some are self-motivated, while others require a centralized computer to give them their instructions."

"Show me how it works."

Car'das turned back to the crate, peering inside. There was no sign of a controller or programming console. "I don't see the equipment I need to start it up," he said, stepping to the other small box and pulling off the front. There were two more folded battle droids inside, and again no sign of a controller. Each of the two larger boxes turned out to contain one of the even deadlier droideka destroyer droids. Still no controller. "I'm sorry, Your Eminence, but without the right equipment I can't start them up."

"Perhaps this would be of use," the Miskara suggested. He gestured, and one of the non-armored Vagaari watching the proceedings pulled a datapad from beneath his robe. Stepping up to Car'das, he offered it to him.

A small ripple of relief washed over some of Car'das's tension. It was indeed a Trade Federation droid controller, labeled in both Neimoidian and Basic. "Yes, Your Eminence, it will," he told the Miskara as he looked over the controls. Activator . . . there. "Shall I try to activate them now?"

"Try?"

Car'das grimaced. "Shall I activate them now, Your Eminence?" he corrected himself.

"Yes."

Bracing himself, Car'das pushed the switch.

The result was all he could have hoped for. In perfect unison the four battle droids unfolded themselves halfway, walked forward out of their crates, and then stood up, reaching back over their shoulders and drawing their blaster rifles. The droidekas were even more impressive, rolling forward out of their crates and unfolding into their tripedal battle stances. Around one of them, as if to demonstrate the full range of its capabilities, the faint haze of a shield appeared.

And suddenly Car'das realized that there were twelve blasters pointed directly at the dais where the Miskara was seated.

Slowly, carefully, he turned around. But the Miskara wasn't cowering behind his soldiers, and the soldiers themselves didn't have their weapons lined up ready to turn Car'das into a cinder. "Impressive," the Miskara said calmly. "Who commands them?"

Car'das peered at the datapad. There should be a pattern recognition modifier here somewhere. "At the moment, whoever is handling the controller, Your Eminence," he said. "But I think they can be programmed to obey a specific individual instead."

"You will order them to obey *me*."

"Yes, Your Eminence," Car'das said, quickly sifting through the datapad's recognition menu. It looked straightforward enough. "Uh . . . I'll need you to come down here, though, so that the droids can see you up close."

Silently, the Miskara stood up and stalked down the steps, motioning his two advisers to stay where they were. He stepped between the two droidekas and stopped. "Do it now," he ordered.

Feeling sweat collecting beneath his collar, Car'das ran through what he hoped was the proper procedure. The six droids turned slightly to face the Miskara; then, to his relief, the battle droids raised their blasters to point toward the ceiling as the droidekas swiveled a few degrees to point their weapons away from him as well. "That should do it, Your Eminence," he said. "Of course," he added as something belatedly occurred to him, "they won't be programmed to understand orders given in Minnisiat."

"You will teach me the proper commands in their language," the Vagaari said. "The first command I wish to know is 'target.' The second is 'fire.' "

"Yes, Your Eminence." Car'das gave him the two Basic words, enunciating them carefully. "Perhaps your people can transcribe them phonetically for you," he suggested.

"No need," the Miskara said. He lifted a finger and pointed to Car'das. "Target."

Car'das jerked backward as all six droids swiveled to point their blasters at him. "Your Eminence?" he breathed.

"Now," the Miskara said, his voice silky smooth, "*you* pronounce the other word."

Car'das swallowed hard. If he'd done this wrong . . . "Fire," he said.

Nothing happened. "Excellent," the Miskara said approvingly. "So you are indeed wise enough not to attempt a betrayal." He lifted a hand. "Bring me three Geroons."

"Yes, Your Eminence," one of the soldiers acknowledged, and left the room.

"Does your Commander Mitth'raw'nuruodo have more of these machines?" the Miskara asked, turning back to Car'das.

"Several hundred at least," Car'das told him. "Possibly as many as several thousand." A movement at the door caught his eye, and he turned as three small aliens were herded into the room. "Who are these?"

"Slaves," the Miskara said offhandedly. "Their pitiful little world is the one currently rolling beneath us. Machines: target."

Car'das stiffened as the droids swiveled toward the three slaves. "Wait!"

"You object?" the Miskara asked.

Car'das closed his eyes briefly. *I will do whatever necessary*—the words echoed through his mind. "I was merely concerned for the safety of your soldiers," he said.

"Let us find out how good the machines' aim is," the Miskara said. "Machines: *fire*."

The salvo from the battle droids' carbines sent the three slaves toppling backward, dead before they even hit the floor. They were still falling when the fire from the droidekas almost literally cut them in half.

"Excellent," the Miskara said into the shocked silence. Not shocked by the deaths, Car'das knew, but by the display of firepower. "Where do the Chiss keep the others?"

"The commander will have them at the base," Car'das murmured mechanically, trying without success to force his eyes away from the charred bodies.

"Then we will relieve him of them," the Miskara said, gesturing to one of the advisers. "Order an assault force to be prepared at once."

"Yes, Your Eminence," the other said. Stepping off the dais, he strode from the room.

"And while we wait," the Miskara went on, turning back to Car'das, "you will teach me the rest of the words necessary for controlling my fighting machines."

Car'das swallowed hard. *Whatever necessary* . . . "As you wish. Your Eminence."

Outside the *Springhawk*'s bridge canopy, the scattered stars and a small but magnificent globular cluster blazed brilliantly out of a black sky. The stars, the cluster, and nothing else.

Surreptitiously, Doriana looked at his chrono. Outbound Flight was late.

Apparently, the look hadn't been surreptitious enough. "Patience, Commander," Mitth'raw'nuruodo said calmly from the captain's chair. "They will come."

"They are late," Vicelord Kav said, scowling at the back of Mitth'raw'nuruodo's head. "More than two hours late."

"Two hours is nothing in a voyage of three weeks," the commander pointed out reasonably.

"Not for Captain Pakmillu," Kav retorted. "Mon Calamari are notorious for punctuality."

"They will come," Mitth'raw'nuruodo said again, half turning to eye the Neimoidian. "The only question is whether or not this system is indeed on the correct straight-line path between their last Republic stop and the system where you were preparing to ambush them."

"Do you dare—?" Kav began.

"The vector was calculated correctly," Doriana interrupted with a warning glare. "*Our* question, on the other hand, is why you think they'll actually stop here."

"They will," Mitth'raw'nuruodo assured him. "The droid starfighters are ready?"

"Very much so," Kav assured him in turn, and Doriana could hear the vindictive anticipation in his tone. The starfighters were ready, all right, complete with the second command layer the vicelord's chief programmer had built in on top of Mitth'raw'nuruodo's close-approach pattern.

The commander inclined his head to the Neimoidian. "Then we have only to wait." He turned back to the canopy—

And suddenly, with a flicker of pseudomotion, there it was, floating in space not five kilometers ahead.

Outbound Flight had arrived.

"The device is called a gravity projector," Mitth'raw'nuruodo said. "It simulates a planetary mass, thus forcing out any ship whose hyperspace vector crosses its shadow."

"Really," Doriana said, trying to sound calm. To the best of his knowledge, no one in the Republic had ever figured out how to turn that particular bit of hyperspace theory into an actual working device. The fact that the Chiss had solved the problem sent discomfiting ramifications ricocheting across his mind.

Kav, predictably, wasn't nearly as interested in such long-term thought. "Then they are in our hands," he all but crowed. "All forces: *attack*."

"Hold," Mitth'raw'nuruodo said. His voice was still calm,

but there was a sudden new edge to it. "*I* give the orders aboard this ship, Vicelord Kav."

"It is *our* mission, Commander Mitthrawdo," Kav countered. "And as we debate, we lose the precious element of surprise." Fishing into his robes, he pulled out a comm activator. "You and your ships may do as you wish. But my starfighters *will* attack."

"No!" Doriana snapped, making a grab for the activator. If Kav fouled up Mitth'raw'nuruodo's plan, whatever that plan was, Outbound Flight might yet slip through their fingers.

But his reach was too short, his grab too late. Twisting his long arms out of range, Kav triumphantly keyed the activator. Swearing viciously, Doriana looked over at the asteroid where the lines of droid starfighters waited.

Nothing happened.

Again, Kav keyed the switch. Again, nothing. "I'm afraid that won't work, Vicelord," Mitth'raw'nuruodo said calmly. "I took the liberty of removing the alternate command layer your programmers had created in the starfighters' systems."

Slowly, Kav lowered the activator. "You are very clever, Commander," he said softly. "Someday that cleverness will turn against you."

"Perhaps," Mitth'raw'nuruodo said. "Until then, allow me to thank you for showing me how such secondary programming is done. That will prove useful today."

"So what now?" Doriana asked cautiously.

"We talk to them," Mitth'raw'nuruodo said, keying his board. "Communications: create a channel."

By the time Lorana arrived, D-1's bridge had become a hive of quiet pandemonium. C'baoth was standing beside Captain Pakmillu's command chair, his back stiff as he gazed out the canopy. Pakmillu himself was over at one of the engineering stations, his flippered hands opening and closing restlessly as he studied the displays.

Outside the canopy, arrayed in the distance in front of them like a pack of hunting howlrunners, were a dozen small ships of a configuration Lorana had never seen before.

"The readback seems to indicate we're in the middle of a planetary mass shadow," the engineering officer was saying tautly as she reached Pakmillu's side. "But you can see yourself that can't possibly be right."

"This is Commander Mitth'raw'nuruodo of the Chiss Expansionary Defense Fleet," a cultured voice boomed over the bridge speakers. "Please respond."

"Who's that?" Lorana asked.

"The commander of that force over there," Pakmillu rumbled, still studying the readouts. "He's been calling every five minutes for the past half hour."

"You haven't answered him?"

Pakmillu's mouth tendrils stiffened. "Master C'baoth has forbidden it," he growled. "He insists we know what happened to our hyperdrive before we reply."

"Maybe the commander could *tell* us what happened," Lorana suggested.

"Of course he could," Pakmillu said sourly. "But I cannot persuade Master C'baoth to that point of view."

Lorana grimaced. "Let me talk to him."

C'baoth was still gazing at the alien ships as Lorana joined him. "So, Jedi Jinzler," he greeted her. "We meet our first challenge."

"Why does it have to be a challenge?" Lorana asked. "Maybe all he wants to do is talk."

"No," C'baoth said, his voice dark. "I can sense a deep malice out there, malice directed at my ships and my people."

"They're alien minds," Lorana reminded him, feeling her pulse starting to pick up its pace. She'd seen C'baoth in this stiff-necked mood before. "Perhaps you're simply misreading them."

"No," he said. "They intend trouble, and *I* intend to be fully prepared to deal with it before I talk to them."

"Command, this is Ma'Ning," a voice came from the command chair speaker. "We're standing ready at D-Four's weapons systems."

"Acknowledged," C'baoth said, giving Lorana a tight smile. "Dreadnaught-Four was the last. *Now* we're ready to talk."

Deliberately, he lowered himself into Pakmillu's command chair and touched the comm switch. "Alien force, this is Jedi Master Jorus C'baoth, commanding the Outbound Flight Project of the Galactic Republic," he announced.

Lorana looked back at Pakmillu, wincing to herself at C'baoth's casual preemption of his command authority. But there was no resentment in the Mon Cal's expression or stance, only a quiet sense of resignation. Apparently, he'd bowed to the inevitable.

"Master C'baoth, this is Commander Mitth'raw'nuruodo," the cultured voice replied promptly.

"Let me see your face," C'baoth ordered.

There was a brief pause; then the comm display came to life, showing a near human with blue skin and blue-black hair and glowing red eyes. He was dressed in a black tunic with silver bars on the collar. "There are matters of great importance we need to discuss at once," Mitth'raw'nuruodo said. "Would you care to join me in my flagship, or shall I come to you?"

C'baoth snorted gently. "I will discuss nothing until you stand away from my path."

"And I will continue to hold here until we have spoken," Mitth'raw'nuruodo replied, his voice as firm as C'baoth's. "Are the Jedi afraid of talk?"

C'baoth smiled thinly. "The Jedi fear nothing, Commander. Come aboard, then, if you insist. A hatchway will be illuminated for your shuttle."

Mitth'raw'nuruodo inclined his head. "I shall be there shortly." He gestured somewhere offscreen, and the image vanished.

"You're going to allow him aboard?" Pakmillu demanded.

"Of course," C'baoth said, an odd glint to his eye. "Or don't you find it curious that this supposed resident of the Unknown Regions *spoke to us in Basic?*"

Lorana felt her breath catch. To her chagrin, she hadn't even noticed the oddness of that fact. "No, there's something more here than meets the eye," C'baoth continued. "Let's find out what that something is."

"Come aboard, then, if you insist," C'baoth's voice echoed from the D-4 reactor monitor room speaker. "A hatchway will be illuminated for your shuttle."

There was a click. "D-Four?" a different voice called. "Any progress?"

With an effort, Uliar pulled his thoughts back to focus. "Still negative here, Command," he reported, running his eyes again over his displays. "There's plenty of power going to the hyperdrive. It's just not doing anything once it gets there."

"That's confirmed, Command," Dillian Pressor's voice seconded from the hyperdrive monitor room half a dozen meters away. "The readouts still insist we're in a grav field."

"So do everyone else's," Command growled. "All right. Keep running your diagnostics, and stand by."

There was a click, and Command was gone. "This is insane," Pressor muttered.

"Maybe more insane than you think," Uliar said, his mind racing. This might finally be their chance. "Or didn't you notice that Commander Mitth-whatever was speaking Basic?"

There was a short pause. "You mean he's from the *Republic*?"

"Well, he's sure not from the Unknown Regions," Uliar said. "We've got to find a way to talk to him."

"Who, *us*?"

"Of course us," Uliar shot back. "You, me—the whole committee. If this guy's from the Republic, maybe he's got the authority to get C'baoth and the rest of the Jedi kicked off."

"It's not all the Jedi," Pressor argued. "Anyway, what would some hotshot from the Republic be doing way out here? It's more likely a pirate who found out about Outbound Flight and decided to grab some easy pickings."

In his mind's eye Uliar saw the firing scores from C'baoth's Jedi meld tests. "Trust me, Pressor, this thing is *not* easy pickings," he said grimly. "But whoever he is, we still have to try."

"Fine," Pressor said. "But how? We're on duty."

"To what?" Uliar countered. "A reactor that's working perfectly and a hyperdrive that isn't working at all?"

"Yes, but—"

"But nothing," Uliar cut him off. "Come on—this may be our last chance to get Outbound Flight back to what it was supposed to be."

There was a short pause. "All right, I'm game," Pressor said at last. "But if this Mitth-whatever's already on his way, we don't have much time. Not if we're going to collect everyone and get all the way over to D-One."

"You just collect them," Uliar said. "I'll make sure he stays put until you get there."

"How?"

"No idea," Uliar said. "Just collect everyone, all right? And don't forget to bring the children. There's nothing like children when you're playing for sympathy."

"Got it."

Uliar keyed off the comm, and for a moment sat gazing unseeingly at his displays as he tried to think. D-1 was indeed a long way away, and if he knew C'baoth the conversation was likely to be short and unpleasant. If he tried to walk or even run, he was likely to miss Mitth-whatever completely.

But there should be one of D-4's swoops parked just a little way aft.

Ninety seconds later, he was racing down the corridor, the wind of his passage whipping through his hair and stinging his eyes. Fortunately, with Outbound Flight at full alert, everyone was either at their battle stations or huddled in their quarters out of the way; the corridors were empty. Reaching the forward pylon, he punched for the turbolift, but instead of leaving the swoop at the way station like he was supposed to, he maneuvered it into the car. Let C'baoth complain about it—let him even lock Uliar in the brig for a few days if he wanted to.

Whatever it took, he *would* see this Mith-whatever before he left Outbound Flight.

* * *

Car'das had been waiting for nearly three hours before the Miskara again summoned him to the throne room.

"All is prepared," the Vagaari informed him. "We fly at once to draw our vengeance from Mitth'raw'nuruodo and the Chiss."

"Yes, Your Eminence," Car'das said, bowing his head and trying not to look at the half dozen fresh Geroon bodies scattered around the throne room. Apparently, the Miskara had been playing some more with his new toys. "I would once again ask you to remember that my companions and ship are also there, and would beg your soldiers to be careful."

"I will remember," the Miskara promised. "And I will do even more. I have decided you will be permitted the best view possible of the forthcoming battle."

Car'das felt something cold run through him. "You mean I'll be on the bridge, Your Eminence?"

"Not at all," the Miskara said calmly. "You will be in the forwardmost of my flagship's external bubbles."

Car'das looked sideways to see a pair of armored Vagaari striding toward him. "I don't understand," he protested. "I've offered you the chance at both vengeance and profit."

"Or the chance to fly into a trap," the Miskara said, his voice suddenly icy. "Do you think me a fool, human? Do you think me so proud and rash that I would simply fly a task force to a supposedly small and undermanned Chiss base in my thirst for revenge?" He snorted a multitoned whistle. "No, human, I will not send a small task force to be destroyed. My entire fleet will descend on this base . . . and *then* we shall see what sort of teeth this Chiss trap truly has."

"The Chiss aren't waiting there with any trap," Car'das insisted. "I swear it."

"Then you should have nothing to fear," the Miskara said. "If we destroy the enemy as quickly as you claim we will, you will be released and your companions freed. If not . . ." He shrugged. "You will be the first to die."

He cocked his head slightly. "Have you anything else you wish to say before you are taken away?"

A confession, perhaps, or an admission of guilt? "No, Your Eminence," Car'das said. "I only hope your soldiers are as capable against the Chiss as they've proven themselves to be against other opponents."

"The Geroons could tell you of our capabilities," the Miskara said darkly. "But you will see them for yourself soon enough." He gestured. "Take him away."

Five minutes later, Car'das was pushed through a narrow doorway in the hull into a zero-g plastic bubble perhaps twice the size of a coffin. Set against the hull on one side of his head was what seemed to be a small air supply and filtering system, while on the other was a mesh bag containing a couple of water bottles and ration bars from the Chiss shuttle, along with a diamond-shaped device of unknown purpose.

And as the thick hull metal was sealed against his back he knew the chance cube had been thrown. From now on, everything that happened would be under the control of others.

He could only hope that the Miskara had been telling the truth about the size of the force he was sending.

21

The fact that Mitth'raw'nuruodo was a near human this far from Republic space had been Lorana's first surprise. More surprising than that were the culture and refinement of his demeanor and speech as he spoke to her and C'baoth from the other side of the conference room table.

His reason for intercepting Outbound Flight was the biggest surprise of all. And the most chilling.

C'baoth, predictably, wasn't impressed by any of it. "Ridiculous," he said scornfully when Mitth'raw'nuruodo had finished. "A mysterious species of conquerors moving across the galaxy toward us? Please. That's the sort of story bad parents frighten their children with."

"You know everything there is to know about the universe, then?" Mitth'raw'nuruodo asked politely. "I was under the impression that this region of space was unknown to you."

"Yes, it is," C'baoth said. "But rumors and stories aren't limited by geographical and political boundaries. If a species so dangerous truly existed, we would surely have heard *something* about them by now."

"What about Vergere?" Lorana murmured from beside him. "Something like this might explain her disappearance."

"Or it might not," C'baoth countered. "It doesn't take a species of conquerors to silence a single Jedi." His eyes glittered. "To silence a *group* of Jedi, of course, is a different matter entirely. And as to this Darth Sidious you cite, I put even less faith in his words than I do in idle rumors. *Darth* is the title of a Sith Lord, and the Sith have long since vanished from the galaxy. That makes him a liar right from the start."

"Perhaps," Mitth'raw'nuruodo said. "But I didn't come here for an open debate. The fact remains that I cannot and will not permit you to continue on through this region of space. You must turn back to the Republic and pledge to never return."

"Or?" C'baoth challenged.

Mitth'raw'nuruodo's glowing red eyes were steady on him. "Or I will be forced to destroy you."

Lorana braced herself for the inevitable explosion. But C'baoth merely smiled thinly. "So says the avian chick to the billinus dragon. Do you truly believe your twelve ships could survive ten minutes against the firepower I hold here in my hand?"

Mitth'raw'nuruodo lifted his eyebrows politely. "Your *personal* hand?" he asked.

"My Jedi are even now standing by in the ComOps Center above us, as well as at the weapons stations of each individual Dreadnaught," C'baoth said. "I'll soon be joining them . . . and if you've never before faced Jedi reflexes and insight, you'll find it a sobering experience."

Mitth'raw'nuruodo's expression didn't change. "Whatever their training, it will do them no good," he said. "Your only choices are to leave now and take your people home, or perish. What is your answer?"

"What if we promised to go *around* this region?" Lorana asked.

C'baoth looked at her, and she sensed his surprise at her presumption quickly turning to anger. "Jedi Jinzler—"

"I mean *all* the way around it," Lorana continued, fighting against the weight of his displeasure pressing against her mind. "We could go to a different part of the Rim and jump off for the next galaxy from there."

"No," C'baoth said firmly. "That would take us thousands of light-years out of our way."

"That would be acceptable," Mitth'raw'nuruodo said, looking at Lorana. "Provided you avoided the entire region lying along your current vector."

"No," C'baoth bit out, his eyes blazing. "Lorana, you will be silent. Commander, you do *not* dictate to us. Not you; not anyone else."

Abruptly, he shoved back his chair and rose towering to his full height. "We are the *Jedi,* the ultimate power in the universe," he declared, the words ringing through the conference room. "We will do as we choose. And we will destroy any who dare stand in our way."

Lorana stared up at him, her heart suddenly pounding in her throat. What was he saying? What was he *doing*?

There is no emotion; there is peace . . .

"In that event, the conversation is over," Mitth'raw'nuruodo said. His expression hadn't changed, but as Lorana tore her gaze from C'baoth and looked at the commander she could sense a hardening of his resolve that sent a fresh shiver up her back. "I will give you an hour to consider my offer."

"No, you will cease whatever you're doing to hold us in this system and move your ships out of our path," C'baoth countered.

"One hour," Mitth'raw'nuruodo repeated, sliding back his own chair and standing up. "Jedi Jinzler, perhaps you'll escort me back to my transport?"

"As you wish, Commander," Lorana said, not daring to look at C'baoth as she scrambled to her feet. "Follow me, please."

Captain Pakmillu had offered some of his security personnel to bring Mitth'raw'nuruodo aboard. Typically, C'baoth had refused, insisting he and Lorana needed no such show of force to keep the alien commander in line.

Which now left Lorana and Mitth'raw'nuruodo alone as they walked back toward the hangar. "Your Master C'baoth is both arrogant and stubborn," Mitth'raw'nuruodo commented as they walked. "A bad combination."

"He is all that," Lorana conceded. "But he's also a Jedi Master, and as such he has knowledge and power hidden from the rest of us. For your own sake, I beg you not to underestimate him."

"Yet if this knowledge is hidden, how can you be sure it is accurate?"

Lorana grimaced. That was, unfortunately, a good question. "I don't know," she said.

"Surely you don't stand alone," Mitth'raw'nuruodo pointed out. "There must be others aboard who oppose to Master C'baoth's tyranny."

Tyranny. It was a word Lorana hadn't dared use even in the privacy of her own mind. Now, suddenly, it could no longer be avoided. "Yes, there are," she murmured, frowning. Directly ahead down the corridor, shifting nervously back and forth between his feet, she could see Chas Uliar from D-4 loitering against the wall. Here to confront her with some new problem, no doubt.

But he said nothing as she and Mitth'raw'nuruodo approached, merely following them with brooding eyes as they passed him.

There was another shuttle parked near the Chiss vehicle, she noted, one of Outbound Flight's transports. Curious; that hadn't been there when the Chiss commander arrived. "We don't intend your people any harm," she told Mitth'raw'nuruodo as they stopped at his shuttle's hatchway.

"I believe you," he said. "But intent alone is meaningless. Your actions are what will determine your fate."

Lorana swallowed. "I understand."

"You have one hour." Inclining his head to her, Mitth'raw'nuruodo turned and disappeared into his vehicle.

Lorana moved back to allow the pilot room to maneuver . . . and as she did so, she sensed a familiar presence. Turning, she saw Uliar walking toward her.

Striding along behind him, a cold fire in his eyes, was C'baoth.

"Jedi Jinzler," C'baoth said as Mitth'raw'nuruodo's shuttle slipped through the atmosphere shield and disappeared out into the blackness of space. "I have another job for you."

The talks had gone on longer than Uliar had expected, and he'd had enough time to get rid of his swoop and find a spot in the corridor outside D-1's forward hangar where he could wait.

He'd been waiting now for nearly twenty minutes. More than enough time for his internal tension to start to fade away and then start ramping up again.

Where in blazes were Pressor and the others?

He could call Pressor and ask, of course. But comlink conversations among different Dreadnaughts ran through a central switching node. If C'baoth had taken over the comm system like he'd taken over everything else, that would show that Uliar wasn't on D-4 like he was supposed to be and tip him off that something was up.

And then, even as he tried to come up with another way to find Pressor, he saw them coming down the corridor: Lorana Jinzler and a blue-skinned, glowing-eyed near human who had to be Commander Mitth'raw'nuruodo.

So he *was* an unknown alien, or at least one Uliar had never seen. More importantly, he didn't have the clothing or other trappings that would indicate he was some official from Coruscant. Uliar grimaced, a part of his hope dying within him.

But only a part. Whether he was a genuine military commander or just some pirate with an assumed title, Mitth'raw'nuruodo seemed determined to keep them from passing through his territory. If Uliar could persuade him to order them back to the Republic—or even if he and his gang were able to plunder enough of Outbound Flight's supplies that Pakmillu was forced to go back for replacements—they might still be able to get Palpatine to do something about C'baoth's growing stranglehold on the expedition.

At the very least, Uliar and the others would then have a chance to jump ship and find something else to do with their lives.

Jinzler and Mitth'raw'nuruodo were coming toward him . . . and with the rest of the committee still absent, it was all up to him. Taking a deep breath, he opened his mouth to speak.

Or rather, he tried to open it. To his horror, his mouth and tongue refused to work.

He tried again, and again, watching as Jinzler and Mitth'raw'nuruodo closed the gap, his throat and cheeks straining with his effort. But nothing worked.

And then they were there, right beside him. He tried to step in front of them, to at least keep them here until he could find a way to unfreeze his mouth. But his legs wouldn't work, either. Silently, he watched them pass him by, oblivious to his urgency and agony and helplessness.

"So you think to betray me, Uliar?" a quiet voice came in his ear.

Uliar's neck still worked, but there was no need to turn around. He knew that voice only too well. "Did you really think you could ride a swoop all the way from Dreadnaught-Four without my people in ComOps noticing and alerting me?" C'baoth went on. "So will treason always betray itself."

With a jolt like that of a suddenly released clamp, Uliar felt his mouth being freed from C'baoth's restraint. "It's not treason," he croaked. "We just want our mission back."

"*My* mission, Uliar," C'baoth said darkly. "*My* mission. Who else is in this pathetic little conspiracy?"

Uliar didn't answer. "Well, let's go see," C'baoth said. "Discreetly, of course, if you please."

As if Uliar had a choice. With C'baoth's hand riding loosely on his shoulder, the two men headed down the corridor after Jinzler and the blue-skinned alien. They reached the hangar just as the others arrived at Mitth'raw'nuruodo's ship. A few meters away was one of Outbound Flight's shuttles . . .

Uliar felt his breath catch in his throat as he suddenly realized why the rest of the committee hadn't appeared. Rather than bringing everyone in along the corridors and turbolifts like an impromptu parade, Pressor had instead loaded them aboard one of D-4's shuttles and had Mosh fly them across.

Which meant there was still a chance. All Pressor had to do was pop the hatch, and before C'baoth realized what was happening they would be in front of Mitth'raw'nuruodo, ready to plead their cause. Surely even a Jedi Master couldn't strangle the words out of all of them at the same time.

But the hatch didn't open. With his tongue frozen again, Uliar watched helplessly as Mitth'raw'nuruodo spoke briefly with Jinzler, then went inside his shuttle and closed the hatch.

And with that, their last chance was gone.

C'baoth's hand prodded at Uliar's back, nudging him forward. "And now," the Jedi said with cold satisfaction, "all that remains is for me to decide what to do with all of you."

Jinzler turned around as they approached, her expression flickering with surprise at their presence. "Jedi Jinzler," C'baoth greeted her. "I have another job for you." He waved a hand casually at the silent shuttle—

The hatch abruptly flew open, spilling Pressor and Mosh out. From the way they sprawled onto the deck, it was obvious they'd been shoving at the hatch with all their weight when C'baoth released his grip on it. "So they *were* trying to open it," Uliar murmured.

"Of course they were," C'baoth said contemptuously. "If a swoop couldn't escape my notice, how did you expect an entire shuttle to do so?" He raised his voice. "You—all of you—come out. I want to see your faces."

"What's going on?" Jinzler asked, staring at the people as they began filing silently out onto the deck.

"This, Jedi Jinzler, is a conspiracy," C'baoth said, his voice as dark as Lorana had ever heard it. "These people apparently don't appreciate all the work and effort we've put into making Outbound Flight as rewarding a place as possible to work and live."

"Maybe we just don't want *your* ideas of what's rewarding," Uliar said. "Maybe we don't want to be treated like children who can't decide for ourselves what we're going to do with our lives."

"Do you have the Force?" C'baoth countered. "Can you tap into that which binds the universe together, and thus automatically defines what is best for us all?"

"I don't believe the Force wants to control every aspect of our lives," Uliar shot back. "And I *sure* don't believe you're the chosen spokesman for that control."

C'baoth's face darkened. "And who are *you* to—?"

"Master C'baoth," a voice called.

Uliar turned. Standing at the entrance to the hangar, gazing at them with a face carved from stone, was Master Ma'Ning. "A word with you, if you please," he said. "Now."

"What are you doing here?" C'baoth called back, and Lorana could sense both surprise and suspicion radiating from him. "You should be at your duty station."

"A word with you, if you please," Ma'Ning repeated.

Snorting under his breath, C'baoth strode across the deck toward him. Lorana hesitated a moment, then followed.

"This had better be important," C'baoth warned as he reached the other Jedi Master. "We have work to do."

"It is," Ma'Ning assured him, his voice under careful control. "I've spent a great deal of time over the past few days considering and meditating on the situation aboard Outbound Flight . . . and I've come to the conclusion that we've overstepped our proper place as guardians and advisers of these people."

"Walk warily, Master Ma'Ning," C'baoth warned, an edge of menace in his voice. "You're speaking to the rightful and duly appointed leader of this expedition."

"That you are," Ma'Ning acknowledged. "But even the most powerful and knowledgeable of Jedi may sometimes stumble. It's my opinion that in your zeal to guide, you've crossed the line into direct rule."

"Then your opinion is wrong," C'baoth countered flatly. "I'm doing what is necessary—and *only* what is necessary—to keep this mission running smoothly."

"Others would disagree," Ma'Ning said, his eyes flicking over C'baoth's shoulder to the crewers and their families gathered together beside their borrowed shuttle. "At any rate, it's now a matter for all of Outbound Flight's Jedi to decide."

C'baoth seemed to draw back a little. "Are you suggesting that a Judgment Circle be convened?"

"In actual fact, Master C'baoth, I've already made the arrangements," Ma'Ning said. "The circle will convene as soon as the situation with the Chiss has been resolved."

For a long moment the two men gazed at each other, and Lorana could sense the tension arcing along the line between their eyes. "Then it will convene," C'baoth said at last. "And when it concludes, you'll understand that I do what is best for Outbound Flight and its people."

He looked at Lorana. "You'll *all* understand."

He turned back to Ma'Ning. "Until then, I am still in command," he went on. "You'll return at once to Dreadnaught-Four and prepare for combat."

Ma'Ning's lip twitched. "The negotiations with the Chiss have failed?"

"There was nothing to negotiate," C'baoth said. "Return to Dreadnaught-Four."

Ma'Ning's eyes flicked to Lorana, as if wondering whether he should ask her opinion on that. But if he was, he left the question unvoiced. "Very well," he said, looking back at C'baoth. Turning, he left the hangar.

C'baoth took a deep breath, let it out in a long, controlled sigh. "Did you know about this?" he asked quietly.

Lorana shook her head. "No."

"A waste of time," C'baoth said contemptuously. "Still, if it'll end this dangerous disunity, he can convene his little circle. Now; come."

Turning, he led the way back to Uliar and the others.

"Wonder what they're talking about," Pressor murmured at Uliar's side.

"No idea," Uliar said, studying the three Jedi closely. Even if they'd been closer, the hangar's lousy acoustics would probably have made their conversation impossible to hear.

But neither distance nor acoustics could disguise their expressions . . . and to Uliar, it was abundantly clear that no one over there was very happy right now. "Maybe they're finally having it out," he suggested.

"I doubt it," Pressor said. "Jedi stick together like molwelded deck plates."

"Yeah, I've noticed," Uliar agreed sourly. "Probably just a difference of opinion on how to swat down this Mitth-whatever."

"Probably." Pressor cleared his throat. "You know, Chas, it occurs to me that we still have one card we could play," he said, lowering his voice even further. "Back in the aft reactor storage area we've got a couple of droidekas packed away for emergency intruder defense. If we pulled them out and turned 'em loose, even the Jedi would have to sit up and take notice."

Uliar snorted. "Oh, they'd notice, all right. All the bodies lying around would be a dead giveaway. Those things are way too dangerous for amateurs to fool around with."

"Maybe," Pressor said. "But still—"

"Break time's over," Uliar interrupted as the Jedi conversation broke apart. Ma'Ning turned and left the hangar, while C'baoth and Jinzler conversed a moment longer and then headed back toward the shuttle. In Uliar's estimation, both looked even less happy than they had before.

They reached the silent group by the shuttle, and for a moment C'baoth sent his gaze around at all of them as if memorizing their faces. "Jedi Jinzler, you'll escort these people back to Dreadnaught-Four," he said at last. "No. On second thought, take them to the storage core and put them in the Jedi training center."

Jinzler turned to him, her eyes widening in surprise. "The *training center*?"

"Don't worry, there's plenty of room," C'baoth said. "I've ordered all the students to Dreadnaught-One's ComOps Center, where they can observe the upcoming meld in safety."

"But they'll be locked in down there." Jinzler's gaze flicked past Uliar, lingering on the children as they clutched their parents' hands. "Besides, we're on full battle alert," she added. "They need to be at their stations."

"Where they can preach their sedition to others?" C'baoth

countered darkly. "No. They'll be out of trouble down there until I've had time to decide on a more permanent solution."

Jinzler seemed to brace herself. "Master C'baoth—"

"You will obey my order, Jedi Jinzler," C'baoth said. His voice was quiet, but Uliar could hear the weight of will and age and history behind it. "Between the Chiss and whatever game this Sidious impostor is playing, Outbound Flight has no time right now to deal with internal dissent."

And as Uliar watched, Jinzler's brief flicker of defiance faded away. "Yes, Master C'baoth," she murmured.

With one final look at the people still lined up on the deck, C'baoth turned and strode away. "If you please, Uliar?" Jinzler said quietly, her eyes avoiding his.

Uliar gazed across the hangar at C'baoth's receding back. *Someday,* he promised himself. *Someday.* "You heard our beloved Jedi slave master," he growled. "Everyone back in the shuttle."

The pulsating hyperspace sky flowed past the Vagaari warship, closer and more vivid and more terrifying than Car'das had ever seen it. With only a single layer of thin plastic between him and the waves, he couldn't shake the sensation that at any moment they might break through and snatch him away from even the precarious safety of his hull bubble, leaving him to die alone in the incomprehensible vastness of the universe. He tried closing his eyes, or turning around so that his face would be to the hull. But somehow that just made it worse.

And it would be a six-hour journey back to the Crustai base, six hours of uncertainty and mental agony along with the emotional strain of the hyperspace sky beating against his transparent coffin. More than once he wondered if he would make it with his sanity still intact.

He never had the chance to find out. Less than two hours after leaving the Geroon homeworld, the hyperspace sky suddenly coalesced into starlines and collapsed back into stars. There was a click from somewhere beside him—

"Human!" the Miskara's voice snarled into his ear.

Car'das jerked, banging his head on the cold plastic. What in the worlds—?

"Human!" the voice came again.

And this time he realized it was coming from the diamond-shaped device he'd puzzled at earlier. The Vagaari version of a comlink, apparently. Reaching awkwardly over his shoulder, he grabbed it. "Yes, Your Eminence?"

"What is this trap you have led us to?" the Vagaari demanded, his tone sending a shiver through Car'das's body.

"I don't understand," Car'das protested. "Did your people get the wrong coordinates from the transport's computer?"

"We have been brought too soon into crawlspace," the Miskara bit out. "The stolen ship net has been used against us."

Behind Car'das came the subtle clicking of locks as someone prepared to open his prison. "But how could the Chiss have planned such a thing?" he asked, fumbling to get the words out before the door could be opened. If he was brought before the Miskara now, he was likely to die a quick and very uncomfortable death. "They must have been using it on someone else, and we just happened to run into it."

"With all of space to choose from?" the Miskara shot back. Still, Car'das thought he could hear a slight dip in the other's anger level. "Ridiculous."

"Stranger things have happened," Car'das insisted, feeling sweat breaking out on his forehead.

Behind him, the hull cracked open. Car'das tensed, but the

Vagaari outside merely thrust a set of macrobinoculars from the Chiss shuttle into his hands. "Look forward," the Miskara's voice ordered. "Tell me the story of this vessel."

The door was slammed shut again behind him. Exhaling some of his tension, Car'das activated the macrobinoculars and scanned the sky in front of him.

The object of the Miskara's interest wasn't hard to locate. It was a set of six ships, big ones, arranged around a cylindrical core with tapered ends.

It was Outbound Flight.

He took a careful breath. "I've never seen anything like it," he told the Miskara. "But it matches the description of a long-range exploration and colony project called Outbound Flight. There are fifty thousand of my people aboard those ships, with enough supplies in the storage core to last all of them for several years."

"How many fighting machines will they have?"

"I don't know," Car'das said. "There'll be some, certainly, mostly those bigger tripod-type droidekas to be used as colony boundary guards. Probably a few hundred of those. Most of their droids will be service and repair types, though. They probably have at least twenty thousand of those types."

"And these mechanical slaves will have the same artificial brains and mechanisms as the fighting machines?"

Car'das grimaced. It was pretty clear where the Miskara was going with this. "Yes, they could probably all be adapted to combat of some sort," he agreed. "But the people there aren't going to just hand them over to you. And those Dreadnaughts pack a *lot* of firepower."

"Your concern is touching," the Miskara said, his voice thick with sarcasm. "But we are the Vagaari. We take what we want."

There was a click, and the comlink shut off. "Yes," Car'das murmured. "So I've heard."

"There," Mitth'raw'nuruodo said, pointing out the *Springhawk*'s canopy. "You see them, Commander?"

"They're a little hard to miss," Doriana ground out, his throat tight as he gazed at the hundreds of alien ships that had suddenly appeared at the edge of Mitth'raw'nuruodo's gravity-field trap. "Who the blazes are they?"

"A nomadic race of conquerors and destroyers called the Vagaari," Mitth'raw'nuruodo told him.

"What are they doing here?" Kav demanded, his voice shaking. "How did they find us?"

"I would imagine we have Car'das to thank for that," Mitth'raw'nuruodo said calmly. "As it happens, this system is on a direct line between the last known Vagaari position and my Crustai base."

Doriana stared at the other. "You mean Car'das *betrayed* you?"

"Car'das has his own concerns and priorities." Mitth'raw'nuruodo lifted his eyebrows pointedly at Doriana. "As do we all."

There was no real answer to that, at least none that Doriana was interested in voicing. "What are we going to do about them?" he asked instead.

"Let us wait and see their intentions," Mitth'raw'nuruodo said, turning back to gaze out the bridge canopy. "Perhaps they will be cooperative."

Doriana frowned. "Cooperative how?"

Mitth'raw'nuruodo smiled faintly. "Patience, Commander. Let us wait and see."

* * *

"They arrived quite suddenly," C'baoth's voice came from Lorana's comlink, calm but with an edge to it she'd seldom heard before. "Some ploy of the Chiss, I imagine."

"What are they doing?" Lorana asked, keeping her voice down as she gazed ahead of her at the line of men, women, and children walking alongside the stacks of storage crates toward the Jedi training center. There was no point in worrying these people any more than they already were.

"So far, just waiting," C'baoth told her. "Captain Pakmillu informs me that their ship design is radically different from that of the Chiss, but of course that means nothing."

"Have you asked the commander about them?" Lorana asked. Uliar, walking at the end of the line of prisoners, glanced over his shoulder and started to drift backward toward her. "Maybe they have nothing to do with him."

C'baoth snorted. "With all of space for them to fly through? Please."

"What's going on?" Uliar asked softly.

Lorana hesitated. But all of Outbound Flight was in this together. "An unidentified fleet has arrived," she told him. "Over two hundred ships, at least a hundred of which seem to be warships."

"Who are you talking to?" C'baoth asked.

"We're trying to figure out whether they're Chiss ships, Chiss allies, or someone else entirely," Lorana continued, ignoring the question.

"What are their reactor emissions like?" Uliar asked. "Is it a similar spectrum to Mitth-whatever's ships, or something different?"

"Who *is* that?" C'baoth demanded. "Jedi Jinzler?"

"Reactor Tech Uliar says we might be able to deduce their identity or affiliation from their reactor emission spectrum," Lorana said.

"And what precisely is Reactor Tech Uliar doing out of the imprisonment I ordered for him and his fellow conspirators?" C'baoth asked acidly.

"We're on our way there," Lorana said, feeling her resolve eroding beneath the weight and pressure of his personality. "I thought that since he's an expert in these things—"

"We have experts up here, too," C'baoth cut in. "*Loyal* experts. You concentrate on putting Uliar where he can't do any more harm and leave the alien fleet to—"

He broke off as a melodious voice, or possibly two of them, began to speak in the background. "What's that?" Lorana asked.

"They appear to be hailing us," C'baoth said. The alien voices grew louder as the Jedi Master moved closer to one of the bridge speakers.

Lorana listened closely. It was a strange language, highly musical, with a distinct singsong component to it. "Uliar?" she whispered.

He shook his head, his forehead creased in concentration. "Never heard anything like it before," he whispered back. "But it doesn't sound like the kind of language near humans like the Chiss would come up with."

Lorana nodded agreement. "Master C'baoth?" she called. "It doesn't sound like—"

"Get the conspirators to their holding area, Jedi Jinzler," C'baoth interrupted. "Then go to Dreadnaught-Four and report to Jedi Master Ma'Ning in the weapons blisters." There was a click as he shut off his comlink.

Lorana sighed. "Yes, Master C'baoth," she murmured as she returned her comlink to her belt.

"We're in trouble, aren't we?" Uliar asked quietly.

"We'll be all right," Lorana assured him, trying to convey a confidence she didn't feel. First Mitth'raw'nuruodo, and now this new threat . . . and with Outbound Flight's defense resting squarely on the shoulders of their handful of Jedi.

And suddenly she was getting a very bad feeling about all of it. "I need to get up to D-Four to assist Master Ma'Ning," she told Uliar. "Get your people inside, and when these other matters are settled we'll get your problem straightened out."

Uliar snorted. "It's not *our* problem."

Lorana grimaced. "I know," she conceded. "Don't worry. We *will* straighten it out."

"They're probably not answering because they don't understand you," Car'das explained as patiently as his pounding heart would allow. "As I said, they're from the same region of space I am, and we don't know the language of the mighty and noble Vagaari."

"You will soon learn it," the Miskara promised him coldly. "In the meantime, you will serve as translator."

Car'das grimaced. That was all he needed: the people on Outbound Flight assuming he was a renegade or, worse, a traitor. *Whatever necessary* . . . "Of course, Your Eminence," he said. "I stand humbly ready to serve the Miskara and the Vagaari people in any way you wish."

"Of course," the Miskara said, as if even a breath of hesitation on Car'das's part would be unthinkable. "Tell me first: how deeply within the vessels will the fighting machines be stored? Will they be at the surfaces, or deeper inside."

"Deep inside," Car'das told him, not knowing whether it was true but not about to take the time to try to actually think about it.

"Good," the Miskara said with satisfaction. "Then we may destroy as we will without risking our prize."

An unpleasant sensation tingled across Car'das's skin. With a hundred Vagaari warships blotting out the starscape around him, the Miskara's words were as close to a death sentence as anything he'd ever heard.

And he was the one who'd pointed the Vagaari in that direction.

"Now: speak this," the Miskara continued. " 'You of the vessel known as Outbound Flight: we are the Vagaari. You will surrender or be destroyed.' "

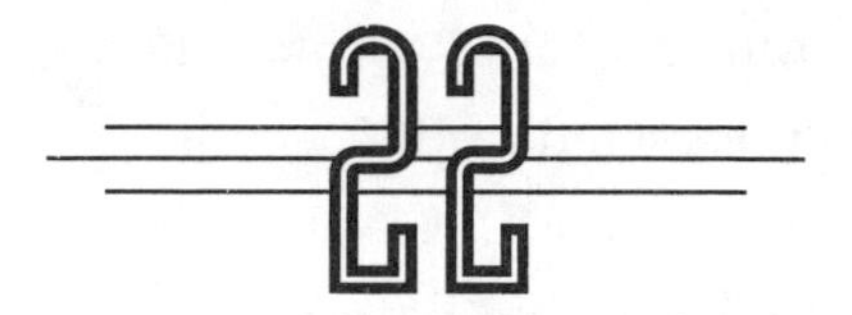

. . . Or be destroyed."

Lorana looked across the weapons blister at Ma'Ning, at the tight set to his mouth. The first voice from the unknown ships had definitely not been human. This one just as definitely was.

And the human had been speaking Basic, as well. This wasn't good. "A captive from the Republic?" she suggested.

"Or a traitor," Ma'Ning said grimly. "Either way, it's going to make this that much trickier."

"Not at all," C'baoth's voice came from the comm speaker. "There's nothing even a traitor could have told them that will have prepared them for the kind of coordinated defense a Jedi meld can offer."

"With a hundred or more warships at their disposal I can't see them worrying overly much about how tight our defense is," Ma'Ning countered.

"Patience, Master Ma'Ning," C'baoth said, his voice glacially calm. "Trust in the Force."

"They're moving forward," Captain Pakmillu's voice cut in. "All weapons stations stand ready."

Lorana took a deep breath as she stretched out to the Force for strength and calm. This was it: the first genuine test of the Jedi control system C'baoth had spent so much of his time teaching the rest of them.

"What in the name—?" Abruptly, Ma'Ning hunched closer to his sensor displays. "Master C'baoth?"

"I see them," C'baoth said. "So this is the sort of enemy we face."

"What is it?" Lorana asked, swiveling her chair to her own displays.

"Look at the warships," Ma'Ning said. "See all those plastic bubbles on the hulls?"

Lorana felt her chest tighten. "There are *people* in there!"

"Living shields," C'baoth confirmed, his voice thick with contempt. "The most evil and cowardly defense concept ever created."

"What do we do?" Lorana asked, a sudden trembling in her voice. "We can't just slaughter them."

"Courage, Jedi Jinzler," C'baoth said. "We'll simply shoot *between* the hostages."

"Impossible," Ma'Ning insisted. "Not even with Jedi gunners. Turbolasers simply aren't accurate enough."

"Do you assume me to be a fool, Master Ma'Ning?" C'baoth demanded scathingly. "Of course we won't fire until we're close enough for the necessary accuracy."

"And meanwhile we just sit here and take *their* fire?" Ma'Ning countered.

"Hardly," C'baoth said, an edge of malicious anticipation creeping into his voice. "The Vagaari have a surprise in store for them. All Jedi: prepare to meld. Stretch out to the Force . . . and then, to the Vagaari."

"They make no answer," the Miskara said accusingly, as if Outbound Flight's silence was Car'das's fault.

"Perhaps they're still consulting among themselves, Your Eminence," Car'das suggested, shifting his eyes back and forth across the sky. The Vagaari ships had started to close the gap between themselves and Outbound Flight, moving together into groups of tight-formation clusters that would provide them the protection of overlapping forward shields.

They were preparing to attack.

And still nothing from Outbound Flight. Or from Thrawn, for that matter. His ships had to be around here somewhere. But where?

"You will give them a new message," the Miskara ordered. " 'The time for discussion is ended. You will surrender now or—' "

And in the middle of the sentence, his voice abruptly dissolved into a confused burbling.

Car'das frowned, pressing the comlink to his ear. The whole bridge seemed to have collapsed into the same helpless babbling, as if the entire crew had had a mass mental attack.

Which was, he suspected, exactly what had happened.

He looked out again at Outbound Flight, an unpleasant shiver running through him. He'd heard the stories about all the ways Jedi could use their mind control tricks to confuse attackers, everything from creating false noises in their ears to making them unable to properly focus on controls or weapons systems. But while the stories also claimed that a group of them together could use that power on this massive a scale, he'd never heard of something like that actually happening.

Until now.

And with that, he knew, it was all over. The final card had come up double-down-nine, and the rest was as fixed and inevitable as a planetary orbit.

With the comlink still pressed to his ear, he settled down to wait for the end.

"So your tales were correct," Mitth'raw'nuruodo murmured. "Your Jedi have reached across the distance to the Vagaari and numbed or destroyed their minds."

"So it would seem," Doriana agreed, feeling a little numb himself. Even if it was just the Vagaari commanders and gunners who'd been affected, and even given the fact that the aliens would have had no forewarning of what was coming, it was still a terrifying feat.

And it was being performed by a relative handful of Jedi Masters and Jedi Knights.

Predictably, it was Kav who broke the awed silence first. "And our part is to sit by and do nothing?" he prompted.

"Our part is to do that for which we have come," Mitth'raw'nuruodo said. Reaching to his board, he keyed a switch. "It is time for the Vagaari to die."

"The *Vagaari*?" Kav echoed. "No! You were given my starfighters for use against Outbound Flight."

"I was not *given* the starfighters at all," Mitth'raw'nuruodo corrected him coolly. Ahead, the droid starfighters were rising in waves now from their asteroid staging area, heading at full speed toward the clusters of Vagaari warships. "*I* will choose how to use them."

Kav snarled something in his own language. "You will not get away with this," he bit out.

"Walk cautiously, Vicelord," Mitth'raw'nuruodo warned, his glowing eyes flashing at the Neimoidian. "Don't forget that the starfighters aren't the only Neimoidian technology I've taken from you."

Doriana felt a sudden tingling on the back of his neck. He spun around, expecting to find the two droidekas Mitth'raw'nuruodo had taken from the *Darkvenge* standing behind them in full combat stance.

But there was nothing there. "No, Commander, the combat droids are not here," Mitth'raw'nuruodo assured him. "They're where they can be of far more useful service."

"And where is that?" Doriana asked.

"Where else?" Mitth'raw'nuruodo said, smiling tightly. "On the bridge of the Vagaari flagship."

The sudden multiple stutter of blasterfire in his ear sent Car'das twitching to the side, and he banged his elbow against the edge of the bubble as he hastily moved the comlink farther away. His head was still ringing as the rhythmic fire of the droidekas was joined by the more deliberate shots from the four battle droids' rifles. Apparently, Thrawn had had a secondary control pattern laid in beneath the program Car'das had set up earlier for the Miskara. The sounds of shooting shifted subtly as the six droids began to move across the bridge, mowing down the helpless gunners and commanders.

And as they systematically chopped off the head of the Vagaari leadership hierarchy, the droid starfighters arrived.

The first and second waves flashed overhead without slowing, skimming the hull barely five meters from Car'das's face as they drove toward the clusters of Vagaari ships in the distance. The third wave arrived in full combat mode, their laser cannons raking the flagship with a brilliant sheet of fire. Car'das flinched back, but almost before he had time to be frightened they, too, were past, leaving torn pieces of shattered hull material and white jets of escaping air in their wake. Blinking against the multiple purple afterimages, he peered through the dissipating gases at the other bubbles around him, half afraid of what he would see.

But the starfighters had pulled it off. In every single one of the bubbles within his view, the Geroon hostages were still alive—terrified, certainly, some of them clawing mindlessly at the plastic as if trying to tunnel their way out. But they were alive. With Outbound Flight's Jedi preventing the Vagaari gunners from defending their ships, and with the sharp-edged precision the droids' electronic targeting systems and close-approach attack had permitted, the starfighters had sliced their way neatly through the warship's hull between the Vagaari's living shields.

And not just aboard the flagship. All around him, Car'das could see clouds of debris and escaping air enveloping the other nearby Vagaari warships, the haze scintillating with the fiery glow of the starfighters' drives as they finished each set of targets and moved on to the next. Already in this first attack, he estimated Thrawn's assault had taken out over a quarter of the alien warships.

And still with no response from the remainder. The question now, he knew, was whether the Jedi control of the aliens would last long enough for the starfighters to finish the job. Switching on his macrobinoculars, listening with half an ear to the one-sided carnage still going on beneath him on the bridge, he focused on Outbound Flight.

It was like nothing Lorana had ever felt before. Like nothing she had ever dreamed she would ever feel, or need to prepare herself for. Even as she submerged herself in the Jedi meld, allowing C'baoth to guide her and the others as they spread confusion across the Vagaari commanders and gunners, the alien minds she was wrapped around suddenly began exploding into death.

Not just a few deaths, either, small ripples of sensation that might have throbbed painfully but controllably against her consciousness. These deaths came in a thunderstorm torrent, wave after wave of fear and agony and rage that hammered against her already overstretched and vulnerable mind. She could feel herself staggering, her hands clutching blindly for something to hold on to as her body reacted to her disorientation. There was a sharp pain in her shoulder and head; distantly, she realized she had fallen out of her chair onto the deck. She could feel herself twitching uncontrollably; could sense the others' reactions flowing through the meld, feeding into her weakness even as her own pain fed into theirs. A thousand alien voices shrieked through her brain as their life forces were snuffed out, with a thousand more waiting behind them . . .

Beside Doriana, Mitth'raw'nuruodo took a deep breath. *"Ch'tra,"* he ordered.

And moving as a single unit, the Chiss fleet surged forward. "Time to join the party?" Doriana asked, still watching in grim amazement as the waves of droid starfighters methodically cut their way across the Vagaari ships.

"No," Mitth'raw'nuruodo said. "Time to start one of our own."

And it was only then that Doriana saw that the *Springhawk* and the rest of the Chiss ships were heading for Outbound Flight. He closed his hands into fists, waiting tensely for the Dreadnaughts' gunners to spot this new threat and open fire.

But nothing happened. The *Springhawk* flew completely through the turbolasers' effective combat range, passed unchallenged through the point-defense zone, and with only minor turbulence passed through the shields near the bow of the nearest Dreadnaught. The other Chiss ships broke from the *Springhawk*'s flanks, spreading out toward the other Dreadnaughts as the *Springhawk* curved from its intercept vector to fly low across its chosen Dreadnaught's hull.

And opened fire.

They hit the weapons blisters first, the brilliant blue fire of the Chiss lasers tearing through armor and capacitors and charging equipment and digging deeply into the blisters themselves. The shield generators were next, the *Springhawk* zigzagging along the Dreadnaught's hull as it targeted and destroyed each in turn. All done with the utmost efficiency, a small detached part of Doriana's mind noted, without a single wasted movement. Clearly, Mitth'raw'nuruodo had made good use of the technical readouts he'd provided.

And then, to his surprise, the *Springhawk* made a sharp turn away from the hull and headed again for deep space. Beyond the expanding cloud of destruction, he could see the other Chiss ships doing the same. "What's wrong?" he asked, his eyes flicking across the sky for some new danger that might have caused Mitth'raw'nuruodo to break off his attack.

"Nothing is wrong," Mitth'raw'nuruodo said, sounding puzzled. "Why?"

"But you have ceased the attack," Kav said, clearly as bewildered as Doriana. "Yet they lie helpless before you."

"Which is precisely why I've stopped," Mitth'raw'nuruodo said. "Jedi Master C'baoth; leaders of Outbound Flight. Your vessel has been disarmed, its ability to defend itself destroyed. I offer you this one final chance to surrender and return to the Republic."

"What?" Kav yelped, his eyes widening. "But you were to *destroy* them."

"If and when you should command again, Vicelord Kav, such decisions will be yours," Mitth'raw'nuruodo said coolly. "But not now. Outbound Flight, I await your decision."

Through the echoing haze of dying minds still screaming at her, through the smoke and debris and distant moans of the injured, Lorana realized she was dying.

Probably from suffocation, she decided as she noticed that her lungs were straining but that little or no air was reaching them. She tried to move, but her legs seemed pinned somehow to the deck. She tried to stretch out to the Force, but with the death agonies of the Vagaari now joined by the much closer deaths of her own shipmates she couldn't seem to bring her thoughts into focus.

Something cold and metallic closed around her wrist.

She opened her eyes to find a maintenance droid tugging at her arm. "What are you doing?" she croaked. It was a matter of mild surprise to discover that she had enough air even to speak. Experimentally, she tried to take a deep breath.

And felt a welcome coolness as air flowed into her lungs.

She blinked away some of the fog hazing her eyes and peered through the swirling debris. There was a long jagged slash through the ceiling above her, undoubtedly the source of the weapons blister's sudden decompression. Stretched across the gash were a dozen sheets of twisted metal that appeared to have been blown or pulled away from the walls. Half a dozen small metalwork droids were climbing across them, filling the room with clouds of sparks as they hastily welded the sheets into place over the gash.

Lying on the deck halfway across the room, his arms stretching toward the ceiling as he used the Force to hold the still-unwelded sheets in place, was Ma'Ning.

Lorana couldn't see very much of his body with the wreckage of the control room scattered across her line of sight. But she could see enough to turn her stomach. He must have caught the full brunt of one of the laser blasts, taking both the agony of the shot itself as well as the impact of the shards of shattered metal it had created. "Master Ma'Ning," she gasped, trying to get up. But her legs still refused to work.

"No, don't," Ma'Ning said. His voice was strained but still carried the full authority of a Jedi Master. "It's too late for me."

"For—" Lorana broke off, a sudden edge of horror cutting through her. With the attack and her own near suffocation, she'd completely lost her connection to the Jedi meld that had so successfully blocked the Vagaari attack.

Now, as she tried to stretch out to it again, she found that it had all but vanished.

"No," she whispered to herself. But there was no mistake. When their attackers had targeted the weapons blisters, they had knowingly or unknowingly targeted the Jedi as well.

And with only one or two dazed and stunned exceptions, they were dead.

All of them.

"I should have . . . tried stop . . . him sooner," Ma'Ning murmured, his voice weakening as he rapidly lost strength. "But he was . . . Jedi Master . . . Jedi *Master* . . ."

With an effort, Lorana pushed back the paralyzing horror. "Don't talk," she said, trying again to move. "Let me help you."

"No," Ma'Ning said. "Too late . . . for me. But not . . . for others." One of his outstretched hands twitched toward her, and a bent section of girder pinning her legs to the deck lifted a few millimeters and clattered away. "You can . . . help them."

"But I can't just leave you," Lorana protested. Again she tried to get up, and this time she succeeded.

"I am far . . . beyond your help," Ma'Ning said, a deep sadness in his voice. "Go. Help those . . . who can still . . . be helped."

"But—"

"No!" Ma'Ning bit out, his face convulsing with a sudden spasm. "You're . . . Jedi. Taken . . . oath . . . serve others. Go . . . go."

Lorana swallowed. "Yes, Master. I—" She trailed off, searching for the right words. But there weren't any.

Perhaps Ma'Ning couldn't find any, either. "Good-bye . . . Jedi Jinzler," he simply said, a ghostly smile touching his lips.

"Good-bye, Master Ma'Ning."

Ma'Ning's smile vanished, and he lifted his eyes again to the repair droids and their work. Turning away, Lorana picked her way through the wreckage toward the door.

She knew she would never see him again.

The door, when she reached it, was jammed shut. Stretching

out as best she could to the Force, she managed to work it open far enough to slip through. The corridor outside was nearly as bad as the blister itself, with buckled walls and chunks of ceiling littering the deck. But here at least the attackers hadn't managed to cut completely through the hull and open it to space.

The blast doors ten meters down the corridor in either direction had closed when the blister had decompressed, sealing away this section from the rest of the ship. But with the breach now sealed and the emergency oxygen supplies repressurizing the area, the forward blast door opened for Lorana without protest.

In the distance she could hear shouting and screams, and could sense the fear and panic behind them. But for the moment, those people weren't her immediate concern. The Dreadnaughts were well equipped with escape pods, where the survivors could take refuge while the droids repaired the hull.

But there was one group of people who wouldn't have that chance: the fifty-seven so-called conspirators C'baoth had ordered locked away in the storage core.

The people *she* had locked away in the storage core.

Her legs were starting to throb now where the girder had landed on her. Stretching out to the Force to suppress the pain, she headed in a limping run toward the nearest pylon turbolift.

"We made a bargain!" Kav snarled. "You were to destroy Outbound Flight for us!"

"I never made any such bargain," Mitth'raw'nuruodo said. "I agreed only to do what I deemed necessary to eliminate the threat posed by the expedition."

"That was *not* what we wanted," Kav insisted.

"You were in no position to make demands," Mitth'raw'nuruodo reminded him. "Nor are you now."

There was a sudden hiss from the comm. "So," an almost unrecognizable voice ground out. "You think you have won, alien?" The display came alive . . . and a cold shiver ran up Doriana's back.

It was Jorus C'baoth, pale and disheveled, his clothing torn and blood-spattered, one side of his face badly burned. But his eyes blazed with the same arrogant fire that Doriana had seen that day long ago in Supreme Chancellor Palpatine's office.

He groped for Mitth'raw'nuruodo's sleeve. "Kav is right—you have to destroy them," he hissed urgently. "If you don't, we're dead."

Mitth'raw'nuruodo's eyes flicked to him, then back to the comm. "I have indeed won," he told C'baoth. "I have only to give a single order—" His hand shifted slightly on his control board, his fingertips coming to rest on a covered switch edged in red. "—and you and all your people will die. Is your pride worth so much to you?"

"A Jedi does not yield to pride," C'baoth spat. "Nor does he yield to empty threats. He follows only the dictates of his own destiny."

"Then choose your destiny," Mitth'raw'nuruodo said. "I'm told the role of the Jedi is to serve and defend."

"You were told wrongly," C'baoth countered. "The role of the Jedi is to lead and guide, and to destroy all threats." The unburned corner of his lip twisted upward in a bitter smile.

And without warning, Thrawn's head jerked back, his whole body pressing back against his seat. His hand darted to his throat, clutching uselessly at it.

"Commander!" Doriana snapped, grabbing reflexively for Mitth'raw'nuruodo's collar.

But it was no use. The invisible power that was choking the

life out of him wasn't something physical that Doriana might be able to push aside. C'baoth was using the Force . . . and there was nothing Doriana or anyone else could do to stop him.

In a handful of minutes, Mitth'raw'nuruodo would be dead.

Lorana was in a turbolift car heading down the forward pylon when she felt C'baoth's attack echoing through her mind like the sound of a distant hammer. For a minute she puzzled at it, sensing his anger and frustration and pride, wondering what in the worlds he was doing.

And then, abruptly, the horrifying truth sliced through her like the blade of a lightsaber. "No!" she shouted reflexively toward the turbolift car ceiling. "Master C'baoth—no!"

But it was too late. In his single-minded thirst for revenge, Jorus C'baoth, Jedi Master, had gone over to the dark side.

A wave of pain and revulsion swept over Lorana, as agonizing as salt in an open wound. She had never seen a Jedi fall before. She'd known it could happen, and that it had in fact happened many times throughout history. But it had always seemed something comfortably distant, something that could never happen to anyone she knew.

Now it had . . . and following close behind the wave of pain came an even more powerful wave of guilt.

Because she'd been his Padawan, the person who'd spent the most time with him. The one person, Master Ma'Ning had once suggested, whom he might have actually listened to.

Could she have prevented this? Should she have stood up to him earlier, with or without the support of Ma'Ning or the others, when he first began to gather power and authority to himself? Certainly she'd tried talking to him in private on more than one occasion. But each time he'd brushed off her concerns, assuring her that all was well. Should she have pressed him more strongly? Forced him—somehow—to listen?

But she hadn't. And now it was too late.

Or was it? "We don't have to kill anyone," she murmured, focusing her mind toward D-1, trying desperately to send the thought or at least the sense to him. She fumbled for her comlink, only to discover that she'd lost it in the attack on the weapons blister. "We don't have to kill them," she continued, pleading with him. "We can just go home. All they want is for us to go *home*."

But there was no reply. C'baoth could undoubtedly sense her protest, but all she could sense in return was his indifference to her anguish, and his determination to continue along the path he'd now set himself upon. It was indeed too late.

Perhaps, a small voice whispered inside her, it had always been too late.

The turbolift came to a halt and the door opened into the storage core. For a long minute she stood in the doorway, wondering if she should leave the prisoners where they were for now and try to get to D-1.

But she would never make it in time. And even if she did, it would do her no good. She could sense the rigid set of C'baoth's mind, and she knew from long experience that even if she were standing at his side there was nothing she could say or do now to stop him. He would continue his attack until he had killed Commander Mitth'raw'nuruodo, then more, until he had killed all the rest of the Chiss out there.

Her heart aching, she stepped out into the storage core and limped toward the trapped crew members and their families. Even a Jedi, she thought bitterly, could do only so much.

But what she could do, she would.

* * *

The bridge crew was on it in a matter of seconds, shoving Doriana roughly aside and clustering around Mitth'raw'nuruodo as they fought to free him from the unseen attack that was killing him. But their efforts were as useless as Doriana's had been.

Standing at the edge of the frantic activity, Doriana looked at the comm display and tried desperately to think. If the Chiss attack had weakened C'baoth enough . . . but there was no sign of weakness in the eyes blazing from that ruined face. Could Doriana shut off the display, then, and at least rob the Jedi of his view of his victim? But Doriana had no idea where that control was, and he didn't speak any language the rest of the bridge crew understood. Besides, he wasn't sure that cutting off the display would do any good anyway.

And then, his gazed dropped from C'baoth's face to Thrawn's control board. The board, and the red-rimmed switch.

It might be nothing. But it was all he had. Pushing past the crewers who stood in his way, he flipped back the cover and pressed the switch.

And then, even as they continued to pound mercilessly against the Vagaari warships, the droid starfighters abruptly turned from their attack and fled.

Car'das frowned, pressing the macrobinoculars tighter against his face. A sizable percentage of the Vagaari fleet was still untouched, the surviving ships scrambling madly for the edge of Thrawn's gravity projector field. Yet all of the starfighters were leaving. Had they drained their solid-fuel engines already?

He caught his breath. No; the starfighters weren't running *away* from the Vagaari. They were running *toward* Outbound Flight.

He was still staring in disbelief when the first wave hit.

Not simply *attacking,* blasting away with laser cannons and energy torpedoes. They literally *hit* the Dreadnaughts, slamming at full speed into their hulls and vaporizing in brilliant flashes with the force of their impacts. The second wave did the same, this group striking different sections of the Dreadnaughts' hulls. Through the smoke and debris came the third and fourth waves, these groups pouring laser cannon fire and energy torpedoes into the damaged weapons blisters and shield generators.

And with a sudden chill, Car'das understood. The first two waves of starfighters hadn't been trying to breach the Dreadnaughts' thick armor plating. Their goal had merely been to create dents in the hulls at very specific points.

The points where the interior blast doors were positioned.

And now, with those doors disabled or warped enough to prevent a proper air seal, the rest of the starfighters were opening the Dreadnaughts to space.

More clouds of debris were blowing away from Outbound Flight's flanks as the starfighters blasted their way through the hulls, sweeping new waves of sudden death through the outer areas of the Dreadnaughts.

But for all the effect the attack had on him, C'baoth might not even have noticed it. His face remained as hard as anvilstone, his eyes burning unblinkingly across the *Springhawk*'s bridge.

And Mitth'raw'nuruodo was still dying.

Doriana curled his hands into helpless fists. So it was finally over. If this second assault had failed to kill C'baoth, it was because he'd hidden himself well away from the vacuum that had now snuffed out all life in the Dreadnaughts' outer sections. Even given the thinner bulkheads and blast doors of the ships' interior sections, there was no way even droid starfighters could clear out the maze of decks and compartments in time.

An odd formation caught his eye as it shot into view outside the canopy: a pair of starfighters flying in close formation with a fat cylinder tucked between them. Not just one pair, Doriana saw now, but ten of them, heading at full speed toward Outbound Flight.

He remembered Kav mentioning this particular project of Mitth'raw'nuruodo's, and the vicelord's contemptuous dismissal of the cylinders as some sort of useless fuel tanks. Frowning, he watched as, in ones and twos, the starfighter pairs drove through the newly blasted holes in the Dreadnaughts' hulls and disappeared inside.

For a moment, nothing happened. Then, abruptly, a haze of pale blue burst outward from the openings, nearly invisible amid the floating clouds of wreckage.

And with a sudden gasp of air, Mitth'raw'nuruodo collapsed forward against his board.

"Commander?" Doriana called, trying to get past the circle of crewers.

"I'm . . . all right," the other panted, rubbing his throat with one hand as he waved off assistance with the other.

"I think you got him," Doriana said, looking over at the comm display. C'baoth was no longer in sight. "I think C'baoth's dead."

"Yes," Mitth'raw'nuruodo confirmed, his voice quiet. "All of them . . . are dead."

A strange sensation crept up Doriana's back. "That's impossible," he said. "You only had one or two of those bombs in each Dreadnaught."

"One was all that was necessary," Mitth'raw'nuruodo said with a sadness that Doriana had never heard in him before. "They're a very special sort of weapon. A very terrible sort. Once inside the protective barrier of a war vessel's outer armor, they explode into a killing wave of radiation. The wave passes through floors and walls and ceilings, destroying all life."

Doriana swallowed. "And you had them all ready to go," he heard himself say.

Mitth'raw'nuruodo's eyes bored into his. "They were not meant for Outbound Flight," he said, and there was an expression on his face that made Doriana take an involuntary step backward. "They were intended for use against the largest of the Vagaari war vessels."

Doriana grimaced. "I see."

"No, you do *not* see," Mitth'raw'nuruodo retorted. "Because now, instead, we'll need to destroy the Vagaari remnant aboard the disabled vessels in shipboard face-to-face combat." He pointed out the canopy. "Worse, some of the war vessels and civilian craft have now escaped to deep space, where they'll have time to rebuild and perhaps one day will again pose a threat to this region of space."

"I understand," Doriana said. "I'm sorry."

To his surprise, he realized he meant it.

For a long moment Mitth'raw'nuruodo gazed at him in silence. Then, slowly, some of the tension lines faded from his face. "No warrior ever has the full depth of control that he would like," he said, his voice calmer but still troubled. "But I wish here that it might have been otherwise."

Doriana looked at Kav. For a wonder, the Neimoidian had the sense to keep his mouth shut. "What happens now?"

"As I said, we board the Vagaari war vessels," Mitth'raw'nuruodo said. "Once they've been secured, we'll free the Geroons from their prisons."

Doriana nodded. And so that was it. Outbound Flight was destroyed, its Jedi—especially C'baoth—all dead. It was over.

All, that is, except one small loose end. *No matter what the outcome,* Kav's warning echoed through his mind, *in the end this Mitthrawdo will have to die.*

And in the swirling chaos of a shipboard assault, accidents inevitably happened. "I wonder if I might have permission to accompany the attack force," he said. "I'd like to observe Chiss soldiers in action."

Mitth'raw'nuruodo inclined his head slightly. "As you wish, Commander Stratis. I think you'll find it most instructive."

"Yes," Doriana agreed softly. "I'm sure I will."

The vibrations from the Dreadnaughts above, transmitted faintly through the metal of the connecting pylons, finally came to an end. "Is it over?" Jorad Pressor asked timidly.

Carefully, Lorana let her hand drop from the bulkhead where she'd been steadying herself. The sudden, awful flood of death from above had finally ended as well, leaving nothing behind.

Nothing.

"Yes," she said, trying hard to give the boy an encouraging smile. "It's all over."

"So we can go back up?"

Lorana lifted her eyes to Jorad's father, and the tight set of his mouth. The children might not understand, but the adults did. "Not quite yet," she told Jorad. "There's probably a lot of cleaning up they're having to do. We'd just be in the way."

"And would have to hold our breath," someone muttered from the back of the group.

Someone else made a shushing noise. "Anyway, there's no point in hanging around here," one of the older men spoke up, trying to sound casual. "Might as well go back to the Jedi school where we can at least be a little more comfortable."

"And where we'll be properly locked in?" Uliar added sourly.

"No, of course not," Lorana said, trying to get her brain back on track. "There's plenty of spare building material crated up in the storage areas. I'll cut a section of girder and prop open the door. Come on—everyone back."

The crowd turned and shuffled back the way they'd come, some of the children still murmuring anxiously to their parents, the parents in turn trying to comfort them. Lorana started to follow, paused as Uliar touched her arm. "So what's the *real* damage?" he asked softly.

She sighed. "I don't sense any life up there. None at all."

"Could you be wrong?"

"It's possible," she admitted. "But I don't think so."

He was silent for a moment. "We'll need to make sure," he said. "There may be survivors who are just too weak for you to sense."

"I know," she said. "But we can't get up there yet. The fact that the turbolift cars won't come implies the pylons are open to vacuum somewhere. We'll have to wait until the droids get them patched up."

Uliar hissed between his teeth. "That could take hours."

"It can't be helped," Lorana said. "We'll just have to wait."

The battle had been over for nearly three hours, and Car'das was starting to get seriously bored when he finally heard the rhythmic tapping at his back.

He half turned over and rapped the same pattern with the edge of the macrobinoculars. Then, turning back around to face the stars, he worked the kinks out of his muscles and waited.

It came in a sudden flurry of activity. Behind him, the door to his prison popped open and he felt the sudden tugging of vacuum at his lungs and face as the air pressure in his bubble exploded outward, shoving him backward out into the corridor. He caught a glimpse of vac-suited figures surrounding him as he was enveloped in a tangle of sticky cloth. Before he could do more than scrabble his fingertips against it in an effort to push it away from his face there was a harsh hissing in his ears, and the cloth receded from him in all directions.

And a moment later he found himself floating inside a transparent rescue ball.

"Whoa," he muttered, wincing as his ears popped painfully with the returning air pressure.

"Are you all right?" a familiar voice asked from a comlink connected to the ball's oxygen tank.

"Yes, Commander, thank you," he assured the other. "I gather it all worked as planned?"

"Yes," Thrawn confirmed, his voice carrying an odd tinge of sadness to it. "For the most part."

One of the other rescuers leaned close, and to his surprise Car'das saw that it was the human who'd introduced himself aboard the *Darkvenge* as Commander Stratis. *"Car'das?"* Stratis demanded, frowning through the plastic. "What are *you* doing here?"

"Luring the Vagaari into my trap, of course," Thrawn said, as if it were obvious. "Or had you forgotten that the Chiss do not engage in preemptive attacks?"

"I see," Stratis said, still eyeing Car'das. "So those spy accusations you were throwing around aboard the *Darkvenge* were nothing but smoke? Something to cover you in case the whole thing fell apart?"

"It was protection, yes, but not for me," Thrawn said. He gestured, and the rest of the group began maneuvering Car'das's rescue ball down the corridor. "It was to protect Admiral Ar'alani, the officer commanding the transport that arrived an hour ago to take the freed Geroon slaves back to their world."

"And who couldn't afford to be even unofficially involved in any of this," Stratis said, nodding. "But who *could* make sure to look the other way at all the right times, leaving you and Car'das to take the blame if anything went wrong."

"Never mind the blame," Car'das put in. "What happened with Outbound Flight? I saw the starfighters take off after it."

Thrawn and Stratis exchanged looks. "We were forced to go farther than I'd hoped," Thrawn said.

Car'das felt his heart freeze in his chest. "How much farther?"

"They're dead," Thrawn said quietly. "All of them."

There was a long silence. Car'das looked away, his eyes catching glimpses of dead Vagaari as the Chiss continued carrying him along. Thrawn had abandoned his attack on known slavers and murderers to destroy thousands of innocent people?

"There wasn't any choice," Stratis said into his numbness. "C'baoth was using his Jedi power to try and strangle the commander. There was no other way to stop him."

"Did you ever give them a chance to just leave and go home?" Car'das retorted.

"Yes," Thrawn said.

"More than just one chance," Stratis added. "More than I would have offered them, in fact. And if it matters any, I was the one who actually pushed the button."

Car'das grimaced. On one level, it did matter. On another, it didn't. "You're sure there aren't any survivors?"

"The Dreadnaughts were taken out by radiation bombs," Stratis told him. "We haven't actually sent anyone over yet to check, but if the commander's weapons stats are accurate there's no way anyone could have lived through that."

"So you got what you wanted after all," Car'das said, feeling suddenly very tired. "You must be happy."

Stratis looked away. "I'm content," he said. "I wouldn't say I'm happy."

* * *

"Well?" Kav demanded as Doriana stripped off his vac suit in the privacy of one of the *Springhawk*'s prep rooms. "I hear no wailings of despair for the fallen captain."

"That's because the captain isn't fallen," Doriana said. "I never had an opportunity."

"Did not *have* one?" Kav asked. "Or did not *make* one?"

"I never *had* one," Doriana repeated coldly. He was not in the mood for this. "You want to try to assassinate a military commander in front of his men, you go right ahead."

He finished undressing in silence. "Yet he *must* die," Kav said as Doriana began pulling on his own clothing. "He knows too much about our part in what has happened."

"Mitth'raw'nuruodo is no ordinary alien," Doriana pointed out. "And there's still a matter of finding an opportunity."

"Or of making one." Stepping close, Kav pressed something into Doriana's hand. "Here."

Puzzled, Doriana looked down. One glance was all it took. "Where did you get this?" he hissed as he hurriedly closed his hand around the small hold-out blaster.

"I have always had it," Kav said. "The shot is small and hard to see, but highly intense. It will kill quickly and quietly."

And would condemn Doriana in double-quick time if he was caught with it. Feeling a sudden sheen of sweat breaking out beneath his collar, he slipped the weapon out of sight into a pocket. "Just let me handle the timing," he warned the other. "I don't want you hovering around like an expectant mother avian."

"Do not worry," Kav growled. "Where is the commander now?"

"Gone to the transport ship to talk to the admiral," Doriana said, finishing with his tunic and starting to pull on his boots. "Car'das went with him."

And that was another problem, he reminded himself soberly. Like Mitth'raw'nuruodo, Car'das knew far too much about what had happened out here. And unlike the Chiss, he definitely *would* soon be traveling back to the Republic. After he dealt with Mitth'raw'nuruodo, Doriana would have to make equally sure that Car'das never told his story to the wrong people.

The rescued Geroons had been herded into the cargo bay, the only place aboard the transport big enough to hold them all. Most were sitting cross-legged in small groups, talking quietly among themselves, the most recent arrivals still working on the food sticks and hot drinks Admiral Ar'alani's warriors had provided them. All of them looked a little dazed, as if having trouble believing they were actually free of the Vagaari.

Standing to the side just inside one of the bay doors, trying to stay out of the way of both the Geroons and the Chiss crewers moving about them, Car'das looked out at the multitude, his heart and mind fatigued beyond anything he'd ever experienced. A thousand times in the past day he'd wondered what he was doing in the middle of this whole thing; wondered how in the galaxy Thrawn had managed to talk him into playing bait for the Vagaari.

But it had worked. It had all worked. The Geroons had been freed, not only these particular slaves but probably their entire world as well. Admiral Ar'alani had already said that when the transport returned the slaves to their home she would bring along a task force of Chiss warships for protection. Any Vagaari still hanging around the system wouldn't be hanging around there for long.

And as for Outbound Flight . . .

He closed his eyes. Fifty thousand people dead, the entire

populace of the six Dreadnaughts. Had that really been necessary? Stratis had said it had, and Thrawn hadn't contradicted him. But had that *really* been the only way?

Car'das would probably never know for sure. Distantly, he wondered what Maris was going to say when she found out what her noble hero had done.

"Even now, they don't seem to believe it," a voice murmured from his left.

Car'das opened his eyes. Thrass was standing beside him, a strange expression on his face as he gazed across the crowded bay. "Syndic Thrass," Car'das greeted him. "I didn't realize you were aboard."

"Admiral Ar'alani suggested I come," Thrass said, his eyes still on the Geroons. "She seemed to think she and I and my brother could now resolve the question of the Vagaari goods being held at Crustai and allow you and your companions to go on your way."

He turned his eyes onto Car'das. "Now that you and I have apparently served our purposes."

Car'das held his gaze without flinching. "I have no problems with having been a part of your brother's plan," he said evenly. "Neither should you."

"I was manipulated and controlled," Thrass said, his eyes flashing with resentment.

"For your own protection," Car'das countered. "If Thrawn and Ar'alani had brought you into the plan, your future would have been just as much on the line as theirs were."

"And as they are now," Thrass pointed out darkly. "The Nine Ruling Families will not stand for such an illegal and immoral attack."

"Number one," Car'das said, lifting a finger. "This system is within the patrol region of the Chiss Expansionary Fleet. That makes it Chiss territory. Number two: the Vagaari arrived in force with the clear intent of causing harm. That makes Commander Thrawn's actions self-defense, as far as I'm concerned."

"They were here only because you had so enticed them."

"I'm not bound by your rules," Car'das reminded him. "Besides, as Admiral Ar'alani will attest, your brother had publicly labeled me as a possible spy. If I got desperate enough to go to the Vagaari for help in freeing my companions, you can hardly blame that on him."

Thrass's lip twisted. "No, Thrawn has always been very good at hiding his hand when he wishes to do so."

"Which seems to me takes care of the legal aspects," Car'das concluded. "As to your other objection—" He gestured toward the Geroons. "—I defy you to look at these people and tell me how freeing them from tyranny could possibly be immoral."

"The morality of an action is not determined by the results," Thrass said stiffly. His face softened a little. "Still, in this case, it's a hard point to argue."

"I saw the way the Vagaari treated their slaves," Car'das said, shivering at the memories of the Geroons the Miskara had murdered in cold blood. "In my opinion, the universe is well rid of them."

"I would tend to agree," Thrass said. "But Aristocra Chaf'orm'bintrano may not see things so clearly."

Car'das frowned. "What does he have to do with anything?"

"He and vessels of the Fifth Ruling Family are on their way here," Thrass said grimly. "I had a brief communication with him just before leaving Crustai. I suspect he intends to place Thrawn under arrest."

Car'das felt his throat tighten. "Does Thrawn know about this?"

"No."

"We need to tell him, and fast," Car'das said grimly. "Do you know where he is?"

"I believe he and Admiral Ar'alani have gone across to inspect Outbound Flight."

"Then let's get over there," Car'das said. "Come on—my shuttle's in one of the portside docking stations."

With a creak of not-quite-aligned metal fittings, the turbolift door reluctantly slid open. "Looks like we've got air seals again," Uliar commented, peering upward into the car. The ceiling was mostly intact, but one of the seams had cracked open and at its edge he could see the faint rainbow discoloration of a massive radiation surge. Had one or more of the reactors gone up? Unlikely. Even down here in the core they should have heard something that catastrophic.

"That shaft's going to be a mess, though," Keely muttered, stepping tentatively up beside Uliar. "And the Dreadnaughts themselves will be worse. This could take awhile."

"Then let's not waste any more time talking about it," Uliar said. He started to step into the car—

"No," Jinzler said, reaching out to touch his arm. She, too, was gazing at the car ceiling, a look of concentration on her face. "I'm going alone."

"Alone's never a good idea in this kind of situation," Keely warned.

"Alone for a Jedi is sometimes the only way," she said. Her eyes came back to him, and some of the concentration faded.

"Don't worry. As soon as I've found someplace safe, I'll come back and get you."

"You sure you don't want at least a little company?" Uliar asked, eyeing her closely. He didn't really want to go poking around up there, not with all the destruction and bodies and all. But he didn't like the idea of letting this Jedi out of his sight, either.

"Very sure," Jinzler said. "Go back and wait until I come for you."

"Whatever you say," Keely said, plucking at Uliar's sleeve. "Come on, Chas."

"Okay," Uliar said reluctantly, stepping back as Jinzler got into the car. "Make it fast."

"I'll try," Jinzler said, giving him a reassuring smile.

She was still smiling as the door creaked shut between them.

They found Thrawn and Ar'alani on the bridge of the main command ship, standing amid a bustling crowd of Chiss crewers methodically checking out the still-active control consoles. There were a lot of bodies there, too, lying haphazardly all over the deck. For once, Car'das hardly even noticed. "Ah—my brother," Thrawn said as Thrass and Car'das made their way through the maze of consoles. "Are the Geroons being properly cared for?"

"Never mind the Geroons," Car'das put in before Thrass could answer. "Aristocra Chaf'orm'bintrano's on his way with a fleet of Fifth Family ships."

"On whose authority do they fly?" Ar'alani demanded.

"The Aristocra's own, I presume," Thrawn said, his eyes narrowed in thought. "How soon until they arrive?"

"They could be here at any time," Thrass said. "I suspect he's coming to raise charges against you."

"In that case he would hardly need a fleet of vessels," Thrawn pointed out. "No, the Aristocra has something far more profitable in mind."

"Outbound Flight?" Car'das asked.

"Actually, I expect he's hoping to take possession of the remains of the Vagaari fleet," Thrawn said. "But you're right. Once he sees Outbound Flight that priority will definitely change."

"He can't do that," Thrass protested. He looked at Ar'alani. "Can he?"

"Not legally," Ar'alani said, her voice tight. "But as a practical matter, if he's brought enough vessels, there'll be no way for us to stop him."

"The Council of Families—" Thrass began.

"—will certainly object," Ar'alani cut in. "But the procedure will be long and complex."

"And in the meantime the Fifth Family will be coaxing the secrets from their new prize," Thrawn said.

Thrass hissed, a startlingly reptilian sound. "We can't allow that," he said. "Possession of Outbound Flight by any one Family could destroy the balance of power for decades to come."

Car'das nodded, a hard knot forming in his stomach. The thought of getting their hands on droid technology alone had been enough to lure the Vagaari to their destruction. How much more of an edge would the droids plus the rest of Outbound Flight's technology give Chaf'orm'bintrano's family?

"We'll have to stall him," Ar'alani said. But she didn't sound very confident. "We must keep his people off this vessel until the Defense Fleet units I've summoned can arrive."

"They won't be in time," Thrawn said. "We need to take Outbound Flight to a military base immediately and have it declared Defense Fleet property."

"How long a trip are we talking about?" Car'das asked dubiously. "This thing's taken a lot of damage."

"It will push the systems to their limit," Thrawn conceded. "But we must try. It would be better for Outbound Flight to be destroyed than to let any single family claim it."

There was a flicker of movement at the corner of Car'das's eye. He turned to the canopy.

Just as the last of a dozen large Chiss ships came out of hyperspace. "Too late," he said. "He's here."

Ar'alani muttered a word that had never come up in Car'das's language lessons. "We'll have to make do with the crewers you already have aboard," she said. "Quickly, before—"

She broke off at a twitter from Thrawn's comlink. Thrawn looked out at the ships, then reluctantly pulled the device from his belt. "Commander Mitth'raw'nuruodo."

"Commander, Aristocra Chaf'orm'bintrano of the Fifth Ruling Family is signaling the *Springhawk*," a voice said. "He demands your immediate presence aboard the *Chaf Exalted*."

Thrawn's eyes flicked to Ar'alani. "Do not acknowledge his signal," he ordered.

"It was not a request, Commander," the voice warned.

"Do not acknowledge," Thrawn repeated, and clicked off the comlink.

"Thrawn, you can't simply refuse an Aristocra's direct order," Thrass objected.

"I haven't yet received any direct orders from the Aristocra," Thrawn said evenly. "Car'das, find me the helm."

"Yes, sir," Car'das said, peering at the nearest consoles.

And then Ar'alani's comlink twittered.

All eyes turned to her. "Clever" was all she said as she removed it from her belt and keyed it on. "Admiral Ar'alani."

"This is Aristocra Chaf'orm'bintrano," a voice boomed. "I've been unable to contact Commander Mitth'raw'nuruodo, and I suspect he's refusing to communicate with me. As an Aristocra of the Fifth Ruling Family, I order you to find and detain him pending a hearing on his recent military activities."

Ar'alani hesitated, and Car'das held his breath. Then, with clear reluctance, she nodded. "Acknowledged, Aristocra. I hear, and obey."

She shut off the comlink. "I'm sorry, Commander," she said to Thrawn. "I have no choice but to place you under detention."

"This will destroy the Chiss," Thrawn said quietly. "The Defense Fleet, and only the Defense Fleet, can safely take possession of this vessel."

"I understand, and I'll do what I can to stall the Aristocra," Ar'alani said. "But in the meantime, you *are* under detention. Order your people to assemble in the hangar to return to our vessels."

For a long moment Thrawn stood motionless. Then, slowly, he bowed his head and activated his comlink. "This is Commander Mitth'raw'nuruodo," he said. "All Chiss warriors aboard Outbound Flight: return to the hangar bay."

"Thank you," Ar'alani said. "Now if you please?" she added, gesturing back toward the blast doors. "You, too, Car'das."

Car'das took a deep breath. "I'm not under Chiss command, Admiral," he said. "I'd like to stay aboard awhile longer."

Ar'alani's eyes narrowed. "What are you planning? Surely you can't fly this vessel alone."

"I'm not under Chiss command," Car'das repeated. "And the Aristocra's order didn't mention me."

Ar'alani looked at Thrawn, then at the incoming Fifth Family ships, then finally back at Car'das. "Permission granted," she said. She started toward the blast doors—

"I'll also stay," Thrass said.

Ar'alani stopped in midstep. *"What?"*

"I'm also not under Chiss military command," Thrass said. "And Aristocra Chaf'orm'bintrano didn't mention me, either."

Ar'alani sent a hard look at Thrawn. "We'll both be destroyed by this," she warned.

"The role of a warrior is to protect the Chiss people," Thrawn reminded her. "The warrior's own survival is of only secondary importance."

For half a dozen heartbeats the two of them locked gazes. Then, with a hissing sigh, Ar'alani turned to Thrass. "Pesfavri is the nearest Defense Fleet base," she said. "You know the coordinates?"

Thrass nodded. "Yes."

"Then we leave you," she said, nodding to him. "May warriors' fortune smile on your efforts."

She continued toward the blast doors. Thrawn lingered for a last, long look at his brother, then followed.

And a minute later, Car'das and Thrass were alone. "You really think we can get this thing all the way to a military base?" Car'das asked.

"You miss the point, friend Car'das," Thrass said grimly. "Weren't you listening to my brother? *It would be better for Outbound Flight to be destroyed than to let any single family claim it.*"

Car'das felt a sudden tightening in his throat. "Wait a second," he protested. "I was just going to try to lock Outbound

Flight down so that the Aristocra's people couldn't get aboard without blasting their way in. I didn't sign up for a suicide mission."

"Courage, Car'das," Thrass assured him. "Neither did I. I assume we can set this vessel's course to intersect the local sun, then escape in the shuttle we arrived in?"

Car'das thought it over. It should be possible, he decided, provided at least one of the Dreadnaughts' drives was still operable and the control cables to it were intact. "I think so."

"Then let us do it," Thrass said. "Your people built this vessel. Tell me what to do."

The turbolift shaft was reasonably clear, and the car reached D-4 with only a few bumps and scrapes. The Dreadnaught itself didn't seem too badly damaged, either.

Except, of course, for all the bodies.

The medical droids had already started clearing them away, probably taking them all to one of the medical labs where, according to the droids' now outdated programming, living beings would be waiting to give orders on how to proceed.

But there was no one to receive the corpses. Lorana stretched out with the Force and worked with the ship's comm system, hoping against all her fears that someone might have miraculously survived the cataclysm that had overtaken Outbound Flight.

But no one answered either call. D-4, it seemed, was dead.

Of defenders and attackers alike; and that Lorana found both curious and ominous. Surely the Chiss hadn't gone to all the effort to destroy Outbound Flight simply to abandon it.

But then where were they?

She spent only a little time on D-4 before continuing on.

The turbolift to D-3 was inoperable, implying damage to the cars or the pylon or both, so she headed instead to D-5. There she picked her way through the same debris and bodies and received the same negative results to her efforts at communication. D-6, the next ship on her grisly tour, was much the same.

Still, all three ships seemed to be mostly airtight again, with adequate light and heat and gravitation. The service droids had used the past few hours well. If the Chiss truly had abandoned Outbound Flight, she and the others might be able to make it at least partially operational again.

She was in the turbolift heading for D-1 when her senses caught the faint whisper of nearby life.

She pressed her head against the wall of the car, stretching out with the Force as best her own injuries and lingering horror would allow. There were definitely living beings out there. Alien beings, and not very many of them. But at least there was someone.

And she and her turbolift car were headed straight toward them.

Stepping away from the wall, she got a grip on her lightsaber. Whether by design or simple blind luck, Commander Mitth'raw'nuruodo had made good on his threat to destroy Outbound Flight. And he had, moreover, destroyed it out from under Jorus C'baoth and the rest of the Jedi.

It was time to see how well the Chiss would do in a face-to-face confrontation.

The turbolift car came up short at the D-1 end of the pylon, blocked by a maze of support girders that had broken loose during the battle. Using the Force to augment her efforts, she pried open the car door and climbed through the twisted metal to the entrance door.

The turbolift pylons connected at the base of each of the Dreadnaughts, serving only Decks 1 and 2. The bridge was another four decks up, and under the circumstances it didn't seem like a good idea to trust the Dreadnaught's own internal turbolift system. Making her way to the nearest stairway, she headed up.

The door opened in front of him, and with a not-very-gentle nudge at the small of his back the pair of yellow-clad Chiss gestured Doriana forward.

He found himself on a command bridge similar to the one aboard the *Springhawk,* only bigger and crewed exclusively by Chiss in the same yellow uniforms as his escort. It made Mitth'raw'nuruodo's black uniform stand out that much more in contrast as he stood in the center of the room before a Chiss in a gray-and-yellow robe. Behind Mitth'raw'nuruodo, a female Chiss dressed all in white stood at stiff attention.

The robed Chiss eyed Doriana as his escort again nudged him forward. He spat something in the Chiss language— " 'So this is your collaborator,' " Mitth'raw'nuruodo translated.

"Hardly," Doriana said, loading his voice with as much dignity and disdain as he could, just in case the robed Chiss was able to pick up on verbal cues. He had no idea of the details, but it was obvious that there was some kind of power struggle going on here.

And Kinman Doriana, assistant to Supreme Chancellor Palpatine, was quite familiar with power struggles. "I'm an ambassador of a vast assembly of star systems called the Galactic Republic," he intoned. "I came here on a mission of goodwill and exploration."

He studied the robed Chiss carefully as Mitth'raw'nuruodo translated. But the other merely smiled cynically and spoke again. " 'You came to bring chaos and war to this region of space,' " Mitth'raw'nuruodo translated. " 'You have brought alien weapons that you intended to use against the Chiss Ascendancy.' "

The robed Chiss straightened slightly as Mitth'raw'nuruodo finished and spoke again. " 'But you have failed. Those weapons are now the property of the Fifth Ruling Family. I, Aristocra Chaf'orm'bintrano, hereby take possession.' "

Doriana nodded to himself. So it was Outbound Flight and its technology that was at issue here. And he knew enough about internecine conflict to know that letting one Chiss group have sole possession of it would probably create terrible conflict with the other groups, up to and possibly including civil war.

Which would, of course, be precisely the situation Darth Sidious would want to see here. A Chiss Ascendancy entangled with its own internal problems couldn't pose a threat to the Sith Lord's plans for the Republic and the New Order he planned to create. Standing here in the middle of Aristocra Chaf'orm'bintrano's people, all Doriana had to do was confirm the Fifth Family's claim and he would help put the Chiss on that long and bitter road.

But as he opened his mouth to speak, he looked at Mitth'raw'nuruodo.

The commander was looking back at him, his face expressionless, his glowing eyes focused unblinkingly on him.

Doriana had already reluctantly concluded that Mitth'raw'nuruodo would have to be killed. But if that death came at the height of a controversy over the disposition of Outbound Flight . . . "I'm sorry, Aristocra Chaf'orm'bintrano, but Outbound Flight is not yours to take possession of," he said instead.

"As a duly appointed representative of the Republic that sent the project on its journey, *I* claim full salvage rights."

Chaf'orm'bintrano seemed taken aback as Mitth'raw'nuruodo finished the translation. He bit something out—" 'Ridiculous,' " Mitth'raw'nuruodo said. " 'An aggressor has no rights.' "

"I deny your claim that either I or Outbound Flight have behaved aggressively toward your people," Doriana countered. "And I demand a full hearing and judgment before any Chiss steps aboard Outbound Flight."

Mitth'raw'nuruodo translated. Chaf'orm'bintrano's eyes narrowed, his glare shifting to the white-clad female. He said something; she replied, and the argument was on.

Doriana looked sideways at Mitth'raw'nuruodo. His face was still expressionless, but as his own eyes shifted to meet Doriana's his lip seemed to twitch upward in a microscopic smile of approval.

Just what the commander would do with the mess that had now been stirred up Doriana didn't know. But to his mild surprise, he discovered he was rather looking forward to finding out.

It had taken longer than Car'das had expected to get Outbound Flight prepped for flight. But at last they were ready. "Okay, get to the helm," he told Thrass, glancing out the canopy at the Chiss ships still hovering in the near distance. Why they hadn't already sent over a boarding party he couldn't guess. Apparently, Thrawn and Ar'alani had found a way to stall them.

"Ready," Thrass called.

Stepping to the navigation console, Car'das gave it one final check. Course set and locked in, ready to take Outbound Flight on its final voyage. Crossing to the engineering console, he settled his fingers on the power-feed controls—

"Watch out!" Thrass snapped.

Car'das spun around, expecting to see a whole squad of yellow-suited Chiss charging in on them.

But to his astonishment, he found himself facing a lone female human. Out of the corner of his eye he saw Thrass snatch a weapon out of concealment in his robe. In reply, the woman produced a short metal cylinder—

And a green lightsaber blade blazed into existence.

"No!" he barked, waving a hand frantically at Thrass.

But it was too late. The other's weapon hissed out a blue bolt, which the woman sent ricocheting harmlessly into the ceiling. "I said *stop,*" Car'das called again. "She's a Jedi."

To his relief, Thrass didn't fire again. "What do you want?" the Chiss demanded instead, keeping his weapon aimed.

"He wants to know what you want," Car'das said, translating the Cheunh for her.

Her eyes flicked to him. "He doesn't speak Basic?"

"No, no one here does except Thrawn," Car'das said. "But he knows some Sy Bisti, if that helps."

"It does." She looked back at Thrass. "Who are you?" she asked, switching to that language.

"I am Syndic Mitth'ras'safis of the Eighth Ruling Family of the Chiss Ascendancy," Thrass identified himself.

"And I'm Jorj Car'das," Car'das added. "Mostly an innocent bystander to all of this."

"Mostly?"

"I got here through a hyperdrive malfunction," he said. "Who are you?"

"Lorana Jinzler," she said. Lowering her lightsaber, but leaving it ignited, she crossed the threshold and continued on into the bridge, limping noticeably. Her eyes flicked across the dead bodies, and an edge of fresh pain crossed her face. "Who else is aboard?"

"At the moment, just us," Thrass said. He hesitated, then slipped his weapon back into his tunic. "But a member of one of the ruling families is trying to claim Outbound Flight for himself. We're trying to prevent that."

Jinzler's eyes narrowed. "How?"

"We're going to have to scuttle it," Car'das said, watching her face carefully. Even with nothing left but torn and broken metal, there was an even chance she would be attached enough to the hulk to object violently to its destruction. People went all weird like that sometimes.

Sure enough, her eyes widened. "No," she insisted. "You can't."

"Look, I'm sorry," Car'das said as soothingly as he could. "But there's nothing left but dead metal and droids—"

"Never mind the dead metal," she snapped. "There are *people* still aboard."

Car'das felt his heart catch. No—that was impossible. A Jedi might possibly have survived Thrawn's attack, but surely no one else could have. "Who?" he asked. "How many?"

"Fifty-seven," Jinzler said. "Including children."

Car'das looked at Thrass, seeing his own horror reflected in the other's face. "Where are they?" he asked. "Can we get them out of here?"

"In that shuttle?" Thrass countered before Jinzler could answer. "No. There isn't enough room for even ten."

"And it would take time to get them up here anyway," Jinzler said. "They're still in the storage core."

Car'das grimaced. The storage core. Of course—the one area Thrawn's attack had ignored. "What do we do?"

"I don't understand the problem," Jinzler said, looking back and forth between them. "Why don't we just leave?"

"For starters, we can't fly Outbound Flight very far, not just the two of us," Car'das said. "Not even if we had time to get your people up here to help us."

Lorana looked around the bridge. "We won't need them," she said, her voice tight but firm. "I can fly Outbound Flight."

"By yourself?" Thrass asked in clear disbelief. "One single person?"

"One single Jedi," Jinzler corrected him. "Master C'baoth insisted we all learn to handle all of the major systems. At least, under normal conditions."

"The conditions here are hardly normal," Car'das pointed out. "And it still leaves the question of where we go. We'll never make it back to the Republic, not with this much damage."

"We have to reach a Defense Fleet base, as my brother originally intended," Thrass said.

"And then what happens to my people?" Jinzler asked. "Would they be prisoners of war? Captives held for study?"

"The Chiss aren't like that," Car'das insisted.

"But the end result might be the same," Thrass conceded. "If the Fifth Ruling Family chooses to press its claim to Outbound Flight, even if we go to a military base they may demand that all aboard be placed in holding until the matter can be decided."

"A prison by any other name," Jinzler said grimly. "How long would this decision process take?"

Thrass snorted. "With a prize such as Outbound Flight? It could be years."

"So we can forget going anywhere in Chiss space," Car'das

said. "Any idea what other habitable worlds there might be out here?"

"Even if I did, I would caution against anything nearby," Thrass said. "This region is dangerous, with pirates and privateers all around."

"Not to mention what's left of the Vagaari," Car'das agreed with a shiver. "Come on, Thrass, think. There has to be *something* else we can do."

Thrass gazed out at the Fifth Family ships. "There's one other possibility," he said slowly. "Within two days' flight is a star cluster that the Defense Fleet has begun to fortify as an emergency refuge. I've seen the data, and there are at least ten habitable worlds within it that haven't yet been explored."

"Kind of an out-of-the-way homestead," Car'das pointed out doubtfully.

"*And* still in Chiss space," Jinzler added.

"But it's a place where vessels of the Fifth Family wouldn't accidentally discover you," Thrass said. "Only Defense Fleet personnel go inside, and only to specific systems as they work on the fortifications."

"So what's the catch?" Car'das asked.

Thrass made a face. "The catch is that I don't have the safe access routes into the cluster," he said. "Are your navigational systems capable of finding such routes on their own?"

"Probably not," Jinzler said. "But I might be able to. There are Jedi navigational techniques that should be good enough to take us through even a star cluster."

"So what happens if she can?" Car'das asked Thrass. "They set up shop and wait for all this to blow over?"

"Or I return after they're hidden and negotiate in secret with the Council of Families for their safe passage home," Thrass said.

"Even if such negotiations take a few months, the survivors will at least have a habitable world to live on." He looked at Jinzler. "There *are* other hypercapable vessels aboard that I could use, are there not?"

"Just one, a two-passenger Delta-Twelve Skysprite," Jinzler said. "But it should have the range you need."

"So that's it?" Car'das asked, not quite believing they'd hammered out something workable so quickly. "We hide Outbound Flight in this cluster, negotiate a deal with the Chiss—*all* the Chiss—and everyone gets what they want?"

"Basically." Jinzler hesitated. "But the *we* won't include you. I have something else I need you to do for me." Her lips compressed. "A personal favor."

"Like what?" Car'das asked cautiously. Doing a personal favor for a Jedi didn't sound very appetizing.

"I want you to find my brother when you return to the Republic," she said. "Dean Jinzler, probably working with Senate Support Services on Coruscant. Tell him—" She hesitated. "Just tell him that his sister was thinking about him, hoping that someday he'll be able to let go of his anger. His anger at me, at our parents, and at himself."

"All right," Car'das said, the hairs on the back of his neck tingling. The fact that she was sending him on such an errand implied she wasn't at all sure she'd be coming back. Given the shape Outbound Flight was in, he wouldn't have bet on it, either. "I'll do my best."

For a long moment she held his eyes. Then she nodded. "You'd better go, then," she said. She looked down at her still-glowing lightsaber, as if suddenly realizing it was still active, and closed it down. "Please don't forget."

"I won't," he promised. "Good luck." He looked at Thrass. "To both of you."

Ten minutes later, Car'das eased the Chiss shuttle out of the Dreadnaught's hangar and flew it clear. Turning the nose toward the waiting Fifth Family ships, he looked back over his shoulder at the magnificent failure that had been Outbound Flight.

He wondered if anyone would ever see it again.

Doriana was gazing out the bridge canopy, listening with half an ear to the argument still going on between Chaf'orm'bintrano, Mitth'raw'nuruodo, and the female Chiss, when Outbound Flight abruptly made the jump to lightspeed.

For a moment he stared in disbelief . . . and then, slowly, he felt a smile tug at his lips. So that was what Mitth'raw'nuruodo had been up to with this confrontation. He'd been stalling for time while some of his people stole the Dreadnaughts right out from under Aristocra Chaf'orm'bintrano's nose.

And even Doriana's own attempt to muddy the Chiss waters had apparently been part of that scheme. Had Mitth'raw'nuruodo anticipated Doriana's efforts? Or had he simply incorporated them into his own plan as they occurred? Either way, it was artfully done. "Excuse me?" he spoke up, lifting a finger. "I believe the discussion is over." He waited until he had their attention, then angled the upraised finger to point out the canopy. "Your prize is gone."

The shimmering hyperspace sky flowed past the Dreadnaught's canopy as Outbound Flight drove onward into the unknown. Lorana knew the sky was there, but had no time to actually focus on the sight. Every bit of her attention was tied up with D-1's systems as she used the Force to both sense the equipment status and keep the controls in proper adjustment.

It was hard work. It was hideously hard work.

Vaguely, she felt a whisper of movement at her side. "Lorana?" Thrass asked, his voice distant in her overstretched consciousness.

"Did you get to them?" she asked. The moment of distraction was too much; even as she finished her question one of the reactor feeds began to surge. Clamping down hard on her lower lip, she stretched out and eased the flow back to its proper level.

"I'm sorry," Thrass said. "I can't even find a way off this ship. All the pylon turbolift tunnels are blocked to one degree or another. Perhaps if you brought us out of hyperspace I could find a vac suit and make my way across to the core that way."

"No," Lorana said. The word came out tartly and impolitely, she suspected, but she didn't have the concentration to spare for courtesy. "Hyperdrive not good."

In point of fact, the hyperdrive was very much not good. It was running blazingly hot, and it was all she could do to keep the circuits from looping and ripping the thing completely out of her control. If she shut it down now, there was every chance it would never start up again. Even if she didn't, it would probably eventually collapse on its own.

On the other hand, with the extra speed the runaway had given them, the edge of the cluster was now only a few standard hours away. If she could continue to fly the ship *and* use the Jedi navigation techniques at the same time to get them safely between the tightly packed stars, they had a good chance of reaching one of Thrass's target systems before that happened.

"I understand," Thrass said. "I'll keep trying to find a communication line that'll get me through to them."

He moved away, and Lorana felt a pang of guilt. If the survivors were still waiting down there like she'd told them to, they would certainly be wondering where she was. They might even conclude that she'd run off and abandoned them.

Across the bridge, a flashing red light warned that the alluvial dampers were drifting. Frowning in concentration, trying to maintain her Force grip on all the myriad other controls she was simultaneously juggling, she reached out a hand and carefully adjusted the dampers back into proper alignment. Once they reached their destination and she could finally let the systems ease down to standby, she and Thrass could make their way back to Uliar and the rest and explain what had happened.

And they would understand. Surely they would understand.

At the other side of the bridge, another red light was flashing. Taking a deep breath, wondering how long she'd be able to keep this up, she stretched out with the Force.

"You will pay for this," Chaf'orm'bintrano ground out, pacing back and forth across the conference room in front of the three prisoners standing silently in front of him. There was a cushioned chair behind the narrow desk, but he was apparently too angry even to sit down. "You hear me? You *will* pay." He leveled his glare first at Doriana, then at Car'das, and finally at Thrawn. "And the charge will be high treason."

Standing behind the desk, well out of the way of the Aristocra's pacing, Admiral Ar'alani stirred. "I don't think such a charge will hold, Aristocra," she said. Her expression, Car'das noted, had maintained a careful neutrality as she listened to Chaf'orm'bintrano's rantings. Still, he thought he could detect a certain relief behind the aloofness.

Small wonder. She'd gotten what she wanted: Outbound Flight was safely out of Chaf'orm'bintrano's grasping hands. What happened to a couple of prisoners was probably a matter of complete indifference to her.

Or at least, what happened to the two non-Chiss prisoners.

"*You* don't think the charge will hold?" Chaf'orm'bintrano snapped, shifting his glare to her.

Ar'alani stood her ground. "No, I don't," she said. "Car'das has already stated that Syndic Mitth'ras'safis and the human Lorana Jinzler were the perpetrators."

"With *his* assistance and advice."

"Advice alone is only lesser treason," Ar'alani said. "And as a non-Chiss, he can't be charged with any level of treason anyway. As for Doriana, he clearly had nothing to do with it."

"What are they going on about now?" Doriana murmured in Car'das's ear.

"The Aristocra wants to roast us over a low fire," Car'das murmured back. "The admiral is suggesting he needs to rethink his charges."

"Ah."

The byplay hadn't gone unnoticed. "Do the prisoners wish to add to the proceedings?" Chaf'orm'bintrano asked acidly.

"Actually, the prisoners will go free," Thrawn said, the first words he'd spoken since they'd all been herded into the conference room where Chaf'orm'bintrano could threaten them in private. "They've done nothing with which they can be charged. If you wish to blame someone, blame me."

"I fully intend to," Chaf'orm'bintrano bit out. "*After* I've dealt with your accomplices."

"They're not my accomplices," Thrawn said calmly. "Furthermore, they're *my* prisoners, and as such fall under the legal authority of the Chiss Expansionary Fleet." He lifted his eyebrows. "As do I, for that matter."

"Not anymore," Chaf'orm'bintrano said. "For the crime of unprovoked attack against sentient beings, I hereby revoke your military position."

"Just a moment, Aristocra," Ar'alani said, taking a step forward. "You can't revoke his position for a crime for which he has yet to be convicted."

"I suggest you reread the law, Admiral," Chaf'orm'bintrano said tartly. "Commander Mitth'raw'nuruodo has pushed the limits for the last time and *this* time we have proof, scattered across the system before us."

"The Vagaari were an imminent threat to the Ascendancy," Thrawn said. "And this system *is* within Chiss space."

"But this time you forgot to let your victim fire first," Chaf'orm'bintrano said, an edge of triumph in his voice. "Don't deny it—I have the records from your own vessels."

"The Vagaari made threats against both us and Outbound Flight," Thrawn said. "I claim that such threats, backed up by their obvious firepower, were sufficient provocation for Chiss action."

"You can claim anything you wish," Chaf'orm'bintrano said. "But the burden of proof is now on you, not me." He looked at Ar'alani. "And until his trial takes place, I can and will revoke both his position and the military protection you so clearly hope to shelter him beneath."

Ar'alani didn't answer. For a moment Chaf'orm'bintrano continued to stare at her, then turned back to Thrawn. "And your fellow prisoners will likewise be taken to trial," he said. "These, along with the other two you have back at Crustai." He paused. "Unless, of course, you have enough concern for their well-being to make a bargain."

Thrawn looked at Car'das and Doriana. "Such as?"

"You will resign your position, completely and permanently," Chaf'orm'bintrano said. "You will likewise renounce your status as Trial-born of the Eighth Family and disappear back into the great mass of Chiss citizenry, never again to rise to a position where you may threaten law or custom."

"You ask my entire life for the trade of a few alien prisoners," Thrawn pointed out calmly. "Are you certain you're willing to live with the consequences?"

Chaf'orm'bintrano snorted. "What consequences?"

"To begin with, the Eighth Family will not permit a Trial-born to simply renounce his affiliation," Thrawn said. "They'll insist on a hearing . . . and I don't believe they'll let me go. Not when they see the prize I'll be bringing them."

Chaf'orm'bintrano stiffened. "You wouldn't dare," he rumbled, his voice dark with menace. "If Outbound Flight reappears at an Eighth Family stronghold—"

"Outbound Flight is gone," Thrawn cut him off. "And I refer to another technology entirely." He waved a hand out at the stars. "To be specific, the device I used to bring both Outbound Flight and the Vagaari fleet out of hyperspace."

Chaf'orm'bintrano sent a startled look at Ar'alani. "The—? Are you saying they *didn't* come here of their own choosing?"

"The choosing was mine alone," Thrawn assured him. "I can provide you a demonstration if you'd like."

"That device is not your property," Ar'alani warned, her neutral expression suddenly gone. "It belongs to the Chiss Defense Fleet."

"And if I remain a member of the Expansionary Fleet, I will of course turn it over to you," Thrawn assured her. "But if my military position is revoked, I will no longer have any official loyalty except to my adoptive family. At that point . . ." He left the sentence unfinished.

Chaf'orm'bintrano was clearly having no trouble connecting the dots. "Admiral, you can't permit him to manipulate you this way," he insisted. "This is nothing less than extortion."

"This is nothing less than reality," Thrawn corrected. "And Admiral Ar'alani has nothing to say about it. *You're* the one threatening to revoke my position."

For a long minute the two Chiss locked eyes. Then, abruptly, Chaf'orm'bintrano turned and stalked out of the conference room.

"That didn't look good," Doriana murmured.

"Actually, it was," Car'das said, looking at Thrawn. "At least, I think so."

"Yes," Thrawn confirmed, his face and body sagging a little. "He's furious, but he doesn't dare revoke my position now." He looked at Ar'alani. "And once the Defense Fleet has the gravfield projector, I'm certain they'll protect me from any future efforts on his part."

Ar'alani's lips twitched. "We'll do what we can," she said. "But understand this, Commander. If you continue to act outside the legal boundaries set by the Defense Fleet and the Nine Families, there may come a point where we can no longer stand with you."

"I understand," Thrawn said. "Understand in turn that I will continue to protect my people in whatever way I deem necessary."

"I would expect nothing less from you," Ar'alani said. Her eyes flicked once to Doriana and Car'das. "I release your prisoners to you. Return to Crustai, and leave me to deal with the rest of the Vagaari debris."

"I obey," Thrawn said, bowing his head to her. "The gravfield projector will be waiting for you at Crustai whenever you wish to retrieve it."

Ar'alani bowed in return and left the room.

Thrawn took a deep breath. "And with that, I believe it's finally over," he said. "A shuttle is waiting to take us back to the *Springhawk*." He gestured to Doriana. "And then I will return you and Vicelord Kav to your vessel."

"Thank you," Doriana said. "We're looking forward to returning home."

And as they filed out of the room, Car'das wondered at the odd stiffness in Doriana's back.

They were passing through one of the systems midway through the star cluster when the hyperdrive finally died.

"No chance of fixing it?" Thrass asked.

Lorana shook her head. "Not by me," she said. "Possibly not by anyone, at least outside of a major shipyard."

Thrass gazed out the canopy at the distant sun. "You have five other Dreadnaughts here, each with its own hyperdrive," he reminded her. "Could we move across to one of the others and use its systems?"

Lorana rubbed her forehead, wincing as the pressure accentuated the throbbing pain behind her eyes. "According to the status readings back in ComOps, none of the other hyperdrives is operational," she said. "And all the control lines to the other Dreadnaughts are down, besides. Whatever your brother used to . . . to stop C'baoth's attack, it scorched a great deal of the delicate equipment aboard. It's going to take months, maybe even years, to tear them apart and fix them."

Thrass tapped his fingers thoughtfully on the edge of the nearest console. "Then this system is where we stop," he said. "We'll shut down the drive, take the Delta-Twelve craft you spoke of, and go try to make a bargain for your people."

"I don't think we should shut down the drive," Lorana said, trying to think. "The shape it's in, if we shut it down we might not be able to start it up again."

"But if we don't shut it down, Outbound Flight won't take long to travel all the way through this system," Thrass pointed out. "We could be away for a month or more negotiating with the Defense Force and Nine Families. By that time, the vessel could have passed into interstellar space, where we would have difficulty locating it."

And if the hyperdrives proved unfixable, interstellar space would be where Outbound Flight would remain. "Then we'd better find someplace here where we can park for a while," she said. "A nice, high orbit around one of the planets, say. Let's fire up what's left of the sensors and see what our choices are."

The survey took most of two hours. In the end, there turned out to be only one viable alternative.

"It's smaller than I'd hoped for," Thrass said as they leaned side by side over the main sensor console. "Less gravity means less stability to the orbit from the perturbations of passing objects."

"But it also means less atmosphere that might cause the orbit to decay," Lorana pointed out. "And it's almost directly along our vector, which means no fancy maneuvering to get us there. I say we go for it."

"Agreed," Thrass said. "Let's hope the drive holds out that long."

They had reached the target planetoid and were on their final approach to orbit when the drive gave one final surge and shut down.

"Report," Lorana bit out as she stretched out with the Force, trying unsuccessfully to coax the system back to life. "Thrass?"

"The red curve bends too far inward," Thrass reported tightly from the nav console. "Fifteen orbits from now, it intersects the surface."

A wave of despair rose like acid in Lorana's throat. Resolutely, she forced it down. After all they'd been through, Outbound Flight was *not* going to end up destroying itself. Not now. "Get to the sensor station," she ordered him. "See if there's a place—*any* place—where we might be able to land this thing."

"This vessel was not designed with landing in mind," Thrass warned as he hurried to the proper console. "Could we possibly still make orbit?"

"I'm working on it," Lorana said, crossing to the cluster of engineering monitors and searching among the red lights for something that might still be showing green. Two of the forward braking and maneuvering jets, she saw, were still operative. If they could somehow rotate Outbound Flight 180 degrees and then use those jets to give them a boost along their current vector . . .

They had slipped into the planetoid's gravitational field and used up the first of their fifteen orbits before she reluctantly concluded that such a maneuver wouldn't be possible. There was simply too much mass to be moved, and too little time in which to move it. "No luck," she said, stepping to Thrass's side. "You find anything?"

"Perhaps," he said hesitantly. "I've located a long, enclosed valley that I believe will be deep enough to hold us."

"I don't see how that gains us anything," Lorana said. "Enclosed valleys imply valley walls, which imply a sudden stop somewhere along the line."

"In this case, the stop would be somewhat less violent," Thrass said, pointing to the display. "This particular valley is full of small rocks."

Lorana frowned, leaning over for a closer look. He was right: the whole valley was filled nearly to the top with what seemed to be gravel-sized stones. "I wonder how *that* happened," she commented.

"Multiple asteroid or meteor collisions, most likely," Thrass said. "It doesn't matter. This is the only place on the planetoid that offers a chance for survival."

Lorana grimaced. But he was right. With the drive gone, coming down anywhere else on the planetoid would mean a full-bore collision at near-orbit speeds. With the gravel, at least they would have a slightly more gradual slowdown. "Can we reach it with the drive gone?" she asked, keying for an analysis.

"The valley is not far off our current orbital path," Thrass said. "I believe the maneuvering systems will be adequate to move us into position, and to give us at least a little deceleration before impact."

The analysis appeared on the display. "The computer agrees with you," she confirmed, looking out at the dark world rotating beneath them as she tried to think. "All right. We're here in D-One, the Delta-Twelve is in D-Three, and the rest of the survivors are in the core. If we want D-Three to end up on top of the gravel heap, we'll need to rotate Outbound Flight to put D-Six at the bottom. It'll hit first, taking the initial impact and hopefully slowing us down enough that the damage to the other ships will be minimal when they dig in."

"Including the damage to this one?" Thrass asked pointedly.

Lorana made a face. "I know, but we have no choice. We need D-Three's hangar bay to stay above the surface if we're going to get the Delta-Twelve out. So we rotate D-Six to the bottom, as I say, then move the people out of the core to—"

"Hello?" a voice came suddenly from the bridge speakers. "Jedi Jinzler? You there somewhere? This is Chas Uliar. We got tired of waiting, so we all came up to D-Four. Jinzler?"

For a stretched-out second Lorana and Thrass stared at each other in horror. Then, snapping out of her paralysis, Lorana dived for the comm station. "This is Lorana Jinzler," she called urgently. "Uliar, get everyone back to the storage core right away. You hear me? Get everyone back to—"

"Jinzler, are you there?" Uliar's voice came again. "Jedi, if you've cut out on us I'm going to be *really* upset with you."

"Uliar?" Lorana called again. *"Uliar!"*

But there was no reply. "He can't hear you," Thrass said grimly. "The comm isn't transmitting at this end."

Lorana twisted her neck to look out at the planetoid, her pulse throbbing violently against the agony in her head. D-4. Why did they have to have gone to D-4?

Because it was the one closest to the Jedi school where she'd left them, of course. And now there were fifty-seven people wandering around down there, completely oblivious as to what was about to happen to them.

Thrass was watching her, a tautness in his face. "We have no choice," she told him quietly. "We'll have to rotate and put D-Four on top."

His expression didn't even flicker. Clearly, he'd already come to the same conclusion. "Which will put D-One—this one—at the very bottom," he said.

Where it would take the full brunt of their crash landing. "We have no choice," Lorana said again. "It's only an assumption that the bottom Dreadnaught will take enough of the impact to leave the others intact. For all we know, they might *all* hit hard enough to be ripped open to vacuum. We have to try to keep D-Four as far out of the rock as possible."

"I understand." Thrass hesitated. "There's still time for you to leave, you know. You may at least be able to get to the core before we hit, perhaps even all the way to D-Four."

Lorana shook her head. "You can't handle the landing alone," she reminded him. "But I could do that while *you* go."

"And who would keep the remaining systems from self-destroying while you cleared a path through the pylons for me?" Thrass countered. "No, Jedi Jinzler. It appears we will both be giving our lives for your people."

Lorana felt her vision blurring with tears. Deep in the back crevices of her mind, she'd wondered why she'd felt so strongly about sending Car'das home with that message for her brother. Now she knew it had been the subtle prompting of the Force.

"This is hardly the temporary home I'd envisioned for them," Thrass went on, as if talking to himself. "It's likely to be far more permanent than I had hoped, too."

"Your people will come here someday," Lorana assured him, wondering why she was saying that. Wishful thinking? Or more prompting from the Force? "Until then, they have enough food and supplies to last for generations. They'll survive. I know they will."

"Then let us prepare for the end." Thrass hesitated, then reached out his hand to her. "I've known you and your people only briefly, Jedi Lorana Jinzler. But in that time, I've learned to admire and respect you. I hope that someday humans and Chiss will be able to work side by side in peace."

"As do I, Syndic Mitth'ras'safis of the Eighth Ruling Family," Lorana said, taking his hand.

For a minute they stood silently, their hands clasped, each preparing for death. Then, taking a deep breath, Thrass released her hand. "Then let us bring this part of history to a close," he said briskly. "May warriors' fortune smile on our efforts."

"Yes," Lorana said. "And may the Force be with us." She gestured downward toward D-4. "And with them."

* * *

"As you can see, we have left your ship and equipment undisturbed," Mitth'raw'nuruodo said, gesturing as he led Doriana and Kav through the *Darkvenge*'s bridge toward Kav's command office. "I know certain of you were concerned about that," he added, looking over his shoulder at Kav.

The Neimoidian didn't reply. "At any rate, I imagine you're looking forward to returning home," Mitth'raw'nuruodo continued as they walked into the office. "There are just one or two points I need to clear up before you leave."

"Of course," Doriana said, taking a hasty step to the side as Kav pushed past him, brushed by Mitth'raw'nuruodo, and circled the desk to drop rather defiantly into his ornate chair. "We'll do whatever's necessary," he added as he took a chair at one corner of the desk.

"Thank you," Mitth'raw'nuruodo said, sitting down in a chair at the other corner and gazing across the edge of the desk at Doriana. "Basically, I believe we both wish to make certain that this one contact between our peoples remains the last."

"I don't understand," Doriana said, forcing puzzlement into his voice. "Our relationship thus far has proved mutually beneficial. Why wouldn't we want it to continue?"

"Come now, Commander," Mitth'raw'nuruodo said mildly. "*My* side of the arrangement is already secure, of course. You have no idea where my base is, or where the worlds of the Chiss Ascendancy lie. We can remain hidden from you as long as we wish." He paused. "It therefore remains only for you to ensure to your own satisfaction that I will never bring news to the Republic of your betrayal of Outbound Flight."

Doriana stared at him, a cold hand closing around his heart. Did Mitth'raw'nuruodo know about his conversations with Kav?

Had he or one of the other Chiss seen Kav pass him that hold-out blaster?

Or had he merely deduced that Doriana would decide to murder him?

Slowly, almost unwillingly, his hand crept toward the hidden blaster, the movement blocked from Mitth'raw'nuruodo's view by the edge of the desk. Certainly it made sense to cover his tracks this way, he reminded himself firmly. Loose ends could be fatal to someone living his kind of double life. Sidious would insist on it, as well, especially given that Mitth'raw'nuruodo had seen the Sith Lord and heard his name.

And after helping to bring about the deaths of fifty thousand people on Outbound Flight, one more death certainly couldn't matter.

Mitth'raw'nuruodo was still waiting, watching him silently. Doriana closed his hand around the grip of his blaster . . .

And paused. Mitth'raw'nuruodo, brilliant tactician. Equally brilliant strategist. A being who could take on Republic warships, nomadic pirates, and even Jedi, and win against them all.

And Doriana was actually considering *killing* him?

"What are you waiting for?" Kav broke impatiently into his thoughts. "You have him alone and unprotected. *Shoot* him!"

Doriana smiled tightly; and with that, the underlying tension that had been nagging at him ever since his task force's destruction finally faded away. "Don't be absurd, Vicelord," he said. Pulling out the blaster, he leaned over and set it on an empty chair between him and Mitth'raw'nuruodo. "I would as soon shatter thousand-year-old crystal as kill a being such as this."

Mitth'raw'nuruodo inclined his head, his eyes glittering. "So I was indeed right about you," he said.

"Eventually," Doriana conceded. "But then, I don't imagine you're wrong very often."

"Then let this be your final mistake," Kav bit out, slapping at his desk chair's arm and popping open a hidden panel. In a single smooth motion he scooped out another hold-out blaster, pointed it at Mitth'raw'nuruodo, and fired.

The shot never reached him. Instead, it struck the faint haze that had suddenly appeared between them, then bounced straight back into Kav's torso.

The Neimoidian had just enough time to look startled before he collapsed forward onto the desk and lay still.

It was only then, as Doriana shifted his stunned gaze from Kav's body to the haze surrounding the desk, that he recognized its shape and coloration.

He looked through the edge of the shield at Mitth'raw'nuruodo. "It was still something of a risk, wasn't it?" he asked, striving to keep his voice conversational.

"Not really," the other assured him. "The shield generator was simple enough to remove from one of the droidekas you provided for me. As I said at the time, we've had some experience with reversing the polarity of such devices." He gestured. "And it was easily predictable that Vicelord Kav would claim his chair and desk for his own, and thus position himself for his own destruction."

"I meant the risk you took with me," Doriana said. "The shield wouldn't have blocked *my* shot."

"No, it wouldn't," Mitth'raw'nuruodo agreed. "But I had to be certain that you were someone I could trust."

Doriana frowned. "Why?"

For a moment Mitth'raw'nuruodo didn't answer. Then,

leaning over, he picked up the blaster Doriana had discarded. "You and your Master, Darth Sidious, told me of a people you call the Far Outsiders gathering at the edge of the galaxy," he said, turning the weapon over in his hands. "Have you ever actually seen these beings?"

"As far as I know, we haven't," Doriana admitted.

"I thought not," Mitth'raw'nuruodo said, suddenly intense. "But *we* have."

A cold chill ran up Doriana's back. "Where?"

"At the far edge of the Chiss Ascendancy," Mitth'raw'nuruodo said, his voice dark and grim. "It was a small reconnaissance force, but it fought with a savage ferocity before it was finally repulsed."

"How many ships were there?" Doriana asked, his mind kicking into high speed. Darth Sidious coveted information of this sort. Enough of it might even persuade him to forgive Doriana the loss of his Trade Federation task force. "What sort of weaponry did they have? Do you have any combat data?"

"I have some," Mitth'raw'nuruodo said. "Admiral Ar'alani was in command of the force that ultimately drove them away. That's why she came personally to investigate Car'das and his companions. We wondered if the Republic they spoke of might be allied with the invaders."

"And that's also why she was willing to look the other way while you dealt with the Vagaari," Doriana said as a final nagging piece of the puzzle finally fell into place. "A two-front war would be exceptionally nasty."

"Correct," Mitth'raw'nuruodo said, and Doriana thought he could hear a note of approval at his quick deduction. "My actions were contrary to official Chiss policy, but she knew as well as I that the Vagaari had to be dealt with, as quickly and decisively as possible. I will speak to her; if she's willing, I'll provide you with copies of the information you seek."

"Thank you," Doriana said. "Now. A moment ago you spoke of trust between us. What exactly did you have in mind?"

"For the moment, nothing," Mitth'raw'nuruodo said. "Each of us has our own peoples to defend and our own politics to deal with. But in the future, who can tell? Perhaps someday our peoples will end up fighting side by side against this threat."

"I hope so," Doriana said. "I, for my part, intend to work with our leaders to prepare as best I can for that day."

"As will I," Mitth'raw'nuruodo said. "Though the obstacles at my end may be difficult to overcome."

Doriana thought about Lord Sidious and his hatred of nonhumans. It wouldn't exactly be easy at his end, either. "I've seen you work military miracles," he said. "I'm sure you can work political ones, as well."

"Perhaps," Mitth'raw'nuruodo said. "My brother may be able to assist in that area when he returns." He stood up and held out the blaster. "At any rate, you and your ship are free to go."

Doriana waved away the proffered weapon. "Keep it, Commander," he said. "Think of it as a souvenir of our first victory together."

"Thank you," Mitth'raw'nuruodo said gravely, slipping the blaster into a pocket. "May it not be our last."

"Indeed," Doriana agreed. "Which reminds me. There's one other small matter I'd like to discuss with you . . ."

"You're joking," Car'das said, frowning at Thrawn. "He's offering me a *job*?"

"Not just a job, but a highly placed leadership position,"

Thrawn said. "He wanted me to invite you to accompany him back to the Republic on the *Darkvenge* so that you could discuss it."

"This doesn't make any sense," Car'das protested. "I'm barely out of school. What kind of high-power position could I possibly be qualified for?"

"Age is not necessarily the best indicator of talent and ability," Thrawn pointed out. "In your case, he was highly impressed by the role you played in luring the Vagaari into position for the attack. You've shown yourself to be intelligent, resourceful, and able to remain cool under fire, qualities he prizes as well as I do."

Car'das rubbed his cheek thoughtfully. It was still ridiculous, of course. But it was also far too intriguing to simply dismiss out of hand. "Did he say what sort of job it would be?"

"I gather it would involve some of the same smuggling work you're doing with Captain Qennto," Thrawn said. "But beneath such surface activities, your primary task would be to create and operate a private information network for him."

Car'das pursed his lips. Smuggling alone he could take or leave, but this other part sounded a lot more interesting. "He's not expecting me to build this network on my own, is he?"

Thrawn shook his head. "He would begin by giving you several months of training and on-the-spot instruction. After that, you would have some of his contacts and resources in the Republic to draw on."

"Which I would guess are pretty impressive," Car'das said, thinking hard. It would mean no more of Qennto's casually lunatic way of dealing with clients and competitors. No more ships falling apart underneath him for lack of funds or interest. Best of all, no Hutts.

"It's your decision, of course," Thrawn said. "But I believe you have the necessary gifts to excel at such a job."

"And as an extra added bonus it would also enhance my usefulness as a possible future contact with the Republic?" Car'das asked wryly.

Thrawn smiled. "As I said, you have the necessary gifts."

"Well, it can't hurt to check it out." Car'das studied Thrawn's face. "Was there something else?"

To his surprise, the other actually hesitated. "I wanted to ask a favor of you," he said at last. "Whichever ship you choose to return on, I'd ask that you never tell Qennto or Ferasi what happened to Outbound Flight."

Car'das grimaced. He'd thought about that himself. Thought about it a lot, in fact. "Especially Ferasi?"

"Especially her," Thrawn said, his voice tinged with sadness. "There are all too few idealists in this universe, Car'das. Too few people who strive always to see only the good in others. I wouldn't want to be responsible for crushing even one of them."

"And besides, you rather liked all that unquestioning adulation coming your way?"

Thrawn smiled faintly. "All beings appreciate such admiration," he said. "You have excellent insight into the hearts of others. Stratis has chosen well."

"I guess we'll find out." Car'das held out his hand. "Well. Good-bye, Commander. It's been an honor knowing you."

"As it has for me, as well," Thrawn said, taking his hand. "Farewell . . . Jorj."

"I don't know," Qennto said, shaking his head. "For my money, it sounds like a really bad idea."

"I'll be fine," Car'das assured him. "Thrawn says Stratis isn't the sort to lure me aboard just to make trouble. It's not his style."

"Maybe," Qennto rumbled. "Maybe not. The last thing a guy like that will want is someone like you planting yourself on a Coruscant street corner and shouting his past activities from the bottom of your lungs."

"And what about us?" Maris added. "*We* knew what he was planning for Outbound Flight, too."

"But you never knew his real name," Car'das reminded her. "All you have is an alias and a rumor. That's not going to get you any traction."

"Even if we were stupid enough to try?" Qennto asked, throwing a warning look at Maris.

"Something like that," Car'das agreed, hoping neither of them would bring up the fact that they *had* known Kav's real name. Still, *Kav* was a common enough Neimoidian name; and since the vicelord himself was dead, that wasn't likely to be too much of a problem. Certainly Stratis himself hadn't seemed worried about it. "Anyway, Thrawn vouches for the man."

"That's good enough for me," Maris declared. "I just hope Drixo the Hutt will be as reasonable."

"Don't worry about Drixo," Qennto said with a grunt. "She won't be a problem, not with all this extra loot to calm her down. In fact, I'll bet I can even talk her into giving us a bonus."

Maris rolled her eyes. "Here we go again."

"Hey, I'm a businessman," Qennto protested. "This is what I do."

"Just do it carefully, okay?" Car'das said. "I don't want to have to worry about you two."

"You worry about yourself," Qennto said ominously, jabbing a large finger into Car'das's chest for emphasis. "Whatever Thrawn says, this Stratis sounds about as slippery as a greased Dug, and twice as unfriendly."

"And having Thrawn foil his attack on Outbound Flight won't have helped his mood any," Maris said. Her forehead wrinkled slightly. "Thrawn *did* stop his attack, didn't he?"

Car'das felt his stomach tighten. Maris had been a shipmate, someone he'd spent half a year living and working and fighting alongside. More than that, he considered her a friend.

He'd never lied to a friend before. Did he really want to start now? And with a lie as terrible as this one?

And then, Thrawn's voice seemed to float up from his memory. *There are all too few idealists in this universe . . .*

The truth wouldn't help the dead of Outbound Flight. All it could do was hurt Maris. "Of course he stopped Stratis's attack," he assured her with all the false heartiness he could create. "I was right there when Outbound Flight flew away."

The wrinkles in her forehead smoothed out, and Maris smiled. "I knew he could do it," she said, holding out her hand. "Good luck, Jorj, and take care of yourself. Maybe we'll run into each other again sometime."

Car'das forced himself to smile as he took her hand. "Yes," he said softly. "Maybe we will."

The shattering impact had passed, the violent shaking had faded away, and the dust was beginning to settle onto the darkened deck. Slowly, carefully, Uliar lifted his head from the mass of chair cushions he'd curled up against, wincing as a twinge of pain arced through his neck. "Hello?" he called, his voice echoing eerily through the silent room.

"Uliar?" a voice called back. "It's—" He broke off as a sudden coughing fit took him. "It's Pressor," he said when he got the cough under control. "You all right?"

"Yeah, I think so," Uliar said, getting up and walking unsteadily toward the voice. All the lights were out except for the permlight emergency panels, leaving D-4 looking and feeling uncomfortably like a tomb. "You?"

"I think so," Pressor said. A pair of shadowy figures crawled out from beneath a desk across the room, resolving into Dillian Pressor and his son, Jorad, as they stepped beneath one of the permlights. "Where are all the others?"

"I don't know," Uliar said. "Everyone scattered for cover when you gave the collision warning." He looked around. "What a mess."

"That's for sure," Pressor agreed grimly, rubbing at some blood trickling down his cheek. "I wonder what happened."

"It didn't feel like laser blasts or energy torpedoes," Uliar said. "Aside from that, I haven't the faintest idea."

"Well, first things first," Pressor said. "We need to get everyone together and check for food, water, and medical supplies. After that, we can see about power and living quarters. After *that,* we can see if we can get to the bridge and figure out what in blazes happened."

He started picking his way through the debris, Jorad at his side, clutching his hand tightly. "Yeah, it's a good thing you gave us that warning, all right," Uliar commented as they reached the door. "How come you knew it was coming?"

Pressor shook his head. "I don't know," he said. "It just sort of popped into my head."

"You mean like some kind of Jedi thing?"

"I'm not a Jedi, Chas," Pressor said firmly. "I probably heard something moving or scraping against the hull. Precursor asteroid gravel, or maybe atmospheric friction. Something like that."

"Sure," Uliar said. "That's probably it."

But whether or not Pressor was a Jedi, there was definitely something strange about him. And after what the Jedi had done to Outbound Flight, Uliar would be watching Pressor and his family. He would be watching them very closely.

In the meantime, there was a little matter of survival to deal with. Ducking under a twisted section of ceiling panel, he followed Pressor down the corridor.